THE TOPAZ SCEPTRE

ANDY STONE

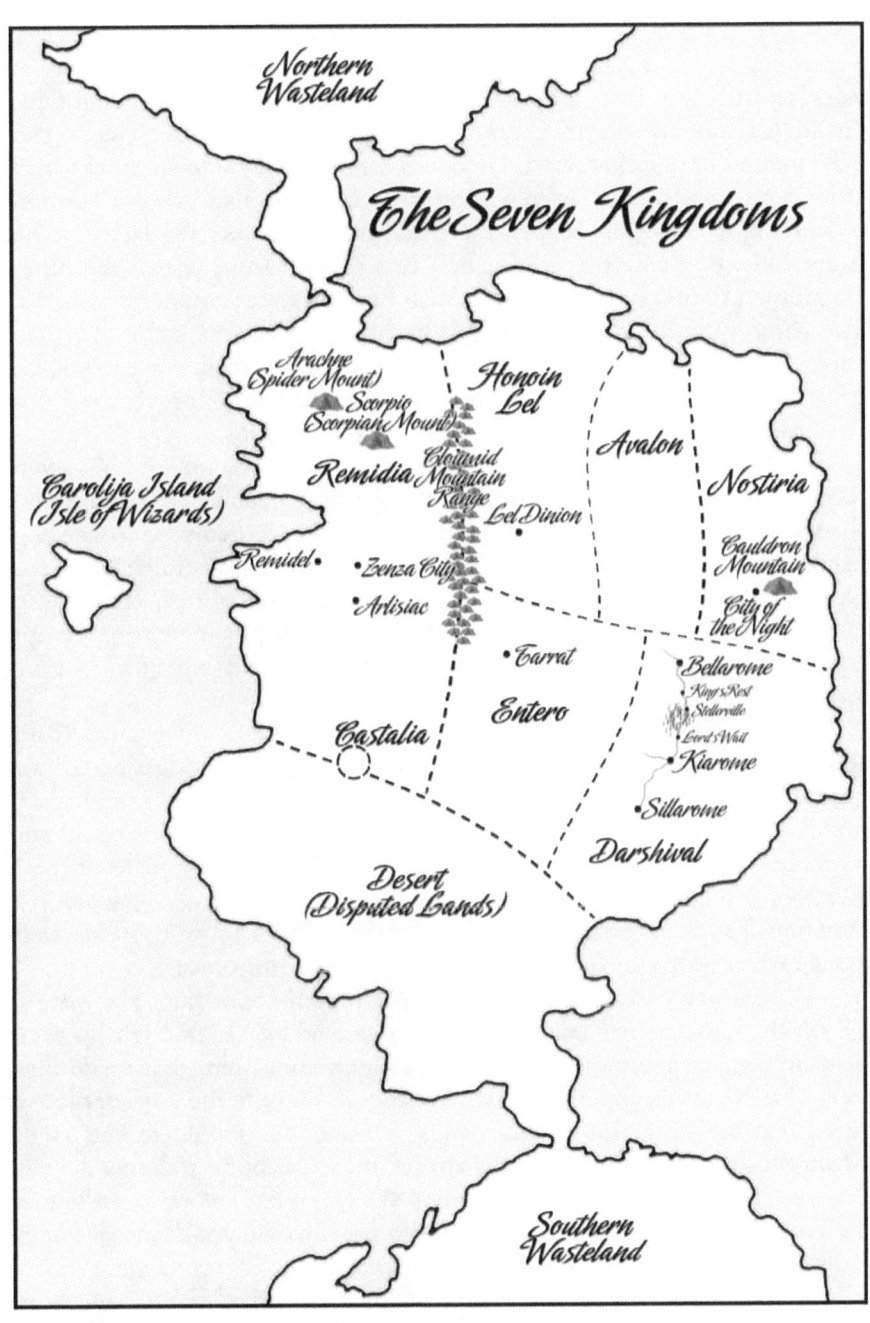

The Seven Kingdoms

Northern Wasteland

Arachne (Spider Mount)
Scorpio (Scorpian Mount)

Honoin Lel

Avalon

Nostiria

Carolija Island (Isle of Wizards)

Remidia
Clounid Mountain Range
Lel Dinion

Remidel
Zenza City
Arlisiac

Cauldron Mountain

City of the Night

Tarrat

Bellarome
King's Rest
Stellorville
Lord's Wall
Kiarome

Entero

Castalia

Sillarome

Darshival

Desert (Disputed Lands)

Southern Wasteland

Prologue: Deceit from Within

The High Chancellor sat on his throne in the Grand Cathedral. Something was seriously not right, but he couldn't quite work out what it was. He had once been a spiritual leader to the entire Seven Kingdoms, but he was not so sure that was the way of things anymore. Things had been getting hazy in his mind. He could no longer feel the spiritual world around him and it had been a long time since he had given a sermon downstairs in the main chapel. He could not remember the last time he had spoken to a citizen from Castalia or a pilgrim from one of the other kingdoms. All his contact has been with his new attendant, Sergio Custos. The name sounded odd to him and he had no idea where the man had come from. Normally those who worked in the cathedral were known only to a small few. They were hand selected from the residents of Castalia. He had no idea where Sergio had come from.

The white robe, trimmed with the seven colours of the seven sects of the city, red, for the God King Ruby, yellow for Topaz, two shades of green for Jade and Emerald, a multi-coloured strip consisting mainly of a light blue for Opal, a deep blue for Sapphire and jet black for Onyx, didn't seem to fit him as well anymore. He thought of removing it, but that would not be appropriate. His thick white hair hung unkempt around his shoulders. Normally his aged body held strength, but he looked just like a feeble old man.

"It is time for you to eat," the all too familiar voice came from somewhere in the room in front of him. The High Chancellor could not focus too far.

The closer Sergio came the more the High Chancellor could see him. He carried a wooden platter in his hands. There was a plate of food and mug of liquid for him to drink. It was the drink that caught his attention. He did not know why, but he didn't want to drink it. He also knew he was going to have to. Something was seriously wrong.

His new advisor had an aura of strength about him. He wore a light, silk shirt that fell around his lightly tanned skin. Although his face held no sign of age there was an ageless look about him that made him look older than his appearance would suggest. Despite the advisors loose fitting clothes and blonde hair falling around his shoulders the High Chancellor could still see he held a strong, muscular body underneath.

"Come on now. The chef went to a lot of hard work to make this for you. You wouldn't want to upset him now, would you?" the question didn't sound right. His words were sickly sweet.

"Of course not," the words came out of the High Chancellors mouth, although he did not know where they came from. Everything inside him cried out for a different response. His lips trembled as his tried to form the words, but they would not come.

All he could do was start to eat the food in front of him. He couldn't quite work out what it was, but it didn't taste bad so he decided to keep going. Even if he didn't want to there was nothing he could have done to stop eating. His body was working of its own accord. The idea to eat was in his mind and there was nothing he could do to stop it. When he was finished he swallowed down the liquid that was in the mug. The taste was foul, but there was nothing he could do to stop himself. He wanted to retch, but nothing would come up.

"There we go, now isn't that all better?" Sergio picked up the platter and turned to walk away.

The High Chancellor wanted to say something, but he could not muster the words. All of a sudden he started to feel tired. The feeling was so overwhelming that he looked around to see if there was somewhere to lie down. He no longer knew where he was, but in the end he figured that he was comfortable enough and nothing could stop the sleep that was on his mind.

Sergio turned around when he heard the High Chancellor lose consciousness. The old man was nothing like what he thought he was going to be. The High Chancellor commanded the largest army in the Seven Kingdoms. The only army bigger was that of the Great Lord himself. He was supposed to be a powerful and commanding man. However he was so easy to subdue and then control that Sergio almost felt sorry for him. It was not an emotion he knew.

When he was happy that the High Chancellor was asleep he let the platter drop to the ground. He looked down at his own body. Although it was a lot younger than the High Chancellor's it was still not suitable. He hated wearing the skin of the silly little creatures. He much preferred what the Great Lord had given him. Some of his brothers liked wearing such skins. He had no idea how they could do it for such long periods of time.

He was sick of running around for the High Chancellor. As time passed he was slowly gaining control of him, but it had taken a long time... too long. It was not suitable for one of the Chosen to be a servant to such a pitiful creature. It would be so much easier to just kill the man and assume his body. Once he was in control of that he could do whatever he wanted. The thought raced through his mind. Each time he thought about it, it seemed a better idea. Eventually he talked himself into it. He took one step forward before he heard a voice from behind him.

"I wouldn't do that if I was you," the voice had a hiss to it. Sergio knew who it was straight away.

"Who asked for your opinion, snake?" One thing he hated more than wearing human skin was serpentants.

Sergio recognised the serpentant instantly. Although he had not met all of the serpentants there was no doubt that it was Cobra before him. Two distinct flaps of scaled skin hung down the side of his head. Even through the black robe, with the hood drawn, he could make out his unique feature.

It could not be a good sign that the Great Lord had sent one his lowly servants to him. Although the serpentants held power it was nothing compared to that held by the Chosen. Za'aroz considered himself to be the most powerful of the seven and he didn't need help from anyone. That could only mean that Cobra had a message for him. He would give the serpentant the benefit of the doubt, but he would remain on edge. There was no way he would be caught off guard. That was the easiest way to end up dead.

"I have some information that you might want to know," there was something strange in Cobra's voice, almost as if he was gloating.

The snake was there for a reason. The Great Lord had been using the disgusting creature for something and he wished he knew what. Until he knew exactly why the serpentant was in Castalia he would have to play along.

"Well I am sure that the Great Lord will not be pleased if you keep me waiting. You can be sure that I will be passing on every detail," he was just as smug as Cobra. He would not show any sign of discomfort. He knew that was what Cobra was looking for.

Cobra hated Za'aroz more than any of the other Dark Knights. He was greedy and self-centred, much like the others, but he would grovel to get in front. There was no doubt that he would go running to the Great Worm if he thought that it would get him ahead. He wanted nothing more than to sink his fangs into the disgusting creature's neck. It would not take long for his poison to take effect. Until the Worm's hold over him was gone he would have to do as he was told.

"I have heard that he is displeased with your so called brother Ra'naroz. My brother Viper is with him, but there is only so much he can do to protect him. The army of the Alliance is on its way from Kiarome. If you have not already heard, your brother Fenaroz has been destroyed. Alaric, who they call the Chosen One, destroyed him. His power is growing by the day. I would say by the time he gets here he will be nearly unbeatable." Cobra was getting off point, but he couldn't resist a chance to provoke the Dark Knight.

"Do you think that I am worried what the Cursed One does? The Great Lord will quickly deal with him, when he is ready of course," Za'aroz didn't sound too disturbed.

He had to admit to himself that he was a little annoyed that his jibe didn't have its desired effect. He always found that it was easier dealing with the Dark Knight's when they were on the back foot. He had travelled a long way and he was not about to let Za'aroz get the better of him.

"Nyrra has decided not to help him. It will not be long before another of your kind is dead. That will leave four by my count. Not to mention the fact that Na'garoz has gone missing. No one knows where he is. I wouldn't be surprised if he was already dead. Now, once the Chosen One..." he didn't believe in the title, but he knew that it annoyed the Dark Knights, so he used it anyway. "Now, once the Chosen One has finished with Ra'naroz in Jarrat how long do you think it will take him to direct the Alliance here?" The question was rhetorical, but he still had to wait for the answer to dawn on him. "That's right. In a month, maybe two, the Alliance will be on your doorstep. To make matters worse he will have reinforcements from Jarrat."

Za'aroz knew about the plans for Jarrat. As much as he didn't believe that Ra'naroz was the right one to lead the plan, he thought that it might just work. If it did work then there was nothing for him to worry about. All his enemies would be dead. If that was true then he did not think his master would have sent the serpentant. He thought he had been safe in Castalia, but it seemed that was no longer true.

"I think that I will wait for it to happen before I get too worried." He was not going to let the serpentant to take the lead. He knew that once he lost the advantage he was going to struggle to regain it. "There is a surprise waiting for the enemy once they reach Jarrat. I am sure that the Great Lord hasn't told you of his plan."

Cobra had to admit that it was true, even though he would not admit it to Za'aroz. If there was a surprise waiting for the Alliance then he did not know about it. It was one of the reasons he didn't like Nyrra. He could not be trusted. He always had intrigues on top of his intrigues. Nothing was ever straight forward. He still didn't know what he was supposed to do in Castalia. Nyrra had told him he would know when the time is right. Until that time he was going to have as much fun as he could.

"I told you that the Great Lord no longer has his back. Whatever surprise he was planning will not happen. It is up to you to prove that you deserve his assistance." Cobra had no idea if what he said was true and he didn't care. He was selling it like he did and that was all that mattered.

He could see that his words had their effect. The Dark Knight was not so sure of himself. If what Cobra had said was true it meant that he was not as safe as he thought. Castalia was still the strongest city to be in, but it was not completely safe. If the Alliance moved through Entero then he would be the next on their list. He had complete control over the High Chancellor, but he was not sure if that was enough to incite the army to defend the city against the Alliance. The High Chancellor was not a military leader like the kings and queens of the other kingdoms. It would be much easier if he did not have to control him. If he could become the old man then everything would be a lot easier, but he had to take on board the serpentant's warning. He still did not, however, believe every word that came out of the snake's mouth.

"I am sure that you think you know what you are talking about, but I will be the judge on what is best for this city. The Great Lord put me in charge here for a reason and I am not about to let him down." It was a weak reply and Za'aroz could feel himself losing the exchange. He had to finish the conversation. "I think that you can go now. If I need you I will summon for you."

"I think not," Cobra was going to have none of that. "I will go to the Southern end of the city. The sun is warmer there and I think that I will be more at home. You can be sure that if I need you I will be able to find you." He was going to leave with the upper hand. He could hear that Za'aroz was about to speak, but he had already left the room. He should have given the Dark Knight more credit than he did, but he still held the advantage. He thought he was going to have fun in Castalia.

***

The Great Lord sat on top of the Mountain. He liked it there. It reminded him of his home at *Crenallous*, the Cauldron Mountain. It had been too long since he had sat on top of the Mountain of Fire. Of course there were differences between the two. The peak where he sat was covered with snow. It was not snowing as he sat there, he made sure of that. Even without the Ruby stone he was still able to control the weather, at least for a short period of time. He hated the cold and would do whatever was in his power to keep it away. There was no snow anywhere on the ground within a dozen paces of where he sat.

It had been a long journey, but he was getting close. The stone was calling out to him. He could feel it. It was pulsating like a beating heart. He thought it was going to be on the peak where he sat, but he had searched and searched, but it was not there. He had been so sure he had gotten his hopes up. Now he had to start again.

He looked out at the peak on the horizon. It was the mountain's twin. He couldn't remember their original names, but he knew they were different to what they were called now. He had to think to remember. The one he sat was Scorpio and the other was Arachne. They were named after the founding brothers of Castalia, the newest of all of the new cities. The mountains were renamed by a King of Remidia who was looking to gain favour by the city's ruler. The Great Lord looked at Arachne and wondered if the stone was there.

There was another reason why he was drawn to Scorpio. It was something he had not felt in a long time. He could feel the beating heart of the great creature in the depths of the mountain. He could feel the pure hatred. He had not felt such malevolence for as long as he could remember. He wanted to wake the sleeping giant, but he knew that it was not the time.

He looked down towards the forest below. He knew it was filled with those nasty creatures that liked to call themselves elves. He knew the evil beneath the mountain could destroy them all, but it was also not the time. The time would come soon enough for the beast to awaken. Then it would be time for destruction. The thought brought an evil grin to his face.

Now it was time for him to leave. Time was running out. His servants were being killed, one by one. It would not be long before he faced the Cursed One in battle. If he did not have the Ruby stone in his possession at that time then he would be destroyed. He had no illusions about that. He would not fail. He knew that he was not going to fail.

He breathed in the evil from the mountain before he blinked out of existence.

***

It was late in the evening and Alaric was still sleeping. His soft blonde hair had grown long and his skin had darkened since their time in the Southern wasteland. Marina, as much as she liked watching Alaric, was becoming hungry. She did not want to leave him alone, but she knew that he would be alright. He had survived so much already and it was nothing compared with what he had been through. He was not in any danger, at least not for the next hour or two.

She wore a deep blue dress, something she had not worn since she had left the palace in Kiarome. Even since she had been travelling with Alaric she had forgotten she had packed it. Despite adapting to life on the road she felt much more comfortable in her princessly dress. She had brushed her long black hair and tied it in a braid before she had left the tent. There was no real reason why she had done so, it was more from compulsion that any real desire. Unlike Alaric her soft white skin seemed untouched by the hard southern sun.

The next problem she had was finding something to eat. She knew that there would be food in the command tent, but she could not remember how to get there. There were no soldiers nearby as they were all busy readying themselves for battle. The next day was not going to be an easy one and she didn't want to distract them for such a minor issue.

"Princess Marina?" an oddly familiar voice came from the dark.

Marina turned around, but she could not see who it was. It seemed odd to her, but that thought was only in her head for a moment. As the figure moved closer she recognised him as Captain Aimon. As he became even closer she felt a slight buzzing in the back of her mind. Her mind started to clear and the feeling that something wrong returned. It only lasted a moment before both it and the buzzing disappeared.

The Captain from Entero was oddly dressed for the eve of battle. Instead of armour he was dressed in soft grey trousers and a pale blue, silk shirt. If they weren't surrounded by tents Marina would have thought they were taking a stroll through the palace gardens. It should have been concerning for her, but for some reason it seemed perfectly normal.

"How are you feeling tonight?" it was an innocent enough greeting.

"I am fine thank you." She thought there was something else, but her mind was so clouded.

"That is good to hear," there was something wrong with his voice. "I was thinking about getting something to eat. Would you care to join me?"

Marina suddenly realised how hungry she was. It seemed pertinent to why she was walking through the campsite. The thought was only there for a moment before it completely disappeared. All that mattered was filling her stomach.

Before she knew what was happening she was sitting in a tent with Aimon and there was a plate of food in front of her. She couldn't remember asking for food or anyone going to get it. Regardless she was hungry and there was something to eat. She didn't wait to be asked to start eating. When she had cleaned her plate she realised that she was very thirsty. Her mouth was dry and she needed liquid. She thought it was odd that Aimon had not given her something to drink with her meal.

"May I have something to drink, please?" she asked softly.

"Of course you can." He smiled.

Before she knew he had moved there was a pewter mug in her hand. She didn't know how it got there, but it was filled with water and that was all she cared about. As she started to drink she thought the water tasted funny, but she could not stop.

When she finished drinking she let the mug fall out of her hand. It didn't seem right, but she couldn't hold onto it any longer. Her eyes were suddenly heavy and she felt very tired. The buzzing suddenly returned and there was nothing that could shake the haziness that she felt.

As her eyes wilted she noticed that the tent was suddenly glowing blue. She looked up at Aimon who was shrinking back away from the light. There was something distorted about his face. He no longer looked like the Captain from Entero. There was definitely something off about him, but she couldn't put her finger on it. Soon enough she could no longer keep he eyes open and the last thing she remembered was the sound of laughter, somewhere in the distance.

Chapter 1: Preparing for War

Alaric woke shortly after sunrise. Marina had given strict instructions that he was not to be woken by anyone. He thought that it would have taken longer for him to feel better, but he woke with a renewed vigour in his heart. It was going to be a trying day and he needed all his energy.

The tent glowed a soft green, emanating from the Emerald stone on the gold bracelet he wore on his right wrist. It was the power of the stone that refreshed him and not the hours of sleep. He knew it was a false feeling, only the Topaz stone could truly heal, but it didn't matter. Returning the stone to its velvet pouch crossed his mind, but the thought he would need it for his upcoming trial.

He sat on a chair and looked down at himself. His skin had browned even more since travelling through the Southern Wasteland. Even with the thick robes he had worn, the sun had still penetrated through. Luckily the Heji, the large, hairy beasts which inhabited the wasteland, had given him a thick paste that had almost instantly healed the burns and boils. He hated to think about how he would have looked without it.

As he pondered his recent adventures his slowly flexed his muscles to make sure they were all working properly. His body had toned since he had left his home in Arsiliac. Running his own merchant business had never stopped him from pitching in and helping move his shipments, but he had never been truly strong. His life, training and trials had toned his body and increased his strength to a level he had never thought possible.

His physical strength was nothing compared to the other attributes he had learned. Within a matter of days he had become more than proficient with the sword, bow and at unarmed combat. But it was his ability with magic that was his true strength. Although he had not come to realise his full potential he had certainly grown in power and control.

Slowly he rubbed his blonde hair as he forced his will onto the Emerald stone. It had been a long time since he had time to have his hair cut. Luckily it no longer needed to be a physical act and as he closed his eyes the length slowly reduced until it was as long as he wanted it to be.

When he was finished with his hair the light in the Emerald stone slowly faded. He didn't want anyone to know he was wearing it and the tell-tale glow would quickly give him away. At first the stone fought his will, but eventually it gave in and the light blinked out.

A fresh set of clothes had been brought for him during the night, a simple leather jerkin and trousers. They were the clothes he had asked for before he fell asleep. He figured it was the most appropriate attire for what he had to do. It had been suggested that he wear some finery, something more appropriate for infiltrating the castle, but he brushed aside the suggestions. He certainly wasn't going to be sneaking around the castle. All he cared about was wearing something comfortable for the battle with the Dark Knight.

Once he was dressed he made his way to the command tent. He assumed that was where all the commanders would be and where he would find breakfast. He was ravenous and could think of nothing else. He didn't even find it odd that Marina was not watching over him. Every other time he had woken he had seen her staring down at him.

He was right on both counts. The command tent was full, not only with the commanders, but also with a number of minor functionaries. The sight was a little overwhelming. In his hungered state he really didn't want to deal with the scene before him. He knew that when they realised he was there he would not have a chance to relax.

"Alaric!" Hulkan was the first to see him. The dwarf seemed excited. "We didn't think we would see you before lunch." He had braided his long brown beard, as was the custom before battle. It was the first time Alaric had seen him in such a manner. He wore thick chain mail and there was no doubt he was prepared for what lay before them. All that was missing was his large double war axe. No one was allowed weapons inside the command tent. It was not that anyone expected any trouble; it was just a matter of space.

Alaric didn't reply as he made his way through the crowd to the table. He didn't mean to be rude, but he needed to be seated before he spoke. It seemed that the effects from the Emerald stone were already starting to wear off. He had been hoping it was not just the stone that had made him feel better, but it seemed as though that wasn't the case. He wanted to draw on the stone's power, but he did not want to answer the many questions that would be asked. In the end he would just have to suffer through the nausea and hope that it would soon pass.

He still hadn't spoken when he had filled the plate with the lavish breakfast before him. The command group had decided they deserved something nice. They had been on strict rations since they had left Kiarome, as had the army. The extra food was not just for them. The soldiers aslo needed all their strength for what lay before them. The decision had gone down well throughout the entire army. There were no delusions that some would die on the battlefield and it was only right that they did so on a full stomach. Soon enough they would either be dead or be able to replenish their supplies from the Jarrat coffers.

As Alaric took his first bite he realised that the entire tent had gone silent. Everyone was looking at him. He quickly swallowed what he was eating and prepared to speak. He would not say much, but he didn't think they would stop staring until he did.

"Sorry, but I need to eat first. Please continue with what you were doing." He continued eating before anyone could reply. The food was starting to make him feel better and he was hoping his nausea was only due to hunger. He didn't like having to rely on the Emerald stone for strength and there was no guarantee he could rely on its power to defeat the Dark Knight. He also had no idea what long term effect it was having on him.

They had been discussing the plans for the rest of the day, which was to say they were just guessing what Alaric was going to tell them. Now there was really no reason to continue with the conversation and they remained silent until Alaric finished eating. It made things a little uncomfortable, but Alaric didn't care. Nothing was going to stop him from filling his stomach.

"What are we going to do now?" Sorrell was the first to speak. The General from Darshival was keen to get moving. He wore his battle breastplate and looked even more ready for battle than Hulkan. A noble and his advisor from his home kingdom had been taken prisoner and he wanted to start the rescue mission. He stroked his closely shaved head in anticipation of Alaric's response.

"I am going into the castle to save the others." It seemed as good a way as any to start. "I need the army to create a distraction."

There was a murmur around the tent. The functionaries were still locked on the conversation, stopping them from their assigned duties. Their silence alerted the others to the fact that they were eavesdropping. When they realised they had been noticed they quickly moved into action.

"So you have nothing better to do than eavesdrop on a conversation that doesn't concern you?" Sorrell's voice boomed. There was no real reason to dress down the servers, but he wanted a chance to think on Alaric's words. "If you've finished your duties then I'm sure I can find something for you to do."

That was enough to make them move even faster. Although no one knew what he would do they didn't want to find out. Before long the table was clean and the servers had all left the tent. If the commanders needed anything then they would call.

"What do you mean 'by a distraction'?" Jarwe asked once the tent was clear.

The question was obvious, but Alaric thought it was better if they asked it first. "The Dark Knight in the castle is using a blocking spell. I will try to explain things as best I can," he was not looking forward to that part. "I have been learning a lot since I left Kiarome. One of the things I can do is travel through the fabric of reality." There were murmurs around the table. "I can't really explain it any better than that. For the moment you will just have to take my word on it. It makes life easier if I can focus on something in the distance. It gives me something to aim for. Anyway that is a story for another time. I have been using Bern as my guide, but since he went into the castle I have not been able to sense him. The Dark Knight is using a spell to cover the castle." He wasn't sure if he was explaining it well, but they seemed to be following. "If the army takes the battlefield then it will force him into distraction. I am hoping that it will allow me to find those who are imprisoned."

Jarwe rubbed his head. It had been a long time since he had had a chance to shave his scalp almost to the skin, and his brown hair was starting to show. It was clearly visible and stubbly under his touch. Jarwe wore his polished silver breast plate. A fox head inlaid over a broadsword, the crest of the Royal Remidian Army, was clearly etched onto its front. It was an odd choice considering they were about to go into battle. The breastplate was only for ceremony and held no real advantage. It was the first time he had worn it since they had arrived at the edge of Jarrat. No one knew what it represented and no one was prepared to ask.

Until Bern returned, Jarwe was the acting commander of the Alliance. The General from Remidia had been the original leader of the army, but he had relieved himself of his command in favour of Bern. At first the other commanders had given Bern the lead when Jarwe could no longer carry out his duties. Something he had seen in Avalon that temporarily taken away his senses. Bern had returned power to Jarwe when he had recovered, but it was not long before he relinquished command of his own volition. It seemed as though Bern was meant to lead and nothing could change that.

There was silence for a short while before Jarwe spoke again. "That seems to make sense, but it's a big risk. Attacking the castle will cost us a lot of men."

"Ah, here is the twist. I don't want you to attack the castle. I want you to provoke the Dark Knight. I need you to taunt him. That will be the way to break his spell," Alaric explained.

There was another awkward silence. They were doing their best to understand what he was saying, but it did not make sense. It seemed as though he was risking the entire army on a feeling. Although they all did not think it was a good idea no one felt as though they could speak. He was the Chosen One and they had to respect him no matter what they thought.

"What is it?" Alaric asked when no had spoken for over a minute. He could feel the tension around the table.

They all looked at each other and in the end the responsibility fell on Jarwe. He certainly didn't want the task, but it was his job as the general. He wished that Bern was still with them, but if that was the case then they wouldn't be having the conversation at all.

"We," he used the term 'we' to bring the others in. He received some cold looks. "We don't think that your plan is going to work. Once we take the field we will be in range of their archers. We will be open targets. I don't know much about the Dark Knight, but I don't think that he will stand on ceremony. I believe that once we are out in the open he will attack." He was a lot happier once he stopped talking.

Alaric silently cursed himself for missing a pivotal part of his plan. He hoped they would find it easier to believe. "Don't worry about the archers. I will make sure the army is protected. This is what will provoke Za'aroz to come out and speak with you."

"What are you talking about?" Sorrell asked before Alaric could continue.

"I told you that my power in the magical arts has increased since I left Kiarome. I won't go into too much detail, but let's just say that most, if not all of the arrows, won't hit their intended target."

Although they did not completely understand what he was planning they were comfortable with his words and were able to relax slightly. It seemed to be a solid plan. There were risks involved, but if all went well then they could get away without a single casualty. They knew it was a long shot, but it had given them more hope than they had had in long time. Ever since they had arrived on the outskirts of Jarrat they had been in disarray. For the first time they had direction.

"What about when you go into the castle?" Hulkan was not as confident of the others. He asked the question that had eluded everyone else.

"I'm afraid there is only so much I can do. Once I have left for the castle there is little I can do to help. I will need all my energy to defeat the Dark Knight. I'm sure you can come up with a good strategy for battle. We have some of the greatest tacticians in the Seven Kingdoms sitting around this table."

They all felt suddenly ashamed, although that was not Alaric's intent. His words were true and it seemed the commanders had forgotten the basics of warfare. They had relied on Bern to make the decisions and without him they didn't know what to do. Alaric's words brought some confidence back to the group.

"I think we should move into action. I am sure that the men will be excited to march out onto the battlefield. Even if they are not going to be doing any fighting," there was a renewed spirit in Jarwe's voice.

There was definitely going to be some fighting at some point during the day. Alaric was about to mention the fact when there came a rustling at the front of the tent. A young looking man had entered wearing a soldier's uniform from Darshival had a short sword by his side and there was a flustered expression on his face. It was obvious that there was something he wanted to say, but he would not speak until he was given leave.

As Sorrell was the commanding officer from Darshival he was the one to address him. "What is it, Private?" he barked.

"I am sorry to disturb you, but this is an urgent matter," he almost stuttered his words. He was clearly nervous.

"Spit it out soldier," it was Jarwe's turn to snap.

"Princess Marina was found weeping in Captain Aimon's tent this morning. She was beside herself. All she was saying is 'she's gone, she's gone'. We tried to move her, but that only made things worse," the soldier blurted the words out.

The look of pure horror on Alaric's face proved that things were worse than they sounded. He wanted to speak, but the thoughts running through his mind stopped him talking.

"All that we could think of was to come here," the soldier ended his barrage of words.

"You did the right thing. Now we have a battle to prepare for, so get back to work." The soldier couldn't be happier to be dismissed.

Once he was gone all eyes returned to Alaric. No one asked the question that was on all their minds. He had to take a deep breath to compose himself. He had a very bad feeling that he knew what had been stolen, but he didn't want to surmise until he was sure. The others would not be happy about him leaving, but they would have to respect his decision.

"There is a lot of work to get done. You need to concentrate on the upcoming war. I will see to Marina," Alaric stood as he spoke.

"I am sorry Alaric, but I need to see that my princess is alright," Sorrell spoke before Wojtek could. They were both equally concerned for Marina.

Alaric felt for the two men, but there were more important matters for them to deal with. He knew there was nothing they could do to help and they would only prove to get in the way. He wasn't even sure what he could do to help. The deed that had been done wouldn't be easy to rectify.

"There is nothing that you can do. You need to keep to the plan. There are many lives at stake. Marina is going to be fine," Alaric raised his voice. There was no doubting his command.

The commanders rushed out of the tent in much the same manner as the young soldier. Alaric had to laugh at the result. He didn't mean to be so hard, but the result was undeniable. He was filling his role quite nicely. If the prophecy was a living being he was sure it would be proud of him. He didn't really know what that meant, but he was sure that it was a good thing.

There was little time to bask in his glory. Marina was in pain and he had to go to her. He berated himself for not sensing her pain earlier. The fact that he still couldn't feel it in itself was disturbing. He did not think that Ra'naroz's power could reach so far. It must have been Argoz. He cursed himself again for leaving the Dark Knight alive. He thought it would give him an insight into the Evil One's mind, but instead it had only caused pain.

Alaric hoped, as he rushed towards Aimon's tent, that he had not taken the Sapphire stone. He didn't know what else he could have taken and he knew his hopes were going to be for nothing. It was the last thing he needed. He needed to concentrate all his energy on the castle not on another Dark Knight. Gathering the stones was key to his victory in the final battle and to lose one to one of Nyrra's agents could prove disastrous for everyone.

Marina was curled up in a ball on the floor in Aimon's tent. She didn't look up when Alaric entered. She was shaking and sobbing. Alaric wasn't sure if he should say something or try and comfort her. He stood in the entrance and just watched her. She didn't seem to notice he had entered and the more he watched the more he didn't know what to do. In the end he decided that it would be best to speak first. He didn't know what her reaction would be if he touched her.

"Marina? It's Alaric here," he kept his voice low and as soothing as possible.

Marina didn't look up from where she was huddled. There was no reaction that indicated she had heard Alaric at all. He watched for a response, but when there was none he thought he should begin again.

"I heard that something has been stolen." He could not see her hand to see if the ring was still there. "Can you tell me what it was?"

Marina slowly lifted her head. Her face was covered with tears, both wet and dry. Her skin was pale, paler than it had been in a long time. Alaric did not think that was a good sign. She looked as though she was about to speak, but she remained silent. It would not be long before the army was ready to take the field. Once that happened he would have no time for Marina. It broke his heart, but he needed to prioritise.

"Please Marina." Alaric took another step into the tent.

Marina shrunk back against his advance. She looked genuinely afraid of him. Alaric was shocked. He didn't understand why she would react in such a way. It only made him want to comfort her more, but he did not continue any further. As she moved back he got a glimpse of her hands. The ring was gone. Alaric's heart skipped a beat. Although he had known it to be true he still hoped that it was not.

"Argoz has taken the ring." It was not a question.

Marina looked up at him with a knowing look on her face. It was the first time that she looked as though she acknowledged his words. She wanted to speak, but she shrunk back at the last minute. Alaric didn't know what he was going to do. If she was not going to speak and she was not going to let him touch her then there was nothing he could do.

"Please, Marina, I need to know what happened. If I am going to be able to help you I need to know."

"How can you help me?" she did not look up as she spoke. "I lost her. She was taken from me and I can no longer feel her."

"What are you talking about?" Alaric took a step closer and then and when she didn't repulse from him another.

She looked up just as he was reaching down for her and she quickly scooted back along the floor until she was up against the tent wall. Alaric let himself drop to the floor thinking it might be better if he wasn't towering over her. He remained seated and she continued.

"He drugged me," she started to explain. "There must have been something in the water. She was trying to warn me, but I could not hear her. He was doing something to block her voice from me," she almost sounded frightened. Alaric wanted to ask who the mystery woman was she was referring too, but he didn't want to interrupt her. "Now he has her in her prison. I cannot feel her anymore. I do not know where she is. You have to help Alaric. I know you can find her." It was with that realisation that she flung herself into his arms.

Suddenly he realised that she was referring to the Sapphire stone as a person. He was going to question her, but her body felt weak as he held her close. She was sobbing again. Alaric slowly stroked her hair hoping it would comfort her, but he knew it was too little. He didn't know what she expected him to do, but he had to try. What he needed was more information.

When she had stopped crying he gently pushed her away from his body, although he kept her within arms reach. She looked a little calmer, but there was still the look of desperation on her face. Her hair fell down in tangled waves and even in such a state he thought she looked beautiful. Without a second thought he pulled her close and kissed her on the lips. He didn't know why he did such a thing, but he knew that he could do nothing else. When he pulled her away again there was a smile on her face.

"Do you know where Argoz has taken the stone?" he spoke softly as he didn't want her to start crying again.

"I can't remember anything. I don't think that he would have told me where he was going. I don't think that he would be that stupid," there was still sobbing in her voice.

"Don't be so sure. There is a chance that you might remember something that he said to you when you were unconscious. The Dark Knights have a tendency to gloat over therir victims. If he thought you couldn't hear him then there is a chance he would have told you his plan."

Marina didn't understand what Alaric was suggesting. She had been unconscious. There was no chance she would have heard what the Dark Knight would have said, but as she thought about it she thought she could hear Argoz's voice, somewhere in the depths of her memory. Whenever she tried to focus on the words they would disappear.

"I think there is something there," she sounded surprised and hopeful for the first time. "But I can't reach it."

Alaric smiled at her. If the words were in her head then he would be able to get them, even if she could not remember. He didn't know what he was going to find, but he had to give it a try. He only hoped that Argoz didn't leave a trap for him. If he did then he did 't think he would have the energy to fight in the castle. It was a tough decision, but he could not leave Marina suffering. If nothing else he could ease her pain.

"Close your eyes and concentrate on your breathing. I will find out what you heard," Alaric explained.

Marina did as she was told without question and she suddenly felt very safe again. She had not felt that way since she had recovered from her unconscious state.

Alaric placed his hands on her temples before closing his eyes. Taking a deep breath he started to draw in the energy around him. The spell he was going to create was not a large one and would not require much energy. It would also be easy for him to mask the spell. Although the Dark Knight would know he had arrived, his exact location would still be a secret. In his weakened state he couldn't risk an attack. Although he didn't believe the Dark Knight would attack him from the castle he still couldn't take the chance.

Once he had finished the spell he released it and Marina felt a warm sensation on the side of her head. At first she felt uncomfortable, but as the warmth started to fill her body she smiled. It was a reassuring feeling. She relaxed and thought that she could do anything. She had completely forgotten what Alaric was doing and what she was supposed to be remembering. She was completely lost in the sensation that filled her body.

"Tell me what happened," Alaric's voice was level, but firm.

"He is taking the ring," Marina's voice sounded frightened. "There is nothing that I can do to stop him. I can't move! Why can't I move?" Alaric wished that there was something he could do to help, but it was her memory speaking. Even if he said something she would not hear him.

"That's right, you fool," the voice was still Marina's, but it was different. There was a rough tone as she recalled Argoz speaking. "Now I have the ring for the Great Lord. He will bestow upon me a great reward. I have succeeded where none of my brothers have." There was a sudden bout of laughter.

"What are you doing?" it was Marina's voice again. "You cannot take her from me."

"Now I need to meet with the Great Lord, the only question is where?" the voice of Argoz was back. It did not take any notice of what Marina was saying. "I can't stay here, I know that much. Where do you think I should go?" there was no response to the question. "I don't think there is any point in travelling further to the west," the voice mused to itself. "I think Lel Dinion might be the place to set up. King Lisle has remained somewhat unmolested to date. I think I should pay him a visit and see if I can talk him into thinking my way," there was another round of laughter before the voice continued. "Yes, I will go there and wait for the Great Lord to send me a sign."

Once he had received the information Alaric released the spell. The longer the spell continued the greater the risk to Marina. He did not want to hold her there any longer. He was glad when he saw the acknowledgement return to her face. He quickly pulled her back to him and he was relieved that she had returned safely.

"What happened?" Marina's voice was muffled against his chest.

He held her for another moment before letting her go. "I know where he is taking the ring." He was debating on whether he should tell her or not. There was a risk that she would go after the stone without him. If the stone was covered by it velvet case then there was no chance of her succeeding on her own. All she would end up accomplishing was to die or worse.

"Don't leave me in suspense. Tell me where it is?" There was excitement in her voice.

Once he had let the cat out the bag he knew he could not keep the location from her. There was a glimmer of hope on her face and he could not be the one to remove it. "He has gone to Hondin Lel." He thought if he could be obscure that might satisfy her.

"Where in Hondin Lel," she would not be dissuaded. "It is a very large kingdom."

Alaric sighed before speaking again. "He has gone to Lel Dinion. I think he plans on entering the palace and trying to take control of King Lisle. If he does this then it will be no easy task in defeating him."

"What are we waiting for?" Marina pushed away from Alaric and jumped to her feet.

Alaric was quick to stand and blocked her from leaving. She tried a number of times to get past, but he would not let her. He didn't have the heart to say anything, but he recognised the look on her face and he didn't want to shatter it.

"Come on Alaric. If we are quick enough we should be able to catch him."

That was not a possibility and Alaric knew it. Unless he was able to find the point where the Dark Knight had started to travel there was no way he could follow. If Marina had been able to sense the Sapphire stone then it would have given him a reference point, but without it there was no point. The only place they would be able to catch him was at Lel Dinion.

"There is nothing we can do about it now," Alaric reached out for her, but she shied away. "There is no way to track Argoz's movements," he explained.

"Then we will wait for him at Lel Dinion," her logic seemed sound.

"You are going nowhere in a hurry. Just because you have been unconscious doesn't mean that you have rested." She could see where Alaric was heading and she would have none of it.

"I cannot rest now. I will not be able to rest until I have her on my finger again," Marina explained.

Alaric was starting to get nervous with Marina referring to the Sapphire stone as a she. There had been a clear connection between the two from the start. He would not have given her the ring if there wasn't, but it was becoming an obsession. He wondered if it wouldn't be a better choice to let Argoz keep the stone for the time being. He quickly scolded himself for thinking such thoughts.

"You have to rest. I have things that I have to do here." He knew that she would not understand.

"There is nothing that you need to do here that is more important than recovering the Sapphire Stone." She stood with her hands on her hips. She was obviously not happy with his excuse.

"I know recovering the ring is important, but it has to wait. Trust me when I say that you need to rest." Alaric had been preparing a spell whilst he was trying to convince Marina.

It was his backup plan to cause her to suddenly feel very exhausted. Again it was a small spell and he felt that he could expend the energy. It was important that she not run off whilst he was in the castle and if he was worried about the fact then his mind would be distracted. He didn't want to trick her, but it was the only option that he had left.

As soon as he released the spell her eyes started to droop. It was a little more sudden that he had hoped, but it was doing the job. She started to wobble on her feet and she looked as though she was about to fall asleep where she stood.

"What were we talking about?" she knew it was important and she didn't want to let it go.

"You need to go to your tent and get some sleep," Alaric caught her as she was about to fall.

"Thank you." She looked up at him with doe eyes.

Alaric half-carried her out. He was happy to be out of the Dark Knight's tent. There was something very disturbing about being inside. It was as if he could feel the hatred emanating from the canvas. He took a deep breath of the morning forest air, the cool air refreshing his lungs.

When they reached Marina's tent she was all but asleep. Alaric didn't like using a spell to control her, but he didn't think there was any other choice. He could not trust her to remain in the campsite by herself. He didn't really want to leave her to go into the castle, but he could not leave his friends inside. There was no telling what they had already gone through. It was that thought that was racing through his mind as he laid Marina down in her bedroll. He was so deep in thought that he didn't hear the tent flap being pulled across.

"I am sorry, Lord Alaric, but the army is ready." He was not used to a title, but he was not going to say anything. "The commanders have requested that you join them."

The time had come for action and Alaric was nervous.

Chapter 2: On the Verge of Battle

"Are you sure you know what you're doing?" Jarwe asked as he sat on his horse at the edge of the tree line.

It was not the first time he had been asked that question since he had returned from Marina's tent. They had to take his word that he was doing the right thing, but they would need more reassurance if they were to believe it. They had no idea what he had planned. His information had been brief and confusing and once they left the protection of the trees they were completely in his hands. They had no idea how Alaric was going to stop the rain of arrows that would meet them on the battlefield, but he was confident enough to convince them.

"I have told you. There is nothing to worry about. Now I can't guarantee you will not have to fight, but you will not get shot by their arrows," he stared out in front of them when he spoke.

The commanders had spent their morning preparing for the fact they would have to fight. When Alaric entered the castle they would lose their protection. The only thing they could think of was to retreat back into the cover of the forest. There seemed to be little reason to remain in the open if Alaric had achieved his goal. From the safety of the trees they could regroup and plan their next attack depending on the reaction from the castle. With a little luck they would remain protected whilst Alaric defeated the Dark Knight. If that was the case then they wouldn't have to fight at all.

There was no time to try and explain his plan any more. He wished he could have reassured them further, but he figured it was the best way to proceed. If he kept repeating the same answer then they could not catch out any inconsistencies. He had too much to think about to worry about changing his answers. All his strengths and abilities would soon be stretched to their limits. He was both excited and nervous with what he had to do.

"It looks so calm," Hulkan wanted to change the subject. "I can't believe it is where the battle is going to take place."

"Some of the most vicious battles have taken place in the most serene of locations," Jarwe explained, also happy with the change of topic.

Something ticked over in Alaric's mind. It was time to move. The assault could not wait another moment and there was no more time for pleasant chit-chat. It was time for action. He took a deep breath before he spoke.

"It is time for you to take the battlefield," Alaric almost couldn't get the words from his mouth. He was about to send a lot of men to their deaths.

"Are you sure this is the right thing to do?" Jarwe wanted to ask the question one more time before he voiced the command.

"There is no more time for conversation." Alaric wasn't going to answer the question.

"Tell us one last time why you are not taking the battlefield?" Sorrell asked from the other side of Jarwe.

"It is important that Ra'naroz doesn't suspect what I am planning. Remember that no matter what happens you have to remain confident. Do not act like anything out of the ordinary is happening."

No one liked what he was saying. The least Alaric could do was to explain what he was planning. It would make it a lot easier for them to lie to the Dark Knight. They were going to be nervous enough as it was. No matter how many times they asked him he was not going to give them an answer.

"Move out!" finally Jarwe called out the order.

The commanders were the first to move out onto the field. Alaric remained inside the forest as the soldiers marched passed him. They kept their eyes straight ahead as they passed. They all wanted to look at Alaric, but they didn't want to risk a reprimand. They all wanted to know why he was not leading the army. It did nothing to increase morale. It was lucky the soldiers were excited at the prospect of battle. When it was said and done they didn't really care who was leading as long as they got some action.

"Are you sure we are doing the right thing?" Sorrell asked Jarwe as they rode out into the open.

"I don't suppose we don't have any other choice," Jarwe didn't sound as though he believed in his words as he kept his gaze firmly on the castle.

There was a delayed reaction, but it seemed as though there was movement across the parapet. Jarwe kept a close eye on what was happening. The further they travelled the easier it would be for the archers to hit them. He could not see if the soldiers were armed with bows and arrows, but he assumed they were. It was a nervous walk and a long wait to see what was about to happen.

They rode their horses until they were within shouting distance. The army had stopped twenty paces behind. It didn't keep them out of arrow range, but it showed they were not about to start an attack. Most of the army was on the battlefield, but there was still a large amount of men in the forest. It was an awesome sight from on top of the castle wall. Under normal circumstances they would surrender to the invading army, but despite the fact that they were hugely outnumbered they had been ordered to defend the castle. Under no circumstances were they to cede control to the Alliance.

"Is there someone who can treat with me?" Jarwe called to the castle.

There was a short silence before a reply came from the wall. "I am Captain Prewitt. Why have you brought an invading army to our land?" It was an honest question, although he already knew the answer.

"We believe you are under attack from within. We are here to liberate you," Jarwe kept his voice strong.

"There is nothing wrong here. If that was the only reason why you marched onto the field then you can just turn around and make your way back." The captain would not be dissuaded.

They all knew that there was no chance of talking them down, but they had to try. It made for a better ruse if they attempted the discussion. It would be all too suspicious if they walked up to the gate and started shouting threats. That's what Alaric wanted. He wanted an excuse for the Dark Knight to enter the discussions.

"I do not believe you are the one that I need to speak to." Jarwe changed his tact. "Bring Prince Leroy out. I will negotiate with him."

There was a round of laughter from the castle. It was a nervous laughter, but it was laughter nonetheless. Jarwe took offence to the sound, but he knew it was not going to be that easy. He would have to get through the captain if he was going to get to speak with the prince. He didn't want to provoke the man, but he didn't have a choice. For the first time he wished Aimon was with them. He thought he would be able to speak to his kinsman, but the captain had not been seen all morning.

"The prince has more important matters to deal with," the captain called back. "If you want to speak to someone then you can speak with me. I am in charge of the army here and I make the decisions." There was little confidence in his words.

Jarwe looked to Sorrell for support. Despite the fact that he saw straight through the captain's bravado he really had no idea what to say next. He knew what needed to happen, but he still didn't want to do it. If he was successful then a barrage of arrows would soon be raining down on them. He hoped Sorrell might have something to say that could avoid the fateful situation.

"I don't think we have a choice. You know what Alaric told us. If we could not get the prince to speak with us then we have to provoke them to attack," Sorrel reassured him.

Jarwe lowered his head before he shook it. He was hoping for a different response. He was hoping for any sort of response that didn't lead to an attack, but he knew it was not going to come. He felt like turning the army around, but that was not the answer either. He was the general of the army, at least until Bern returned, and he needed to start acting like it. He had fought battles before. He had led men to their deaths. He did not know why he suddenly felt so responsible.

"If your prince will not come out to meet us then we have no choice, but to attack"

Jarwe wanted to give the captain on last chance to change his mind. He also wanted the captain to attack. The battering rams had been finished and were being carried onto the field. Alaric had given strict instructions they were not to be used, but their appearance would signify their intensions better than words ever could. Jarwe didn't know what they were going to do if the captain did not give the order to attack. Their entire plan had been to ram the castle gates and he did not think the soldiers would accept things if he told them not to.

"Do your worst," the captain didn't sound interested.

"What do we do now?" Jarwe looked at Sorrell.

"I guess we could give our own archers a shot at the castle. I hear the elven archers are exceptional shooters. I am sure that once they lose a few men they will attack back," Sorrell actually sounded pleased with himself. Jarwe didn't think it was the time or the place, but he was happy for the advice.

"Lord Pernian," Jarwe called to the elven lord.

"Yes, general!" he called back.

"I think that you should have your archers fire a few volleys over the wall. Let's see if we can get a reaction from that." The more he thought about it the more he liked the idea.

Lord Pernian rode back to where his elves were positioned. He was looking forward to unleashing his archers and they would definitely provoke a response. Once he explained their plan the elves moved forward.

There were not as many archers as Jarwe would have liked for a proper attack, but that was not what they were there for. There were going to be casualties, but that could not be stopped. At least it was the elves who were doing the killing. It would be a little easier on the army.

Pernian rode back to his place with the other commanders and raised his right hand above his head. It was the signal for his archers to nock their arrows and prepare to fire. He would not give the signal to fire until Jarwe had made his final decision. He knew the general was having second thoughts. He didn't like the plan in the first place, but Pernian had a little more faith in Alaric than Jarwe had, but he was not going to subvert the general.

"This is your last chance to surrender," Jarwe yelled.

"Do your worst. Even with your numbers you will not breech our walls," the captain called back.

"Fire!" Jarwe called out at the top of his lungs.

Pernian lowered his arm, giving the signal to shoot. Although Jarwe had shouted the command the archers would not fire without the signal from Lord Pernian. As soon as it was given the elves reacted in a heartbeat. Almost as one there was a loud twang of bowstrings and a volley of arrows was sent sailing into the air. It was as if the soldiers on the parapet did not believe they were going to shoot. It wasn't until the arrows were in the air that they decided to protect themselves.

When the arrows fell a number a screams could be heard from inside the castle. Jarwe cringed. He didn't know why he felt so bad. He had battled against Entero in the past and he had killed many Enteroites. There was something different about the battle before him. Those inside the castle were not his enemy. He did not want to see anyone die, anyone except for the prince.

"Another volley," Jarwe called out when there was no reply from the castle.

Pernian signalled for another volley. He was surprised the first attack did not warrant a response. He didn't really want to signal another attack as it meant that there would be more deaths. Normally he wouldn't mind killing the men, but if they were to succeed then those inside the castle walls would have to become allies.

The arrows again flew through the air and over the castle wall. There were fewer screams than the first time, but there were still screams. Jarwe really wanted to know what was happening on the other side. He hoped they were preparing for a counter-attack. The last thing he wanted to do was to send another volley.

"What are you going to do now?" Sorrell asked. He kept his voice low so none of the soldiers could hear him.

"We wait for a response," Jarwe replied, keeping his voice at the same level.

"I don't know if that is such a good idea. The soldiers will see that we hold the advantage now. If we wait for them to attack then I feel they will lose faith in your leadership." Sorrell's council was wise.

"This was never a great plan from the start, but we have to stick to it now that we have started. Alaric warned to only send two volleys over the walls and that is exactly what we are going to do," Jarwe replied.

Sorrell knew there was going to be no other response. They had to do what Alaric had told them, but he still didn't like it. He could see in Jarwe's face that he also didn't like it. He would have to keep his mouth shut for the moment, but he would look for his opportunity in the future.

He did not want to subvert Alaric, but he did not believe the man knew what he was talking about. He had absolutely no experience with war and none with the Alliance. The plan sounded like it was going to get them all killed.

"What do you say about that Captain Prewitt?" he called to the castle.

The army seemed confused at his words. It was not normal that the generals would stop to talk at such a time in the battle. They had the advantage and it was time for them to continue the attack. With no defence coming from the castle it was the perfect time to besiege. They had the battering rams ready and it was time to use them.

The captain popped his head above parapet. Even from the distance they could see the confused look on his face. He was obviously expecting another attack. When there was none coming he brushed off his surprise and did his best to regain his command.

"Is that all that you have? Well I think you should see what a real army does." He looked behind to see where his archers were. They were busy running around trying to avoid being shot. When they realised the arrows had stopped they composed themselves. "On the wall you wretched men. Show some backbone."

There was silence as Prewitt waited for his men to get into position. He was surprised there were no more attacks from the army on the field. He knew General Jarwe, by reputation; he was a renowned general and a man to be feared of on the wrong side of the battlefield. He wondered if the stories he had heard were true. The man across the field from him could not be the same master tactician. If he was then Prewitt had a feeling he was walking into a trap. Nevertheless he was not going to look a gift horse in the mouth. He had been caught off guard and there was a very good chance the army could have breeched the gates. His soldiers were taking a long time to ready themselves. He cursed himself for being taken off guard, but since he had been given a chance to recover he was not going to waste it.

"Move into position. Do you want me to get the prince? I could tell him how slow you are at taking orders." The threat of the prince was enough to make any man move.

Prewitt watched the opposing army carefully. If they fired again then he would lose a lot of his men. He could not work out why they were waiting or what they were waiting for. The way things were going his archers would be in position without another loss of life.

That was in fact the way it happened. His archers were ready to fire and the army had not moved. It took all of Jarwe's self-control to keep him from giving the order. The enemy was taking a long time to get ready. Every time he thought of giving the order to attack he remembered he had to do what Alaric had said. He knew he had no other choice.

"Now, I will give you one last chance," Captain Prewitt called from the castle wall. "My archers will be a lot more efficient than yours."

"Stand strong men," Jarwe called to the soldiers who were in the firing line. "Stand strong and we will be victorious," he kept the strength in his voice, even though he did not completely believe in his own words.

"Ready," Prewitt called when it was clear that they were not going to surrender. "Aim... Fire!"

The twang of bowstrings was louder than those of the elves, although they were not as synchronized. The arrows flew over the castle walls. Some were shot from the walls themselves whilst others were shot from the ground behind. Jarwe looked in horror as the arc neared its pinnacle. It was the time for Alaric's plan to come to the fore. If it didn't then they would soon all be dead.

Just before the arrows were about to land on their heads the strangest thing happened. They suddenly bounced off an unseen shield. As they returned skyward they disappeared. None of the arrows made it through the shield towards their target. The sight shocked both sides of the battlefield. No one knew what was happening or what they should do.

"It seems as though Alaric knows what he's talking about," Jarwe was glad he could act superior. No one cared about his attitude, however, they were just happy to be alive.

"I am quite happy to stand corrected," Sorrell's voice was filled with awe. He had no idea Alaric was capable of such a feat.

By himself Alaric was not capable of such a spell. He knew this when he made the plan. He also knew that with the aid of the Emerald stone he could do what needed to be done. Despite the urge to put the stone in its velvet pouch he had kept the bracelet on his wrist since they had left the wasteland. He had to trust the conversation inside his mind. The voice had said it was going to help. In the end he didn't think he could have accomplished both what he had and what he needed to do without the stone's help.

Ever since they had reached the forest Alaric had felt something new inside the stone. It was something he had not felt before. It was almost like the stone was at peace. Alaric also felt a renewed strength that was more powerful than he had felt from it before. In the end it made what he had to do much easier.

The shock took a moment to register on the captain's face as he watched what should have been a deadly rain of arrows, but was in fact a completely futile attack. He had been prepared to signal a second attack once the first had struck, but instead he just stood there. It took him more than a moment to recover his senses.

"What are you looking at?" he yelled the question to no one in particular. "Fire your arrows!" he was starting to lash out at his subordinates.

There was only a short pause before the bowstrings started to snap again. There was no order to their shooting. Each time the arrows came close to hitting their target they bounced off the invisible shield. Once they were back into the air they completely disappeared again.

Alaric hoped the captain would soon send for the Dark Knight. The strain of keeping the protective shield up was starting to weigh on him. Although he could keep it up all day he needed his energy to save his friends trapped in the castle dungeons.

The disappearing arrows caused more confusion than anything else within the castle grounds. Those at the base of the wall could not understand what was happening on the other side. The archers on the wall had stopped shooting after their second arrows had had no effect. They could not comprehend what was happening. The sight did nothing to reassure those who could not see. They kept shooting until Prewitt called for them to stop.

"What do you think you are doing? Stop wasting your arrows," he was fuming as he barked the order.

The archers did as they were told, but they did not know why he had spoken to them so harshly. They wanted nothing more than to climb the stairs to the parapet, but they did not want to suffer the captain's wrath. Something bad was happening on the other side of the wall and until they knew what it was they would have to rely on instructions from their leader.

Captain Prewitt stared out at the untouched army before him. He was not sure if what he had seen was the truth or if he had been dreaming. He was hoping he was still asleep and he was going to wake up at any moment. As much as he wanted it to be true he knew it was not. There was simply an impossible situation before him and he had to work out what to do. He had to admit he had underestimated General Jarwe's abilities. He still didn't completely understand the manoeuvre, but now he had a lot more respect for the man.

"Somebody go and get Prince Leroy." He kept his gaze out in front.

Nobody moved. No one wanted to be responsible for fetching the prince. No one wanted to be in the same room as the prince, let alone be the one to summon him. It was the reason that Prewitt did not want to speak the order, but there was no other option. There was magic at work and the prince was the only one capable of dealing with it.

"Move!" he screamed at the nearest soldier, who was already trying to sneak away.

Jarwe could see that Captain Prewitt was not enjoying the situation. He had to admit to himself he didn't completely understand what was happening, but he had a lot more faith in Alaric than he did a few minutes before. The next part of the plan was not going to be easy. Alaric had told him he had to provoke the prince. They did not want the prince to attack, but merely lose his temper. That was not going to be easy. Once the prince was on the parapet there was a limited amount of time he could protect them. Once Alaric was gone it was up to them. If the prince was provoked enough to attack himself then the casualties would increase.

"We need to prepare the soldiers," Jarwe spoke to Sorrell. "The archers have done their job. We need to be ready for an attack."

"If the prince is standing on the wall there is a chance we can shoot him," Sorrell suggested.

Alaric had told them under no circumstances were they to shoot at the prince. Even though the start of his plan had worked there was still a long way to go. Sorrell thought it would be better if they just did away with the prince when they had the opportunity. Jarwe was able to read between the lines and knew what Alaric was talking about.

"If Alaric could protect us from the barrage of arrows I think that a Dark Knight would be able to do the same. I am sure not one of our arrows would touch him. If Alaric says not to shoot then that is what we are going to do," Jarwe returned. He was glad he was in charge, although if he wasn't he would probably be thinking the same as Sorrell.

The fact of the matter would prove firing arrows would be the best way to distract Ra'naroz. He would have to move his attention from the prisoners and use it to stop them. The only problem was if he was physically attacked then there was a good chance that he would respond in kind. Once the spell shrouding the castle had dissipated he would have to move into action. He would not be able to protect his army from a magical attack. He was not prepared to take that risk with the soldiers' lives, although if it came down to the crunch he would have to consider it.

Alaric continued to watch from the edge of the forest. There had been no action for too long. He only hoped they were getting the Dark Knight. Everything was going to plan, but the easy part was over. He was not looking forward to Jarwe taking on Ra'naroz. He didn't think the general would be a match for the Dark Knight. There was not much he could do about it. If he tried to help then he was sure that Ra'naroz would know where he was. If that was the case then there was little hope he would be able to rescue the prisoners.

There was a long wait whilst the soldiers went to get the prince. Captain Prewitt stood nervously on the parapet and stared out to the army before him. They had made no further move to attack. There had been no word from General Jarwe. The sudden pause was disturbing. There had to be a reason why they were waiting, but he couldn't figure out what it was. He was not looking forward to trying to explain the situation to the prince.

"Get down from there," the voice did not sound happy.

Captain Prewitt did not have to look to know who was speaking and who he was speaking to. He did not want to leave the battlements, but he had no choice. To disobey the prince meant a trip to the dungeons. He would rather die in battle than be imprisoned.

Taking a deep breath he prepared himself for what he knew was going to be an ordeal. The prince would not be happy with what he had done, not that he knew what he should have done. There was nothing he could do to stop a magician. There was no other explanation.

The sight before the captain was not at all what he was expecting. He thought the prince would be dressed for battle, but instead he wore a light blue, silk shirt and thin linen trousers. It looked as though he was out for a friendly stroll.

"Why have you disturbed me from my entertainment?" There was a sullen look on the prince's face.

Prewitt cringed at the prince's reference to entertainment. He had heard what the prince liked to do for his entertainment and it was not something he wanted to think about. If what he had heard was only half true then it was still too much.

"I am sorry, your majesty," Prewitt wished that he did not have to speak to him, he always made him feel uncomfortable. "There is something that you need to hear."

"Well spit it out. I don't have all day." the prince did not look impressed.

Slowly Captain Prewitt explained what had happened. He wanted to be careful to explain the entire situation. He knew if he forgot something then it would come back to haunt him. He wanted nothing more than to relinquish control to the prince and return to the barracks.

"I am sure it is not that bad," Prince Leroy did not sound convinced. "Let's take a look at it."

Leroy led the captain back onto the top of the wall. He was not going to let Prewitt go until he was sure of what was happening. If there was something off with the captain's story then there would be trouble. He did not like bad news.

He could not believe what he had been told. He knew the Cursed One had arrived. He had felt his presence as soon as he made it Jarrat, even sooner in fact. What he didn't understand was why he hadn't used his strength to attack the city. Ra'naroz had been expecting him to try and rescue the prisoners, but this was something else. If he wanted a battle then that's what Ra'naroz would give him.

When he reached the top of the castle wall he looked out over the battlefield. He was angered to see the army standing there. There should have been dead bodies strewn across the land. He wanted nothing more than to strike down at the silly little ants standing before him. Fire would work nicely. It had been too long since he had brought fire down from the heavens. It would make such a nice display.

Slowly Ra'naroz started to fill himself with the energy around him. Alaric watched on from the tree line. He did not expect such a reaction from the Dark Knight and was not prepared for an attack. If he mustered a quick defence then Ra'naroz would know exactly where he was. If he did not then the army would be slaughtered.

As the energy filled the Dark Knight's body he suddenly let it go. He could not feel Alaric on the other side of the field and that was not what he was expecting. He had to be smart, he had to be cautious. There was only one reason he could think of why he could not feel Alaric. He would be preparing for an attack and was masking his presence. He could not fall into a trap.

He scanned the army for a sign of Alaric, but there was no sign of the man. If he was indeed planning an attack then it would make sense for him remain hidden. As he continued to look through the army he knew that it would be a fruitless exercise. All he could do was be prepared for when the attack came. He would need to speak with the head of the opposing army to get an idea of what was happening.

"Who is it who believes that he can bring an army to the doorstep of my castle?" his voice boomed throughout the battlefield. Everyone could easily hear his words.

"You have usurped power that is not yours," Alaric made sure that Jarwe's words could be clearly heard by everyone. It was a simple spell and one that the Dark Knight would not be able to sense. "I have come here for your surrender. The rule of Entero will return to the queen."

The sound of laughter resonated around the battlefield. It was not the response that Jarwe had been expecting. His job was to enrage the

Dark Knight, not to entertain him. All he could do was to wait for the laughter to die down and Leroy to respond.

"The queen is quite happy for me to be here. In fact she is quite happy on a daily basis." The comment passed over most of the army, but the command group knew exactly what he was talking about. The thought of what the Dark Knight had been doing to Queen Oriana almost made them feel sick. "It is you who is the invading army. It is you who is in the wrong. Leave my land now and I will let you live. Stay, and I will see that you are all dead by nightfall."

"You are hereby required to surrender to the Alliance. You will face trial in due course for your crimes. From there I have no doubt you will be executed for what you have done." Jarwe ignored the Dark Knight's taunts. He would not be able rile the Dark Knight if he engaged in futile conversation.

"I will face no trial. I do not live by your rules. I live by the rules of the Great Lord. In his name you will all burn today," Ra'naroz was starting to become more enraged.

Jarwe was starting to run out of ideas. Alaric had told him under no circumstances was he to attack the castle, but it was not as easy as he thought to rattle the Dark Knight. If things did not turn around soon he didn't think that he had any other option but to attack. It was not something that he wanted to do, but he could not lose the advantage.

"This is your last chance," Jarwe warned. "If you do not surrender we will be forced to attack."

Ra'naroz was still nervous that Alaric had not shown himself. He had no doubt that he was stronger than the Cursed One, but the element of surprise could be dangerous. If he was to use his power to defend the castle then there was a chance that Alaric could attack him directly. That was a risk that he could not take. In the back of his mind he felt the spells he was holding. They were becoming more of a strain as time passed. He didn't think too much could go wrong if he released them and it would not be long before he could create them again. There was still the surprise waiting in the forest. That thought made him smile.

"Then I think that you should attack. There is nothing more that I need to speak with you about," Ra'naroz spoke with a grin.

Jarwe looked at the other commanders for support. They didn't seem to have any answers for him. In his life as a general it was the hardest decision that he had to make, although he felt as though he had no other choice. He had painted himself into a corner. If he did not give the order to attack then Ra'naroz would know he was bluffing. If he did attack then he would be going against what Alaric had told him.

"What should I do?" he asked the question to himself more than anyone else.

No one wanted to answer and the question was lost on the wind. The army was starting to become nervous. The gauntlet had been thrown down, but no action had been made. They were starting to doubt their leader. It was time to take action and there should have been no hesitation. The battering rams should have been moved into place.

"Bring up the rams!" Jarwe called out. There was no other choice. All he could hope for was that Alaric was able to protect them again.

***

Alaric watched the exchange from the edge of the forest. Things had not gone as well as he had hoped. There was something wrong with Ra'naroz. He was not as aggressive as Alaric had thought he would have been. He didn't think that the Dark Knight would be able to control himself being goaded by a mere man and it seemed as though they were in risk of having to siege the castle. It was something that Alaric wanted to avoid. He was between a rock and hard place and he didn't know what he should do. If he protected the army then his friends were as good as dead. If he tried to rescue his friends then the army would suffer horrendous loses. If the army attacked the castle then he did not think that Ra'naroz would spare them.

Slowly he could feel the cover over the castle start to waver. He could still not sense anyone inside, but it was a good sign. Ra'naroz's attention was starting to slip from the spells he had in place. It was a good sign and a bad sign. Whichever way things went Alaric had to make up his mind. If he waited much longer then the decision would be made for him. He wished he had Eldred or Heryion to ask advice. Life was so much easier when he did not have to make all the decisions by himself.

Suddenly Alaric got a feeling that something was wrong, something was different. He had a bad feeling that he was missing something. There was something bad in the near future and there was nothing he could about it until he knew what it was.

He returned his attention to the scene in front of him. He had to focus on the task ahead. The sound of the over-accentuated voices had died down. He had no idea what the last words had been spoken and he cursed himself for losing perspective. All he could do was wait to see what was about to happen.

"Bring up the Rams!" he heard Jarwe shout the command.

It was the time to make his decision.

Chapter 3: Into the Castle

The sound of the battering ram pounding on the castle gates echoed throughout the battlefield. To everyone's surprise there was no sign of a counter attack from the castle. Alaric could easily see Ra'naroz on the battlements scanning the army for someone. He was surprised there had been no attack. He was sure once the assault had started then all hell would break loose. It was as if Ra'naroz was waiting for something to happen. The worst part was that the shroud over the castle was still up. Until it was gone there was nothing Alaric could do but wait.

The makeshift battering rams did not seem to be having any affect on the heavily constructed castle gates. Without iron to tip the rams it would be a difficult task breaking them down. Alaric thought Ra'naroz might be under the impression the gates would hold, but the army had a least a dozen more rams in reserve. One way or another they would make their way into the castle. That was the reason why Alaric could not understand why Ra'naroz did not attack. He knew the Dark Knight's could be arrogant, but they were not stupid.

There was another option Alaric had available to him, but it was risky. With Ra'naroz's attention on the army there was a chance Alaric could break the spell and enter the castle before Ra'naroz realised what he was doing, but there was little chance of Ra'naroz not realising it. It was a move he would have to make if the shroud did not lift soon, but it would be a last resort.

It was not long before the second ram was brought up into place. No one could believe there were no ramifications from their attack. It was becoming one of the strangest sieges of all time. Even after the surprises at Kiarome the soldiers could still not believe what they were witnessing. The army in the castle still made no move to counter-attack.

Alaric watched on from the tree-line as the bazarre situation continued. Shortly after the second ram had come out Alaric had made his decision. Regardless of what happened he would have to save those trapped in the castle. The soldiers were used to war and knew that there would be casualties. As much as he didn't want to sacrifice the valiant men in the Alliance he had to rescue the prisoners. He knew that deep down in his heart and he knew he really did not have any other option.

As the second ram was wearing down a loud creak could be heard from behind the wall. It was obvious, even without hearing the command from within the castle, what was about to happen. The portcullis from behind the castle gate was being raised. Although nothing would surprise them now, it was clear that Ra'naroz planned on fighting the Alliance. It was a bold move that baffled everyone, except Alaric.

The Dark Knight had no allegiance or compassion to those inside the castle. If he believed all was lost then there was no reason why he would keep the soldiers alive. There was something else that Alaric could not put his finger on. He knew it related to the bad feeling he had felt earlier. There was a terrible surprise waiting for them, but he still could not work out what it was.

The soldiers using the ram simply dropped it to the ground and retreated. If there were soldiers about to spew forth from the castle then there was no reason for them to be there. They did not need to wait for the order to come from the commanders. They had been soldiers long enough to know what to do.

A hush had fallen over the Alliance as they waited for the gates to open. There was a long pause as the portcullis screeched to a halt. Those on the other side were not so sure it was the right decision. They also knew that there was no point in disobeying an order from prince Leroy. He would be quite happy to kill everyone until he found someone who would open the gate. If they were to die then they would do so on the battlefield.

Alaric let his attention stray from the Dark Knight to the gate. He was also waiting to see what was about to happen. He hated to think the Alliance would have to fight those in the Enteroite army, but there was no other choice.

He did not have a chance to see the gate fully open. Before he knew what was happening the shroud had disappeared. In a flash he could feel the location of Bern, Alena and Eldred. He could not pinpoint them exactly, but it was enough to go on. With a little luck he could rescue them and be back in time to help the army. In his excitement he almost forgot to mask his spell. Although he would not be able to completely hide what he was doing he was hoping that Ra'naroz would be too distracted to notice.

Alaric heard the creak of the gates starting to open as he disappeared from the tree-line. The jump through reality was only small, but it would still have an effect on him. The spell he used to deflect the arrows had drained a small amount of energy and although the jump would not drain much it all counted. The last thing he wanted to do was to face the Dark Knight in a weakened condition. In the end he would have to rely on the power of the Emerald stone if he was going to succeed. The Jade dagger hung in its sheath on his belt, but he had no intention of using it.

There was a strange feeling as he travelled. It was a different experience jumping through the threads of reality; travelling through stone rather than open space. With more time he would have studied the moment, but there were more important matters to deal with. He took a deep gasp of breath as he suddenly returned to the world. As soon as he did he wished he had not. His lungs filled with the stench of the dungeons. The hot, stale air stunk of rotting flesh. He involuntarily dropped to his knees and started coughing. It was obvious that no one else was in the room or he would have been attacked. He had been prepared to come out fighting, but the rotten air had stopped him. His eyes had started to water as he continued to cough. The noise would draw attention to himself, but there was nothing he could do.

The sound of loping footsteps could be heard coming towards the small cavern he was in. Slowly he came to his feet and looked around to judge his surroundings. In the centre of the cavern was a dead body, hanging from chains from the roof. The body had been there for a long time and had obviously not died well. The feet had been eaten away by rats and the skin hung off its bones. Alaric did not have time to feel sorry for the deceased. He had to prepare himself for the attack.

"What's going on here?" a deep, slovenly voice spoke as a large man moved into the doorway.

Luckily for Alaric there was no door at the entrance to the cavern or there was a chance he could have been locked in. The man looked surprised when he saw Alaric standing at the far side of the cavern. It was obvious he was not expecting to see a live body. The shock almost made him drop the large cudgel he held in his right hand.

Alaric's first reaction was to run the man through. There was no chance the prison guard could defend himself with a cudgel. It would take a lucky blow to knock Alaric out, but he knew it would only take one. The guard's arms were as thick as his cudgel and one hit to the head would crack it wide open, but that wasn't the reason why he stayed his attack. With the guards help he would be able to find the prisoners a lot quicker. His wits would be more pertinent than his skill with the sword.

"There you are!" Alaric put on his most officious voice, that is to say that he sound annoyed. "I tell you these dungeons are like a maze."

Alaric took a step closer, but no further. The guard had a confused expression on his face. He didn't know what to think. He had not been expecting someone from the castle. In fact the only people he saw from the castle were prisoners, the soldiers escorting them and the prince. He definitely did not recognise the man before him. He thought the warden would have told him if they were expecting someone and the man did seem like he knew what he was doing. He knew not to upset those of a noble birth. It would not be unheard of if he ended up next to one of his victims.

"I have been looking everywhere for you," Alaric kept up the façade when the guard did not speak. "Prince Leroy wanted you to show me the new prisoners."

There was truth in his words, but they did not make complete sense. The warden was the only one who was allowed to see the new prisoners. He had been quite strict about that and the prince did not want anyone to see them. But the man standing before him did seem to know what he was talking about. The only thing he could think of was to get the warden. He knew he was going to be in trouble either way and it seemed like the most obvious solution.

"Are you just going to stand there looking like an idiot or are you going to take me to the prisoners?" Alaric took another step forward and placed his hand on the hilt of his sword. He did not want to get too close. If the guard did not believe him there was a good chance he would receive a knock on his head. "I do not have all day." Alaric was starting to get really annoyed, making it easier to play the part. He did not know why the guard wasn't responding.

"Very well. I cannot take you to the prisoners myself, but I will take you to the warden. If you are who you say you are then he will know." The guard was starting to regain control.

Alaric didn't think that the warden would approve his request. He had one more card to play, but he really didn't think it would work.

"I do not have time for this. If you like I would be happy to tell the prince that you have disobeyed his command. I am sure that he will want to come down and reward you personally," Alaric barked the words, firmly gripping the hilt of his sword.

The guard was taken aback by Alaric's abruptness. He was not expecting such a response. He was not a quick witted man, but he would not be bullied by nobility. Down in the bowels of the castle he was royalty. Even with his small mental capacity he could tell there was something different about the man standing before him. He could sense Alaric's power.

"What is your name?" the guard realised he had no idea who he was talking to. The name wouldn't make much difference as he didn't know any noblemen, but he thought that it was an appropriate question.

Alaric took another step forward as he was about to speak, moving within striking distance. The guard made no move to attack, but Alaric could tell that he was thinking about it. He had no idea what name he should give. Although he didn't think the guard would recognise a name, there was a chance that he could.

"My name is..." Alaric took another step forward.

The guard became nervous as Alaric didn't answer straight away and before the guard could move Alaric drew his sword. The movement was as quick as lightning and the shock was clear on the guards face as Alaric stabbed him through the heart. The look remained on the guard's face as his life blinked out. Alaric pushed the guard backwards before he had a chance to collapse on him. If the guard had fallen then it would take a great effort to get out from underneath.

Before he left the cavern he wiped his blade on the dead guard's grubby shirt. The action didn't do much to remove the blood, but it was better than nothing. Alaric knew he would be shedding more before he left the dungeons. He would worry about cleaning his blade properly later.

The feeling that Bern was close was unmistakable, but his connection to Alena and Eldred was not as strong. They were still quite a distance away. Alaric was amazed at what that meant. The dungeons of Jarrat were more extensive than Alaric had originally thought. He had to keep moving if he was going to rescue everyone before Ra'naroz realised he was there.

The air outside the cavern was not much better than inside. Alaric assumed that the entire dungeon must have the foul smell of death. He could not imagine the suffering and pain of those who had died. He knew if he concentrated enough he would be able to feel it, but that was not something he really wanted to do. The pain and the suffering could easily overwhelm him. He could feel the pure malevolence emanating from the walls. He felt as though the pure evil surrounding him could consume him at any moment and that was why he had to hurry. He did not think that he would be able to fight the Dark Knight in such a place.

It did not take long for Alaric to realise that finding the prisoners without a guide was not going to be easy. His sense of Bern's location was strong, but that was not really helping. His sense of Bern was in a straight line, whereas the prison tunnels were not. Just when he thought he was travelling in the right direction he came to a dead end. The worst part was the dead ends always ended up in a torture cavern. Most of the inhabitants were already dead, some by more than a week. They were bad enough but occasionally he stumbled across a cavern where the victim was still alive. The almost inaudible moans cut through Alaric's heart like a razor blade. The only humane thing for Alaric to do was to kill them. There was nothing he could do to save their saves and to leave them hanging was cruel. The trail of death he left behind would alert the guards to his presence, but he could not leave them alive.

After an hour of searching through the tunnels Alaric stopped to rest. He was starting to become frustrated. With the shroud gone he thought that he would be able find his friends quickly. He did not think it would be such an ordeal. With every new cavern he could feel himself slipping into the darkness. The pure evil was starting to get to him, suffocating him like someone was holding a pillow over his mouth.

As he stood and sucked in the evil around him he heard the sound of footsteps. The last thing he wanted was another confrontation. He was getting nowhere fast and the more dead bodies he left behind the greater the chance that Ra'naroz would realise he was there. There was a cavern not far from where he was standing and there was no other choice but to hide there.

The footsteps stopped directly outside the cavern and Alaric's heart started to race. His hand went to the hilt of his sword and he realised for the first time his hand was starting to shake. He would have to calm himself if he was going to complete his task. He knew he would be able to draw strength from the Emerald stone and as the thought entered his mind it started to glow softly. Alaric could only hope those on the other side of the door wouldn't be able to see the green light.

"Do you hear something?" the warden asked.

"No, sir," the second voice sounded submissive.

"Something strange is happening here and I don't like it." The sound of the warden moving around was a clear sign he was looking for the noise.

"What do you mean?" the guard sounded as though he didn't want to ask the question.

"There are a string of dead prisoners behind us. I am sure that some of them should still be alive," he sighed as he thought. "It just doesn't make sense."

There was a moment of silence as both men thought. The guard did not want to speak as he knew the warden could be a vengeful man when he wanted to be. It would not be the first time the warden had sent one of his guards to the torture chambers. On the other hand if he kept quiet then there was also a good chance he would also end up in chains.

"Do you think someone might be coming to save the new prisoners?" the guard didn't sound confident with his suggestion.

There was another moment of silence as the warden thought. Alaric's ears pricked up at the mention of his friends. There was a good chance he could gain the information that he needed and all of a sudden his dire situation was looking promising.

"I think that you might be right," the warden sounded impressed. "It's the only reason that makes sense." There was another pause as the warden thought again. The guard was pleased he had said the right thing and he was not going to ruin it by speaking again. "I will check on the prisoners. You will go and find the prince and advise him on what is happening."

At the sound of the warden's words the guard's heart sank. The last thing he wanted to do was to deliver bad news to the prince. He thought it might be better to be hanging from the chains than to face the prince's wrath.

"I don't think the prince would like to hear about this. I am sure that we can sort this out ourselves," speaking out of turn was a risk, but it was one he had to take.

"Do you dare question my judgement?" the warden yelled. "See that you do what I tell you or you will face the most terrible of punishments."

It was the tone in the warden's voice that convinced the guard to do as he was told. The sound of his hurried footsteps was heard shortly after the warden's tirade

Time was against Alaric. It would not be long before the Dark Knight came to investigate. Ra'naroz would not be stupid enough not to realise Alaric was there. He needed to move quickly, but he was bound by the warden's pace. There was nothing else he could do to speed things along.

"I can help you." Alaric jumped as the voice came inside his mind. It had been a long time since the voice had come and he wasn't expecting it.

"There will be time," Alaric returned. "Now is not the time for rash actions."

There was something inside his mind that didn't agree with his words, but there was no response. That last thing Alaric wanted to do was fight with the voice inside his head and he was grateful it seemed to accept his answer.

Alaric waited in the cavern until the footsteps were almost inaudible. He had to be careful if he was going to follow the warden and not be discovered. Despite the fact that time was against him it would be even worse if he was caught. All he could do was hope his friends were not far away.

As Alaric moved out of the cavern he just glimpsed the warden before he disappeared around a corner. The movement made Alaric feel a little better. He did not think he could have remained in the cavern a second longer. The stench of death was really getting to him.

The warden kept a painfully slow place. He stopped regularly to check the many caverns to see if the intruder was hiding. On more than one occasion Alaric nearly walked around a corner into him. If the large man had been paying attention he would have easily realised he was being followed. The warden was too concerned with what was happening in front of him to take any notice of what was happening behind.

After, what Alaric thought were hours, they finally reached the prison where Bern and the others were being held. The warden marched inside, brandishing an angry looking cudgel. He looked as though he was ready to bash everyone.

"Have you missed me?" the warden asked when he entered.

Alaric remained out of view. He did not want to risk the lives of his friends by rushing in. The warden could easily club any one of them before Alaric had a chance to attack. It was hard for him to wait, but the risk was too great.

"We have told you already. There is no point in torturing us. There is nothing that we can tell you." Alaric could clearly make out Bern's voice. It still sounded strong which lifted his spirits.

The warden didn't speak straight away. It was as if he was waiting for something. When nothing happened he returned his attention to the man who had spoken. An evil grin crossed his face.

"That is not for you to decide. I have been given instructions from the prince. I just can't wait for the time that I get you in the middle. I have something special waiting for you," there was a nervous tone to the warden's voice.

"I have told you already. I am ready to take whatever you can hand out." Bern picked up on the nervousness. "But I do not think that is why you are here." Bern paused for dramatic effect. "Something has happened. I can smell the fear."

"I would not speak so brazenly if I was you. Just because the prince has told me not to torture you now doesn't mean he will not change his mind in the future. The more you provoke me the more I will enjoy getting you." The warden didn't sound too convincing.

"I think you're right Bern. There is definitely something wrong with our good warden," Hadar's voice was weak, but it still had a certain strength to it.

"Now I don't think you should be saying anything. I would be more than happy to give you another beating." The warden turned his attention to Hadar.

"We have taken your beatings this far. You are not as good as you think." It was obvious the warden was becoming flustered and they all wanted to get into the act. Alaric realised Richmond's voice was weaker than Hadar's, but he was trying his best to sound powerful.

"That's right. You are not as tough as you think you are. We will not be bullied by you," Tancred added his piece.

The warden looked around the room wildly. He did not know what was happening. His prisoners had never spoken to him in such a manner. Something was not right, he was losing control of a situation that he should clearly be commanding.

The taunts started coming from all around the cavern. They did not seem to fear the reprisal of such actions. When he spun around to see who had just spoken, another prioner attacked him. The cavern was starting to spin and he didn't think he could stay there any longer. It was obvious the intruder was not in the cavern, so he still had time to wait for the prince to arrive.

As the warden backed out of the room he realised there was someone else in the tunnel. He thought it was of one of his guards. That thought in itself was enough to enrage him. He had given strict instructions that no one was allowed in this area of the dungeons.

"You better have a good reason for being here. You have a second to respond or you will hang from the chains," the warden didn't even look at Alaric when he spoke.

Alaric was taken aback by the warden's words, but it did not take him long to realise what was happening. He almost laughed when he realised the warden didn't know who he was. The thought of playing along was too irresistible.

"The prince sent me," Alaric kept his voice level. "He told me he believes there is someone trying to infiltrate the prison. He wants you to meet him in the castle."

If the warden had been thinking properly he would have realised the words did not make sense. There was no way Prince Leroy would call the prison warden to the castle. However the warden's mind was still filled with the prisoners' taunts.

"Very good, I will be along shortly," the warden still did not look at Alaric. "You should leave here now." The warden said as he collected his thoughts before he left the prisoners.

"I do not think that the prince wants to be kept waiting," Alaric pushed the warden.

The warden had taken two steps away from the cavern giving Alaric the perfect opportunity to block the entrance to the torture chamber. The time was right for him to make his attack.

"I know, but I need time to…" The warden finally took a moment to think on what was being said. When he looked at, who he assumed was a guard, he almost fell over backwards. He took two stumbled steps before he composed himself. "Who are you?"

"I am Alaric and this ends now," Alaric drew his sword as he spoke.

"You will not free those prisoners." The warden brandished his cudgel, but he was no longer sure of himself. "The prince will be here any minute. I have no doubt that he will dispose of you."

Alaric took a step forward. All of a sudden he could feel the death and pain that the warden had dished out. He could not say the warden was evil, but when it was said and done he was just doing his job and there was a chance he was only doing what he thought was right. One thing that he was sure of was the warden enjoyed the pain he created. That fact alone was enough for Alaric to condemn the man to death. He had no qualms in dealing out revenge for all who had suffered under his hand.

The warden saw the look in Alaric's eyes and knew he was not going to back down. Normally he commanded a presence that scared most people, but then most people before him were in chains. He was not sure how to handle an armed man. All he needed was one blow with his cudgel and Alaric would be his.

Alaric easily dodged the first swing aimed at his body. He could not retreat too far or else he would leave the entrance to the cavern open. He swung a wide arc with his sword. It was not really designed to do any damage but to force the warden further back down the dungeon tunnel. Although he was sure he could defeat the warden quickly he did not want to be over confident. It would only take one mistake for him to end up on the dungeon floor.

The weak attack had its effect and the warden who took a number of steps backwards. He also knew that one mistake would take his life. The last thing he wanted to do was to die. He thought the best way to stay alive was to wait for the prince to arrive. He would have preferred to escape, but the tunnel he was in led to a dead end. He would have to play for time.

Alaric noticed the warden made no move to attack. After his first aggressive move he thought it was out of character. It didn't take long for him to realise what was happening. The warden was clearly not going to attack; he was waiting for Ra'naroz. Alaric had to change his plan. He could no longer defend and wait for an opportunity to strike. He needed to finish with the warden before the Dark Knight arrived.

Without a second thought Alaric moved to attack. The warden was a little surprised to see Alaric move towards him, he thought he would be able to wait for the prince to save him.

Alaric formed a tentative attack. He wanted to gauge the warden's skills at fighting before he did anything drastic. The cudgel was not the easiest of weapons to use in a battle, it was more of a bashing weapon when an opponent was unarmed or otherwise defenceless. All the warden could do was retreat further and swat at Alaric's sword. It didn't take Alaric long to realise the warden wasn't going to put up much of a fight.

With renewed confidence Alaric went on the offensive. Each swing pushed the warden further and further down the tunnel. When there was nowhere else for him to go he knew his time was running out. The only advantage of the cudgel was to delay the inevitable. The warden was able to use the bulky weapon to stave off any killer blows. What it couldn't stop was the side attacks. With every swing Alaric was able to draw blood. At first it was a cut to the warden's left arm. Next was a slash across his right cheek. As the blows came the blood started to flow. Soon enough the warden held the cudgel limply in his right hand. The time was perfect for Alaric to administer the killing blow, but he didn't. He was starting to enjoy giving the warden pain. The man had created hell for his prisoners and it was time for revenge. Alaric knew it wasn't the right way to go, but he could not help himself. There was a feeling of righteousness that he could not ignore. What he didn't notice was the Emerald stone pulsating on his wrist.

"Please!" The warden dropped to his knees. He knew defence was no longer an option. All he could do was beg for his life. "I don't want to die."

The irony was not lost on Alaric. He felt nothing but contempt for the grotesque man grovelling before him. He wanted to strike him down, but there was still an opportunity to make him suffer. Those who had died before him deserved their retribution and it was Alaric's job to make sure that they received it.

"What about those who asked you for mercy? Did you give it to them? Or did you give them more pain? I think that you wallowed in their misery," Alaric was gloating.

The warden lunged at Alaric. He knew what was happening. Alaric was going to make him suffer. The only way he was going to get a quick death was to force the inevitable. Unfortunately for him Alaric was ready for it. He simply side-stepped the attack and then cracked him on the back of his head with the hilt of the sword. The blow was not enough to knock the warden out, but it was enough to knock him to the ground.

Alaric was not going to give the warden a chance to recover. He slashed at the back of the wardens legs, severing various muscles and tendons. There was no chance the warden would be able to attack again. The man was completely at Alaric's mercy, for which he would receive none.

As Alaric continued his torture of the warden he realised he was wasting time. Not only that, but he could feel the evil of the dungeons consuming him. The situation was wrong. It was not something that he should be doing. The warden was sobbing on the floor beneath him. The man was pitiful. Alaric almost didn't have the heart to end his life, but he knew the warden did not deserve to live. A quick death would be a mercy, but he couldn't bring the man to suffer anymore. If he left the man to die a painful death he would be no better than the Evil One himself.

He had already wasted enough time and he did not want to waste anymore. Taking a deep breath he plunged his sword through the warden's heart. There was a gurgle from the warden's throat as blood dripped from the corner of his mouth. He twitched once before laying completely still. Alaric thought the world would be a better place without the warden in it.

There was no time for retrospection. His four friends were still hanging from the chains in the torture chamber. He quickly searched the warden's body for the keys. They were drenched in blood, but Alaric did not flinch. There was nothing that would stop him from freeing them.

There was a huge sigh of relief when they saw Alaric enter the chamber. They had heard the commotion, but had no idea what was happening. Bern was the only one who knew Alaric had been there. His connection with Alaric was strong and he had felt his old friend long before he arrived. He had no doubts Alaric would overpower the warden.

"I can't tell you how good it is to see you," Hadar's voice almost sounded jovial as he saw him.

The duke's words were echoed by Richmond and Tancred, but Bern remained quiet. He knew their ordeal was not yet over.

Eldred and Alena were still hidden somewhere in the dungeons. They had still not managed to gain any information about their whereabouts. All they knew was that the pair was buried deep within the dungeons. He could only imagine what they had been through. Bern knew what had happened to them when they were only captured for a day. He did not want to think about what had happened to the two for over a month.

"We need to find the others," Bern was the first to speak once they had all been released.

"Of course," Richmond's voice was weak.

Alaric wasn't sure if the three men were up to the challenge. He also didn't believe they would be able to leave on their own. Even if they didn't run into any guards on the way out they would definitely run into trouble once they were out of the dungeon.

"We will do our best not to slow you down," Tancred said.

"Maybe you should wait here," Alaric suggested.

"No!" they all said in unison.

The last thing they wanted to do was remain in the place they had been tortured. As soon as the words came out of Alaric's mouth he realised what he had said and wished he hadn't. There was nothing else he could do. He would have to take the three with him. He knew time was running out, but he could not abandon one group of friends for another.

"Okay, then, let's get going," Bern was quick to change the subject. For whatever reason he had not been tortured, but his wrists were sore from the shackles.

"Do you know where they are being held?" Alaric asked as they started down the tunnel.

"Not exactly," Bern replied slowly.

Chapter 4: A Tough Rescue

The pace was frustratingly slow. Alaric wanted to be out of the dungeons as quickly as possible, but that wasn't happening in a hurry. Richmond and Tancred needed to rest often. The torture had taken more out of them than they had been willing to admit. At first they were trying to be strong, but they could only suffer the pain for so long. With each passing moment a feeling of dread filled Alaric. He wished he could leave them behind and come back for them later, but that was not an option. Alaric had seen the bloody gashes on their backs. Pieces of flesh hung from their bodies. He could not imagine how much it must have hurt. He was not even sure how they managed to continue. The thought of leaving Bern to look after them crossed his mind, but without a weapon there would be little he could do if they were attacked and Alaric needed to keep his sword.

Every now and then one of them cried out as their tattered shirts grazed across their open wounds. They did their best to keep their voices low, but that was not easy. Each time they heard it both Alaric and Bern cringed.

Alaric wondered how Bern had managed to escape without a scratch, whilst the others were in so much pain. He didn't think the Dark Knight would have spared him out of compassion. There was something not right with the situation. As much as he didn't think Bern would have made a deal with Ra'naroz he could not dismiss the idea. Once he had seen to the other three men being beaten then it was completely plausible that he would cut a deal. He wanted to ask the question, but he felt uncomfortable speaking about it with the others within earshot.

"Does anyone have any idea where the other two are?" Alaric asked after they had been walking for about half an hour.

"All I know is that they are kept in a place reserved for the vilest of prisoners. It is not in the regular dungeons," Tancred explained, although he started panting half way through. "I do not think we are going to find it just by wandering around."

Alaric stopped and sighed as he heard Tancred's words. It was not what he wanted to hear. He had started to sweat as they walked through the stale dungeon tunnels and hearing that made him feel even more uncomfortable. He was starting to struggle to feel Eldred and Alena and all he wanted was to wash himself clean from the evil that was infesting his body.

"Do you have any ideas?" Bern asked Alaric when they didn't keep moving.

"I have to think," it was clear that thinking was a strain. "I know that I can find them, but it is not clear. It is as if there is a fog in my mind and the fog is pure evil."

No one responded. Bern thought on his words. He could feel the other entity that shared his body starting to stir. The feeling was not pleasant. He had grown used to the fact that there was someone, or something, else inside his body, but what was happening was something different. There was a pain inside him that he had never felt before. He hoped it would not become a common occurrence.

"I think we need to get these three out of the dungeons," Alaric didn't notice the change in Bern's voice at first. "Their wounds are still open. It will only be a matter of time before they become infected."

There were no arguments from the other three. At first they had been keen to find Alena and Eldred, but all they wanted to do was rest. Their pain was increasing the further they continued. They hoped Alaric agreed with Bern's suggestion, they did not know how long they could keep travelling through the tunnels.

"I think you're right," Alaric conceded the point. "You take these three to the castle. Do your best not to get caught. I am sure you will be able to find somewhere for them to rest. I will continue on alone and find the others."

There was a glimmer of hope in the three wounded men's faces. They had not dared to hope that Alaric would let them leave without Alena and Eldred. It looked as though they would survive the ordeal that would have claimed a lesser man's life.

"That is not a good idea," Bern's words dashed their hopes. "I do not think you could fight a Dark Knight in your condition, at least not in this place." Alaric knew he was speaking with Heryion. He was glad to hear from the strange little man. "This place is pure evil, which has been multiplied since Ra'naroz has been increasing the tortures. The Dark Knight will be too powerful for you down here. You have to fight him above ground. I think you should do this before you rescue the other two."

"I don't think I can take that risk. I am sure that once Ra'naroz realises I am here he will kill Eldred and Alena."

"I can't see Ra'naroz taking it upon himself to kill Nyrra's prisoners. If the Evil One wanted them dead then they would already. There is a reason why he wants them alive," Heryion explained, hoping to persuade Alaric.

Alaric had to admit that Heryion's words did make sense, but there was still something in the back of his mind telling him that he had to continue. He knew in his heart that their lives were not as safe as Heryion claimed. He didn't know if that was the case, but he was beginning to resign himself to the fact that he was destined to fight Ra'naroz in the dungeons. He didn't think that there was any way around it now.

"Be that as if may I have to keep going." Alaric would not be dissuaded.

"Then I guess we will have to continue with you," Heryion sounded defeated. He knew it possibly meant the death of his three brave companions.

"No, you have to get these three out. I will not risk their lives. I will do just fine by myself," Alaric returned, giving hope to the three men.

"You will need my help if you are to defeat Ra'naroz. You cannot defeat him by yourself. Not in this place," there was no confidence in his voice.

Alaric laughed softly. He would have laughed out loud, but he didn't want any guards to hear. There was still a chance they could get caught and he did not want to kill anyone else.

"I think you would be surprised with what I am capable of. I have a few surprises left," Alaric almost sounded jovial.

"Very well. I suppose I will have to trust your judgement," Bern's voice had returned, although there was still a hint of Heryion. "Are you sure you will be able to find them?"

"If I have a moment to concentrate I am sure that I will be able to find the way," Alaric reassured him. "Now I think it is time you get these men out of here. They need to see a surgeon and have those wounds stitched up."

There was no room for arguments. Alaric had made up his mind. Bern was grateful he was able to leave the dungeons, but he wished Alaric was going with them. He truly believed he was in no state to face a Dark Knight, but he knew better than to try and argue with him. It was obvious he was being led by the prophecy and that was not something he could ignore. Bern could not feel himself being tugged in either direction and he wished the answer was there for him. In the end he would have to make his own decision. If Alaric was confident in continuing alone then he had to respect his judgement.

"Okay then," Bern did not sound happy. "We will head for the castle."

Bern took a step forward before he felt Alaric grip his arm. "Be careful. The castle is a dangerous place."

Bern nodded and Alaric let him go. The men were happy to be on the move again. As much as they wanted to rest they did not want to stay in the dungeons longer than they had to. No one looked back at Alaric as they made their way forward.

"Do you know the way out?" Tancred asked as they rounded a corner.

"Not exactly," Bern replied from the lead. "But I have faith we are going in the right direction."

Ever since he had made the decision to part from Alaric he had felt a pull. He was amazed at how the prophecy worked, or at least he assumed it was the prophecy leading him out of the dungeons. He could think of no other explanation.

"I think we should think about it for a minute," Hadar barked, his voice regaining some of its boisterous strength. "I don't think wandering around aimlessly is going to do us any favours."

"Don't worry, Hadar. Have some faith in the world around you." It was not the most reassuring comment Bern could have made. There was little to have faith in their current surroundings. "I have a good feeling we will be out of here very soon."

The other three had little confidence in Bern. The man had done some amazing things in the short time they had known him, but there was something different about their current situation. He had confidence in his voice, but it seemed as though it was forced. They did not have time to be relying on a hunch by someone who had not been tortured. At the time they had not resented Bern for not being beaten, they knew what the Dark Knight was trying to do. But since they had been freed the animosity was starting to build. The man was obviously not suffering like they were. It was not a logical thought, but they all felt the same.

Bern failed to notice the angst from behind him. He was more concerned on getting them out. The feeling he was travelling in right direction was only subtle and he had to concentrate hard. One wrong turn and there was no telling where they would end up.

As they continued they all noticed the air was not quite as stale as it had been. That was enough to lift their spirits. The stale air and the heat was starting to make them feel sick. Their heads were spinning as they walked. All Bern could do was focus on the task ahead him.

"I think we should be out of here soon," Bern spoke to the others as they walked, but he did not look around.

When there was no response Bern suddenly became concerned. He thought they would not be able to contain their excitement. When he turned he found that all three men had collapsed on the ground. They were sucking in air, but the air on the floor was worse than that above and gave them no relief.

"I said I don't think we are that far from the castle." Bern walked back to where they were lying.

Again there was no response. The three men looked as though they were in agonising pain. Bern didn't know what he could do. They were so close to their end, but if they could not walk then it was futile. There was no way Bern could carry all three of them to safety. He didn't think he would be able to help any of them. He needed all his attention to find the exit. He knew they were close, but he also knew they were not out of danger.

"I don't think we are going to make it," Richmond was the first to speak.

"What sort of talk is that?" Bern could not believe what he was hearing. "We are so close to our destination. This is not the time to give up. I know you are in pain. If I could trade places with you then I would, but that is not the case. It is my job to make sure we all get out alive and that is exactly what I am going to do."

"It's too late," Tancred tried to push himself off the ground, but he did not have the strength. "The pain is too great."

Bern could not imagine what they were feeling. He felt sorry for them, but if he left them there then they would be dead in no time. The only thing he could do was to try and motivate them into rising.

"I know you are in pain, but this is not the end. I will not let you give up. No come on. Let's go." Bern moved to Hadar's side. He figured the duke had yet to complain, so he was the best to start with.

The large man from Hondin Lel was harder to pick up than Bern had originally thought. As soon as he placed his arm around Hadar he could tell that the man was weak. There was very little strength left in his body. Bern had no idea exactly how bad they were. Even though they had only spent a day and a night in the dungeon he doubted they would survive. He had to wonder how the other prisoners had lasted so long. He shook his head as the thought came into his mind. If he lost faith then it would spell doom for them all.

"We are going to get out of here, but I cannot carry you. You have to muster all the strength you have left. I promise you that it will not take long for us to reach the castle," Bern urged them on.

Although their goal was to reach the castle there was no guarantee that would lead to safety. Unless Alaric was able to defeat the Dark Knight by the time they arrived then they could be walking into more trouble. The thought weighed heavily on Bern, but he wasn't going to share his fears with the others.

Hadar had to admit he did feel slightly better when he was off the ground. He still had an urge to empty his stomach, not that there was anything in there, but he held on. Bern's words had given him strength. The thought of lying on a soft bed inside the castle was a pleasant one.

Bern helped the others to their feet. They all felt just as weak as Hadar, but better for being off the filthy floor. He was pleasantly surprised to see that Hadar was on his feet when he lifted Richmond. All three were standing, albeit that their legs were wobbling and they looked as though they could collapse at any minute.

"Let's get moving," Bern sounded excited.

The tunnel they were walking through had a gentle upward slope. Walking upwards was a good sign, but Bern still had to concentrate to regain the feeling of which direction they needed to travel. In his strain to lift the men from the ground he had lost the sensation, but by the time he reached the end of the tunnel he knew which way to turn.

As he turned the corner he was hit in the face by a blast of cold air. The air filled his lungs and forced him to cough. He had been so used to the filth of the dungeons that the fresh air was a shock to the system. Once he had cleared his throat he felt much better. Not only was the fresh air a relief to his lungs it also meant they were near the exit to the castle.

At the end of the tunnel they came out into a small room. It was neither a cavern nor a prison cell. At the far end of the room there was a flight of stairs leading upwards. The room had a number of tables and chairs and Bern thought it must be a common room for the guards. He was surprised it was vacant.

"I don't think this will be a good place to rest. I am sure there will be guards here soon." Bern read their minds. He could tell they wanted nothing more than to collapse in one of the chairs.

"Yes, but I think it would be a good idea if we rest here for a moment," Hadar made the suggestion.

Bern turned around and looked at the three of them. Their skin was pale and they were all sweating profusely. They looked as though they could lose consciousness at any moment. He knew it was not a good idea to leave them in the guard's room, but he had no other choice. They had to rest.

"Okay, stay here. I will scout the castle and find a better place for you to rest." Bern resigned the point.

"And if you could find something to eat or drink?" Tancred asked as he collapsed onto a chair.

The next sound resonated throughout the room. Without thinking Tancred had leaned back and a great pain ripped though his body as his exposed flesh touched the back of the chair. The scream that came out of his mouth made everyone in the room cringe. Richmond and Hadar were thankful they had not made the same mistake. Tancred started whimpering. He had never felt such pain in his life. All he wished was for it to be over He didn't know how much longer he could survive.

"I will be back as soon as I can," Bern tried to reassure them, but his words were weak.

He paused when he reached the door leading into the castle. If there were guards on the other side then his mission would shortly be over. It was at this point he realised he did not have his sword. It would be pointless to enter the castle unarmed. He looked around the guardroom for something he could use as a weapon. In the far corner there was a weapon rack that had a number of short swords hanging from it. They were not his weapon of choice; he still preferred the extra weight of the war axe. He had been relatively proficient with the sword when training at Elhjem, the elven village, but it was more with the double handed broadsword. He could hold his own with the short sword, but not against a trained soldier.

The sword felt reassuring in his hand, even if it wasn't his preferred weapon it was better than nothing. He was a little more confident to enter the castle. At least if he ran into trouble there was chance he could defend himself. He passed the three men and they moaned as he walked by. Although they did not speak he knew what they were thinking. If he did not return soon then there was a good chance that at least one of them would die.

Slowly Bern pushed the door open and poked his head around the other side. To his relief he found the hallway was empty. There was a real chance his plan was going to succeed. The feeling was still inside him telling him which way he should go. He could feel there was a safe room not too far away and he could only hope the prophecy was leading him in the right direction.

The battle outside the city walls had emptied the corridors. Those who were not taking part in the fight were hiding in their rooms. It gave Bern the run of the castle. He started to relax a little, but not enough to make him complacent. He could hear the sound of battle coming from outside. He hoped not too many people were being killed. It was a sad affair that they were forced to fight each other.

He walked for fifteen minutes before he stopped suddenly. He was at a door, which looked much the same as the other doors he had passed, but there was a strong feeling their salvation was waiting for him on the other side. His hand rested on the knob. He didn't know why he was waiting. He was sure there was nothing dangerous inside the room, yet he could not bring himself to open the door. As his hand started to twist the knob he heard someone approach. His heart missed a beat before starting to pump faster.

"What are you doing there?" a man's voice asked as the footsteps came nearer.

Bern didn't want to turn around, but as he stood there an idea suddenly came into his mind. He knew why he hadn't entered the room straight away.

"Where is the physician?" Bern turned and barked at the man.

When he turned around he saw a young man dressed in a soldier's uniform.

"I am sorry sir, but what are you talking about," the soldier was taken aback by Bern's tone. Although the man did not look as though he was a noble, he definitely spoke like one. The soldier knew better than to upset nobles.

"I sent someone to fetch a physician almost an hour ago. I was just coming by to see what had happened. I have a number of friends who are deathly sick inside," Bern continued with his ruse.

"I think all the physicians are busy with the war," the soldier sounded confused.

"I am sure that there is one physician left in the castle," Bern was hoping his logic was right. "I don't think the queen would be left without help."

"Of course, but I don't think that I would be able…" the soldier was cut off by Bern.

"I don't care what you think. If my friends die then I think the queen would be most upset!"

The soldier bowed his head and quickly disappeared down the hallway. Things were working out better than he thought. With a little luck they might be able to get out of the castle without having to fight.

Once the soldier had disappeared Bern opened the door. The room was dark inside. Once he became accustomed to the light he saw the room had recently been packed up. All the owner's possessions were in boxes. It seemed that the owner was on the way out. Things could not have worked out better. There was a large bed in one of the rooms and a couch in the front room. They would do perfectly for the injured men. Now all he had to do was get them safely inside.

Bern did not waste any time. Once he was sure that the location was safe he returned to the guard room. He was relieved to see that the three men were still conscious. He was not sure what state he was going to find them in. They did not look well, but they were alive. He only hoped that they were able to walk. Things would turn nasty if the soldier was to return with the physician and no one was there.

"Are you able to walk?" Bern asked the question to everyone.

There was no response. The men were too weak to speak. It was not a good sign. They were so close to their destination, yet they still might fail. Bern looked at the three men. It seemed as though Hadar was the fittest of the three. If he could get Hadar to his feet then it might motivate the other two.

"Come on Duke Hadar," Bern moved to the great man's side. "I have found somewhere better for you to rest and have sent for the physician. Nothing is going to happen if you stay here."

Bern tried to lift Hadar from where he was seated, but he was a dead weight. There was no strength in the great man's body. Bern tried his hardest, but he was unable to rouse him. His spirits had been lifted just to be doused again. If he couldn't get the three men to the empty room then it was all for nothing.

"Come on!" Bern said, still puffing from the effort. "This is the last thing you have to do. Once we are in the room you will be able to rest all you like, but we have to get moving now."

Richmond was the first to move as Bern's words took effect. He was not about to give up and die. There was still work for him to do. Slowly he pushed himself to his feet. Bern could see the strain on his face and knew the effort it had taken.

"That's the way. Now you two, come on!"

Bern had to help the other two, but soon enough they were all standing. Richmond looked shaky on his feet and Bern didn't think it would be long before he collapsed again. They had to get moving. He hoped the movement would keep them all on their feet.

Bern led the way out of the guard room. Once they were in the corridors Bern went from man to man giving them assistance when they required it. The travelling was slow and it took nearly twice as long to reach the room as when Bern was by himself. When they eventually reached the door there was a sound resembling a squeal from Tancred.

"What's wrong?" Bern asked as he opened the door.

"Is this some kind of a joke?" Tancred's voice was weak and he forced the words from his mouth.

"What are you talking about?" Bern opened the door as he spoke. He didn't think that there was any point in having the conversation in the hallway.

"This is Amilie's room," Tancred didn't look like he wanted to enter.

"I know that it's difficult." Richmond said also recognising the room. "But we need to get out of the corridors. It's not safe here. I am sure she would forgive you."

Hadar paid no attention to Tancred, he wanted to get off his feet as quickly as possible. If he remained in the hallway he wasn't sure he would make it inside. When he saw the bed he almost fell over in relief. Once he was near it he collapsed, face first, onto it. He almost lost consciousness when he did.

Bern helped Richmond to the couch before helping Tancred to the other side of the bed. The lord's advisor looked deathly pale, more so than the other two. He could understand his point of view. Tancred felt responsible for Amilie's death and it would be hard for him to return to this place. In the end there was no other choice and Tancred would just have to deal with it.

As Bern stood over the bed he heard a rushed knock at the door. His heart jumped for a moment before he realised it must be the soldier returning with the physician. He quickly moved to the door and opened it. There was an elderly man on the other side. There was no sign of the soldier, but Bern didn't think he would hang around.

"I hear you require a physician?" the man pushed his way into the room without waiting for a response.

Bern quickly shut the door behind him. He knew once the physician recognised the wounds there would be trouble. He made sure he blocked the only exit from the apartment. The physician already seemed like an arrogant man and Bern didn't want to leave anything to chance.

"I take it the three lying down are those you want me to look at?" again the physician did not wait for a reply before looking at Richmond's wounds. "These look familiar. They do not look like they have been done in battle," the physician thought for a moment. "Who are you?" there was a slight amount of shock in his voice.

"It is not necessary to know who we are. All that you need to do is tend to their wounds," Bern's voice was hard.

"These marks were done in the prisons. I would recognise them anywhere. These days no one returns from below, which means you have escaped," he was putting the pieces together as he spoke. "You are escaped prisoners. I will not help you."

Bern drew his short sword. He was glad he was able to secure a weapon. He did not want to threaten the physician, but he was quickly running out of ideas. He could not wait much longer.

"I assume you have been in the castle for a long time. If that is the case then you will know that not all the people in the dungeons deserve to be there. We need your help and you are going to give it to us," Bern hoped that his words would work.

The physician thought for a moment. He obviously didn't look happy with the situation. He had been enjoying a nice lunch when he had been summoned. He hated being interrupted during mealtime, but the soldier had been very persistent. He knew he would not receive any peace until he followed the man. He wished he had remained where he was. If the prince found out what he was doing then he would be the one in the dungeon. On the other hand the man standing before him looked as though he knew how to use the sword in his hand.

"Very well. I will do what I can, but I need to get some more equipment. I do not have enough thread in my pack to sew all those wounds. I will go and get the rest of my instruments and then I will return," the physician made his way to the door, but Bern did not yield.

"I don't think so," Bern was not going to be duped. "I think we can have a servant collect what you need."

The physician seemed offended at what Bern was suggesting, but Bern was not going to be dissuaded. He was not going to let the physician leave the room until he had attended to the injured men.

"I do not trust a servant to handle my instruments. There is no telling what they would do to them," the physician wanted to move closer to the door, but another step would bring him within the striking distance.

"You will just have to trust they will get what you need," Bern was starting to become annoyed. "Ring the bell pull and then get to work."

It was not the best of ideas to upset the physician, but there was nothing else for it. The man would bolt at the first chance he could get. If Bern had the physician fear for his life there was a better chance of him doing a better job.

The physician resigned himself to the fact that he had no choice. He only hoped the prince would see it the same way. As soon as he was able to the leave the room he would go straight to him. At least then he could plead innocence.

Once he called for a servant he started to look at Richmond. He winced at the wounds when he removed the man's shirt. He had only managed to sew one of the wounds when there was a knock on the door.

"Needless to say that if you say the wrong thing you will end up worse than my friends," there was no nonsense in Bern's voice.

The physician didn't look up from what he was doing. He waved for the door to be opened. Bern took his arrogance as a sign that he would do the right thing.

When Bern opened the door he saw a young woman starting to walk away. Bern called out for her to return. He was surprised to see her leaving without orders.

"Where do you think you are going?" Bern sounded annoyed.

"I am sorry, sir," the girl sounded embarrassed. "I didn't realise that the Lady's quarters were being used again."

"Get in here," the physician barked at the door. "You are not paid to think, you are paid to do what you are told."

"Of course, doctor. I didn't mean anything," she was now fumbling over her words.

"Here is a list of what I need from my office, you do know where that is don't you?" The physician handed her a piece of paper. "Be sure that you hurry back. I do not have time to wait for you to dawdle," he didn't wait for her response

"Yes, sir!" She snatched the paper and quickly left the room.

Bern thought he was too rude to the young woman, but that seemed to be in his nature. As long as he got the desired response Bern didn't really care how he did it. Things were starting to look up.

"Now I won't be able to stitch all these wounds. Some of them just don't have enough skin left," the physician spoke so matter-of-factly that it caught Bern off guard.

"Do whatever you have to do," Bern didn't know how else to respond.

The physician had almost finished with Richmond when the young woman returned. She had a glimmer of sweat on her brow. It was obvious she had rushed to get the physician's things. Bern was grateful she returned so quickly.

Bern watched as the physician did his job. He worked on the three men as if it was nothing out of the ordinary. He was glad when the job was finished and all three men were asleep, or at least unconscious.

"They will need to rest for a while. The wounds were deep and they will take a long time to heal. They are also suffering from shock. There is no telling how long it will take for them to recover. I have left some clean bandages and some salve. You will need to change their dressings once a day. If you do that they should be fine," the physician explained as he packed up the remainder of his things.

"Thank you for your help," Bern was truly grateful.

The physician simply grunted as he left the room. Bern hoped the man did not tell anyone they were there. He had gone too far to lose now. All he could do was keep an eye on his friends and hope they all survive.

Chapter 5: The Battle Begins

Something was wrong, Ra'naroz was sure of that. He didn't know what it was, but he knew it was there. The creaking of the castle gates opening distracted him from his thoughts. Things had been going so well, but he had a bad feeling that was about to change. The castle guard was marching to their doom. It was unfortunate he was going to lose so many men, but when it was said and done they were not really his allies. Either way it was a victory for the Great Lord. There was still his little surprise that was waiting in the forest to the north. He licked his lips at that thought. There was going to be a lot of delicious death.

A subtle breeze touched his blonde hair. Unlike everyone else he didn't wear any armour. It was almost as if he wasn't keen for battle, but they all knew that wasn't the case. His face was uncommonly beautiful and if it wasn't for the fear he caused the courtesans would be throw themselves at him.

The thought of death raced through his mind and distracted him from what he was doing. He had to physically calm himself to remember where he was and what was expected of him. He knew the Cursed One was with the army somewhere and he would need to be careful. As much as he didn't think he was going to lose, Ra'naroz wasn't that arrogant to not realise it was a possibility. Some of his brothers had already fallen to the Cursed One and he wasn't going to make the same mistakes.

"Prince Leroy?" a voice came from behind him, just as he was about to regain his composure.

"What is it?" he snapped.

He didn't like the pitiful human creatures at the best of times, but now he was really starting to lose his patience. He still enjoyed the pleasures of the flesh, but that was it. He wanted nothing more than to strike the man down, but that was not appropriate. He would only have to suffer them for a short while, at least that was something.

"We are waiting for your command. The soldiers will be assembled shortly," the soldier sounded nervous.

His initial thought was the tell them to charge in. He didn't care if they were all annihilated. But he needed to think before he made any rash decisions.

"And you will continue to wait until I give you an order. Now leave me," his words were enough to send the soldier running.

There was no doubting the prince was in one of his moods. The last place the soldier wanted to be was anywhere near him. Although death seemed like a certainty, he would much rather die on the battlefield than in the dungeons.

Ra'naroz returned his gaze to the battlefield. The soldiers from Entero were filling the space between the Alliance and the castle. There would be bloodshed very soon. The Dark Knight shook his head as the thoughts of chaos filled his mind. He had to concentrate on what was wrong. The battle could wait, but something important had happened that required his full attention.

Something had happened. He had let the grip on the queen slip and the cover on the castle, but he needed all his energy for the upcoming battle. He was starting to think it was not the right decision to make. He knew Alaric was out there somewhere, but he had not made his presence known. It was odd. Not only that, but he hadn't seen his brother, Argoz, either. It wouldn't be out of the realm of possibilities for Argoz to betray him. He would need to be very careful.

He looked out over the battlefield to see if he could see the answer there. As he glanced over the field something twinged on the back of his neck. He spun around quickly to see who it was, but there was no one there. He knew the feeling was pertinent to what he was trying to figure out. It was as if the answer was just on the edge of his mind.

Suddenly he realised what it was. It had only been subtle and that's why he hadn't noticed it straight away, but someone had used magic. He couldn't be certain, but he didn't think it was his brother. The magic was cleaner. It didn't have the same taint that he used. The question was... what did it mean? He was sure if it was Alaric then the spell would be apparent. There would have been an explosion or something of that magnitude to kill the approaching soldiers.

There had to be another reason, but he couldn't work it out. It didn't make any sense for Alaric to try and mask his spell. Suddenly it dawned on him what was happening. He had been so focused on the battle ensuing in front of him that he had completely forgotten about his prisoners in the dungeons. That was the only thing that made sense. Alaric must be trying to rescue them and that was something he could not allow to happen. In an instant he disappeared from the wall.

***

The army remained where it was as the soldiers from the castle assembled themselves. The entire idea was absurd. Whilst they were protected by the castle walls there was a chance they could survive. In open combat there was no chance. Something had to be wrong. Jarwe was not looking forward to giving the order to attack. He would wait until he was given no other choice. He only hoped he had achieved what Alaric had wanted him to.

It took almost an hour for the soldiers to fill out onto the battlefield. The soldier's in the Alliance had started to become restless. As much as they were keen for battle they were starting to understand the gravity of the situation. They were about to fight allies, not enemies.

On the opposite side of the field the Enteroite soldiers looked just as enthusiastic. They could not understand why they were ordered to march out from behind the safety of their walls. Although the battle had not gone to plan they did not have to act so rashly. Many of the soldiers were still not sure what they had seen. They could not believe the arrows had just disappeared. It was not something that should have happened and yet they were marching out to fight an unaffected army.

"I suppose I should go and speak to the captain," Jarwe spoke when the soldiers had stopped moving.

No one from the Enteroite army had made a move to attack or negotiate with the Alliance. There didn't seem to be any reason why they had left the castle. They all looked as though they didn't know what they were doing. Jarwe thought it was one of the most bazarre situations he had been in.

General Jarwe took General Sorrell and Lord Pernian with him to the other side. They moved cautiously as they approached the opposing army. They could not take anything for granted. Although the doctrine of war dictated they were safe that was now no guarantee. He only hoped they would stick to tradition.

As they approached, the middle three men started riding out to meet them. The sign relieved the two men and the elf as they approached. At least it seemed they were going to get some answers to their current situation. There was still a chance they would not have to fight.

"General Jarwe," Captain Prewitt was the first to speak. He did not introduce the two men on either side of him.

"Captain Prewitt," Jarwe didn't feel it necessary to introduce Sorrell or Pernian either. "I must admit that I didn't expect this move."

"You can quit the pleasantries," Prewitt did not sound happy. "Nothing has changed. You are a foreign army invading our soil. Now I implore you to leave our land."

Jarwe was taken aback by Prewitt's attitude. The man didn't seem to understand the gravity of the situation. There was no way they would be able to survive against the might of the Alliance. The pure numbers would overrun them.

"That is enough Prewitt," the large man sitting on a horse to the left of the captain spoke.

"This is Captain Tyson," Prewitt introduced the man, although it was obvious that he was not happy about it.

Captain Tyson was an imposing figure. Even on horseback they could tell he would stand at least six and half feet tall, possibly taller. His thick physique was not hidden under his large steel breastplate. He held his helmet by his side revealing a completely shaved head. It was obvious his nose had been broken more than once, but he didn't seem to care. He was a consummate soldier and there would be no talking over him.

"I am sorry for Prewitt's attitude, but you must understand that things are not what they should be," Tyson explained, his voice was very deep. His words belied the fact that he looked ready for battle.

"I know that you are under the control of a Dark Knight, but now is the time to break free," Jarwe spoke. "You do not have to do what he says anymore."

"That is all well and good," Prewitt replied. "But it is not the prince who we take our orders from. It is Queen Oriana who we obey."

"And it is the queen who is under the control of the prince," there was an obvious tension between the two captains.

"That is semantics," Prewitt retorted. "The point of the situation is that if we do not do as the prince commands he will kill our queen. She is transfixed by him and she will do nothing to save herself. Either way there is nothing we can do. We have to do as he commands," Jarwe had found a new respect for Prewitt. At first he had thought the man was an upstart, but he realised that the man was quite intuitive.

"We have people on the inside. It will not be long before the Dark Knight has been defeated and the queen has been rescued," it was all Jarwe could say to reassure them.

"Be that as it may, we still have to do what we are ordered," Prewitt would not be dissuaded from his train of thought.

"Then why have you not already attacked?"

"We have not been given the order to attack," Tyson explained. "The last order we were given was to take the field, but that was it. The prince has disappeared without giving further instructions."

"So you will not attack unless the prince gives the order?" Jarwe was starting to understand the situation.

"The prince or Queen Oriana herself," Prewitt cut in.

"We do not want to fight you, Jarwe. We are not stupid enough to believe that we are able to defeat you. We know it is a suicide mission, but as I have explained we do not have a choice," Tyson explained further.

There was hope they would not have to fight, but it was a slim one. He didn't understand what was happening, but things were looking better. If Alaric was distracting the Dark Knight then there was a very good chance that they would not get the order to attack. All they could do was wait for something to happen from inside the castle. The wait would be infuriating, but it was better than the alternative. For some reason the idea didn't make Jarwe feel any better. He had a bad feeling they would need to fight before the day was done.

"So what do we do now?" Jarwe asked.

"I suppose we just wait," Tyson added. "And hope your people can succeed. If not we will be going to war."

"Very well, I hope it does not come to this," Jarwe ended the conversation.

The men returned to their respective armies. Although not much had been resolved at least they had an idea of what was happening.

Jarwe explained the situation to the other commanders once they had returned. The information was then passed on to the sub-commanders. He figured the soldiers would be calmer if they knew the full story. It would be a tense wait to see what would happen. Anything to calm the soldiers' nerves was worth while.

"There has to be something we can do," Hulkan spoke after another hour had past.

"I don't see how," Sorrell replied. "All we can do is stay here and wait.'

"I don't like it any more than you, but the alternative is much worse," Jarwe added.

"If all we have to do is take out the prince then shouldn't we storm the castle whilst the gates are open?" it seemed logical enough to the dwarf.

"I don't think the army is going to let us march into the castle," Jarwe sounded a little annoyed at the suggestion. "They will defend it to the last and that is not a result we want."

"Then why don't we leave the battlefield, if you can call it that, and return to camp. I don't see the point in standing out here all day," Hulkan was equally annoyed.

"I have to admit he does have a point," Sorrell had to agree with Hulkan. "We have done what we came here to do. We have distracted the Dark Knight and Alaric has successfully entered the castle. There is little point in just standing here."

Jarwe did not like what he was hearing. He knew they made good points. On any other day he would gave agreed with them, but he had information the others didn't know. Alaric had told him not to say anything, but it didn't seem like he had a choice. If he did not explain the situation to them then there was a chance there would be a mutiny.

"Alaric told me not to leave the battlefield. He said I would know when the time was right to lead the army back to camp and I don't feel it," Jarwe did his best to explain.

"That doesn't make any sense," Sorrell didn't like what he was hearing.

"I know that it doesn't, but it does to me," Jarwe was not doing himself any favours. "I have a feeling we must stay. It is hard to explain, but I do not think leaving the field is the right thing to do."

His words were not making a great deal of sense, even to himself. No one spoke because they didn't know how to respond. It was as if he was talking gibberish. They knew what his words meant for them. It meant they were not going anywhere. They would just have to wait until Jarwe got his feeling.

They did not have to wait long for something to happen. From their vantage point atop their horses they could see a man running from the castle. They could not see the look on the man's face, but the sight did not give them a good feeling. They hoped it was a message to the captains that they were to stand down.

The discussion was heated between the captains and the messenger. Occasionally Tyson looked across at the Alliance's commanders. The look on his face did nothing to ease their nerves. Jarwe knew something bad was about to happen. But he did not want to give the order until he was sure.

The conversation between the messenger and the captains lasted for about fifteen minutes. Whatever the man was saying the captains did not want to listen. When they had finished talking the man ran back towards the castle. He did not want to be on the battlefield when the fighting started. Once he had entered the castle the gates slowly started to creak shut. The action shocked both sides of the battlefield. The prince was effectively cutting off any chance of retreat for the Enteroites. In essence, he was sealing their fate.

"Prepare for battle," Tyson yelled out the command, although it was obvious his heart was not in it.

Jarwe raised his hand. He did not want the Alliance to make the first move. He needed his soldiers ready, but the longer he could hold them back the fewer casualties there would be. He did not want to completely annihilate the Enteroites.

"Charge!" The order came from Prewitt.

Charge was not quite what came next. The Enteroites started to advance, but not at a great speed. It was not going to be the most intense battle in history. The Alliance stood their ground, but made no move to advance. They would defend, but not attack. Earlier the soldiers had been keen for battle. They had almost insisted on it. Now they realised they were not fighting a powerful enemy their enthusiasm had gone. They would, however, defend their lives if that was what was required.

"Forward line," Jarwe barked the command as the Enteroites came within fifty paces.

The command echoed throughout the Alliance and the soldiers at the front started their own slow march. It was one of the strangest things Jarwe had ever witnessed in his many years in the army. It was as if he was watching the progress in slow motion. It was frustratingly slow and yet he wished both sides would move slower.

There was almost no noise when the two armies finally met. Normally when two opposing armies met in battle there was a loud crash. The sound was usually thunderous. The fighting was slow and cautious. No one wanted to die, but they also did not want to take a life. It was one of the strangest things that Jarwe had ever witnessed.

"It looks at though we might get away unscathed after all," Sorrell commented in a jovial tone as he watched the battle unfold.

Unfortunately Sorrell spoke too soon, or perhaps his words cursed the battle. A young Enteroite soldier was fighting with a soldier from Hondin Lel. The two were very careful not to do any damage to the other, or expend much energy. They were quite happy making sure neither of them got injured. Unfortunately the Enteroite soldier slipped on a loose piece of dirt and stumbled forward onto the point of the Alliance soldier's blade. There was nothing either man could do about it, but it was enough to get the battle started.

The soldiers fighting next to the pair only saw the end result. If they had seen the accident occur their reaction would have been different. Instead they saw the action as an act of war. They would not let their comrade die without retribution and suddenly the battle became heated.

It started around the dead man and slowly worked its way out. Once a number of soldiers saw there was real fighting they followed suit. Jarwe could not believe what he was seeing. He had not seen the death of the Enteroite soldier and therefore had no idea what had sparked the serious fighting. He watched from his vantage point as his soldiers rushed around him.

"What is going on?" Sorrell asked, his voice a lot graver than before.

"I don't know, but our soldiers are out of position. We need to get them back into line or it is going to cost us a lot of lives," Jarwe's voice was thick with concern.

Jarwe cursed himself for not being prepared for such an occurrence. The entire situation had been so strange he had forgotten what he was doing. He was so transfixed by the sight he could not think about anything else. He was in a position he did not want to be in.

"Get the soldier's to reform the line," Jarwe called at the top of his voice.

He looked around after he spoke, but his flag bearers were nowhere to be found. They were the best way to relay information to the front line. Without them the only way to communicate was by runners. It was not as efficient, but it would still do the job.

"Where are the runners?" Jarwe asked Sorrell. He had to raise his voice to be heard over the sound of battle.

At first Sorrell did not hear him. He was transfixed by the scene. He could not believe the ferocious level the battle had taken. He watched as the Enteroites and the Alliance fought to the death. What had first seemed to be a completely benign battle had turned to complete mayhem.

"Where are the runners?" Jarwe yelled again.

"Sorry," Sorrell shook his head before facing Jarwe. "What was the question?"

Jarwe asked the question a third time. He was not happy, but he could understand why Sorrell had been so distant. The situation was not at all what they were expecting. They had been caught out in some unforseen ruse. Jarwe wondered if it was what the Dark Knight had planned for all along. With the gates to the castle shut there was nothing else to do except fight to the death.

"I don't know," Sorrell looked around, but there was just a mass of soldiers moving around them. "I can't see any of them."

Without the flag men or the runners there was no way to get word to the front of the line. Jarwe looked around again, but he could not see what he was looking for. Without thinking Jarwe kicked the flanks of his horse. He could not let the slaughter continue. If the soldiers were able to reform their line then it would be harder for the Enteroite army to attack. It would stem the flow of blood and give them back the advantage.

Jarwe yelled out as he rode toward the front of the battle. There were now skirmishes breaking out all over the place. Jarwe could not believe what a mess it had become. He couldn't move his horse quickly through the mass of soldiers. He had to carefully pick his way through. Occasionally he was stopped by a wayward Enteroite soldier. As much as he did not want to kill anyone he was given no choice. His skill on horseback made it an impossible task for his opponents. His progress was frustratingly slow. He was too keen a soldier to rush his attack. He knew it was the best way to end up dead. As much as he wanted to move on there was nothing he could do. He had to fight each battle as it came.

There was a slathering of blood on Jarwe's horse as he made his way towards the front of the line. As he neared the front of the battle the soldiers started to reform their line. They were starting to look like an army again and not just a rabble.

"Lieutenant!" Jarwe called out as he recognised the uniform of a Remidian lieutenant. The man had just killed a Enteroite soldier and was looking for his next fight.

The lieutenant spun around quickly as he heard Jarwe's voice. He recognised the general's commanding tone and was surprised to see his general so close to the action. He instantly thought something was wrong.

"Get your men back into line. We are an army not a bunch of mercenaries. This is no way to conduct a war," Jarwe's tone was harsh.

"Yes, sir!" the lieutenant saluted before returning his attention the soldiers around him.

Jarwe had done what he had set out to do. It would not be long before the army was assembled again. It would stem the flow of blood and bring order to proceedings. He would also be able to buy Alaric a little more time to succeed in his task. Things were not looking good, but Jarwe still had faith they would leave with more men than they did when they arrived. With that thought in mind he returned to where the other commanders were waiting.

When he arrived back he found that only General Sorrell and his advisor Wojtek remained amongst the sea of soldiers. The two dwarves had gone to the front line to join the battle, whilst Lord Pernian had gone to lead his Elven warriors. Although his Elves were better known for their skills with the bow they were also skilled with the sword.

"Things should calm down a little now," Jarwe explained. "Once we have a solid line it will be harder for them to attack."

"You have done well, but you really shouldn't risk your life like that," Sorrell commended him.

"There is no point giving orders if the soldiers can't hear them. I did what I had to do," Jarwe explained.

The soldiers were doing as Jarwe had commanded and as expected the fighting was reduced. The Enteroite soldiers could not break through the Alliance's line of defence, which limited the amount of soldiers who could attack at one time. It would slow down the amount of death and that could only be a good thing.

Just when things were starting to become under control an awful screech came from the forest to the north. It was a multitude of voices coming from creatures that Jarwe couldn't hazard a guess what they were. The sound sent a chill down his spine. It also caused the entire battlefield to stop. Everyone who had been fighting lowered their weapons and looked to the north. No one took the opportunity to attack their distracted opponent.

"What in the God Kings' names made that noise?" Sorrell asked in shock.

"I don't know, but I have a feeling we are about to find out," Jarwe replied, not taking his eyes from the forest.

***

"What is it that you want, my prince," the man grovelled in the space before him.

Ra'naroz wanted nothing more than the slaughter the man. The creature made him sick, but he was loyal. He knew his true identity and he wanted to serve. For now he needed all the allies he could get. The war had not truly started yet and there was something he had forgotten to do. He had to rectify the situation before anything else happened. Too much time had passed since there had been a mass death. The Enteroites had no chance of defeating the Alliance, but then they were not supposed to. The surprise he had waiting would kill the Enteroite army as easily as they would kill the Alliance. If he didn't have them fighting each other they would turn on his true army.

Things were happening too quickly and they were not going to plan. He did not like it when that happened. He was not a quick thinker, but given enough time he could come up with a mastery of plans. He would have to do whatever came into his mind first and hope that it was the right move. The danger ahead of him was more important than what was happening outside the castle walls.

As he went to check on the queen, he realised something was amiss. She was still seated on his throne where he had left her and although he had let the spell he had over her lapse it would still take her a while to recover her senses. She still smiled, her comatose smile, when she saw him enter the room. To his surprise he was relieved to see her still there and still in her current state. Whoever it was who had cast the spell was not after the queen, which only left one logical explanation. In fact there were many explanations, but only one that had come to Ra'naroz. Whoever it was must be after the prisoners. That end was worse than the queen's state-of-mind, but it did not seem to register in the Dark Knight's mind.

"See that only those who are loyal to the Great Lord remain in the castle. I want everyone else on the battlefield. Once that is done send word to the captains they are to advance. Tell them the order has come from the queen herself. She is not happy they have let a foreign army onto her soil without her permission. That should keep them in order. Once that is done have the gates shut. We don't want any of them getting back inside," Ra'naroz seemed quite pleased with his plan. He thought that he might be a little quicker of mind than he originally thought.

"I will do so at once," the man bowed a number of times as he backed his way out of the throne room.

Ra'naroz returned his attention to the queen. She still had the glazed over look on her face, the one that he liked so much. He thought about having some fun with her before he continued down into the dungeon. The thought was overwhelming in his man-like body. He wanted to give in to his urges, but hismind remained strong. He knew there was a great threat in his castle and he must stay in control.

"I think it is time for you to retire. I will meet you in the bedroom when I am done," he had to send her away if he was going to think. The thought of such a reward would make him work even harder.

The queen did as she was told without question. Although Ra'naroz was not paying attention there was a slight confused look on her face. It was only there for a second, but if he had noticed it he might have changed his plan. Instead the Dark Knight decided the save his strength and not to reapply the spell on her. He didn't think she would be able to recover in the time it would take for him to hunt out the spy.

When she had left the room he sat down on the throne. He pushed out his senses down into the dungeon to try and find the spy. He should have known before he started that it would be a pointless exercise. There was too much residue from all the pain and suffering for him to be able to pinpoint the location of anyone. The feeling was glorious, but that did nothing to help him. He would have to move quickly if he was going to locate the spy.

He wished that he was able to remain and watch the carnage that was about to occur outside of the castle, but he knew he could not. He hated the person who had caused him so much grief. He would have to devise a new kind of death, something to remember him by. It was time for the Cursed One to meet his end. With that thought in his mind he disappeared from the throne room.

Chapter 6: The Rescue

As soon as he left the others Alaric's senses increased. He had a stronger feeling of where Alena and Eldred were being held. It was not strong enough to give him the exact location, but it was enough to get him started. His feeling gave him renewed strength and for a while he was able to block out the pure evil that surrounded him. He moved on with renewed vigour.

As time slipped away he could feel he was getting closer to his destination, but he also knew that he was getting closer to a confrontation with the Dark Knight. He was both nervous and excited at the same time. It had been too long since he had seen his two friends. Eldred had looked after him ever since he had left Arsiliac. Alena… He let the thought of Alena drift away. He dared not think about her until they met again.

Throughout his travels through the vast tunnel system of the Jarrat dungeons he did not run into another guard. He was thankful for small mercies. He did not feel like dishing out any more death. There had already been so much death in the dungeons that he did not think the place could handle anymore. The only other death would be that of the Dark Knight. But with a little luck that would happen inside the castle.

As he passed by a small door Alaric had a strange feeling. He could not bring himself to take more than a couple of steps past before he had to stop. It was as if the door itself was calling to him. He felt the two prisoners where in the direction he was travelling, but he could not bring himself to continue. He stood in the one spot longer than he should before he conceded the fact he would have to investigate what was behind the door.

The door was not locked as Alaric had expected it to be. For such a strong feeling he thought the door would be secured tightly. He was very surprised to see that he could simply push the door open. The doorway itself was about half the height of Alaric and he had to crouch down to walk through. He was grateful to see the tunnel on the other side was not as low. It was, however, different to the other tunnels in the dungeon. The main dungeon tunnels where build out of stone. This tunnel had simply been cut out of the ground. Every now and then there were wooden beams for support, but that was it.

He knew, after he became accustomed to his surroundings, it was the right tunnel. He was sure that he would find his friends at the end of it. There was torch in a sconce a couple of paces in and Alaric assumed the tunnel would not be lit like the rest of the dungeon. He took the torch as he didn't want to waste energy having to create light.

The tunnel narrowed in places and widened in others. It was clear it had not been built by professionals. In fact it was originally dug out by prisoners trying to escape. They had made it as far as the chamber at the end of the tunnel before they were caught. The chamber and the subsequent cells were made to house and punish those who tried to escape. It was then used only for the most evil of prisoners.

At least the air wasn't as stale in the makeshift tunnel, although it was just as hot. He was glad to be away from the stink of death. If he had have known what he was about to walk into he would not have been so relaxed. The pure evil of the secret chamber of horror, as it was known to the locals, was double that of the rest of the dungeon.

Alaric almost fell over when he stepped into the chamber. Alaric hated to think how much work was involved with building such a place. At least he would have if he had been able to think. The room was made from the same stone as the main dungeon, but the first sight that hit his eyes were the piles of dried blood on the floor. He could not imagine how many people would have been tortured to create such a mess.

The next sight was just as horrifying as the first. A large stone slab stood in the middle of the chamber. There were ropes to secure both the prisoner's wrists and ankles. There was another pool of dried blood on the slab. It was obvious that was where the bulk of the torturing had taken place. He started coughing uncontrollably. He gasped for air, but all he could breathe in was the filth. He stumbled forward and put his hand out to settle himself. The only thing he could find to help was the slab. He felt the congealed blood between his fingers, but he did not let go. It would be worse to fall onto the bloodied floor. Suddenly he felt another presence in the chamber.

"What do we have here?" Alaric recognised the arrogance of a Dark Knight.

The appearance of Ra'naroz was enough to make Alaric calm himself. It was not the reaction he thought he would feel when the two finally met. The fear he had felt had completely left him.

"Where are Alena and Eldred?" Alaric kept his voice level.

The Dark Knight walked around the chamber, his eyes never leaving Alaric. Alaric remained where he was, his hand remaining on the stone slab, not for support, but = because he didn't want to move it. He let his body move only enough to keep his eyes on the Dark Knight. He knew Ra'naroz was just trying to sum him up, but he also knew better than the turn his back on such evil.

"Ah! I see. It is all starting to make sense," his words were confusing. It was obvious from the start what Alaric was doing there. "I suppose it would be cruel of me not to let you see them before you die."

Alaric didn't know what the Dark Knight's plan was. He couldn't see any reason why he would show him where the two where being held. It didn't make any sense to give him two allies. He was up to something and he had to be very careful. On the other hand Ra'naroz knew what effect seeing the state of the two prisoners would have on Alaric. It was going to give him a greater advantage.

"What are you playing at Ra'naroz?" Alaric let his hand leave the slab and stood up tall. It was time to show Ra'naroz the strength he held.

"Let's just say that being in this body has made me sentimental," there was an evil grin on his face.

Although Alaric didn't like the situation he had to admit he wanted to see that his two friends were still alive. There was no point in forcing the issue. There was plenty of time for the two of them to attack each other. He would wait until he knew that his friends were alright.

"Okay then, lead the way," Alaric resigned the fact he had no other option.

Ra'naroz laughed before he replied. "I don't think so. They are at the end of the middle passage. You can go down there. I will be waiting for you when you get back."

Alaric was even more suspicious. Once he had his friends he could easily disappear out of the dungeon. Things were looking up, but he still had to be careful. There had to be a trap somewhere.

Slowly Alaric started down the tunnel. He made sure he backed out of the chamber. He was not going to turn his back on the Dark Knight. As much as he didn't know what he was planning he wasn't going to give him a chance to attack. It wasn't until Ra'naroz was out of sight that Alaric turned around. When he did he saw there was only one door at the end of the tunnel and it was no more than a dozen paces away. Suddenly he became nervous. He didn't know what was waiting for him on the other side.

As Alaric put his hand on the doorknob he suddenly got a very bad feeling. Something was very wrong. He was trusting that a Dark Knight was giving him the right information and that was not something he should have done. He couldn't believe he had let himself be tricked so easily. He quickly took his hand off the door before the urge to open it overwhelmed him. He did not know what was waiting on the other side and he really didn't want to know.

He could not believe he had let his guard down so much that he didn't realise that the Dark Knight was messing with his mind. The spell would have been subtle, but not that subtle he shouldn't have felt it. The radiating evil from the chamber was having a greater effect than Alaric had thought.

Before he returned to the chamber he would have to find the spell and remove it. To break the spell he would need to draw on the energy around him. He would need to suck in the pure evil. Luckily he didn't need a lot to achieve his goal. Once he knew what he was looking for it would not be hard for him to fix it. Alaric steeled himself as he drew on the evil, he knew it was only the beginning. Once he removed Ra'naroz's spell it would get much worse.

As Alaric had expected he was overwhelmed by a feeling of nausea when he plucked away the threads of the Dark Knight's spell. He felt the evil coursing through his body. He could no longer hold back the urge to vomit and it continued for a few seconds before he was able to stop. He had to admit that he felt better for it. Ra'naroz burst out laughing, but made no move to leave the cavern and attack.

The sight that met Alaric's eyes when he returned made his heart sink. He knew why the Ra'naroz had sent him down the wrong tunnel. He could not believe that he had been so stupid.

Lying on the slab in the middle of the cavern, both wrists and ankles firmly tied, was Alena. She did not look at all like he remembered her. Her skin was deathly pale. There seemed to be no colour left in her face and her body was skin and bones. She was skinnier than he had ever seen before. Alaric had to wonder at the last time she had eaten. Her breathing was slow and shallow. There was only a very subtle rise and fall of her chest. If he was not looking directly at her there is no way he could tell if she was dead or alive.

The sight made his heart ache. He could not imagine the pain she had gone through. Her dress was so ripped there was very little cloth left. What material was left was soaked in blood. He could see the scars on her skin through the holes in her dress. They looked as though they were just as bad, if not worse, as the three he had rescued earlier. It almost made him sick to look at her. It also built up the rage inside his body. All he could think of was making the Dark Knight pay for what he had done.

"So I see that you can fill with rage as well," Alaric looked up from Alena's body when he heard Ra'naroz speak. The look on his face made the Dark Knight take a step backwards. He was not expecting such malice, but he did not stay on the back foot for long. "It is good. I think there is hope for you yet. At least there would be if I wasn't about to kill you." When he recovered from his initial shock Alaric stepped back to the slab.

"I don't think you are going to leave this place. I think it is quite fitting that you will be put to death here," Alaric spoke between clenched teeth. He wanted nothing more than to start his attack, but there was something in the back of his mind telling him to wait. He wanted to shut it out, but it would not go away. He knew better than to go against his feelings.

Ra'naroz started laughing. He found Alaric's threats too amusing. The man did not realise what a position he was in. There was nothing he could do without risking the woman's life and he knew Alaric wouldn't do that. When there was no recognition on the man's face he knew he would have to explain. He could not believe how dense the Cursed One was.

"I have a feeling you will willingly hand your life over to me," there was an evil smile on Ra'naroz's face.

"And why would I do that?" Alaric still asked the question through clenched teeth.

"Because you are not quick enough to kill me before I kill your she-elf. I don't think you will risk attacking me. I think you will do exactly what I say," Ra'naroz drew a small dagger and waved it threateningly over her body.

Alaric watched in shock as the realisation dawned on him. He had not thought about Alena's safety, only his vengeance, there was still a chance the Dark Knight could kill her. There was no way he could allow that to happen. He hated to admit it, but Ra'naroz was right. There was no way he could attack with Alena trapped as she was.

"What do you want?" Alaric was resigned to ask, but he had to play for time.

"Now that is the question," Ra'naroz made a sign of thinking, although it was clear he knew what he wanted. "I believe that you have a *Stone of Power* or two," Ra'naroz did not have to finish for Alaric to know what he was after. "I think that I will take them off your hands."

Alaric felt something spark in the back of his mind at the mention of the stones. He pushed the feeling aside. There was no time to fight with voices inside his head. All his attention was needed on the Dark Knight. The stone on his wrist suddenly felt very heavy. He wanted to look down to see if it was glowing, but he didn't want to draw any attention to it.

There was nothing he could do about Ra'naroz's request. He could not sacrifice Alena and he could not relinquish the stones. There had to be another solution. There had to be a third choice. He had to keep the Dark Knight talking until it presented itself.

"You know I cannot willingly give you the stones," Alaric started.

The Dark Knight was a little taken aback at his response. He thought the Cursed One would instantly back down. He thought about plunging the blade into Alena's chest, but that would not prove anything. If he was able to get the stones then he would be able to kill Alaric and then he could do what he liked with Alena. If he killed Alena then all he would gain was another dead body. He would give her a stay of execution, but not for much longer. The Great Lord had told him that she needed to be alive for the final battle, but if the Cursed One was dead he didn't see the point. It would not be long before it would all be over and he would be victorious.

"So you will sacrifice the life of your she-elf?" Ra'naroz smiled.

Alaric thought it was a rhetorical question, but he thought he should answer it anyway. "You have not given me a choice. There is nothing I can do," Alaric's rage had abated.

"Then I guess you leave me no other option," Ra'naroz did not like Alaric's answer. He was going to have to kill the she-elf and then take his chances against him

.He turned to Alena "If you have anything to say now would be the time," he spoke to her, but there was no response. "It seems as though she is ready to die." He looked at Alaric.

When he finished speaking Ra'naroz thrust the dagger down towards her chest. Just before the blade was about to strike Alaric called out. Ra'naroz stopped just as the point touched her. It did not break the skin, but a moment longer and she would have been dead.

"This is your last chance," Ra'naroz was yelling. "Give me the stones or she will die."

"Okay!" Alaric held up his hand in a signal to get him to stop. As Ra'naroz pushed down on the blade a trickle of blood appeared between her breasts and trickled down towards her stomach. "I admit. I have the Emerald stone. If you let her go I will give it to you."

Ra'naroz pulled the blade back. There were a couple of drops of blood on the blade and Ra'naroz could not help himself. He had to lick it off. He knew that it would have an effect on Alaric and he loved the taste of fresh blood. It was a win-win situation.

"I know you have more than one stone, but at least it is a start," Ra'naroz seemed happy with himself.

Alaric pulled the velvet pouch out of his pocket. It seemed extra heavy in his hand. He wondered if the stone knew what was happening. He was sure the Jade stone would not be happy if it knew it was going to a Dark Knight. It was that thought that gave him an idea. Slowly he made a move to open the pouch, but Ra'naroz was getting impatient.

"I don't think that you need to open that. I am not a complete idiot," Ra'naroz spoke. "Just throw me the pouch. I will check for myself to see if it is indeed the Jade stone."

The Emerald stone, covered by the sleeve of his shirt, suddenly made his wrist itch. He wanted nothing more than to rub it, but he couldn't bring its attention to the Dark Knight.

"Let's finish this," the voice came unbidden in his mind. "Give me control and I will destroy him."

On face value it was a promising offer, but Alaric knew there was something underlying in the words. He steeled himself and pushed the voice to the back of his mind. He could sense a feeling of anger and unrest, but he couldn't let it distract him from the scene in front of him.

"I wouldn't do that Alaric," the voice was weak, but it was unmistakable. Alaric was relieved to hear Eldred's voice.

"Stay out of this, wizard," Ra'naroz didn't like the new arrival. He had thought Eldred was unconscious when he retrieved Alena. If he had known Eldred would surface he would have been more careful.

"I don't think so," Eldred spoke as he entered the chamber.

The wizard was in a bad state. He had a multitude of scars across his body. His shirt had been completely stripped, as had most of his skin. The skin that wasn't scarred was pale and he looked as though he was having trouble breathing. The only real difference between him and Alena was that Eldred was conscious and on his feet. It did not look as though he would remain that way for much longer.

"But he will kill Alena if I don't give him the stone," Alaric's voice was strained. He was still fighting with his decision.

"Is that right Ra'naroz?" Eldred asked the question.

"I don't know what you are talking about. All I know is if I don't get the stone in the next second your friend will be dead," Ra'naroz did not sound as confident anymore.

"And I think you would be following shortly after," Eldred warned.

There was something about the way that Eldred spoke that made Ra'naroz nervous, but he was not completely beaten. Even without the aid of two stones he was still confident he could beat them.

"I think I will be able to hold my own. You are not as strong as you think you are," Ra'naroz returned.

"I think you are forgetting a very important player in all of this," Eldred was not going to give any information away. He wanted to play for time, although he did not know how much longer he would remain conscious.

"I would just tell me what you are talking about or she gets it," Ra'naroz warned.

"Okay, but I think you will kick yourself when I tell you," Eldred paused to give him another chance to realise the answer. "There is a reason why Nyrra did not want you to kill us. He wants Alena to be kept alive and it seems as though you are not doing a great job. I don't think that your Great Lord would not be too pleased to find out you have killed his prize."

Eldred's word hit the mark. Ra'naroz knew he was right. If he killed Alena then the Great Lord would quickly kill him, but he didn't know if he had a choice. Alaric would not simply hand over one of the stones of power, let alone two, but he needed to get them somehow. The longer they remained in Alaric's possession the greater the chance of him ending up dead. Surely the Great Lord would understand his reasoning.

Alaric fingered the Emerald stone with his free hand. The offer was becoming more and more tempting. With the aid of the Emerald stone he knew he could kill the Dark Knight. Slowly he pulled his sleeve back to reveal the stone.

"Be that as it may, I will do what I have to do to survive and if that means killing her then I will," the logic seemed solid to Ra'naroz, although he was trying to convince himself more than the others.

There was a small buzzing in the back of Alaric's mind as the stone was out in the open. There was a gentle glow coming from the centre of the bracelet. In the back of his mind was a feeling of content which quickly changed when it realised Alaric was not about to attack.

The Dark Knight had not realised that Alaric was wearing the Emerald stone, even though the green glow could easily be seen. He had been so focused on the Jade dagger that he had not thought about the bracelet. With the Jade stone sill in its pouch he had returned his complete attention to the woman bound in the middle of the room. Eldred's words had done nothing to convince him that killing Alena was the wrong idea. What he had done was distract Ra'naroz so Alaric had enough time to plan his attack.

Ra'naroz plunged the dagger downwards to kill Alena. He had given up on waiting for Alaric to hand over the stone and he was filled with a murderous rage. The old wizard could not know the will of the Great Lord and he silently cursed himself for letting himself be delayed. The Dark Knight would kill the elf and prove he was still in the Great Lord's favour. Just before the blade stuck his arm froze in midair. No matter what he did he could no longer move it.

"I can kill him now," the voice cooed in the back of his mind. "Just give me the word and I will do it for you."

"Be quiet," his mind's voice snapped.

"I don't think that is the greatest of ideas," there was something different in Alaric's voice. Ra'naroz did not like what he was hearing. "Get her off the slab," he spoke to Eldred.

Alaric could not feel the sickness from the energy he had drawn in from the room to create his spell, but he knew it was there. The

Emerald stone was keeping him from feeling sick, protecting him from the evil. Alaric was grateful for the help, although he knew he would suffer once it was all over.

"It doesn't have to be like this," a voice spoke inside his mind.

Alaric blinked once and put the thought out of his mind. He needed to concentrate on the job in front of him if he wanted to defeat the Dark Knight. There was little strain in keeping the spell up, but he knew that Ra'naroz was working on a counter spell. If Eldred was not quick enough then Alena would soon be dead.

Eldred worked as quickly as he could to untie Alena, but he was very weak. What would have normally taken a few seconds had already taken over a minute. There was still no life in Alena, which was a concern to both men. There was a good chance that she would die before they were able to defeat the Dark Knight.

Just when Eldred was able to roll Alena's body off the table Ra'naroz was able to break the spell. His dagger came crashing down onto the stone slab taking a small chip off the top. When the initial shock had passed he focused his attention towards Alaric. Alena was out of striking distance and any move to attack her or Eldred would leave him defenceless against any further attack from Alaric.

"Then this is where it ends for us, Cursed One," Ra'naroz sneered. "I will see that none of you will leave this chamber."

"I think that the time for talking is over. I am sick of the sound of your voice. It will be a pleasure for me to destroy it," Alaric knew the Dark Knight was only speaking to give himself more time to create a spell. Alaric was not going to get caught off guard.

Ra'naroz had to give Alaric credit for realising his plan, but the damage had already been done. The Dark Knight was able to create a small spell that would distract Alaric whilst he drew in more energy. A small ball of fire shot from Ra'naroz's hand. Alaric hardly had time to think to deflect the ball. It simply struck the wall before it fizzled out. He did not like the elementary style of the initial attack. He knew there was something more powerful waiting for him.

"Do not risk it," the voice pleaded inside his mind. "Give me control and I will defeat him."

"I can do this myself," Alaric's voice inside his head barked. "You will do what I command, not the other way around."

As he had defeated the other Dark Knights Alaric didn't like attacking early in the battle. He found it was better for him to defend then he wouldn't be taken off guard. This time it was different. The rage of the treatment of Alena and Eldred had bubbled to the surface. The evil of the energy was starting to play a role and it was causing him to remember his rage. It also helped to increase the intensity. There was no way he was going to let the Dark Knight live.

Alaric threw a crackle of lightning in the Dark Knight's direction. His attack was wild and not very effective. His rage had brought strength to his spell, but very little direction. The sparks flew around Ra'naroz's ears, but did not damage him. It was more of a light show than anything else.

Ra'naroz had not been expecting such an attack. At first it was a shock, but when he realised the futility of it he started to laugh. He could not believe that the Cursed One, the man they were all supposed to fear, could throw such a weak spectacle. What made it even more amusing was the fact he was using the Emerald stone. Killing him was going to be easier than he thought and then he would sit on the right hand of the Great Lord, above all of his brothers.

Eldred was sitting against the far wall watching the display. He had Alena's head cradled in lap. He wanted to help, but there was nothing he could do. If he tried to create a spell it would drain the life from him. All he could do was sit and watch.

"If that is the best you can do then I think that you should give up now. I am sure that the Great Lord could find some use for you," Ra'naroz sounded smug.

Alaric did not like what he was hearing. His face felt hot. He did not know if it was through embarrassment or rage. All he knew was that he could not let the Dark Knight get away with such a jibe. He would make him pay. Without thinking he drew in more power. He knew it would take a greater effort if he was going to bring down the Dark Knight.

Alaric tried to suck in as much energy as his body could hold. As he did the stones in the wall started to shake. Grains of dirt started to trickle down from the roof. Eldred did not like what he was seeing. Although he could not feel the energy around him, he knew what was happening. He knew that Alaric was drawing in too much power.

"Be careful Alaric," Eldred's voice was weak.

"Yes, be careful Alaric," Ra'naroz taunted. "You know you are not strong enough to hold that much power."

The jibe only made Alaric want to draw in more. He would not let the Dark Knight get the upper hand. He knew he could handle more power, but as he did he had a feeling that something wasn't right. The buzzing returned to the back of his mind. He wanted to dampen the noise, but he couldn't. Something was holding him back.

"Be careful," the voice came inside of his mind. "Ra'naroz is trying to bait you. He wants you to burn out. Doing this will prove nothing."

The voice made sense, but Alaric did not want to back down. Suddenly a realisation came to him. The voice was right. There had been plenty of time for the Dark Knight to attack, but he was waiting for Alaric. He had a bad feeling that he was walking into a trap. With a deep regret he stopped drawing in energy. He was brimming with power, but he still had the urge for more.

Once he had stopped drawing in power he had another realisation. The amount of energy he was holding would be enough to blow up the entire castle and half of Jarrat. There was little he could do without bringing the roof down on top of them. He only hoped that Ra'naroz didn't realise the fact. Alaric could not risk attacking. He could hold a defence, but that was it. He would have to wait for the Dark Knight to attack. He knew if he let a little energy dissipate then he would lose the lot and would risk collapsing to the ground.

What Alaric did next surprised both Ra'naroz and Eldred. Neither of them were expecting his reaction. He did the only thing that he could think of and that was to draw his sword. The sound of steel sliding out of its scabbard resonated throughout the chamber. He took a strong stance and waited.

Ra'naroz did not know how to respond, but he knew not to trust Alaric. The move was not what he expected and therefore could not be trusted. He knew that Alaric had drawn in a great deal of magical energy. He could feel the stagnation in the room, although the evil was starting to seep in from the rest of the dungeon. He had to be holding onto the energy for a surprise attack. For the moment he would play along with Alaric's game and be prepared.

The Dark Knight was not wearing a sword, but that was not a problem. Creating a sword of fire, or from some other material was an easy enough spell, but to do it properly was an art form. Ra'naroz had decided to go with a sword of ice. Normally an ice sword would shatter the moment it was struck with steel, but the ice was just for show, like with fire, it was the magic that made the sword and gave it strength.

Once Ra'naroz was armed Alaric did not wait to attack. He had to admit he was somewhat surprised with his choice of weapon, but that thought was not in his head for long. It was time for business. If he could kill Ra'naroz without using the power inside of him then it would be a good thing. It wasn't long before Alaric knew that would not be the case.

There was no doubt Alaric was a more accomplished swordsman than Ra'naroz. The Dark Knight was competent with the sword, but that was about it. At one stage in his life he had been a master, but that was a long time ago. He had not kept up his training over the years. He found it much easier to use magic to get others to submit to his will. In Alaric's state they were evenly matched. Whilst he was holding onto the energy and the power flowed through his body he found it hard to focus on his swordsmanship.

Ra'naroz did not realise what was happening with Alaric. He just assumed that he was stronger with the sword than him. Alaric went on the attack early. The Dark Knight was able to fend off the attacks without too much trouble. There was little room in the chamber for a sword fight, which made the battle even more difficult. That fact also favoured the Dark Knight. Alaric, although he had trained in such a manner, was not used to fighting in such a cramped space. To make matters worse Alaric had to make sure the Ra'naroz was not able to manoeuvre his way over to Eldred and Alena. If that happened then the battle would be over and he would have lost.

The battle was somewhat lacklustre compared with his battles with the other Dark Knights. Neither combatant ever looked like killing the other. The attacks had no substance and were easy to defend. It was like there were two beginners fighting for the first time. They did, however, fight for almost half an hour before they realised the futility of what they were doing. As much as Alaric did not want to have to use the energy stored in his body he knew if he wanted to kill the Dark Knight he would have to find a way.

"It seems we are well matched with the sword," the words were as much as a surprise to Ra'naroz as they were to Alaric as they came from the Dark Knight's mouth.

Alaric knew it was not the case, but he did not want to explain the fact to Ra'naroz. If he did then the Dark Knight would feel as though he still held the advantage. For the moment he was happy to let Ra'naroz think what he wanted. It was time to concentrate on the real battle.

"It seems as though it is time to stop playing with you," Alaric's voice was not as strong as he hoped it would be. It seemed as though the strain was starting to get to him.

"Now is the time to strike," the voice came inside of his head. "Give me control, you are too weak to defeat him on your own."

He knew the voice was right, but he still did not know what he could do. If he released the power he would kill them all. That was not something he wanted to risk. He had to find a way to destroy the Dark Knight and then get them out of the dungeon. He couldn't give up the fight to the Emerald stone and in his weakened condition he didn't think he would be able to regain his conscious state.

Ra'naroz did not wait to see what Alaric had in store. He was sick of being on the defensive. It was not in his nature to defend. He was the one who was the aggressor. He was the one who set the tone of the battle. He had let Alaric lead the dance for too long. It was his turn to show Alaric the might of the Dark Knights. He too was aware of the precarious situation they were in, but he was not as concerned.

The chamber shook as Ra'naroz released his spell. The air shimmered in front of Alaric, but that was the only sign the Dark Knight had started his attack. The sign was so subtle that Eldred was not sure he had seen it. Alaric felt the attack before he saw anything coming. If he had not diverted the attack then he would have been consumed by the spell. Ra'naroz was a little surprised to see Alaric still standing before him. He thought his spell would have been strong enough to kill him.

In defence Alaric was able to use a small amount of energy he had stored in his body. He felt a little better once it was gone. Instantly he saw a way out of his current situation. If he was able to keep the Dark Knight attacking then eventually he would have a safe level of energy. He would only need one attack to destroy the Dark Knight. He was sure of that.

"Is that the best you can do?" Alaric's voice was weaker than he felt. He thought that would drive the Dark Knight harder. The more aggressive the attack the stronger his defence would have to be and therefore the quicker he would be able to counter-attack. "I thought you were supposed to be one of the Great Lord's Chosen. It seems that you are just one of his pets."

Alaric's words hit their mark. There was no way that Ra'naroz was going to let a snivelling human speak to him in such a manner. He would make the Cursed One pay for such insolence. He no longer thought about the consequences of his actions. He had forgotten about the amount of energy Alaric had drawn upon before they had started their sword fight. All he could think of was killing him. Even Eldred and Alena had gone from his mind.

His next attack was a lot stronger than the first one. The chamber started to rumble and more dirt fell from the roof. Alaric was concerned the Dark Knight was going to bring the roof down on top of them. He did not have enough strength to keep the roof from collapsing and save himself from the impending attack. All he could do was hope Ra'naroz wouldn't try and bring the ceiling down on them.

The air started to crackle around the chamber. Alaric was not sure what was about to happen, but he knew that he had to defend himself. All of a sudden small bolts of electricity appeared from the space around him. Once they were formed they shot towards him, striking his skin. One of the electric bolts, although would not have killed him, would have caused pain if Alaric had not cast his defensive spell. Ra'naroz did not know that Alaric had completed his defence and laughed wickedly when the first of the bolts struck. Alaric feigned distress which caused the Dark Knight to increase his attack. With each moment that passed the electric bolts were appearing more frequently and from more and more locations. Soon Alaric's body was completely engulfed by the magical storm.

Ra'naroz kept up the attack until he consumed all the energy he had drawn around him. There was still more power for him to draw upon, but he figured that he had done the job. When the last of the energy left his body he felt exhausted. The only thing that kept him going was the knowledge that Alaric would be lying on the ground, dead. His body would be a smoking mess. With any luck he would not be able to recognise the wretched creature's remains.

The sight that met his eyes brought fear into his heart. It was not at all what he had been expecting. Instead of a smouldering corpse Alaric stood before him, not a single scar on his body. It was as if nothing had happened. Ra'naroz could not work out what had happened. It was like he was waking from a bad dream. He tried to draw in the remaining power around him, but he could not. There was something blocking his ability. When he realised what it was the shock he had been feeling intensified.

"What is going on?" there was fear in the Dark Knight's voice.

"It seems as though you have underestimated my abilities. Now it is your turn to suffer," there was pure malice in Alaric's voice. Eldred did not like the sound of it, but he did not have the energy to do anything about it. All he could do was sit and watch and hope he did not do anything stupid.

Alaric knew exactly what he was doing. Defending against the barrage of electricity had drained just the right amount of energy from him. Now he could cast a spell and not risk bringing down the entire cavern. All he had to do was work out the exact manner of the Dark Knight's death. He did not want to make it too quick, but on the other hand he knew that he did not have time to waste. As he watched the trembling Dark Knight he finally knew the suitable punishment.

Ra'naroz's eyes shot open, wider than what Alaric would have thought possible. Fear was obviously written on his face. He tried to move, but his body was stuck. There was nothing he could do. Alaric had him completely trapped. He could do nothing to defend himself, neither magically nor physically. He was completely at Alaric's mercy.

"Now you have him, now it is time to end it," the voice came again.

"Enough from you! If you don't be quiet the stone is going back in its pouch."

The voice didn't know if Alaric was serious or not, but it didn't want to take a chance. It would was a double edged sword and there was no good end. If the Emerald stone was in the pouch it would be trapped again. It would also mean that it could no longer help Alaric and he would be at the mercy of the Dark Knight. Neither result was worth risking.

"Please, don't kill me," The Dark Knight begged. Begging was his last hope. The only chance he had of remaining alive was to convince Alaric that he needed him. "I have information that will be useful to you."

Alaric drew his sword and walked to where the Dark Knight was frozen. He wanted nothing more than to draw his blade across Ra'naroz's throat and watch the blood spill to the floor, but something was holding him back. He knew the Dark Knight would say anything to stay alive, but there was something in his voice that made Alaric want to hear more. He knew he was not being manipulated by magic because Ra'naroz could not create any spells, so it had to be something else.

"Tell me what you know and I will decide if it is worth keeping you alive."

"There is an army of orglin in the forest to the north. At any moment now they will be crashing into your army. Your army has no idea that they are coming. Leave now and you might have a chance to save their lives," the words rushed out of Ra'naroz's mouth.

Alaric had stopped no more than a step away from the Dark Knight. He held his blade precariously close his throat. He thought on the information. There was a chance Ra'naroz was lying, but he did not think that was the case. It was insignificant either way. Now that he had the information there was no point in leaving the Dark Knight alive. He would dish out some of the evil creature's own medicine.

"Wait, there is more." Ra'naroz saw the look on his face and realised what he was about to do. "Your she-elf," Alaric stopped when he heard his words.

"What about her?" Alaric's sword was about to cut into Ra'naroz's neck when he stopped.

"She is sick and I do not think your physician's will be able to cure her." There was a wry grin on Ra'naroz's face. He knew his words were having their effect. "I know how to cure her, but I won't be able to if she is dead."

"Tell me what you know?" Alaric didn't like what he was hearing.

"I do not think this is the place to speak of such matters," Ra'naroz knew that he had just saved his life, or at least had prolonged his death.

"Tell me now!" Alaric shouted.

Ra'naroz kept his mouth shut, knowing that it could be his last mistake. It was a risk he was willing to take. He did not think that Alaric would kill him whilst he knew Alena's life was at stake. At least he would die knowing she would share the same fate soon enough. There was little comfort in that thought, but there was some.

"I will not speak until we are out of the dungeon," Ra'naroz was adamant.

Alaric did not know what to do. He looked at Alena, who was still lying in Eldred's arms. She did not look well. She did not look as though she would survive for much longer. As much as it pained him he had to admit that the Dark Knight had won. He could not kill Ra'naroz until he knew what was killing her.

"Okay, you have your way," Alaric resigned.

It would take a lot of energy to move all four of them out of the dungeons. The only way he would be able to do such a task was to tie off the spell he had cast on Ra'naroz. That meant it would be possible for the Dark Knight to break it. It was not an easy thing to do, but he was sure Ra'naroz would have the skill. At least the Dark Knight was weakened from the attack. If he was able to break through the spell then it would not be for a few days. It was with that thought that he made the decision. He took a long time to tie off the spell. He wanted to make sure it would be as hard as possible for Ra'naroz to break free. He also left a number of nasty surprises along the way.

Once he was done he concentrated on the job at hand. He needed more energy to complete the spell to get them all safely out of the dungeons. If he was able to touch all of them at once it would be an easy task, but the Dark Knight and the other two were on separate sides of the room. He had never attempted such a spell before, but he was sure that he knew how to fashion it.

He started to draw in more of the sickening energy around him. Again the Emerald stone blocked any adverse affects. It helped his current situation, but it would come back to hurt him later. Just as he was ready to cast his spell a voice came within in mind.

"You should not do this," the voice was almost panicked. "You should not leave him alive. This is a bad mistake. Dead he is no threat, but alive he could kill you at any moment."

"I have no choice," Alaric spoke aloud, although he did not have too. "I have to save her."

Ra'naroz was surprised to hear Alaric speak as there didn't seem to be a reason why he should. He didn't think the man was speaking to him, so he did not answer. He would wait for a direct question before he spoke again. He did not want to risk his life.

"She is insignificant. Let her die. Kill the traitor before he kills you," the voice was very persistent.

"Don't worry, I will not let him live long," Alaric controlled himself and used his mind voice to speak. He did not want Ra'naroz to know what he was thinking.

Alaric had made his decision and he would not be dissuaded. He would not risk Alena's life. She had been through too much for his sake for him to leave her now. If it wasn't for him then she would not be in such a state. Deep down he knew it was not really the case, but he was willing to believe it anyway.

The strain was clear on his face as he released his spell. In a moment they blinked out of existence. There was a short rush before they reappeared in the castle hallway. Instantly he collapsed to his knees. There was little energy left in his body, even with the added help from the Emerald stone. As he looked up he saw a number of armed men moving towards them. His heart sank as his eyes closed and he lost consciousness.

Chapter 7: Surprise Attack

Suddenly orglin started to rush out of the forest and onto the north of the battlefield. With the sound of the screaming creatures both armies had stopped fighting. They were so perplexed with the noise they wanted to see what was making it before they started fighting again. There was an entirely new chaos to deal with and no one knew what to make of it.

The flank of the Alliance had quickly regained their composure and started fighting the wicked creatures. The Enteroite army did not know what to think. They were not sure whether they should continue attacking the Alliance or whether they should help. The captains did nothing to help the soldiers. They also did not know what they should do. Initially they just stood and watched the battle.

It was not only the surprise of a new army taking the battlefield that confused the Enteroite soldiers, but also the nature of it. Most people had heard of orglin in tales or books of old, but no one really believed they were true. The creatures ran hunched over, unable to stand fully upright. Their thick, leathery skin hung tightly on their bones. The only clothes they wore were dirty loin cloths.

At first the orglin had the better of the army. The creatures threw themselves at the soldiers with a ferocity they had not been expecting. They did not have any weapons, but that did not stop them causing havoc. They scratched with their claws, taking out chucks of flesh as they did. They also used their teeth, which were as sharp as razors, to bite into their victims. They could rip out a human's throat with one bite.

If the soldiers had been prepared for the attack they would have been able to use their armour in defence. Despite their sharp teeth and claws the orglin could not penetrate hardened steel. Instead the soldiers just stood, perplexed at the rampaging creatures.

It took Jarwe a few seconds to recover from the initial shock. It was much the same with the rest of the army. They could not believe what they were seeing. They had just managed to regain control of the battle only to lose it again. All of a sudden there was an entirely different mess to sort out. The soldiers, who had previously been in a solid, almost unbreakable line, were all over the place. They had been taken by surprise and it showed in their lack of formation. Jarwe did not know what he was going to do. He was unsure what formation his soldiers should take. This was like nothing he had ever experienced before.

"What should we do?" Jarwe could tell by Sorrell's voice he was just as surprised as everyone else.

"I don't know," was all he could reply.

The command group stared at the horror that was unfolding before them. The soldiers fought valiantly, but they were outmatched by the orglin. They were out of formation and taken by surprise. It was a deadly combination. The orglin had a thirst for death they had never come across before.

The orglin were suffering casualties, but for every one that went down there seemed to be another dozen spew out of the forest. Jarwe did not know if it was ever going to stop. They were starting to over run the army. If he did not do something to stem the flow they would inevitably lose.

"We need to fall back and spread out," Jarwe spoke the order, which was only just audible to the other commanders.

"What about the Enteroites?" Sorrell asked? "We are still at war with them as well."

With the horror in front of him he had completely forgotten about the original army they were fighting. He looked over to where the Enteroite army was standing and watching the horror. They did not look overly excited about fighting either side. If they remained where they were it would not be long before they would be forced to fight one of the armies.

"Send word to Captain Tyson that we do not want to fight with them anymore," Jarwe explained.

"I don't think they will just accept that," Sorrell replied. He was not happy with what Jarwe was suggesting.

Jarwe took a moment to think. Even though the battle was getting closer by the minute he had to make the right decision. Things had not gone to plan from the start and they were only getting worse. He was normally quick to come to a decision, but he didn't know what to do. He knew that the wrong decision would see them all dead. He was beginning to doubt himself as a general, something he had never done before.

"Tell them that we surrender. Once we have defeated the army of orglin then we will surrender control to the queen," Jarwe didn't like what he was saying, but it was the only thing he could think of. The worst thing that could happen was to get in-between the two armies. Surrender was better than death.

Sorrell shook his head, but he did not argue. When it was said and done he knew that Jarwe was making the right decision. He was glad he was not in charge of the army. Passing the message along was bad enough. He only hoped that the rest of the soldiers understood their reasoning. If word got out before the battle was over then it would do nothing for moral and they needed all they could get.

Jarwe watched as a runner took the message to Captain Tyson. When the captain had received the message he looked over towards Jarwe. He saluted quickly before returning his attention to his soldiers. With the threat of attack from the Alliance gone there was only one command he could make. It was time for his army to get involved. Jarwe could see he was having a heated discussion with Captain Prewitt. The general hoped that Tyson would be able to make the man see sense.

"Tell the soldiers to fall back. We need to stop the carnage. We need to spread out," Jarwe barked the orders.

Eventually the word made it to the front line and soldiers started to fall back. At the same time the Enteroite army started to move forward. The orglin did not realise what their opposition was doing and continued their frenzied attack without a second thought.

Jarwe watched the battle and tried to work out some tactic that would sway the advantage back in their favour. There was no rhythm to the orglin's attack. They were just throwing themselves at the men. It was an unconventional battle, but it was one he would learn by. If they were fortunate to be able to survive he would have to come up with an entirely new plan. For now it was a matter of survival.

"Charge!" Jarwe called when he realised the retreat was finished.

The line was solid again, but that was not going to be much help. The wave of orglin struck as hard as they did from the start. The Alliance had managed to stem the flow of death and were starting to kill more orglin. Jarwe hoped that he had done the right thing.

It was not long before the general worked his horse towards the front of the line. He had watched too much. He could no longer sit and watch his men get slaughtered. The command work was complete. It was time for him to shed some blood. He only hoped that it wasn't his.

"Where are you going?" Sorrell asked. Even if it seemed his command was done there was no telling what else would happen. It seemed as though he was content to leave Sorrell in charge and the General from Darshival wasn't too happy about it.

"There is nothing more I can do here. It's time to join the battle." His horse raced away before Sorrell could say anything else.

Sorrell looked to his advisor, but didn't say anything. As he returned his attention to the battle he wanted nothing more than to follow Jarwe, but that wasn't a choice. Someone still needed to command the Alliance and he couldn't leave it to anyone else.

From horseback it was a lot easier to kill the orglin. As they approached he slashed from above. His experienced warhorse was able to manoeuvre around to make his job a lot easier. Jarwe hacked at the creatures who charged at him with no fear or remorse. The feeling of battle was euphoric. As a general it was very rare he would actually take the battlefield anymore. There was nowhere else he would rather be. His sudden appearance also raised the morale of the soldiers fighting around him.

As the battle continued there was suddenly another noise coming from the forest to the north. It was not as terrifying as the first, but there was something disturbing about it. It was the sound of war horns being blown. Jarwe did not recognise the sound of the horn, which in his mind meant that it was another ally of the Evil One. It was only then that he realised what he had done. He had left his position of command to fight and that was unacceptable. As much as he wanted to return to the command group he knew he couldn't leave the battlefield.

Jarwe wanted to see what was about to come forth from the forest, but he could not divert his attention from the orglin. After the initial shock he continued slashing at the evil creatures. As soon as one died there was another to take its place. On occasions he would have to fight two or three at a time. No matter what he did there was no break from the attack. In his peripheral vision he could see his fellow soldiers going down around him. Slowly he had to get his horse to go backwards. The last thing he wanted to do was to get surrounded. That would mean certain death.

Suddenly there was a break in the onslaught. At first Jarwe thought the battle was over, but when he looked up he could still see a swarm of orglin in front of them. Something had changed. They were no longer powering forward with the insatiable hunger for death. If anything they looked confused. Another horn sounded from the forest behind them, but Jarwe still could not see who was blowing it.

"Hold!" Jarwe called out as the soldiers started to press forward.

He did not think that it was a good idea to advance until he knew what was waiting for them. There had already been too many surprises. The sudden change in the orglin's demeanour was a good sign. Jarwe was beginning to hope there was help on the other side of the trees.

All eyes were locked on the forest. A safe distance had opened up between the orglin and the two armies. The orglin seemed almost scared of what was hiding in the trees. Jarwe could not believe what he was seeing. He held the belief that there that there was an unknown ally in the forest. There was a new hope they would survive. They had lost some serious numbers.

Suddenly arrows started raining down from the sky. They struck the orglin making the creatures go wild. They had not been expecting an attack from behind. They didn't know what to do and there was still no sign of the secret saviours. Another hail of arrows shot down. There was no co-ordination within the evil creatures. No one would be able to bring them back into control. It was the one flaw in the Dark Knight's plan. The orglin did not handle surprise at all well.

After a number of volleys hit the orglin there came another high pitched cry from the forest. It was obvious that another attack was about to start. It was the perfect time for Jarwe to start his own attack again, but he did not give the order. The order to attack came from Sorrell and Jarwe was grateful for his attentiveness.

The first to come out into the open was a young looking man. He had long flowing blonde hair and a long, slender sword raised above his head. It only took a moment for Jarwe to realise that it was not a man, but an elf. It was not long before more elves crashed through the edge of the forest. They looked as though they were hungry for battle.

"Charge!" Jarwe echoed the order before he moved forward.

It was time for the Alliance to go on the offensive. The tide has turned. The soldiers were keen to get back into the thick of battle. Now that they held the advantage they were keen to seek revenge for their fallen comrades. They would fight the orglin with no mercy.

The battle was fierce, but quick. In less than an hour the orglin had been completely annihilated. Even if they had wanted to retreat there was nowhere to escape to. With the addition of the elves they were completely surrounded.

When the battle was over Jarwe made his way through the corpses to the elves. He was greeted by an elderly looking elf. Jarwe assumed that he must be the leader of the group. There were fewer elves than he thought there were and he could not see any dead elves on the ground.

"I am Jarwe, interim General of the Alliance." He thought he better make the point that he was just filling in. "I must thank you for your assistance. I do not know what we would have done if you had not come along when you did."

The elf did not look impressed with his words. "I am Orric, is Eldred with you?" he did not sound hopeful.

Jarwe was only just recovering his breath from battle, whilst Orric did not sound puffed at all. It was strange, but it was something Jarwe noticed nevertheless.

"I am sorry, but I don't recall the name," Jarwe knew he had heard the name somewhere before, but he could not place it.

There was a concerned look on the elderly elf's face. It did not instil any confidence in Jarwe. He tried harder to remember, but after the heat of battle all he could concentrate on was the rushing of blood through his head. He could find no answer. All he could do was wait for a response from the elf.

"Do you know if Alaric is here?" Orric asked when he was sure there was not going to be any further information.

"He is in the castle. There are some friends of ours who are trapped there," Jarwe did not divulge anything further.

If it was possible there was an even more concerned look on Orric's face. He did not like what he was hearing. Things had gone to plan, more or less, but that was little reassurance. He had been expecting to find Alaric and Eldred fighting with the Alliance. He knew Eldred was one of those trapped inside the castle, but the most disturbing part was the he did not feel that anything was wrong. He was starting to lose his connection with the prophecy. That could only mean one thing, but it was not something he was willing to consider.

"What is the situation inside the castle?" Orric asked, although he had a bad feeling that he already knew the answer.

"We believe there is a Dark Knight controlling the queen," Jarwe kept his brief short, mainly because he didn't have much more information to give.

"This is not good news…" Orric was about to continue, but a young soldier, wearing the uniform of a Remidian private, rushed over to them.

"Sir," he saluted in a manner fitting of a victorious general.

Jarwe actually recognised the private. He could not recall how he knew the man's name, but he did. "Get on with it Private Dawson, I don't have all day."

"I am sorry to interrupt, but the other commanders demanded that you get the information," the Private didn't sound too sure of himself.

"Well, spit it out man." Jarwe was starting to become annoyed.

"Captain Prewitt has called for your surrender." Private Dawson took a step backward when he delivered the news. It was at that point he realised he was within striking distance.

"What is he talking about?" Orric sounded shocked at the announcement.

"It's a long story, but needless to say that I need to get going. Your elves are more than welcome to make camp with the Alliance," Jarwe was about to move off, but something stopped him.

"My elves will wait here for my command. I will join you when you meet with this captain," there was strength in Orric's voice. Jarwe knew that there was no point in arguing.

Jarwe kept a brisk pace on the back of his horse. He made out he was in a hurry to meet the captain, but in reality he wanted to try and leave the elf behind. To his surprise Orric didn't seemed worried keeping up the pace. He thought about increasing the speed to see if he could keep up, but he thought that would be too obvious.

When they arrived Jarwe was pleased to see Tyson was standing with Prewitt. There was a chance they would get out of surrendering. He knew it had been the right decision to make. In the end it could have been the difference between those surviving and everyone dying. With the battle won he was beginning to regret the decision. If the Dark Knight was still in charge of the city then there was still a good chance they would all end up dead.

"Well, you do not look as sombre as I would have thought, considering you have just lost," there was a smug look on Prewitt's face.

What happened next surprised everyone. Tyson swung his right arm and struck Prewitt right across the mouth with his fist. It was obvious the blow was meant to hurt. It was only after Prewitt was knocked backwards did Tyson look at him.

"I think you should leave," he spoke between clenched teeth.

"You have no right," Prewitt drew his sword.

Jarwe noticed that there was no blood on his blade. It seemed as though the captain had remained behind his soldiers when the fighting broke out. Jarwe almost spat in disgust at the realisation. The man did not deserve to wear the rank of captain. If he was under Jarwe's command he would be struck down to the lowest rank possible.

"Put your sword away, Prewitt," Tyson didn't even bother to draw his own. Jarwe could see the blood on his uniform. It was clear he had taken part in the battle. "You know you are no match for me. Now run along and let us get down to business."

"I am the one that the prince placed in charge of the army. You have to do what I command," there was no power in Prewitt's voice. It sounded as though he was a spoilt brat trying to get his own way.

"I don't care what the prince has said. Run along or I will take your head here and now," Tyson barked.

"I...I...I will see that you are arrested for this insolence. You will be resting in the dungeons by nightfall," Prewitt raced away before Tyson had a chance to react.

"You wouldn't, would you?" Jarwe asked when Prewitt had disappeared.

"As much as I would like to, no. He might be a snivelling worm, but it wouldn't set a good example for the other soldiers. But don't worry, if he did anything untoward I would be the first one to run him through," there was no lie in his voice.

"So about this surrender?" Orric said.

Jarwe introduced the elf when Tyson looked confused. He seemed happy enough with Jarwe's explanation and comfortable to answer the elf's question.

"I don't think that will be necessary. We have bigger problems to worry about. With the gate locked shut we are as much outsiders as you are. The prince holds the castle, but at least the city is free now," Tyson explained.

"What about Prewitt?" Jarwe asked. "I think he is looking to cause trouble."

"Don't worry about him. He has little support out here. In fact I think he has little support amongst the prince's loyal soldiers. The men will do what I tell them," Tyson was confident.

"Okay, so what do we do now?" Jarwe asked.

Things were not quite going to plan. He had not expected things to go so easily. He wanted to be careful. The surrender would still stand if Tyson decided he wanted to enforce it. He would play along until everything was over.

"I think we need to work out how to get into the castle. prince Leroy has had the run of the place for too long," Tyson sounded like a man on a mission. His blood was still pumping from the first battle.

"I don't think that is the best of ideas," Jarwe spoke. "We have people inside. We have to give them a chance to get out. I also don't think it is a good idea for you to attack your own castle."

"Then how do you suggest we get rid of the prince?" Tyson did not sound convinced.

"I think we should convene in our command tent. There are others who might be able to shed a little more light on the matter," Jarwe suggested.

"Okay, but I don't think it's a good idea to keep the two armies together. We do not need to give Prewitt any more ammunition."

It did not take long for the command group to be assembled. They were all keen to formulate another plan. The sooner they were able to gain entrance into the castle the better. The battle outside the castle was over, but it was not to say that they had won. Until they heard from Alaric there was no telling what the end result would be. If the Dark Knight was successful then the army had little chance of survival.

They had picked up one more elf on the way back to the command tent. Orric introduced him as Kilean. The elf held himself in the same fashion as Orric, yet he looked as though he was considerably younger. Jarwe simply said hello and moved on. He did not really care about the new arrival; he was already starting to plan an assault on the city. Things seemed more clear-cut. The Evil One's followers held the castle and the only remaining allies inside were Alaric, the prisoners and the queen. The rest were fair game and deserved to suffer a painful death.

The other commanders were waiting for them when they arrived at the tent. Lord Pernian looked both excited and relieved when he saw Orric. He rushed over to the elderly elf and gave him a warm embrace.

"It is good to see you, my lord," Pernian spoke as he took a step backwards.

"And you too Lord Pernian. I see you have served me well," Orric replied.

"But what brings you here?" Pernian sounded somewhat confused.

"That story will have to wait. We have more important business to take care of," Jarwe interjected before they could continue their conversation. "We have won a great battle, but the war is not over. Our friends are inside and we need to get them out."

The realisation of the situation brought them down from the ecstasy of victory. They had achieved what they had set out to do, but the result was still unknown. There was a completely different situation they needed to try and figure out. Jarwe wished Alaric had given him more information on what he should do.

"I don't know if we can do anything without knowing the situation inside of the castle. We cannot risk the life of our queen," Tyson did not sound happy with what Jarwe was suggesting.

"Then what do you suggest that we do?" Jarwe shot straight back at him.

Tyson did not have an answer. He knew there was not going to be a solution to his problem, but he had to voice it anyway. When it was all said and done what he did he did for his queen. He knew his soldiers felt the same way. If Jarwe led the Alliance in an assault on the castle then he would have to stop him. He knew what that meant. It was not something he wanted to do, but if he had to then he would.

"I think that we have to have faith that Alaric will succeed. It is not that I am afraid of a suicide mission, but I don't think there is any other way," Hulkan spoke when everyone else was silent.

"This is not an easy situation," Orric spoke. "I think that Hulkan is right. We have to have some faith."

Jarwe did not like what he was hearing. It was not a solution. It was not an answer. It was nothing. He was a man of action, but he had to admit they were right. Alaric had told him what was expected of the army.

He had not said anything about their current problem, but he had not told him to attack the castle. Even that thought wasn't enough to convince him it was the right thing.

"How can we sit here and do nothing?" he asked himself more than anyone sitting around the table.

"Because we do not have a choice," Kilean spoke and everyone looked at him. There was something in the way he spoke that demanded respect, more so than Orric. "We have to wait. We will know when the time is right."

There was something on Orric's face that only Jarwe saw. It was like the elderly elf was jealous of his companion. He knew there was more to the story than what he knew. He wanted to ask the question, but it didn't seem as though it was appropriate. He would have to wait for a better time.

"Then what do we do in the meantime?" Jarwe was looking for answers.

"There is a field strewn with death. I think that it would be a good idea to clean it up," Sorrell suggested. It seemed as though the General from Darshival was still thinking straight. "Then I think the soldiers deserve to celebrate."

The first idea was great, but Jarwe did not agree with the second. There was a distinct possibility they would still have to fight those in the castle. If the soldiers celebrated throughout the night then they would be good for nothing in the morning. He wanted to reach across the table and throttle the man for making such a suggestion.

"I think we should wait until everything is over before we celebrate," Wojtek said.

Jarwe was grateful the man had spoken. He didn't think he would be able to voice his opinion in such a diplomatic manner. He wished Bern was back. He'd had enough of leading the Alliance. He thought about passing control to Sorrell, but he didn't want to think of the ramifications of such an action.

"We shall wait out the night," Jarwe spoke with a definitive voice. "If there is no sign from the castle then we will attack at first light."

"But…" Tyson was about to interject, but Jarwe would have none of it.

"I have made my decision. We cannot wait out here for ever. The longer we leave the Dark Knight in charge the more chance the queen will die," Jarwe's raised his voice, almost to the point of shouting.

"Then I think we should order the burning of the dead bodies," Sorrell added quickly before Tyson had a chance to reply.

"What do you want me to do with the Enteroite army?" Tyson resigned himself to the fact that Jarwe was in control. He knew deep down he would eventually have to assimilate the Enteroites into the Alliance. There was little point in trying to defy him.

"The Alliance will remain camped in the forest," Jarwe started. He was thinking as he spoke. "I don't think there is much point in getting your men to join us now. If we have to attack the castle then I think it would be better if your soldiers are not on the battlefield."

"Is there room for them inside of the city?" Wojtek asked.

"I think so. There should be," Tyson sounded unsure of the question.

"I think that is a great idea," Sorrell voice his opinion. "I am sure there will be agents of the Evil One inside the city walls. The presence of the army will dissuade them from starting any trouble."

Tyson had to admit it was a good plan. He silently cursed himself for not thinking of it himself. He had been so concerned with the castle that he had forgotten about the city. He himself had not been in the city since the prince had arrived. He had no idea what condition it was in.

"You are right. The army should regain control of the city. Our citizens deserve that much," Tyson conceded.

"Well I think we are done here. There can't be more than two hours before sunset. We all have a lot of work to be done before then," Jarwe stood and the meeting was over.

It had been one of the quickest meetings they had in a long time. Jarwe was grateful they were able to come to a decision so quickly, even if the main point was to do nothing. All he could do was hope that Alaric had succeed in his mission. If he had not then Jarwe didn't want to think of the consequences.

Chapter 8: Questions

Alaric woke with a start and looked around in a hurry. He had no idea where he was or how long he had been unconscious. A feeling of panic raced through his body. He knew something terrible had happened, but he couldn't remember what it was. He reached out for the energy around him for protection, but as he did he suddenly curled up in pain. He let out a terrible cry as the energy released from his body. Once it was gone the pain disappeared, but he was left with a feeling of nausea. Without control he vomited over the side of his bed.

When he was able to recover he took a better look at his surroundings. Things were not at all like he expected. He was in an ornately presented bedroom. The sheets on which he lay were silk. It was a four poster bed with lace curtains tied up to each post and two large drawers on either side. The floor had a soft white carpet, which quickly soaked up the pure liquid vomit. The entire situation didn't make any sense. He was sure he shouldn't be in such luxurious surroundings.

It took longer that he thought for the sickness to leave his body. It happened so suddenly that Alaric wasn't sure what had happened. He felt bad about the mess he had made on the floor, but until he could remember where he was there was nothing he could do about it. He had more important matters to deal with.

When he rose from the bed he realised he was almost naked. All he was wearing were pants made out of light material. They were obviously designed for sleeping in. In the normal wear and tear of life they would soon fall apart. He looked around the room for his clothes and his weapon and something else he should have, but he couldn't remember. He knew it was important. He wished he knew why his head was so cloudy.

He looked around the room for answers, but it didn't take him long to realise he was not going to gain anything. The drawers were filled with clothes, but they did not look as though they were something he would wear. There was nothing in the room that looked familiar to him. The situation was not getter any better.

When he had finished his inspection of the bedroom he knew the only way he was going to find answers was to leave. He figured it would be the first main test to find out if he was indeed a prisoner. If he was not then he had to work out where he was and who had saved him.

When his hand touched the doorknob he paused. He was not sure if he wanted to know what was on the other side. He took a deep breath before he quickly turned the handle and yanked the door open.

To his relief he found the room in front of him was empty. He felt rather foolish for the way that he had acted. He knew there were not going to be any answers in the room he was in. He would have to leave the safety of the apartments and find someone to speak with.

He slowly opened the door and stuck his head out. The corridor was empty. It was longer than he had been expecting. The possibilities of where he was became even narrower. He knew he must be in a mansion, a castle, a palace or something of similar status. When the thought of a castle passed through his mind it sounded familiar. It still didn't narrow anything down enough to jog his memory.

Alaric took a step out into the corridor before he realised he wasn't wearing much clothing. He did not want to be caught half naked roaming the corridors of a strange castle. He returned to the bedroom and searched the drawers until he found some suitable clothes. They were a little big on him, but they were the best he could find. He didn't think he looked too conspicuous.

Once he was dressed Alaric returned to the corridor. He needed to find someone who could explain where he was and what had happened. He was still not completely sure he was not a prisoner and therefore had to be careful. He peeked around each corner before proceeding. If he saw someone who looked hostile then he would have to run.

He rounded a corner and then quickly returned. He saw a pair of soldiers walking towards him. Luckily the two men were deep in conversation and had not noticed he was there. Alaric did not like the look of them. He stood still as he heard the sound of footsteps get even closer. If he had moved from the start he could have disappeared down the other end of the hallway, but he had waited. He was unsure if flight was the right choice. As the soldiers approached he had a sudden feeling of dread. The only escape was through one of the many doors in the corridor.

Without really thinking about the consequences Alaric started trying the doors. The first two were locked, but the third was open. He did not bother on ceremony as he pushed the door open and quickly moved inside. He shut the door and rested his back against it. It was at that point he realised the room wasn't empty.

He had entered a single roomed apartment. On the far side of the room was a bed. In the bed was a woman, at least that's what Alaric thought initially. He soon realised that she was an elf. She looked deathly pale and her chest hardly moved as she breathed. An elderly man sat by her side. There was a look of concern of his face. Alaric thought he looked exhausted, yet there was an air of determination about him. He felt bad for rushing in, but he did not feel threatened. The man looked up slowly when Alaric entered the room.

"Ah, Alaric it is good to see you. I don't really think you should be up and about. I don't know what you've been doing, but when you collapsed I thought you were dead," the old man spoke in a familiar tone.

Alaric didn't know how to respond. The man looked very familiar, but he couldn't place where he knew him. It was the same with the elf in the bed, although he didn't think she normally looked so wane. They didn't seem as though they were going to attack him so he thought he should be honest.

"I am sorry, but I don't seem to recall you," Alaric took a step into the room as he spoke. His head suddenly started to spin and for a moment he thought he was going to collapse, but the feeling only lasted a few seconds.

The concerned look returned to the old man's face. He had looked hopeful when Alaric had entered the room, but that was all gone. He looked at Alaric carefully as if he was trying to read his mind. Alaric was starting to become uncomfortable. He didn't like the situation, yet he felt compelled to stay. For some reason he needed to know if the elf was alright.

"This is disturbing," the old man spoke before Alaric had a chance. "I am Eldred and this is Alena. Does that help at all?"

The names did sound familiar. It was like they were on the edge of his memory, just out of reach. The harder he thought the further away the answers were. In the end he had to stop as his head was starting to hurt.

"I'm sorry. I am sure I know, but I just can't place you," he explained.

"That's alright. I am sure that it will come to you in time. I don't think we will be leaving here for a while," Eldred spoke in a grave voice.

Alaric didn't like the sound of what Eldred was saying. It certainly sounded as though they were prisoners. He needed answers.

"Are we prisoners?" he asked.

Eldred had a confused look on his face. It only stayed there for a moment before he realised what Alaric was asking. He couldn't help himself, but laugh. It was not really appropriate, but he was glad the mood was lightening, if only for a moment. By the look on Alaric's face he knew that he had to answer the question sooner rather than later.

"We are not prisoners. We are a guest of the Queen of Entero. We are in her castle in Jarrat," Eldred explained.

His words were a relief to Alaric, but something still didn't make sense. The more he thought on it the more confused he became, but he had no idea why. For some reason the idea of being a *guest* of the queen, and not her prisoner didn't seem right. He smacked the side of his head to try and bring his memories to the front, but instantly realised that was a bad idea. His head started to reel with pain and he had to take a seat or else he would have collapsed on the ground. Eldred looked concerned, but waited for Alaric to recover and speak.

"The last thing I remember were a number of soldiers walking towards me and a feeling of dread," Alaric explained his last memory. He kept his head down in his hands, which seemed to ease the pain.

"There is much to be explained, but I do not know if there is much point until your memory returns." Eldred returned his attention to Alena.

Alaric was not satisfied with the answer. He felt if he could hear about the events that led to his collapse he might be able to remember more. He did not appreciate Eldred ignoring him. It didn't seem as though the elf's situation was changing. He didn't want to sound rude, but he needed answers.

"I think you should tell me what you know. I know it will help me to remember." Alaric lifted his head and looked at Eldred. His eyes were bloodshot and he looked strained.

"I think you should go back to the apartment set for you and rest some more. It's late in the night and there is nothing to be gained now," Eldred replied as he let his head drop into his hands. "I don't think I have the energy myself. I need to rest."

Alaric seemed perplexed. If the man needed to rest then why was he sitting by the elf? He wanted to ask the question, but he didn't know if Eldred wanted to answer. He still needed answers, but he also needed rest.

"Then what am I supposed to do?" he asked. "I need answers."

Eldred lifted his head and looked at Alaric. The man looked as though he aged fifty years in a second. The look on his face was enough to tell Alaric he wasn't going to get any more from him. Eldred looked as though he was about to lose consciousness.

"Do you want me to find someone to help you?" Alaric asked, suddenly concerned for Eldred's wellbeing.

"I will be fine, thank you. I just need to sit here for a while. If you won't rest you should go and see Bern, he will be able to fill you in on the details."

"Bern is here?" Alaric sounded surprised. He had not expected to recognise a name.

"Yes. I expect he will be in the throne room," Eldred replied.

Alaric didn't respond. He wanted to ask for directions, but he didn't think Eldred really want to speak any further. He was sure it would not be too hard to find the throne room. Since he knew he was not a prisoner he could freely ask for directions from anyone he met in the corridors. He took one last look at Alena before leaving the room.

He felt upset she was in such a condition, but he could not work out why. He could not recall ever meeting an elf and yet she seemed so familiar. He hoped his old friend could shed some light on the situation. He couldn't imagine what Bern was doing in Jarrat, but for that matter he didn't know why he was there either. Nothing was making sense.

Alaric walked for about fifteen minutes before he realised he had no idea where he was going. It didn't take long for him to find a soldier walking the halls. He was surprised the man was so helpful, especially at such a time of day. In fact if it was indeed so late in the evening as Eldred had said why were there were so many people.

There was something in the way the soldier addressed Alaric that seemed even stranger. It was respectful. Almost like Alaric was someone special. That only confused the situation even more. When it was clear Alaric didn't want anything further he saluted and then continued on his way. Alaric would have shaken his head in dismay, but he didn't want the sickness to return.

The throne room was a hive of activity. As soon as Alaric entered he felt his head swim and he stumbled slightly. He felt the bile rise up from inside him and he had to force it back down again to avoid vomiting. He didn't think it would be the best way to remain inconspicuous.

Once he had settled himself Alaric made his way through the crowd. He was grateful that no one noticed him enter, not that he really thought they would know who he was. The room was noisy. Everyone was trying to talk over everyone else. He had hoped it would be easy to find his friend, but he could not see Bern anywhere amongst the throng of people.

He walked aimlessly through the crowd. He bounced off people as he passed through. They didn't seem happy, but all they did was look at him in disgust. If he was not someone they thought was important then they didn't want to know. It was a good time for minor nobles to prove their worth and scurry for the many vacant positions of power within the castle. That was what most of the squabbling was about. Who deserved what and why. Everyone came to plead their case with the queen, who had yet to join them.

As Alaric neared the centre of the crowd he saw there were two people standing on the throne dais at the far end of the room. At first he could only see the tops of their heads, but as he neared he recognised the man standing on the right-hand-side. He was grateful to see his old friend. The next problem was being able to make his way to the dais. The closer he came to the front the thicker the crowd became. Not only that, but they were also unwilling to move out of his way. Although they did not know who he was they did not want to give up their position. Once the queen entered the room they wanted to be as close as possible.

"Excuse me!" Alaric called out when he could get no further.

The two men who were blocking his path looked over their shoulders at him. When they didn't recognise him they both sneered and turned away. They didn't even respond to his request. Alaric had remained calm until that point. It was not the ideal situation and he was not willing to except it. The utter distain that the two men treated him with was not acceptable regardless of who he really was.

"Excuse me! I need to get to the dais," Alaric called again. He wanted to give them one more chance to move out of his way.

"You and everyone else," one of the men called out without turning around.

"You wait your turn like everyone else. We were here first," the other man said.

That was all Alaric needed to hear. He reached out and grabbed the man on the left by the shoulder. Before the man could react Alaric gripped hard and dug in with his thumb. The man's legs crumbled underneath him and he dropped to the ground, crying out in pain.

The second man was slow to react. When he saw what Alaric had done he lashed out. The attack was a feeble one and Alaric was easily able to deflect the blow. He then struck out himself without thinking. He caught the man square on the neck. The man grasped at his throat before dropping to the ground, gasping for breath.

With the two on the ground he was able to pick his way past them. Those around had seen what had happened and pushed their way backward. The ferocity and suddenness of the attack had taken them by surprise. They did not want to do anything to enrage the man further.

"Alaric!" Bern called out when he saw his friend.

The crowd had parted to try and get a better look at the commotion. As they did they inadvertently opened a corridor towards the dais. Alaric looked up at his friend and slowly approached. Relief filled him and the sickness he had been feeling suddenly washed away. He didn't think he was as glad to see anyone in his life as he was to see Bern.

"It is good to see you are up," Bern embraced Alaric when he reached the dais. "I wasn't sure if we were going to see you today. How are you feeling?"

"I feel fine," Alaric said, but he wasn't sure that was the truth. "Do you think that we could go somewhere to talk?"

The crowd had gone suddenly silent. They were all focused on what Alaric was doing. He was on the dais and that meant that he was somebody important. Those who had been rude to him wished they had not. They waited, desperately trying to hear what was being said and to find out who the mystery man was.

"I can't go anywhere right now," Bern was apologetic. "We have to announce something to the audience. It should not take long and then we can go and talk."

Alaric did not like what he was hearing. It was late into the night and everyone should be in bed and he could not come to think why Bern needed to address a room full of noblemen. Especially not in the queen's throne room in Jarrat. He was thinking he had lost more of his memory than he initially thought. He didn't want to be brushed aside. He needed answers, but Bern had already turned to face the crowd.

"Now I have your attention we have some news," Bern used the nobles' distraction to his advantage. There was no way they were going to listen to him whilst they were squabbling amongst themselves. He doubted that any of them would know who he was. All they knew was that he was standing with Duke Xarles, the man who had freed the castle. "The queen is not well at the moment. It is hard to say when she will be better." The nobles started to mutter amongst themselves at the news.

"Quiet down!" Bern boomed his request for silence which was instantly met. "As I was saying. The queen is not well and we do not know when she will be fit to rule. In the meantime Duke Xarles will assume control. He will manage all the day to day business of the castle. He will also take control of the army."

The second announcement brought a jeer from the crowd. They did not like the sound of what was being said. It was not like there was anything wrong with Xarles taking control, he was the logical choice, he was a high ranking noble and he was the one who had liberated the castle. Their main concern was that they were not mentioned at all. They were all filled with their own self-importance.

"Who are you to give us orders?" the noble who shouted out the words didn't expect them to be so audible.

The entire crowd went silent. There was a mixture of embarrassment and curiosity. Mostly they wanted to hear the answer. They all wanted to know who the man was and it was their chance to find out.

"I am General Bern. I am the leader of the Alliance," Alaric nearly fell over when he heard his friend speak. "I can quite easily order the army to storm the castle, but I figured this was a better solution." He had no intention of ordering the army to attack, but the nobles did not know that. "Now I think that we are done for the day. The castle will remain locked for the night. In the morning I will send word to the Alliance that we have been successful."

The crowd of nobles still wanted more answers, but Bern just ignored them. If he gave them his ear then he would be there all night. Since he had passed control over to Duke Xarles all he wanted to do was to see how Richmond, Tancred and Hadar were fairing. Although they were resting peacefully there was still a chance they could die. The physician had done all that he could, but he was not confident.

Bern stepped down from the dais and left Xarles to deal with the nobles. He motioned for Alaric to follow him and they exited through the door at the back of the room. He didn't think it was a good idea to cross through the throng of nobles. They did not seem too happy with what he had proposed.

"Now, tell me how are you feeling?" Bern asked as they walked through the corridors.

The question stuck in Alaric's head. He could not bring himself to answer. He suddenly felt very dizzy and his legs started to wobble. He did not know how much longer he could remain on his feet. He opened his mouth, but no words came out. His eyes rolled back into his head and he fell to the floor. Bern moved to try and catch him, but there was nothing he could do.

"I need some help," Bern called out.

It took a moment for a number of page boys to appear from around a corner. Bern didn't think the small group of boys would be able to lift Alaric. He could do it himself, but he didn't know if that would make him worse. The only thing he could do was get the boys to go for help.

"Fetch a stretcher and some men to lift it," all of the boys started to race off. "One of you find the court physician," he called after them. He hoped that one of the boys heard him.

He did not have to wait long before some men returned with a stretcher. Bern made sure they were careful with the way they handled Alaric. There was no sign of the physician as they carried him away. He was hoping the man would be waiting for them once they reached Alaric's apartment. He didn't know if he would be too helpful after their last encounter. Now that they had control of the castle he was hopeful the doctor would realise his place.

When they arrived at the apartment there was no sign of the doctor. The men placed Alaric in his bed before taking their leave. It was late and it had been a long day. All they wanted to do was return to their own beds and rest their heads. Bern wanted to send them to find the physician, but he let them go. He did not want to keep them with such a trivial task. He would have to wait. Alaric was breathing steadily. He was pale in the face, but he looked peaceful. Bern did not think it was a life and death situation. The thought made him want to leave Alaric and go and check on his other three friends. He had not seen them since the physician had been with them. All that he knew was that they were still alive.

There was an impatient knock on the door before it was pushed open. Bern jumped up from where he sat and rushed to the front room to see who it was. The physician moved in with his head down. When he heard Bern he looked up. It took him a moment before he recognised the man, but when he did he made a move towards the door.

"Wait!" it was a cross between a plea and an order.

The physician's hand was on the door when he paused. There was something in Bern's tone that made him stop. He had heard what had happened in the throne room. He knew the prince was no longer in power. He also knew that Bern was a man of importance. There was a good chance that doing a favour for Bern could do wonders for his status. He had never really liked being a physician. He wanted to be noble, but he had been born into poverty. Studying to be a doctor was the closest he could get. If there was a chance he could be raised into the nobility he would be a fool to pass it up.

"I will help you friend," the physician turned around when he spoke.

Bern thought the man was going to say something more, but no words came out. He wondered what he was going to say, but it was obvious that the physician had thought better of it. Instead he moved towards the bedroom to check on the patient. Bern waited in the front room as the physician did his job. He didn't think there was any point in looking over the man's shoulder.

When the physician returned he had a grave look on his face. It did not instil any confidence in Bern. There was going to be some bad news. He only hoped that it was not the worst.

"I have never seen anything like this before in my life," the physician scratched his head as he spoke. "I cannot find anything wrong with him and yet he does not respond. I am afraid there is nothing that I can do."

"Surely there is something," Bern said, he didn't sound as concerned as the physician thought he should.

The physician simply shook his head.

"Is he going to be alright?" Bern asked as the physician started to make his way towards the door.

"I just don't know. As I said, there does not seem to be anything physically wrong with him," the physician was about to leave, but a thought came to his mind. "I will check on him later, if you want."

Bern was concerned at the physician's sudden change of attitude. He wasn't sure what his motives were, but it was a good idea. He could not refuse the physician's offer.

"Yes, I think it would be a good idea for you to come back," Bern was grateful.

The physician took his leave and left the room. Bern walked into the bedroom to look over Alaric. He looked surprisingly peaceful. If Bern didn't know any better he would have thought Alaric was simply sleeping. He wondered what had happened in the depths of the dungeons. That thought was only able to stay in his mind for a short period of time. His other friends were in a much more precarious position.

Bern quickly made his way to the room where the other three men were resting. He had another two beds brought in so they could rest more comfortably. The physician had given them something to help them sleep before he left. Without it there was no way they would be able to rest without suffering great pain. Against his better judgement the physician also called for a nursemaid to look after them. Bern found the woman sitting in a chair, knitting what looked to be a scarf.

"How are they?" he asked quietly, not wanting to wake the sleeping men. In reality he could have yelled at the top of his lungs and he would not have woken the three of them.

"They are still sleeping. I don't expect that they will rouse before morning. The physician gave them all a heavy dose." There was a concerned look on Bern's face. "Don't worry. I would have done the same thing. Their wounds are like nothing I have ever seen before," she continued. "I think they will be alright, but I can't be certain."

Bern was grateful for her words, but he would have been happier without the last ones. No one would commit to the fact they would survive. Even if they didn't think that would be the case Bern would have liked to have been told.

Without waiting for her to continue Bern went to check on them. They looked just as they had when he had left them. Their wounds had been patched and were all covered with bandages. He was glad he wasn't able to see the wounds. The memory of them alone was enough to make him cringe.

It was at that point he realised how tired he had become. The trials of the day had finally got to him. He was not sure he would be able to make it to the apartment he had been assigned. He stumbled out to the front room where the nursemaid was seated. She didn't look up from her knitting. Her many years of experience tending the sick and dying made her very good at ignoring the little movements of people around her. She knew that when she was needed they would call for her. Until that time she was happy giving them what privacy she could.

He collapsed into a chair. It was the noise of him hitting the chair that made her look up. She recognised the sound and realised he was not just simply sitting down. He had not lost consciousness, but he was not far from it. If he had not seated himself then he would have collapsed onto the ground.

"Are you alright?" she placed her knitting on the table in front of her and stood as she spoke.

"It has been a long day. I think that I need to get some sleep," he yawned as he spoke. His voice was weak.

"I shall have someone help you to your apartment," she moved towards the bellpull, but Bern stopped her.

"I will be alright in a moment. I just need to rest for a minute or two, then I will walk there myself," a little strength returned to his voice.

She looked at him carefully before returning to her chair. She had known too many men who would not ask for help until it was too late. She didn't think the Bern was in any immediate danger. He was exhausted, but that was it. She believed he would be able to make it down the hallway to the apartment he had been given.

He waited in the chair for almost fifteen minutes. The nursemaid thought he had gone to sleep for a moment and was going to get him a blanket. When she stirred he lifted his head and she returned to what she was doing. It was not long after that Bern lifted himself from his chair. He knew he would get a much more comfortable sleep in a bed. He had a feeling that he was going to need all the sleep he could get.

It was a slow and stumbled walk towards the end of the corridor. If anyone had seen him they would have assumed he was drunk. He almost didn't have the strength to push the ornate timber door open.

The apartment he was in had once belonged to a very powerful duke. The man had turned and followed the prince when he had arrived in the palace. Now he was imprisoned in the barracks with the other traitors. It was not that the man was a follower of the Evil One, like most of the traitors, he just knew that the prince held power. If he wanted to continue in the life he was accustomed to he would have to follow the prince.

Bern hardly noticed the wealth of artefacts and trinkets in the room. The only thing that was on his mind was sleep. He stumbled and weaved his way into the bedroom. He didn't worry about taking off his clothes. He even kept his boots on as he dived, face first, onto the bed. He was only able to move his head to the side to stop him from suffocating on his pillow before he fell asleep.

Chapter 9: A New Day

Alaric rubbed his head as he woke. He had a slight headache. He looked around the room and although it seemed somewhat familiar to him he did not know where he was. He did not feel panicked, which he thought was strange. Something was missing, he knew that much.

Once he had risen from his bed he found a pile of his clothes neatly stacked on a chair. He could not remember leaving them there, but then he could not remember going to sleep. He quickly pushed the thought out of his mind and dressed. He was not going to get any answers moping around his bedroom.

He walked outside into a long corridor. For some reason that did not seem strange to him either. He knew he was not in his house in Arsiliac, that fact was obvious. He also knew that his friend Bern was somewhere in the building, which for some reason he knew was a castle. He didn't know which castle he was in, but he knew it all the same. There were large gaps in his memory and he needed answers.

It did not take him long before he ran into a serving woman, rushing around on her morning duties. He didn't want to disturb her, but he needed to find his friend. At first she seemed annoyed at being stopped, but when he asked for Bern she quickly changed her attitude. Alaric thought it was strange. There was something happening that he could not explain. He was sure his old friend would be able to shed some light on the situation. The serving woman raced away to find him after Alaric had stopped speaking.

Alaric returned to his apartment to wait for Bern. The serving woman seemed confident she knew where he was. It was a nervous wait. The longer he was awake the more things did not seem right. He could not remember why the room felt so familiar. He was sure that he had never been there before, but the feeling was so strong. It was an impossible situation.

"Are you feeling alright?" Bern asked when he entered the room.

"I don't know," Alaric replied. It was a truthful answer. Although he felt fine, physically, he could not shake the feeling that something was not right. "My brain seems, well, fuzzy. I can't seem to remember anything."

Bern did not like what he was hearing. It seemed as though Alaric had already forgotten what he had learnt the night before, not that it was a great deal. There was only one person he knew who would have the answer. In fact there were two, but the second one was a lot harder to contact. He hoped Eldred was awake. No one had seen him that morning. Bern knew he had stayed up late watching over Alena and would have only fallen asleep as a last resort. He didn't want to wake the wizard, but there was no time to waste.

"Can you tell me what happened?" Alaric asked when Bern didn't answer.

Bern recalled what he could about what had happened. There was not a great deal of information he could tell, but all he knew was that Alaric had rescued them from the dungeons before going after Eldred and Alena. Bern surmised it was his battle with the Dark Knight that had caused the amnesia.

"So I killed the Dark Knight?" again this didn't seem strange to him, which was even more disturbing.

"No," Bern replied. "For some reason you kept him alive."

It didn't sound like something that he would do. Why would he keep such a deadly enemy alive? He suddenly remembered something.

"I had a spell to stop him using magic. I can no longer feel it," there was panic in his voice.

Before Bern could explain the situation Alaric reached for the power surrounding him. As soon as he sucked in the energy he fell off his chair and curled up on the floor. Every muscle in his body suddenly seized. A great wave of pain ripped through him. He wanted to cry out, but his jaw was locked. All Bern could do was watch. He didn't know what he could do to help.

Alaric started to convulse. With the change he was able to cry out. The sound that came from his mouth was like nothing Bern had ever heard before. He was not sure what he should do. He didn't know if helping was going to do any good. There was a good chance it would make things worse. In the end Bern remained where he was and watched.

As soon as the convulsions stopped Alaric lost the contents of his stomach. There was nothing he could do to stop it. The best he could do was to make sure he did not get any vomit on himself or Bern. When he was done he pulled himself back onto his seat. As he did, the memory of the same thing happening the day before returned to him. He didn't know what it meant, but he knew it was not a good sign.

"What was that?" Bern asked, ignoring their previous conversation.

"I don't know, but I can't draw in magic. Every time I try, that happens," Alaric explained.

"That is definitely not a good sign," Bern replied.

"No, which leads me back to my question about Ra'naroz." He didn't know where the name came from, but he knew it was the Dark Knight. It was a good sign his memory was starting to return. "What happened to him?"

"It seems as though there is a herb that grows locally. When it is chopped and brewed with hot water it blocks a person's ability to create magic. That is what they were feeding Eldred all this time. It seems it works quite as well on Dark Knight's as it does on wizards. Now I don't understand magic all too well, but it seemed as though when you passed out the spell you created started to wane. It would not have been long before Ra'naroz was able to break free," Bern explained.

Alaric remembered returning from the dungeons. The last thought that went through his mind was that he had lost. Why? He racked his brain and finally it came to him. The castle was in the control of the Dark Knight. He could remember seeing armed men rush toward him before he blacked out. It didn't really make any sense. He quickly explained his last memory to Bern.

Bern couldn't help himself, but laugh. He had to admit if he did not know the full story he would have thought the same thing. Either way it did not help Alaric. He could not understand what he said was so funny. He wanted to say something, but it looked as though Bern was ready to give him an answer.

"That is quite a story," Bern started. "But I don't suppose we are going anywhere in a hurry. When the battle started between the Alliance and the orglin, something else was happening. Duke Xarles led his band of rebels in through the secret entrance and into the castle. It did not take long for him to gain control. Those soldiers left inside were not prepared for an attack. They were caught off guard and soon imprisoned. Those armed men you saw where part of the rebel force."

Alaric could see the funny side of things. What he thought were soldiers coming to the aid of the Dark Knight, were in fact men coming to help him. Things were slowly starting to make sense. With each realisation another memory returned to him. There was hope he would soon have his full memory back, unless he lost consciousness again and with it his memories.

"That is good to know. Where…"

"I am sorry Alaric." Bern cut in. "I would love to stay and reminisce, but I have work to do. The gates to the castle will be opened soon and I must meet the army. There is still much to be done," Bern stood as he spoke. "I will have a servant come and show you to where Eldred is staying. He will be able to give you some more insight into your situation."

Alaric remembered Eldred from the previous day. He also remembered Alena, the elf. She had not looked well. There was a connection between the three of them, but he still didn't know exactly what it was. If Bern thought that he would have answers then he would have to trust his friend. He didn't really feel like explaining the situation again, but if he was to regain his memory it was what he had to do.

It was not long after Bern had left that a serving woman arrived at the door to take him to see Eldred. She kept her head lowered and seemed to be nervous to be around him. He knew it must have something to do with his past, but he still could not remember. For the moment he was happy to play along. Although it did not feel comfortable it was better than the alternative. He could not explain what he did not know.

He was grateful when she left him at the door to Eldred and Alena's apartment. He waited a moment before he knocked on the door and entered. When he entered he found Eldred sitting by Alena's side again. He did not look up when Alaric entered the room. At first Alaric thought that he might be asleep, but as he moved closer he saw that he was still awake.

"How is she?" Alaric asked.

"There is no change. If she does not wake soon then she will die of starvation," Eldred's words did not sound promising.

"Is there anything we can do?" although Alaric did not completely remember the elf, he did feel as though it was the right reply.

"I do not know. I do not know what the problem is," Eldred looked up for the first time.

Alaric thought he looked much better. He must have slept for most of the night. He looked more refreshed than he had the day before. He was happy the man looked better. Again he did not know why, but it just felt right.

"I can call for the physician if you like," Alaric suggested, not knowing what else to say.

"That's alright. There is nothing he can do for her," Eldred responded before Alaric had a chance to act. "There is only one idea that I have, but that is not something I want to do."

"What is it?" Alaric was starting to become frustrated with the lack of answers.

"I think we need to speak with Ra'naroz. There is a reason why you kept him alive and I think this is it," Eldred looked at Alaric to try and gauge his reaction.

It was not what Alaric had wanted to hear. In his condition he was no match for the Dark Knight. His inability to remember and tap into the magical energy around him was not something he wanted Ra'naroz to know about. The serious look on Eldred's face showed there was no other option.

"What is it, Alaric?" Eldred asked when there was no response.

Slowly he started to explain what had happened. He felt as though he could trust Eldred. With each word he felt better about himself. No memories returned to him, but he felt as though they were close. The more he talked the better he felt.

"This is disturbing, but it is not unexpected. When you draw in such raw, evil energy it can have a terrible effect on your body. I was worried this was going to happen when the Emerald stone protected you from its filth," it sounded as though Eldred wanted to continue, but Alaric had stopped listening.

The words 'Emerald Stone' echoed throughout his mind. At first it did not register, but slowly he remembered. He not only remembered the Emerald stone, but the others as well. With a shock he realised he had no idea of the location of the Emerald or the Jade stone. He was suddenly filled with panic. He could not feel the two stones. He had no idea where they could be.

"It is alright Alaric. The stones are safe," Eldred stood as he spoke. "I had them brought here when you were rendered unconscious. I didn't think it was worth the risk of leaving them with you. Sometimes castle staff can have sticky fingers. I did not think it was worth the risk."

Alaric's heart slowed when Eldred dropped a velvet pouch and a velvet sheath on his lap. He knew instantly what was inside and which one was which. He wanted to open them and have a look, but he knew that was not the right thing to do. Things were starting to come back to him and he didn't want to risk an adverse effect. There was no telling what the stones would try when they realised his weakened state.

"Thank you," Alaric spoke softly. "Things are starting to come back to me."

"I will try and do something to help," Eldred stood over him.

There was a sudden itch on the back of his neck and a sick feeling in his stomach. He knew he was not going to vomit, but it was not pleasant all the same. Soon he felt a warm sensation fill his body. It started at his toes and worked its way up. As it did Eldred slowly waved his hand over Alaric's head. The warmth took almost a full minute to fill his body, but when it was over it left in a heart beat. When it was gone Alaric had hoped his memory would have come back, but it hadn't.

"It's alright Alaric. It will take a while for your memory to return, but it will come back in time," Eldred explained. "Now we need to go and see Ra'naroz."

Alaric did not like the idea, but he knew that Eldred was right. If the Dark Knight had answers then they would have to ask the questions. Alaric felt he needed to do anything in his power to help Alena. He did not know why, but he knew the answers would soon come to him. In the meantime he would just do what felt right.

The Dark Knight was being held in a room two apartments down from the one Eldred was staying in. Alaric thought it was strange. He thought that the Dark Knight deserved to be in the dungeons. The thought suddenly brought back the memory of what had happened. It came back so suddenly and in such a rush that it nearly knocked Alaric off his chair. He was thankful he was still sitting down.

"What was that?" Eldred asked.

"That was a memory coming back, or a few of them," Alaric explained.

"Oh, well, we better get moving. I don't think Alena has much time left," Eldred explained.

Alaric quickly came to his feet. He knew what had happened with the Dark Knight and he was not happy. He wished he had killed Ra'naroz when he had the chance. He knew the Dark Knight would be no end of trouble, but at least he might have his uses. It would take all his self-control not to kill him now.

Alaric burst into the Dark Knight's apartment.

"I did not think it would take this long for you to come to me," Ra'naroz didn't sound like a prisoner.

The Dark Knight was seated on the bed at the far end of the room. His arms were bound behind his back and his ankles were chained to the bedposts. They were not taking any chances. If the Dark Knight escaped then there would be no end of trouble. There were two soldiers standing guard on the door and one in the room. When Eldred and Alaric entered the guard left at Eldred's suggestion.

The Dark Knight was dressed in a simple red linen shirt and brown trousers. Although Alaric couldn't be sure he thought he had changed his clothes since their last encounter. He didn't know why it would be important, but it was.

"Let's get down to business. You said that you knew how to heal Alena," Eldred kept his voice level.

"So it seems that you need my help after all," Ra'naroz smiled. "But don't think I will make it easy for you."

"The only reason you are alive is for this information," Eldred reminded him.

"Then it would be remiss of me to give you all the information right now," Ra'naroz kept the smile on his face. "If you want the information that I know then you will have to do something for me."

"I knew I should have killed him," Alaric spoke to Eldred. "Move out of the way and I will finish the job."

Eldred thought about moving out of Alaric's way. He did not like being in the same room as the wicked creature. He had been tortured more times than he cared to remember. It was Ra'naroz who had started the beating, and then it was his orders that made them continue. He wanted nothing more than to inflict the same pain, but then he would be no better off and Alena would surely die.

"If you kill me then she will die and you have not even heard what I want," Ra'naroz showed no sign of fear.

"Fine," Eldred relented. "What is it that you want?"

Ra'naroz looked at Alaric when he spoke. "I want him to ask. No, I want him to beg for my help." The evil smile remained on the Dark Knight's face.

Alaric did not know how to respond. It was an easy enough request, but there had to be something else. The Dark Knight was not to be trusted. There had to be an ulterior motive. He wanted to wait for Eldred to respond, but it was clear the wizard was leaving the decision to him.

"Will you please let us know how to save Alena's life?" His begging was not genuine.

"I don't think so." The smile disappeared from Ra'naroz face. "I think you can kill me now."

"What are you playing at?" Eldred asked.

"It is a simple request," Ra'naroz replied. He was not going to give anything away.

Alaric looked at Eldred. "I don't suppose it will hurt," he didn't bother to lower his voice.

"Do what you think is best," Eldred replied.

It was not the response Alaric was looking for. He wanted Eldred to tell him to run the Dark Knight through, not that he was wearing his sword. The only option would be to try his hand at torture.

"I don't think that will work." It was like Ra'naroz was reading his mind. "I will not give in to torture."

There was no lie in Ra'naroz's voice, but Alaric was unsure whether it was the truth. He was sure he could make the Dark Knight talk. It would be the easier if he used one of the *Stones of Power*. That thought made him smile, but in the back of his mind was the feeling of absolute pain when he tried to use magic.

"I would be eternally grateful if you were to tell me how we can save Alena." Alaric tried his best to sound genuine.

"Well, I still have my doubts, but it was a much better effort. I will do what I can to help you, but I do not think you are going to like what you hear." The smile had returned to his face. Alaric wanted nothing more than to walk over and wipe it off.

"Spit it out or you will not speak another word," Eldred spoke between clenched teeth.

"There is only one way you can cure Alena and that is with the Topaz stone." He felt as though he was winning when he saw the look on Eldred's face.

"That is easy to say. You know that we do not have the Topaz stone," Eldred replied. "You better come up with a better story if you want to live."

"I know you don't have the stone because *I* know where the stone is." Alaric wanted to move across the room and throttle him. He was deliberately being obtuse. No one responded. They knew he was waiting for them to speak. When there was still no response he continued. "It's in Castalia!"

The Dark Knight waited again, but this time it was for the information to sink in. He was surprised it took longer than he expected. It was Eldred who was the first to respond.

"There is no way we can get to Castalia and back again before she dies."

"That is true, but I see that you are not thinking. I am sure that a wizard of your calibre should be able to see where the solution lies." Ra'naroz was not going to give the answer away.

Slowly it dawned on him and he did not like it. He wondered if it was the Dark Knight's plan all along. He didn't think Ra'naroz would plan for defeat. It must have been pure luck, or the prophecy rearing its head again.

"What?" Alaric asked when he saw the answer dawn on Eldred's face.

"I can create a spell that will keep Alena in stasis. It will keep her from dying," Eldred explained.

"That's great. How long can you keep her alive?" Alaric asked, a little confused at why Eldred was not pleased.

"Forever, or at least as long as I live. The only problem is I can't be more than a few hundred paces away for the spell to work. I will be linked to her in more ways than one. It means that I will not be able to go with you to Castalia."

Alaric thought for a moment. "Do we still need him alive?"

"I wouldn't get too far ahead of yourself. One of my brothers is in control of Castalia. It will not be as easy as walking up to the gate and asking for them to hand over the stone. If you do then you are dumber than I thought. You need my help if you are going to successfully retrieve it." Ra'naroz was sure of himself.

Alaric had to think. His memory was still hazy, but things we starting to come back to him. He knew that Ra'naroz's words were not right, but he didn't know why. He wanted Eldred to refute them, but the words didn't come. For the moment he would have to play along, even if that meant he would have to take the Dark Knight along for the ride.

"Very well, but don't think that your life doesn't hang in the balance," Alaric reluctantly agreed. "I think we should be leaving now."

Despite Alaric's memory not having completely returned and the fact he couldn't draw any energy he knew it was the right thing to do. He still couldn't place where he knew Alena, but he knew he couldn't let her die. As long as he had enough of the herb to keep Ra'naroz unable to use magic he thought he could handle the rest.

They waited for the guard to return before they left. The last thing they wanted to do was to leave Ra'naroz by himself. No matter how much they wanted to leave the room they could not forget the big picture. Just because the Dark Knight was willing to help didn't mean he was not still looking for his chance to escape.

They walked the corridor in silence. Even though they were only travelling two doors down there was still a lot of traffic moving through. What they had to discuss was not for anyone else to hear, court gossip was the last thing they needed.

"I don't like this Alaric," Eldred said as he closed the door to the apartment. "You should not let Ra'naroz travel with you."

"Then why didn't you say something?" Alaric replied, a little hurt at the allegations.

"Because the Dark Knight was looking for a weakness, he knows you are not completely fit and he is looking for something to hold against you. I had to make him think that he was in control."

It made sense and yet it didn't. Eldred knew that Alaric's memory was still sketchy. He should not have let the Dark Knight take the advantage. If anyone was at fault it was Eldred. Something had changed in the wizard he had once put all his faith in. He did not know what Eldred had suffered in the dungeons, but it had affected him more than he thought. He did not think it was such a bad thing he would have to stay behind. Time to rest could be just what he needed. He knew he would need the wizard to be at full strength before his time was over.

"There is not much choice now," Alaric said. "Until my memory returns completely I am going to have to keep Ra'naroz with me," even as the words came out of his mouth he knew it was not a greatest of ideas.

Eldred returned his attention to Alena. There was not much else to be said. The plan had been made and it was the Dark Knight who had made it. That thought in itself was disturbing. There was nothing to say the information he gave them was even remotely correct. There was a greater chance there would be a trap waiting for them once they had left the safety of the castle. They had no other option. Eldred could not leave the castle and Alaric could not do it on his own, at least not until his memory returned.

Alena had not changed. She did not look any worse, but Eldred did not think she could get any worse and still be alive. If she was just suffering the strain of what they had been subjected to then bed rest should be enough to revive her. There had to be another possibility, but he could not think of it. She had to have been poisoned; he didn't know what poison it could be. He didn't even know where to begin and he knew that Ra'naroz would not divulge anything.

"Then I guess there is nothing left to discuss," Alaric spoke to Eldred's back. He did not like being ignored.

"I wouldn't say that," Eldred turned around when he spoke. "There is still much for you to know. Until your memory returns you are at your most vulnerable."

Alaric had to agree. There were still many people who wanted him dead. There was still a chance there were assassins in the castle. He guessed that was what his life was like before he lost his memory. The only difference was that he could defend himself. He guessed that the stones would be his best form of defence, but in his current state he knew there were great risks involved.

"What do you have in mind?" Alaric asked.

"There are a few things you need to know. Now unfortunately I don't know what happened to you since I was taken prisoner. Someone else will have to fill you in on that. What I can do is warn you to be careful with what you do with the stones. There is a reason why they are in the pouches. Until you get your memory back I suggest that you leave them where they are," Eldred suggested.

"Why do you say that?" Alaric asked. Although he knew Eldred was right.

"You will just have to trust me. When you know what you are doing you will understand why. I think that is the safest way for the moment," Eldred returned. "You have friends as well as enemies. I think you should keep the stones private to everyone. No one needs to know that you have them."

Alaric wasn't overly happy with the explanation. He knew he had a connection with the stones, but he did not know what. He knew they were powerful magical artefacts and they were very dangerous, but that was it. It seemed as though that was all the information he would get for the meantime.

"I think I should return to my room now. I am feeling a little tired." Alaric had a lot to think about and thought that he needed time to reflect.

"Of course. You need to rest," Eldred didn't look further into the comment. His focus was more on the task at hand. He wasn't sure if he was strong enough to do what was necessary.

Alaric took his leave. He was happy to be on his own. Eldred had given him a lot to think about. His memory was slowly starting to drift back and he needed time to himself to collect his thoughts. The memories were returning scattered. A lot of them were not making sense to him. The most disturbing was his yearning to look at the stones.

He quickly made his way back to the room. He kept his head down so as not meet anyone's eyes. On the off chance he met someone who knew him he didn't want to make conversation. He had a strange feeling he was more than just one more man wandering the corridors. Every time he passed someone he felt uncomfortable.

There was a certain relief when he arrived at the safety of his apartment. He moved straight into the bedroom. He wanted privacy, but he did not want to lock the door. He thought it would be all too suspicious. He did not want anyone to know what he was doing inside. A locked door would get people talking.

He sat on the bed and tossed the two velvet pouches in front of him. He was surprised to see that they did not bounce up as they hit the bed. It was like they were a dead weight, yet they were light to hold. The dagger obviously held more weight than the bracelet, but not enough to have that effect. He knew the stones were effecting the situation, even from within their velvet prison. Alaric wondered if the supposed protection was just a placebo. If that was the case then he could be in a lot of trouble.

The compulsion that had slowly been growing inside of him when he had received the stones from Eldred was coming to a head. He wanted to see the stones. He had to see the stones. He knew that it was not a good idea, but he didn't know if he was able to control himself. The stones were calling to him and he wanted to answer.

He didn't know how much time had passed since he had started staring at the velvet cases. He had been transfixed by them for a long time, he knew that much. He felt tired. More tired than he had felt in a long time. He couldn't recall what had happened. He did not feel as though he had just been sitting on a bed. He felt as though he had been running all day. His eyes started to droop. He thought the two pouches in front of him had been moved as he picked them up. If he was going to sleep he would have to leave them on the small table next to the bed.

As he pulled back the covers there was a fog in his mind. It was like his memory was going again. The last thing he wanted to do was to lose what he had just regained. It seemed to happen every time he fell asleep, or at least when he lost consciousness. It was that point that was thick in his mind as he tried to stay awake. He had only just started to regain some of his memories and he was not going to let him go.

The fight was a futile effort. There was nothing he could do to stave off the sleep that was hunting him down. Eventually he had to let his head hit the pillow and his eyes close. He was asleep before he knew what he was doing. There was no telling what would be waiting for him in the morning.

Chapter 10: Reconciling the Alliance

Bern didn't want to leave Alaric, but he had other matters to attend to. The Alliance had successfully defeated Ra'naroz's army of orglin. It seemed as though the Enteroite army was prepared to join the Alliance, but there was still unrest. The two armies had clashed and people had died.

The thoughts of what might be happening raced through his mind as he crossed the courtyard towards the main gate. He had heard a rumour that Jarwe had surrendered the army to the Enteroite captains. He did not believe that story. Captain Prewitt, who had started the rumours, was safely locked up with the other traitors. The most disturbing part was he was not the only one he had heard the rumour from.

Once he was past the gate he saw a large billowing cloud to the north. The smoke was coming from a fire near the edge of the forest. Bern didn't think it was a good idea the burn the pyres so close to the trees. The wind had changed direction and was now blowing back towards the castle. The smell of burning flesh had yet to penetrate the walls, but it was only a matter of time. Outside the walls was another matter all together. Bern almost gagged when he took his first breath.

Bern didn't think it was such a bad idea, the smell of the pyre reaching the castle. It would give some of those noblemen who did not fight an idea of what had been happening whilst they were safely tucked behind their walls. It was too easy to sweep away the dead bodies and pretend that nothing had happened. With the smoke creeping in there would be no hiding it. It would be a while before the stench of death would leave the castle and even longer before it left their minds.

The next problem they had was what to do with the orglin. It was not that they really cared what happened to the bodies of the creatures, but there were too many to leave lying on the field outside the city and castle. At first they had tried burning them on their own pyres, but it gave off an incredible stench. A burning human corpse would stink at the best of times, but the smell of a burning orglin corpse was something again. Even the most hardened of soldiers were on their knees releasing the contents of their stomach. It was not a pleasant sight.

When they finally became accustomed to the acrid smell it was time to make a decision. They could not just leave the orglin to rot in the sun. They were sure that smell would be even worse. The most tempting of ideas was to drag their bodies deep within the forest and leave them there, but in the end the decision was made to bury them. So the job of digging a mass grave had started that morning and it was no small task. All soldiers, who were not overlooking the pyre or on other duties, were given the job of grave diggers.

Bern looked out over the scene as he made his way to where the army was camped. He knew he would find the other commanders in the command tent. He had told them to wait there for his arrival and they would do what they were told. By what he had heard Jarwe had not been enjoying himself back in command. He had heard stories, but he still did not have the full information. Before he made his decision he would have to wait and hear what the others had to say and even that might not help.

There were few soldiers on the field between the castle and the campsite. Bern thought there would be more men around, but then he figured that they were all busy elsewhere. He was glad he did not get stopped by anyone. He much preferred to be left with his own thoughts. There were many in his head and the slightest of distractions could unravel them all.

"Welcome, General Bern. It is good to see you return to us and unharmed by the looks of things," Sorrell was the first one to speak when he saw Bern enter the tent.

"Thank you, but unfortunately I was the only one. Richmond, Hadar and Tancred are resting in the castle. They made it through the night, which is a good sign, but it is still touch and go. They are not out of the woods yet," Bern's words were sombre. He thought it was better to get it out of the way early in the conversation, that way they could move onto business.

There was a moment of silence as everyone thought about the men. Some of them wanted to ask what had happened, but they didn't know if it would be appropriate. They figured Bern would have told them if he wanted to speak about it. They could not imagine what pain they had gone through if their lives were at risk in such a short period of time.

"Now I need some information. There have been a number of rumours passing through the castle. I need to know which ones are true and which ones are false," he figured it was the best place to start since no one else had spoken.

There was a new man in the room and someone was missing. Jarwe introduced Captain Tyson as he started to explain the events of the previous day. What he had neglected to mention was what had happened with Captain Aimon. He knew the man was in fact a Dark Knight and he didn't like the knowledge that he did not know where the man was.

"What of Captain Aimon?" Bern asked.

The tent went silent as everyone looked around at each other. It was clear that no one wanted to answer the question.

"I will tell you what happened," the voice was feminine and it sounded familiar, but there was something wrong with it. "Since no one else here has the strength to tell you."

Bern looked around to the front of the tent where the voice was coming from. He recognised the woman as Princess Marina, but there was something wrong with her. Her face was drawn and pallid. Her normally beautiful pale skin looked haggard. Bern felt as though he was not going to like the explanation.

"Captain Aimon, is not in fact Captain Aimon," Tyson was about to speak, but Jarwe stopped him by placing a hand on his forearm. Jarwe knew that Tyson would get his answers soon enough. "He is the Dark Knight Argoz and we have all been duped, no more so than myself. He has stolen my ring and gone and no one did anything to stop him." When she finished she walked towards the head of the table where Bern was seated. Before she reached her destination she stopped.

"That is indeed disturbing news," Bern spoke when it was clear she had finished. "Does Alaric know?" he asked.

She laughed loudly, but it was not the joyous laugh they had heard in Kiarome. There was something sickly about, almost mocking. Bern didn't know what to think. He thought it would be a good idea if someone took her to the castle. It would be better if she was near Alaric.

"He knows and has done nothing about it," the more she spoke the worse her voice sounded and the more concerned Bern became. "He goes off to rescue his friends when he needs to take care of business. He will not defeat the Evil One with that attitude. He has to make sacrifices if he is going to succeed."

Bern could not believe what he was hearing. This was not what he was expecting to hear. If it wasn't for Alaric then he would still be chained in the dungeons, if he wasn't already dead. He could not sit by and listen to Marina bad mouth him. He was sure Alaric had done the right thing, even if a Dark Knight did have one of the *stones of power*. When he thought about it he was no longer sure he was correct, but he was going to stick with the plan anyway.

"Alaric did what he had to do. He always does what he has to do. If he did not then we would still be prisoners and there is a good chance we would not have won this battle. All the events of our lives are intertwined with his," Bern tried to explain.

"That is all well and good, but you are not seeing the big picture. This is just a small battle in the entire scheme of this war. This decision may just have sealed our fate," she sounded as though she believed what she was saying, although there was a touch of mania in her voice. Bern did not think that she was thinking straight.

"I am sorry you feel this way, but for now we have other issues to discuss. It looks as though you could use some rest," Bern dismissed her, but she would not be so easily brushed aside.

"Where is Alaric now?" she had been the first to ask the question.

Bern had been hoping to avoid that conversation, although he knew there was no chance. Everyone would want to know where Alaric was and why he was not with them. He had just hoped if he was able to distract them enough then he would be able to leave without having to speak about it.

"Alaric is still in the castle. He is recovering from his attack with the Dark Knight Ra'naroz," Bern explained without giving away much information.

"So another Dark Knight is dead," Marina sounded somewhat relieved. "I suppose something good has come from this."

Bern did not want to reveal the truth. The lie would mean she would be appeased for the moment, but he didn't think it would serve its purpose in the end. She would not be happy, but they would all find out soon enough that Ra'naroz was still alive.

"That is not exactly what happened," Bern didn't know what to say.

"What do you mean?" Sorrell asked before Marina had a chance to speak again.

"Alaric has kept the Dark Knight alive. He believes there is information he has that is vital to our cause. Unfortunately I do not know any more than that," he wanted to avoid any further questions.

"That doesn't make any sense," Hulkan brought his fist down hard on the table.

"Why would he trust a Dark Knight?" Pernian asked.

"I will tell you," Marina spoke. "Alaric is starting to turn. He has spent too much time with the *Stone's of Power*. They are starting to take control of his mind. He is no longer the man he once was," there was something fanatical in her eyes.

"That is enough talk, Princess Marina," all eyes moved to Orric. His voice commanded respect. "You are not yourself and should not be speaking in such a manner."

"Who are you to speak to me in such a manner, elf?" Marina fired back. She was not going to be submissive just because everyone else was. "I will be heard. My opinion is just as valid as yours, more so. I have been travelling with Alaric since we left Kiarome and I have seen the change." There was some truth to her words, but she was twisting them to her advantage.

Orric shook his head. He knew there would be no convincing her. For some reason she had it in her head that Alaric was playing against them. The worst part was that there were some sitting around the table that were starting to believe her. He had to get rid of her before she was able to continue with her train of reasoning.

"I think it is time that you leave us Marina," Orric suggested. "You look as though you need rest."

"I will not be brushed aside by you," Marina raised her voice until she was almost screeching. "I have every right to be in this tent."

"Please," Bern stood as he spoke. "This is not the time for such conversations. I am the leader of this army and my ruling is final." He could feel his control slipping. "We can continue this debate later, but for now we need to figure out what to do next." He did not dismiss Marina, but it was obvious that he would if she did not leave on her own recourse.

Marina stood for a moment and thought. She was happy to go up against the elf, but she was not so sure about Bern. He was the General of the Army and he had control. She could try to pull rank, she was a Princess of Darshival, but she didn't think it was worth the argument. She didn't really care what they were planning. All she cared about was the Sapphire stone. One way or another she would get it back.

"I think that I will lie down. I need to get some rest." She did not wait for anyone to respond. She simply walked out of the tent.

When they were sure she had left Sorrell spoke first. "What was that all about?"

"She is not well. I am sure all she needs is some rest," Orric explained, although no one really believed his words. They were all happy to let the subject rest.

"The question that needs answering is what are we going to do now?" Jarwe asked.

That was the question that Bern was dreading the most. He had no idea where the army was going to travel to next. He had no compunction to leave. There was no sensation drawing him in any direction. It could only mean they were meant to stay. It was not the answer anyone was looking for and would make things even more difficult for him to explain.

"There is still work to be done here," Bern was desperately thinking as he spoke. He paused for a moment and Tyson took the floor.

"I believe that there are still agents of the Evil One inside the city. Once they have heard what has happened I am sure they will try and leave. That is something that we cannot allow. They must pay for the crimes they have committed against the queen," Tyson's voice increased in intensity the more he spoke.

Tyson's comments brought some heated discussions around the table. Some believed his intensions were just to keep the Alliance in Jarrat. Others thought it was time for the army to move on. There were more important places for them to be than where they were. Bern kept quiet and listened to the argument. He thought it was better to listen to their thoughts before he told them what they were going to do.

"Tyson is right. We need to remain here until we are sure the threat is gone. There is no point leaving an enemy behind us," Bern spoke with strength in his voice. There was no doubt he was there to command. His confidence soon brought the room to order. "We have to make sure all the agents of the Evil One have been rooted out and properly dealt with. Besides we have too many injured to leave just yet. We need to completely assess the damage of this battle before we race off to the next one." His words made sense.

"Very good then and how do you propose we go about this little task?" Sorrell, who was against the decision, spoke.

"We will have the army set up a perimeter around the city. No one can leave unless they check out," Bern suggested, or more so commanded.

"The army is already stretched with the clean up," Hulkan added. He was also keen to be on the move again.

"The soldiers from Entero will be more than adequate to do the job," Bern replied.

Everyone had assumed that the Enteroite army would assimilate itself into the Alliance, but no one had actually asked the question. Tyson did not look pleased with what Bern was assuming. He held his tongue for a moment, but he could not resist.

"The people of Jarrat have been enslaved for too long under the yolk of the Evil One. All we are doing is taking away one enslaver and replacing it with another." Tyson wasn't happy with what Bern was suggesting. He wanted to tell Bern that he was not in command of the Enteroite army, but that would not be productive. He could still use that card if he didn't like the general's answer.

"That is not what we are trying to do," Bern replied. He could see Tyson's point. "There is no other way to find the traitors. If the city gates are open then they can just freely leave whenever they want to. Until we are confident that they have all been captured we must hold the city. I am sure the citizens would feel more comfortable if it was a local army watching the roads than a foreign one."

Tyson had to admit that Bern was right, but he still wanted to press him. "And how long do you think this is going to take? What happens if you don't find all the traitors?" Tyson hoped he had made a valid point. "By the sounds of it you want to have a long term occupation of Jarrat."

Bern had to think for a moment. He had to admit he had not made a plan. He was just guessing and he would need another solution. "We have a bounty of prisoners in the castle. I am sure they will talk sooner or later. It should not be too hard to find those who have betrayed us."

Tyson had to admit that Bern had come up with a great plan. He had forgotten about the traitors who were inside the castle when the fighting had started. They were now prisoners of the rebellion. From what he had heard those who openly opposed the prince had been taken to the dungeon and tortured. With the tables turned there was no reason why they could not use the same tactics.

"Only as a last resort," Orric spoke as if he read the captain's mind.

Tyson had almost forgotten where he was. He realised there was a smile on his face and everyone was watching him. That made him feel very self-conscious. He had to say something to try and recover.

"Why would you say that? The prince has been using those tactics against us. In fact I believe he was administrating torture just for fun."

"I agree," Hulkan was the first to agree, shortly followed by Sorell and his advisor.

Bern sat back and listened as the table started to argue amongst itself. He thought Tyson's reasoning had been logical. It did seem like the best solution to their problems. The traitors certainly deserved no less than what they had administered. He could not understand why the three elves were so vehemently against the idea. Just when the argument was about to become physical Bern called for silence.

"Arguing is not getting us anywhere. We need rational thinking. Now why is it that you don't want us to interrogate the prisoners?" Bern addressed his question to Orric.

"That is easy. The Evil One thrives on pain and anguish, as do his followers. Now I am not saying that those you have captured will thrive by the torture, but the Dark Knight will. You run the risk of giving him more strength, by creating more suffering. I do not think that is what we are trying to achieve," Orric explained.

Bern did not know why Orric had not just mentioned that fact in the first place. He was sure that it would have avoided all the heated words. Now the tent was filled with angst and it would take a lot to calm the situation. The elf made sense, but it did not solve the problem at hand. They needed to root out the enemy. He was sure there was some vital information to be gained.

"So what do you suggest we do?" Tyson asked when no one had responded.

"We have to wait," Orric was quick with his response. "There is time yet and we do not want to rush into anything."

"That is not an answer," Tyson barked back before Orric could continue.

Things were looking as though they were about to start again. The last thing Bern wanted was for another argument to break out. He would have to think quickly if he was going to avoid it.

"Be calm." It seemed as though it was as good a place to start as any. "There is a solution to be had here. Orric is right, we do not want to rush to a rash decision."

His words did nothing to settle their nerves, but at least it brought silence. It gave him a chance to take control of the meeting. He thought the best way was to get Orric to continue with his line of thinking.

"Thank you Bern," Orric started when he was given the floor. "We have time to wait. I know some of you are keen to keep moving. Your own home kingdoms are still in danger, but now is not the right time to be brash. We should give the prisoners a chance to speak without the threat of torture. Some of those imprisoned my not have chosen sides. They may give us the information we seek willingly."

"And they may give us false information." Tyson was still not happy with the situation.

"They may do that under torture," Orric replied.

The argument started again and this time Bern did not have the heart to stop it. They had just won a great victory and all they could do was argue. It was not a good sign for the Alliance. If they could not decide on relatively simple matters how would they go when it counted? Although the decision was not simple it should not have gone so far. With the addition of another major army it would only get worse.

"We are forgetting one important matter," it was Hulkan's words that stopped the yelling.

"What are we forgetting?" Bern was the only one with a calm voice.

"Tancred, Hadar and Richmond. They infiltrated the city before we arrived. I am sure they have contacts." Hulkan sounded proud of himself.

"That is a brilliant idea," Sorrell agreed with him.

There were a number of other agreements voiced around the table, but there were no arguments. It seemed as though the dwarf had come up with the solution. Only Bern knew what was wrong with his idea. It seemed as though they did not remember what he had told them when he arrived. He didn't want to remind them, but he could see no other choice. It would only be a matter of time before they remembered and he thought it would be better if they heard it from him.

"That is a great idea, but we will have to wait for them to recover. I do not know how long that will take. We need a back up plan," Bern cringed as he spoke the words.

The tent went silent. Everyone was thinking about what Bern had said and no one wanted to speak. Eventually Tyson broke the silence.

"I think we have our plans," he spoke slowly so everyone had a chance to listen. "We wait for Tancred and Richmond to recover. Until then we surround the city and don't let anyone leave." He was beginning to like the plan. "If that fails we start interrogating the prisoners. Nicely at first, but if they refuse to give us the information we need then we take more drastic measures."

It did not please everyone, but it was enough to appease them. It was a good plan and they had all played their part. Bern was happy with the result. The tension had left the room, if only for the time being. There was still another problem they had to deal with and that was Marina. Hopefully she had gone to rest and not tried to enter the castle. No one was allowed in or out of the castle unless under the duke's or Bern's specific instruction. He could see she would cause trouble if she tried to enter.

"I think that is enough for one morning," Bern stood as he spoke. "There is still much to be done. For now the castle will still be closed to everyone," his last words brought a rise from around the table. Tyson was the loudest.

"Who are you to say who can enter the castle?" he boomed above the other voices.

"The castle is under the control of Duke Xarles until the queen is fit to rule again. He takes my advice on the matter, but this is something we are both agreed upon. There are still spies and enemies about. It is not a good idea to open the gates with a Dark Knight prisoner in the castle." Bern was not to be dissuaded.

"When will we be able to return?" Tyson asked, a little calmer this time.

"Very soon. But for now you will have to remain out here." Bern didn't know what else he could say.

Tyson was about to refute the decision, but instead he huffed and crossed his arms across his chest. If it wasn't for the seriousness of the situation Bern would have laughed. It seemed like such a childish reaction for a war meeting.

Bern knew his next comment would enflame the situation further, but there was nothing he could do. "Now I must return to the castle. There is work to be done. Get to it!"

No one appreciated being spoken to in such a manner, but his words served their purpose. No one spoke as Bern left the tent. They were so angry they didn't know what to say. Everyone wanted someone else to start the conversation. Bern would have none of it. He quickly left before anyone could speak.

The meeting, although it had taken most of the morning, had yielded some positive results. He knew they needed to remain in Jarrat, but he did not know why. Seeking out the agents of the Evil One was an important job and it would keep everyone busy while they waited for their next move.

He saw the soldiers of the Jarrat army start to move into position around the city gates. It would not keep all his agents inside, but it would keep most of them. Those who tried to escape would run the risk of death. The soldiers were not told straight out to kill those who left without permission, but they were smart enough to read between the lines. Death was not the first option, but no one was to be outside of the city walls without the appropriate paperwork.

The guards by the castle gate stood up straight when they saw Bern approach. Everyone in the castle knew who Bern was. It was well known that he was responsible for freeing the castle from the prince. They did not know the full story and the role Alaric had played, but it was more pertinent he kept that quiet. The less everyone knew about Alaric the better.

Bern made his way straight to the throne room. He knew the duke would be there, still dealing with the minor nobles. He thought it would be best if he explained the situation to Xarles before he went to check on the patients. He didn't think they would be in a position to speak anyway.

As he expected he found the duke surrounded by a myriad of people all shouting at him at once. He had done what he had told himself he would not do and that was sit on the queen's throne, but he had no choice. The nobles had beaten him down with their inane banter and he had collapsed on the throne. No one even seemed to notice or else they might have become offended. They just kept yelling their requests in a hope the duke might listen to one.

He looked up from where he sat when he saw Bern enter. The general had made no movement towards the throne. The duke had a pleading expression on his face, but then he had a thought. When he was sure that it was going to work he stood from the throne. On the dais he loomed over the crowd. The nobles were not expecting such a move and were suddenly quiet.

"That is it for the day. I have important matters to discuss with the general." There were protests from the crowd. "This will take all day, now leave!" he boomed the last part at the top of his voice.

There was no doubting he meant want he said. Although the nobles did not want to leave him alone they knew they had no choice. They did not want to risk the wrath of the duke. There was no telling what he would do. Slowly they started to filter out of the room past Bern. He could hear their snide comments as they left. He felt like calling them all back into the room and berating them, but he did not have the time or the energy. There were more important things for him to do.

"Thank you," the duke greeted Bern as he stepped down from the dais. "I think I have had enough of this room for one day. Would you like to join me for a drink in my apartment?"

"But it is only just past lunchtime." Bern tried to hide his surprise.

"With the morning I've had it is never too early to drink," there was little humour in his voice.

"Well then it would be rude of me to let you drink alone." Although Bern knew it was not a good idea he decided that he deserved a little break.

The corridor was a buzz with the leaving nobles and the soldiers passing by. Bern had wanted to explain what was happening on the way back to his apartment, but he could not with so many ears listening to what they were saying. They were all trying to gain whatever little advantage they could get, but Bern was not going to give anything away.

"Is this place secure?" Bern asked when they returned to his apartment.

"I would like to think so," Bern wasn't sure if Xarles was offended or not. He spoke as he poured two glasses of wine. "These are my private apartments. You can say whatever you want here."

Bern took a glass goblet from Xarles before he took a seat. He looked around the room. The sitting room seemed secure enough. There were paintings on the walls of past battles and two couches and a coffee table. Nothing looked out of place, but he had a bad feeling that someone was listening. The last thing he needed was for the enemy to get the information. If they warned who were going to be questioned then they could go to ground, but if Xarles said that it was safe then Bern had to trust him. Bern started to explain what they had decided.

"I think that is a good idea," Xarles spoke as he poured them both another glass of wine. "I don't know about holding the city prisoner though."

"There is no other way to stop the traitors from leaving. I wished there was, but there really isn't," Bern explained. "How is the queen?" Bern thought it would be wise to change the subject.

"She seems to be getting better, although she is still in bed. I am wondering if it is more embarrassment than illness." Xarles recognised the deliberate change in subject, but let it slide. He knew there was no point in continuing their previous conversation. "It did not take long for King Unwin to recover." Bern remembered Unwin's recovery from the control of Na'garoz.

"I am sure that Unwin did not have to suffer the same as Queen Oriana. I am sure it will take her some time to recover completely." Xarles did not look happy with Bern's response. He was very defensive with his answer. He did not like what Bern was insinuating.

"I am sorry. I did not mean to insult anyone." Bern didn't know what else to say. He had heard the rumour of what had happened between the queen and Ra'naroz. He wished he had not made such a flippant comment.

"No, of course not." Xarles controlled himself. "It will take a long time for Queen Oriana to recover, but I will be here for her. I'm not going anywhere."

Bern finished his drink and motioned for Xarles to pour him another. He thought it was the best way for him to break the uncomfortable silence. He made a comment on the quality of the wine. He figured it might lighten the mood. It was a feeble attempt, but it was worth a shot. Xarles appreciated the effort.

They spent the remainder of the afternoon avoiding the subject. There were plenty of other topics for them to discuss. By they time they had finished their fourth drink the tension had been forgotten. The wine was starting to have its effect on Bern's mind and he liked it. The idea of visiting Tancred, Richmond and Hadar had completely gone. He was set for an afternoon of drinking.

Xarles was glad he had found someone to drink with. He had known that running the kingdom would be an arduous task, but he had know idea just how painful it was going to be. The snivelling noblemen and women would have to wait another day. He was not going back to work. Too much had happened recently and he thought he deserved to a little time off.

"To success!" Xarles raised his glass after pouring another drink.

"To freedom!" Bern returned.

"I think I should get someone to bring some more wine," he spoke when he sat down. "I think this is going to be a long afternoon," there was a big smile on his face as he spoke.

Bern returned his smile and nodded his head. There was now definitely no chance of any work getting done. Whatever was out there would have to wait for the next day. For the moment Bern was content in continuing to get drunk. He could not remember the last time he had a full afternoon to enjoy himself. He made a silent promise to make more time for such matters, although he knew there was little chance of him keeping his word.

Chapter 11: Devising a Plan

Bern woke with a terrible headache the next day. He looked around the room, but he could not focus on anything. The urge to retch was becoming uncontrollable. He leaned over the bed and was grateful to find someone had placed a bucket there.

When he had finished he wanted to roll back into bed and fall asleep, but he knew that was not an option. There was too much work to do. He had to see if the three patients were ready to talk. There was a lot riding on their recovery. He did not like the sound of Orric's warning. The last thing he wanted to do was make the enemy stronger.

As soon as he stood up his head started to swim. He felt as though he was going to be sick again. The feeling only lasted a moment and the contents of his stomach remained intact. The more he stood the better he started to feel. The next thing he had to do was put something in his stomach. He realised in their haste to drink they had not eaten. At that thought his stomach started to growl and didn't feel as good.

Before he could leave the room there was a knock on the door. When he opened it he found a young serving woman on the other side. She held a plate filled with bacon, eggs and crusty bread. He almost forgot his manners as he took the plate out of her hands. He could not be more grateful for the food. He thanked the serving woman before placing the plate on the table.

When he had finished eating he felt much better. He could not believe his luck when the food had arrived. He did not know how far he could move before the hunger pains got to him. After a good meal he was ready to face the challenges of the day, or at least more so than before.

When Bern went to leave the room again there came another knock on the door. This one was a lot firmer. He knew it was not the serving girl, but he did not know who it was. The door was pushed open from the outside before Bern had a chance to reply. A slight rage started to build up inside him until he saw Alaric walk into the room. He was glad it was his old friend and not some pesky noble come to annoy him.

"Good morning Alaric, how are you feeling this morning?" Bern spoke first.

"Feeling a lot better today, and you?" Alaric replied.

"A little under the weather, but that is another story all together. How about your memory? Is that returning?" Bern quickly changed the topic from his hangover.

"It is better than what it was yesterday, but it is still not all there," Alaric replied honestly. "Which I suppose is one of the reasons why I came to find you this morning."

Bern did not like the sound of Alaric's voice. He was sure there was going to be some bad news and bad news from Alaric was the worst kind. His mind was racing with all the different scenarios of what could be wrong. The worst one was that the Dark Knight had escaped. It was apparent on his face the torment running through his mind. It almost made Alaric laugh.

"Relax, my old friend, things are not that bad. As I said my memory is slowly starting to return, but there are still quite a few gaps. I need to speak with Marina."

Bern thought for a moment. He wasn't sure if she was the best person Alaric could be speaking with. She was not in a good frame of mind. He had to explain this to Alaric before he divulged her location.

"She is not well Alaric. She is acting strange," Bern didn't know how else to explain things. "I know the two of you have been through a lot since I last saw her, but the other commanders have said that same thing. I don't think it is a good idea for you to speak with her at the moment."

"I appreciate the concern and I am sure it is warranted, but unfortunately I do not have the time to wait. I have to be leaving soon and I need to speak with her before I do." Alaric knew something had happened to Marina. Deep inside he felt it, but like most things he could not remember the details.

Bern was surprised to hear Alaric's words and he was not happy. There was no way that he could let his friend go back out in the world in his current condition. He knew Alaric was strong, but at the moment he was in no condition to travel. The problem was that he had no idea how he was going to stop him.

"I do not think it's a good idea. I think you should remain in Jarrat until your memory returns," Bern suggested.

Alaric knew that Bern was only doing what he thought was best, but he did not have all the information. He wished he could remain in Jarrat. What he had to do was more dangerous than anything he had done before and in his current condition it was all the more so. The problem was he didn't have a choice. If he did not go then Alena would die. Although he could not completely remember the elf, he did know she was important to him. He could not let her die.

"There is more to this that you know, Bern. If only I could remember I could tell you, but again I must ask for you to trust me."

"Very well. Marina is in the army camp. I think it is best if I have someone bring her to the castle," Bern suggested.

Alaric thought for a moment. He had to admit that Bern was right. If he was to walk into the army then he would be hit with a hundred and one different questions, not all of which he would be able to answer. It was those sorts of situations that would start the gossips talking. It would not be long before the entire castle knew that something was not right with him.

"That's a great idea. I will wait in my room," Alaric replied. "I do not know if I will see you again, before I return from Castalia," Alaric spoke as he was about to leave. "You have to make sure that nothing happens to Alena whilst I am gone."

Bern thought it was a strange comment, but he agreed nevertheless. With that organised, Alaric left the room. Bern had hoped for a little more information, but he didn't have the heart to push any further. He would have to surmise on the information at hand. Alaric was going to Castalia and it had something to do with Alena, further details would just have to wait. For the moment he had other matters to deal with, things that were in his control.

Finally Bern was able to leave his room. He was half expecting someone to knock on the door as he reached for the handle. His hand paused for a moment before he pulled the door open. There was no one waiting for him on the outside. He looked left and right before he was confident no one was there. He felt uncomfortable setting foot outside of his room. His initial reaction was to return to the safety of his apartment, but he swallowed it down and continued. He had to see the three injured men, he owed them that much. He hated the Dark Knight more for not including him in what he had subjected the other three to. He felt as though he deserved the same treatment. He only hoped they would be able to forgive him.

Bern found the physician coming from the room just as he was about to enter. He was happy that he caught him before he left. He was also glad the physician was on the way out. He did not like the man and if he was still inside it meant that he would have to make small talk.

"How are they?" Bern did not bother to ask how he was.

"They are stable, but still unconscious. I don't know what happened to them in the dungeons, but it wasn't good." The physician shook his head. He genuinely looked stumped. "I don't understand. They should be fine by now. Their wounds are starting to heal and there doesn't seem to be any mental damage. If there is something causing their state then I have no idea what it is. I will check on them later in the day, but I fear there is nothing more that I can do." The physician didn't wait for Bern to respond. He knew there was no answer he could give, no matter what the question was.

Bern didn't worry about calling after him. He could tell by the physician's body language the man had no answers. That was indeed disturbing, but it was not the end of the line. There was still one place he could go. If the physician was not able to help then he was sure Eldred could.

He didn't bother entering the room. There was no point in visiting the sick men if they were not able to speak. He needed answers and sitting around would not get him any. Time was slipping away. If he did not have something for the command group soon then they would start the interrogations. That was something he needed to avoid. Not only would it cause great suffering, but he also didn't believe it would get the results they were after.

Eldred was sitting by Alena's bed. Bern had not had time to visit, but he wished he had. Alena looked deathly ill. Bern could not believe she was still alive. Eldred looked up when he heard Bern enter. His face looked drawn and faded. He did not look as though he was well himself.

"Are you alright?" Bern asked when he gained Eldred's attention.

"I will survive. It is an arduous task keeping Alena alive. I am afraid that the task may be too great for me alone," his voice was strained.

Bern almost didn't have the heart to ask Eldred the question, but he had to. "The three men who were with me in the dungeons have also not recovered. The physician said that there was no reason why. I don't think their condition is natural. Is there anything that you can do?" Bern held his breath and waited for Eldred's response.

"I am afraid that there is nothing I can do." Eldred's head dropped into his hands. "It is taking all my energy to keep Alena alive. If I divert some for just a moment then all is lost," there was a great sorrow in his voice.

Bern wished he had not asked the question. Eldred did not need to waste his energy on such matters. Bern didn't worry about saying goodbye. He simply left the room. He didn't think that Eldred noticed him leave. Bern didn't think that Eldred would even remember that he was there.

Now there was only one more option left to him and that was Alaric. He didn't know what his old friend could do in his weakened state, but there was nothing else for it. He had already requested Marina be brought to the castle, but he did not think she would be arriving for a least another hour. The decision would bring angst amongst the command group, but there was nothing he could do. He was not going to let Alaric leave the castle unnecessarily.

He found Alaric waiting in his room. He knocked, but didn't wait for a response. It was a little pay back for Alaric barging into his room earlier. He knew it was childish, but he did it anyway. Alaric didn't respond to his entering the room, which was a little disappointing. It was not that he was expecting much of a reaction, but some response would have been nice.

"I have sent for Marina. I would be expecting that she should be here soon," Bern started.

"That is not the reason you have come here," there was something cold in Alaric's voice, something that Bern had not heard before.

At first he was taken aback, but the he thought it might just be the hangover having an effect on him. "No, of course not," he continued to speak. He paused and thought for a moment before he started to tell Alaric about the other three.

"Unfortunately there is nothing I can do for them," Alaric looked as though he was deep in thought as he spoke. "There is one thing though."

Bern was becoming frustrated. He should not have to push for answers. He wanted to walk across the room and throttle some sense into his old friend, but that would not prove anything. He knew there was a reason why Alaric must be acting the way he was, but he had no idea what it would be. He decided he would just ignore it as much as possible and continue with the conversation.

"Is there something you think you can do to help?" Bern asked, a little more hopeful of a positive response.

"Well, yes and no," his tone had changed and he sounded more responsive. "It is a theory I have, but I am fairly sure it will work." Alaric paused again.

Bern was becoming annoyed again, but he took a deep breath and then asked the question. "What is your theory?"

"I believe that Ra'naroz is the problem. He is doing something that is causing the three men to remain unconscious," Alaric explained.

"I thought the herb that he was drinking was stopping him from creating spells," Bern replied.

"That is true, but I do not completely understand the power of the herb. The point is that I have a theory. I believe once the Dark Knight is away from the three men they will start to recover," Alaric explained.

"Then we are still at an impasse. We can't let the Dark Knight go and I don't dare move the men." Bern's hopes were dashed. He almost wished that Alaric had not said anything.

"That is not exactly true," there was a wry smile on Alaric's face, but his tone sent a shiver down Bern's spine.

"I hate to ask, but what is it?" Bern cringed as he waited for Alaric's response.

"Ra'naroz is coming with me." Alaric paused once he had broken the news. From his initial reaction he knew Bern was not happy. "There is a good reason for it." Alaric tried to reassure him.

"Are you out of your mind? I don't think this can happen. We can not let the Dark Knight leave the castle. He will soon be put to death."

Alaric knew he wasn't going to get a favourable response from Bern, but he couldn't think of another way to break the news. His next problem was telling his friend, the General of the Alliance, that he didn't have a say in the matter. He would not be happy, but there was nothing he could about it.

"I am afraid that he is coming with me. That is the reason why he is still alive. There is information he has and I need it," Alaric explained.

"But…" Bern let his objection trail away. "Surely there is another way. In your condition there is nothing you can do to stop him if he breaks free."

"I am glad you have such faith in me. I know I can't use magic at the moment, but neither can he. The advantage I have is that he doesn't know that. The other side is that I still remember how to fight. I will able to kill him if he tries to escape," Alaric explained, trying to ease Bern's nerves.

"I don't like it, but I suppose I don't have a say in the matter." Bern knew his place. "I guess you have your reasons. What should I tell the rest of the army command?" It was not going to be an easy conversation. They would want to know why he let the Dark Knight go free. Although it was not the case he knew it was the way they would see it.

"As little as possible," Alaric retorted. "There are still many enemies within the castle walls. If they found out where I was taking Ra'naroz then there is no telling who would be coming after me. The least amount of people who know what I am doing the better."

"You are not making my life any easier." Bern smiled as he realised Alaric was right. He wished he could tell the truth, but it would cause more damage down the track. He would have to soak up the anger that would come his way. In the end he would know he was doing the right thing.

Suddenly there was a knock on the door. Before either man had a chance to react, the door was pushed open. Marina stormed into the room whilst a serving woman tried to halt her progress. Once she saw Alaric she moved over and collapsed into his arms. She held onto him tightly.

"I am sorry, I tried to stop her," the serving woman sounded afraid.

Alaric could feel Marina starting to rise to confront the woman. He increased his grip on her so she couldn't say anything. He didn't think it would be appropriate for her to speak.

"That's alright. I am on my way out anyhow." Bern rose from where he had been seated. The conversation was over whether he liked it or not. He could not discuss the matter further in front of Marina. That was Alaric's call on how much she would know. "Please, we shall give them some privacy." He smiled a warm smile and nodded at Alaric on the way out. Alaric returned his goodbye in the same manner. It would be another long time before they saw each other again. It seemed as though there should be longer farewell.

When the two had left the room Alaric lifted Marina's head off his chest. The tears rolled freely down her cheeks. He didn't know if it was sadness or relief that caused the tears. She looked wild. Even when they had been travelling through the wasteland he did not think he had seen her hair in such a state. She had always been so proud of her appearance. Even without the tears he would have realised that something was not right.

"What's wrong?" he asked.

The tears suddenly stopped and there was a confused expression on her face. It was as if she was seeing him for the first time. She couldn't work out what was happening.

"Why do you tease me?" there was hurt in her voice.

"I am sorry. My memory is a little all over the place since I fought with Ra'naroz," he explained, without giving too much away. There was something not right with Marina. Alaric could feel it in his bones.

Marina pushed herself up and out of Alaric's arms. She wanted to get a better look at him. Something was different. She had felt it as soon as she entered the room, but she had been too grateful to see him alive to pay any attention to it.

"Please tell me what it is that you are missing?" He didn't know why he worded his question in such a manner, but it seemed appropriate.

"Missing!" Marina sounded shocked. "I think you mean, what was stolen." It was at that point that Alaric remembered what had happened. He knew why she was so upset. "Argoz has stolen the Sapphire ring, my ring!" He had expected Marina's voice to crack with sadness, but instead it was full of rage. Alaric was taken aback.

"I remember now. He has taken the stone to Lel Dinion," Alaric cringed at the thought. Now another Dark Knight had a *Stone of Power*.

"We have to go after him. We have to get the stone back. If we leave now I am sure that we will be able to catch him before he reaches Lel Dinion," there was renewed hope in Marina's voice.

Alaric's heart sank when he heard Marina's words. He had forgotten all about the Sapphire stone. He did not know how he was going to tell her they could not go after the Dark Knight. He had to travel to Castalia. He knew that deep within himself. He didn't have to consult the prophecy to know that Castalia was where his destiny was taking him.

"We will have to wait before we regain the Sapphire stone," Alaric just blurted the words out.

Marina stood and stared. There was a look of pure horror on her face. She knew Alaric was not at his peak, but she had not expected such a response. She could not understand why he could not see what she saw. There was nothing in the world that was more important than regaining the Sapphire stone. She had to find out what he thought was more important and then refute his claims.

"Where is it you are planning on going?" she asked, an accusatory tone in her voice.

Alaric chose to ignore what was not said and concentrate on her question. "We are going to Castalia." He thought if he used the word 'we' then it would include her in his decision.

"And what is in Castalia that is so important?" She was not going to let him slow down.

"We believe that the Topaz stone is there. We need to get the stone if we are going to save Alena." Alaric thought it was best that he didn't add himself to the cause, the least amount of people who knew his secret the better.

"And why do you believe the Topaz stone is in Castalia? Is it written in the prophecy? Is the Jade stone showing you the way?" Marina fired the questions. She was trying to catch Alaric out.

Alaric knew she was not going to like the answer to her questions, but he did not think lying was the answer. "Ra'naroz told us it was there."

"And I am sure there is a very good reason why you would trust a Dark Knight. Have you consulted the prophecy?" Marina asked, knowing full well that he had not.

"There is no time to consult the prophecy. We have to leave today."

"I am not going anywhere with you, unless it is to Lel Dinion," Marina barked.

Alaric didn't think that things were going to be so difficult. He was beginning to wish he had not sent for Marina. The problem was that he had a feeling he would need her on his journey. He almost thought of giving in to her demands and hunting down Argoz before travelling to Castalia, but he did not think Alena had the time. The other problem was Ra'naroz. It was a stretch taking him to Castalia. He could not drag him around the Seven Kingdoms.

"I wish you would reconsider. I need you to come with me," he wasn't pleading, but he was not far off.

"I do not think this conversation needs to go any further," there was a coldness in Marina's voice that sent a shiver down his spine.

There was a hardness to her face he had not seen before. Alaric did not like it. He had been warned about the power of the stones. He knew they could be possessive. It seemed as though the Sapphire stone was trying to take control of Marina. It was not a good sign, but there was nothing he could do. He thought at the very least the Sapphire stone would protect her against Argoz. It was that thought that solidified his resolve.

"I want you to come with me. I promise once we have the Topaz stone we will go after Argoz."

"That's okay. I see where your priorities lie now. I will regain the Sapphire ring without you." Marina was about to storm out of the room, but something made her stop.

"Please. I need your help." Alaric finally resorted to pleading.

"Fine. I will go with you, but I do not like it," with that Marina walked out of the room.

Alaric didn't know if it was a good thing or a bad thing. He needed Marina's help, but he did not know if he could trust her. There was something very wrong with her. At least he would have a chance to figure it out on the way to Castalia. With any luck the Topaz stone would be able to cure her cravings towards the Sapphire stone.

He took a deep breath when he was sure Marina was gone. It had been an ordeal talking her into coming with him. He wished he could take someone else, but all those he trusted were either injured or busy. He felt a lot better knowing she was coming. There was no doubt in his mind she was supposed to travel with him again. The last thing he had to do was get Ra'naroz ready to leave. It would not be an easy task getting him out of the castle, at least not without everyone knowing. He wished that he had more time to devise a plan, but he had to get moving.

There was only one person he knew who could get him out of the castle. He didn't know if he trusted the man, but he seemed to have Bern's confidence and that was enough for him. The duke had proven to be worthy when he led his little band of rebels into the castle. If he had not done so then Alaric and his friends would surely still be prisoners. It was with that thought in his mind that he decided to take the plunge. At some stage he would have to take a risk on someone's trustworthiness and it seemed like a good a time as any.

The next problem he had was that he knew the duke would be holding court in the queen's throne room. He would be surrounded by a myriad of nobles vying for his attention. There was no way he could enter the room and speak with the duke unnoticed. What he needed to do was speak with Xarles so no one else could hear. If someone found out what he was doing then it would all be for nothing.

As he expected the throne room was full. The duke was slumped on the throne. He did not look like he was paying attention to what was being yelled at him. He did not look happy. Alaric did not think that this was a good sign. Xarles did not look as though he would be too receptive to his plight. That was not going to stop him though, he had to at least ask.

The crowd grew denser the closer he came to the throne dais. At first he just got strange looks from those he passed, but the further he travelled the worse it got. As he tried to make his way through some of the noblemen pushed him back. They gave him rude looks. It was obvious they had no idea who he was. Bern had made a point to keep his identity secret. It was a good idea, but it didn't help him in his current situation.

"Wait your turn," one noblewoman screeched at him as he tried to get past.

"We have been here since dawn. You will just have to wait," a nobleman spoke harshly at him.

Alaric wanted to gain access to Xarles without drawing attention to himself, but it seemed as though that was a fruitless exercise. He had no choice but to fight his way to the dais. It was not something he wanted to do, but he could see no other way.

Alaric reached out and grabbed the nearest man in-between his shoulder and neck. When he had a firm grip he squeezed as hard as he could. The nobleman instantly sunk to his knees and cried out in pain. Alaric didn't know if it was movement or the noise that brought the attention of the other nobles around him, but it worked. A nobleman to Alaric's right, when he realised what had happened, swung a punch at his head. Alaric simply deflected the attack and struck out with his own fist. He caught the man on the nose and he crumpled to the floor. This caused the crowd to step away from him. Some, who didn't see what had happened, wanted a better view and those who did wanted some distance.

Alaric quickly looked around to see if anyone else was going to attack. He was confident he could take out everyone in the room if necessary. His strength was returning, but it was not something that he wanted to do.

The commotion brought the attention of Xarles. He had to admit he was happy to see something break up the monotony. At first he didn't care that it was a fight, but he soon realised that he was going to have discipline the guilty parties.

"You, come to the dais," he boomed at the top of his lungs whilst he pointed at Alaric.

Alaric breathed a sigh of relief. Things had worked out better than he thought. He was prepared to take out another half dozen nobles before he could make his way to the front. Now he was getting a free pass. The other nobles stepped aside as Alaric walked towards the dais. It wasn't until he was almost at the front before Xarles recognised who he was. He instantly wished he had not spoken so brashly.

"I am sorry, Alaric, I did not know it was you," he apologised in a soft voice so no one else could hear.

The throne room had gone suddenly quiet. Everyone was transfixed. They were waiting to see what punishment the stranger was going to receive. They did not know exactly what it would be, but in their current situation it was likely to be severe. Those who had seen what had happened were hoping for a public flogging. It was a punishment that suited the crime. They did not like they way Alaric treated their fellow nobles, even though they had no respect for the nobles in question.

"I need to speak to you in private," Alaric also kept his voice low.

"Then I think that we should get out of here. I don't know if you planned this, but it has worked out quite nicely." Xarles smiled as he turned to address the crowd. "I will take this foreigner to my chamber and discuss his punishment. I will make an official announcement once I have made my decision," he spoke in his most commanding voice.

There were a few cheers, but more jeers from the crowd. They wanted the trial to be made public. They did not know what the duke had in mind, but private trials were never good. Most felt that justice was a public matter, not a private one.

"Be sure that I will not be lenient," he added before he led Alaric from the dais.

Alaric had to use a great amount of self-control not the smile as the crowd cheered. They would be disappointed when they found out he had not been punished. He had to admit that things had worked out well. The only problem was that he would stand out in a crowd. At least they did not know who he was. If they found out then it would be almost impossible to sneak out of the castle.

"Again I must apologise, but to leave any other way would have looked too suspicious," Xarles apologised again when they were alone.

"No need to apologise. I think it was a brilliant plan." Alaric smiled warmly. He wanted to laugh, but he did not think that it would be appropriate.

"Now what is it that I can do for you?" Xarles asked as he went to his table and poured himself a goblet of wine. "Would you care to join me?" he asked as an after thought.

"No thank you. I still have much to do today and I don't think it will end soon," Alaric replied.

"I don't normally drink this early, but the nobles are really getting to me." Xarles felt as though he needed to make an excuse for his drinking.

"That is quite alright. I am sure you are not going to like what I have to say, but I can assure you there is no other option." Xarles didn't like the sound of Alaric's words. "I need the take Ra'naroz out of the castle."

"I don't understand. Where are you planning on taking him?" It was not the response Alaric was expecting.

He wasn't expecting the question. He had not planned on telling Xarles where they were travelling. He thought for a moment, but decided it would be safer if he didn't know. 'I can not tell you that. It is safer for everyone that you don't know. All you need to know is that I need to leave with Ra'naroz and Princess Marina will be leaving with me." Alaric hoped he would understand.

"I do not think it is a wise decision. Prince Leroy will need to stand trial and pay for what he did to the queen. I do not think my people will just let you walk out of the castle with him, even with my instructions." Alaric didn't know if it was genuine concern or just an elaborate ruse.

"We are not going to walk out of the castle. No one must know. We have left this for as long as possible. We have to leave in complete secrecy. The only other people who know are Eldred and Bern. That needs to stay the same," Alaric explained.

"I don't think anyone is going to miss you, but they will notice if Leroy is no longer in his room," Xarles explained.

"You will just have to say he is now in solitary confinement. No one is allowed contact with him, except for you and Bern. That way there will be no one to notice he has left. I will need at least a week, but anything more would be great," Alaric added.

"Hmmm." Xarles thought for a moment as he drained his glass. "There is a way, but it will not be easy." He paused as he double checked his plan. "There is a secret way out of the castle through the stables. It is how I brought the rebels inside. The only problem is that I now have it heavily guarded. I will not make the same mistake that Leroy made."

"Then I won't be able to use that way." Alaric didn't not know why Xarles had mentioned it at all.

"That is not exactly true. Shortly after dusk there is a changing of the guard. Things have not exactly been running smoothly at that time. It is something I have been meaning to work on. Anyway, there is a chance that the three of you will be able to escape unnoticed," Xarles explained.

"I don't know," Alaric did not think that the plan sounded solid. "A chance to escape unnoticed is not the same thing as leaving unnoticed. It sounds too risky for my liking." It was the best plan so far, but there had to be a better way.

"That is true, but the plan continues." Xarles paused to pour himself another drink. "As I said the changing of the guard has been quite sloppy. I think tonight I shall have a meeting with the guards and berate them for a little while. That will give you all the time to sneak out." Xarles seemed quite pleased with himself.

Alaric had to agree the plan seemed secure. There would still be a risk walking through the castle, but he thought it might just work. There was only one thing left.

"What about the horses?" Alaric asked.

"That's an easy one. I will have Bern get the horses for you and meet you outside the castle. He can freely move between the castle and the army campsite." Xarles was very pleased with himself.

Alaric was grateful that the duke had come up with the answers to his problems. He felt relieved that Xarles was left in charge of the castle. He seemed like a smart man although Alaric was a little concerned with his drinking. He felt he should comment, but then decided that it was not his place. He was sure Bern would be able to keep him in check.

"I also need all the herbs that block the Dark Knight's power. I will need that for my journey." Alaric was almost about to leave when the thought came to his mind.

"Of course, they are all stored in the castle. It will be a little suspicious, but I will be able to get it for you. Is there anything else that you need?" Xarles asked as he poured himself another glass of wine.

"No I think I should be able to manage everything else, by myself. I will need to raid the kitchens, but that should be fine," Alaric replied.

"Then I will bid you goodbye. Now remember to be at the stables on nightfall. I will have the guards distracted by then," Xarles stood and shook Alaric's hand.

The duke remained in his apartment when Alaric left the building. He hoped Xarles did not drink himself into a stupor. A lot was riding on his ability to be a leader. If he was not on time then all was for nothing and the castle would know exactly what he was doing. He knew he was not going to be able to relax until he was out of the castle.

Chapter 12: The Journey Begins Again

The plan went off with out a hitch. Xarles looked a little shaky on his feet, but Alaric was sure none of the guards noticed. He put on a riveting show. The duke was able to kill two birds with one stone. He had been meaning to speak to the guards ever since they started guarding the stables. The three of them were able to easily sneak past the guards without anyone seeing them.

The three wrapped themselves in dark robes so no one would recognise them as they walked through the castle. Alaric was worried the Dark Knight would try and reveal his identity, but it seemed as though the threats Alaric had made hit home. Marina also seemed sullen at having to cover herself in such a fashion. She had made a big effort to improve her appearance and felt the robe would mess it up.

In the end Alaric was able to convince her to remain hidden and they successfully made their way through the stables and out the other side of the castle. Once they were there it did not take them long to find Bern. He was waiting with Adelanta and two other horses as Xarles had suggested. There was also a donkey with their packs tied on.

"Be warned, Ra'naroz, if you do anything untoward I will hunt you down and kill you." There was a spark in Bern's eyes as he dealt out the threat. Alaric wasn't sure if it was just a reflection of the firelight from the torch he held or it was something else.

The Dark Knight did not back down. He had a straight look on his face. There was no telling what he was thinking until he spoke. "I know you have won. All I want to do now is stay alive. These ropes that you have bound me with are unnecessary, but I will understand if you wish to keep them on." His deference was surprising, but Bern was not convinced.

"Don't treat us like fools. We know you have no remorse for what you have done. Remember my words because they will haunt you for the rest of your short life." Bern kept a calm demeanour despite his words.

Instead of responding to Bern the Dark Knight turned to Alaric. "We should be on our way. We want to be well away from the castle before daybreak."

Alaric had to admit that Ra'naroz was right. They did not have time to stand around whilst Bern dished out threats. He turned to his old friend. If he said a few words of good bye before they left then it would not seem as though it was the Dark Knight's idea.

"I will be able to look after him," Alaric reassured Bern. "You need to focus on your job at hand. The city is rife with evil. You need to find them all and deal with them before my return."

Bern had been ignoring the fact he had his own problems to deal with. Whilst he could concentrate on Alaric's troubles he could forget his own. He wished Alaric had not mentioned them, but it did bring him back to reality. He needed to be getting back to the castle. He needed to see if there was any change in the health of Tancred, Richmond and Hadar.

"I will be ready for when you return." Bern shook Alaric's hand and turned and left.

"Let's get moving," Alaric suggested when the light of Bern's torch disappeared.

Marina had already removed her robe when Alaric turned around. She would not wear it for a minute longer than necessary. Alaric had wished she kept it on. It was not that he thought they would meet anyone who would recognise them, but he still didn't want to take the risk. He thought about telling her, but in the end he figured that it would be easier if he kept his mouth shut.

Alaric had to help Ra'naroz onto his horse. With his arms tied behind his back it was an almost impossible exercise by himself. Alaric didn't feel right touching the Dark Knight. A shiver ran down his back and he didn't feel right again until he moved away. There was something very wrong about the situation. He wished he had time to ponder on it, but he had to get moving.

They travelled at a steady pace throughout the night. They did not stop for a break until the sun crept above the horizon. Alaric wanted to keep going, but he figured they had travelled far enough. Duke Xarles had assured Alaric it would be a long time before anyone knew the Dark Knight was missing. With any luck he would already have returned before anyone did.

The ride to Castalia from Jarrat was about half that of the journey from Kiarome to Jarrat. At a good pace Alaric thought they would be in Castalia in a week. He would not let the fact that the Dark Knight was bound slow them down. He could suffer like he had made so many before. He wanted nothing more than to strike out against the evil creature, but that would prove nothing. He would have to wait for the chance to kill the Dark Knight and there was no doubt in his mind he would.

When they made camp they still had the protection of the forest. They would only remain in it for another day and a half, after that were rolling grasslands. Trees were few and far between from the edge of the forest to Castalia. The only protection they would have from prying eyes were the hills. They did have some advantages. Only two people knew they had left the castle and knew where they were going.

Once they had all eaten their fill Alaric gave Ra'naroz the mixture that blocked his ability to use magic. The Dark Knight didn't do anything to thwart him. He drank the potion without question. Although he was being amicable Alaric didn't like it. He couldn't work out why he was being so compliant. There had to be an ulterior motive. It was that thought that was racing through his mind when he fell asleep.

Ra'naroz smiled when he saw that Alaric had fallen asleep. He looked across and saw that Marina was still awake. This was the opportunity he had been waiting for. He did not think it would have come so quickly, but he was not going to look a gift horse in the mouth.

"So why is it that you have come with us?" he asked casually.

Marina looked at him with a sneer. She was not in the mood to talk. The situation was still not what she was hoping for. She thought that it was more important to recover the Sapphire stone than it was to save Alena's life. She didn't know why the elf was so important to Alaric. She would be quite happy to watch her die if it meant the return of her property.

"I mean I think it would be better if you were to go after my brother." It was those words that made her take notice.

"What do you know?" she asked with an accusatory tone in her voice.

"I know that Argoz has the Sapphire stone. I know that he has left for Lel Dinion." there was a wry smile on the Dark Knight's face.

Marina shuffled the deep blue skirts of her riding dress in anticipation of the conversation. There was something in his words that made her listen. It was possible that if she played her cards right she would be able to gain some insight. She needed to catch him out. Little did she know that Ra'naroz wanted to give her the information that she required.

"What of it?" She was not going to show her true interest, although it was written in her body language. She leaned forward, waiting for his response.

Ra'naroz paused for dramatic effect. His plan was starting to work. He could tell she was interested in what he had to say. All he had to do is keep her interest piqued and she would do exactly what he wanted.

"You have a connection to the stone. It calls to you. I can see it on your face. There is something magnificent about a person who is linked to a *Stone of Power*. You should not be apart." Ra'naroz baited her even further.

"You are right. I should not be separated from the Sapphire stone. Alaric should be travelling with me to Lel Dinion." Marina was sucked into what the Dark Knight was saying.

"Why is it that he is wasting his time on an elf? I think there is something going on between the two on them."

Marina looked away from the Dark Knight. Her face had gone red, but she did not know if it was from rage or embarrassment. Either way she did not want Ra'naroz to see. He looked at something to the left in an attempt to make her feel more comfortable. It was his time with the queen that gave him the ability to sense what a woman was feeling.

"I have seen the way he looks at her." He continued when she did not respond. "They were not just travelling companions." He had no idea if he was right, but that didn't matter.

"I don't know what you are talking about." She didn't want to divulge her relationship with Alaric to the Dark Knight, but she did not like what he was insinuating.

"Then why is he going so far to make sure that she is alright. I am sure there is time. Her condition is stable. There is no real hurry to save her." It was a lie, but he was sure that she would not pick up on it.

Marina didn't know what to think. Alaric had told her that Alena did not have time to waste, but then again it might have just been ploy to get her away from the Sapphire stone. She had always thought he was jealous of her connection to the stone. It seemed as though the Dark Knight was making sense. She was beginning to trust Ra'naroz, even though every fibre of her body was telling her not to.

"That is a very good question. There is no reason why he should be going to Castalia." It seemed as though she was going to get the answer on her own.

"Then he must only be doing it to keep you from the Sapphire stone. I am sure he is plotting against you." Ra'naroz pushed a little harder.

"You are right. He is trying to keep the stone for himself. It is the only reason why he will not help me get it back. I cannot believe that he would do such a thing, but there is no other explanation." Ra'naroz leaned backwards. He knew he had won. Marina was going to do exactly what he suggested.

"There is only one thing you can do now."

"What is that?" Her mind was so full of deceit that she did not notice the slight change in the direction of the conversation.

"You must go to Lel Dinion yourself and recover the stone. If you do not then surely Alaric will take it from you." He could see the realisation cross her face.

"You are right. I must leave now." She thought for a moment. "But I don't think that I am strong enough to defeat Argoz." Her excitement suddenly dwindled.

There could be no way around her little dilemma, but Ra'naroz would not be beaten. It would take a number of lies to convince her, but that was his forte. He would stop at nothing to see her on her way to Lel Dinion. He thought it might be a good idea to let her sleep on the idea, but that quickly left his mind. The risk of a confrontation between her and Alaric was too high. If he did not get rid of her that morning then he did not like his chances. That thought strengthened his resolve.

"I believe you are strong enough to defeat Argoz. He is the weakest of my six brothers. Once you have the Sapphire stone back in your possession then nothing can stop you." Marina was not convinced, although she was yet to become suspicious of his motives.

"He has the stone concealed. I can not feel her at the moment. If he keeps her confined then I have no hope of defeating him."

"Do not sell yourself short. Now, I am not saying it is going to be easy, but I am sure that you will be able to use your guile to get him to show you the stone." Ra'naroz would not let up. If he kept hitting her with answers then she would not have a chance to dwell.

"I do not…"

"You cannot doubt yourself. That is what Alaric is hoping for. He will use your doubt to his advantage and he will take the stone from you. Once he has it then there will be no chance for you to get it back." It was not a complete lie.

If Alaric was able to get his hands on the Sapphire stone then there was a good chance he would not hand it over. She knew it was true and it was something she could not risk. With the Dark Knight there was a chance she could recover the stone, with Alaric there was none. It was a long ride to Lel Dinion, so she would have time to devise a plan.

"You are right. I have to do this or I will never see her again," it sounded as though Marina had her mind made up.

Ra'naroz didn't say anymore. He had done what he had set out to do and he didn't want to ruin it. He knew he would suffer a great punishment when Alaric found out what he had done, although if he was smart enough he might be able to talk his way out it. Either way he was not too worried. It would not be the first time he had been tortured. He had spent many years in the dungeons of a city that had long been destroyed and its name forgotten.

Marina had not noticed the large grin on the Dark Knight's face. If she had she might have thought twice about his motives. Instead she busied herself packing her supplies. It would be a long ride to Lel Dinion and she did not want to waste time hunting or foraging for food. She felt bad leaving Alaric without food or water, but he was not doing her any favours.

She moved around quietly. If Alaric woke then she was sure he would not let her leave. She had made up her mind and she did not want anything to change it. There was nothing more important to her than recovering the Sapphire stone.

Just before she was about to leave she looked down at Alaric. The morning sunlight bounced off his face. He looked somewhat peaceful, but Marina could not find any pleasant feelings for him. She could not believe he was a man who she used to love, or at least she thought she loved. Their relationship had been quick and passionate. Now she felt nothing but contempt. It was that thought that was deep in her mind as she rode away from the campsite.

***

Alaric woke with the sun in the afternoon. He instantly knew something was wrong. His first reaction was to see if the Dark Knight was still bound on the other side of their campsite. His heart rate slowed when he saw him sitting peacefully staring at the ashes of the fire. He didn't seem to notice that Alaric had woken.

Even though the Dark Knight was still there he could not shake the feeling that something was wrong. Something had happened during the night. He thought Marina would be able to shed some light on the situation. When he looked over he could not see her or her bedroll. Even then it didn't dawn on him that she had gone. It was not inconceivable that she had woken and already packed her things, ready for a long day and night's ride.

"Do you know where Marina is?" Although he didn't want to speak with Ra'naroz it was the easiest option.

"I don't know. She was not here when I woke." There was something wrong with Ra'naroz's comment, but Alaric gave him the benefit of the doubt.

It didn't take long for Alaric to realise what had happened when he saw that Marina's mare was also missing. He searched the ground and found the horse's tracks out of the campsite. The track led off to the North-East. There was no doubt in his mind she had gone to chase Argoz and the Sapphire stone. He cursed quietly to himself. He did not know what she was thinking. She was no match for a Dark Knight on her own without the aid of the stone. He knew something was not right. She could not have made that decision on her own. He was sure the Dark Knight was somehow involved. He would get to the bottom of it before they left for the day.

"What have you done?" there was an edge to Alaric's voice that made the Dark Knight look up.

"I don't know what you are talking about?" Ra'naroz knew he was in trouble.

"What did you say to Marina to make her leave?"

"I said good night to her and then I went to sleep." He feigned confusion on his face and in his voice.

Alaric calmly walked across to where Ra'naroz was still seated and kicked him across the side of the face. The move was so calm and unexpected the Dark Knight did nothing to defend himself, not that he would have been able to do much. The blow knocked Ra'naroz to the ground, although it did not draw blood.

"I do not want to ask you again. Tell me what you did to Marina?" Alaric spoke between clenched teeth.

Ra'naroz knew there was no chance of escaping without a beating, but he would not make life easy for Alaric. He would keep his mouth shut for as long as he could. He thought there was a good chance he could outlast Alaric's punishment. If he was able to keep the information to himself then it would be a successful exercise. He knew either way he was in for some serious pain.

"I can't tell you what I don't know." He tightened his body, waiting for the next blow.

Alaric brought his foot down hard on the Dark Knight's stomach. Even though he was prepared for the blow he had the wind knocked out of his lungs. Alaric did not let Ra'naroz rest as he tried to suck in the air around him. He picked the Dark Knight up and punched him in the face. The blow was enough to knock him to the ground again.

"Anytime you want to change your story feel free to do so." Alaric was true to his word. He was not going to re-ask the question.

Ra'naroz knew he could not back down yet. If Alaric knew he could get answers with an easy beating then he would do it all the time. The Dark Knight could withstand a great deal more pain, although in the past he was able to use magic to protect himself. Without that aid it was a completely different feeling.

The beating lasted for almost half an hour before Ra'naroz broke. He thought Alaric might have started to tire, but his attack was relentless. He did pause for a moment to catch his breath, but it did not last long. In the end the Dark Knight was beaten into submission. The pain ripped through his body and there was nothing he could do the make it better.

He slowly started to explain what had happened, leaving out certain details. Alaric didn't seem to pick up on the missing information.

When Ra'naroz had finished confessing Alaric drew his sword and placed the blade against his throat. He wanted nothing more than to slit it. It had been a mistake bringing Ra'naroz with him.

"You can do that, but there is still information that you need from me." Alaric thought that there was a slight amount of fear in Ra'naroz's voice, but he was not sure.

Alaric gripped the hilt even harder. He knew Ra'naroz was right and that made it worse. There was a reason why the Dark Knight was travelling with him. If he killed Ra'naroz then it would defeat the purpose and Marina would be gone for no reason. In the end he knew it would be better to keep the Dark Knight alive.

The effort of torturing the Dark Knight had made Alaric hungry. They had already lost time, but he needed to keep his strength up. If Ra'naroz saw any weakness then Alaric would lose his advantage. The last thing he wanted to do was to give the Dark Knight the upper hand. It was only when he started looking for food did he realise that all the supplies were gone. Marina had taken the lot. The only thing he had left were the water pouches that were strapped to Adelanta. Things had just gotten much worse. He would have to go hunting for his breakfast. He did not have the time or the energy to waste, but again he had no choice.

As he searched the ground to see if there were any animal tracks he couldn't believe that Marina would do such a thing. He could understand that she had to leave to find the stone, but she did not have to leave them with no food. He could not believe Ra'naroz could be stupid enough to convince her to do that. He would do him no favours to starve to death.

It took an hour before Alaric was finally able to find a small herd of deer. Once he had found them it did not take him long to kill a young doe.

By the time he had skinned the animal and taken the meat it was almost dusk. He cursed Marina inside his head as he worked. She had cost him a lot of time. If Alena died then it would be on her head and he would see that she would pay for it.

"I don't think Marina was really thinking about us when she left," Ra'naroz tried to make conversation as they ate.

With his arms bound it was difficult for Ra'naroz to eat. The easiest thing would be for Alaric to feed him, but that was not going to happen. Alaric didn't really care to make the Dark Knight's life any easier than he had to. In the end he just threw a slab of meat on the ground in front of him. The Dark Knight had to lay facedown to eat the deer.

Alaric ignored Ra'naroz's words. He did not want to speak with the Dark Knight, but he had to admit his words made sense. Even though Ra'naroz claimed his innocence Alaric knew he played a big part in Marina leaving. With Ra'naroz as his only travelling companion it was going to be a long ride. He did not want the Dark Knight to get a chance to mess with his mind. Even in his weakened state he knew he could still be very dangerous.

The next problem that Alaric faced was the lack of water. The key to keeping the Dark Knight's power in check was the evil brew he had been feeding him. Without water he didn't think that the herb would have the same potency. The two water pouches he had left would only last for two or three days. He would need to stop to refresh the pouches as often as possible. That would again slow their journey. He had to wonder why he brought Marina in the first place. It seemed his feelings were only bringing him more and more trouble.

"What does the prophecy say about this? Surely it would have given you an idea that this was coming?" Ra'naroz kept pushing the issue. If he could keep Alaric's mind distracted then there was greater chance for him to escape, not that it would happen for a while.

Alaric again chose to ignore the comment. Ra'naroz did not need to know that he had left the *Prophecy of the Stone* in Jarrat. He did not want to risk the prophecy being stolen again and he did not think it would be good to take it to Castalia. He had to admit that Ra'naroz had gotten to him. He did like the comfort of being able to consult the prophecy, even if it did not it gave him straight answers. He wished he could open the great tome and see what the future had in store for him. He had a bad feeling it was going to be his greatest challenge yet and he was at less than full strength. If only he knew what to expect then he would be able to prepare for it. At least he would have the two stones in reserve if he needed them, although he was still not sure if they would be a help or a hindrance.

"Should we get on the move? It will be morning before we know it." The comment was dripping with sarcasm.

Alaric felt like hitting the Dark Knight again, but he had to admit that he was right. The day was getting away from them and they needed to be on the move again. It was imperative they reach Castalia as soon as possible. There was no telling how long it would take for Alaric to find the Topaz stone, not to mention the fact that there was another Dark Knight in the mix.

It did not take long before Alaric realised he was wasting time in thought. There would be plenty of time for thinking whilst he was riding. The first thing he had to do was make sure Ra'naroz was secure on his stallions back. Alaric could not risk wasting time haing to pick the Dark Knight up off the ground.

Ra'naroz did nothing to help Alaric get him on his horse. Of course he did nothing to deter him either. He knew it would cause him more pain and gain nothing. It was in his best interest to make his way to Castalia. With Marina gone he would have more time on his own and that would be the best time for him to escape.

The first thing Alaric did once Ra'naroz was sitting on the saddle was to securely tie his legs to the stirrups. Although he would still be able to ride he could not do so at any great pace. He thought about leaving it at that. At least if he fell from his saddle his horse could still drag him along the ground. In the end he stuck with his original idea of lashing the Dark Knight's hands to the horse's reins. He tied them tightly so there was no chance Ra'naroz could escape. There was a chance he could steer his horse off the path, but Alaric was quite confident Adelanta could easily catch the stallion. He did not think Ra'naroz would be silly enough to try and escape in his current condition. All it would achieve in the end was another beating and Alaric was not so sure he would be able to control himself. He thought the Dark Knight would definitely taste the bite of his sword.

Once he was sure Ra'naroz was secure he mounted Adelanta and started towards Castalia. His first mission was to try and find a source of water. With a little luck he would be able to find one they could follow all the way to Castalia. He tried to remember back to his studies of the maps of the Seven Kingdoms, but he could not remember ever seeing anything. He knew there were rivers and streams nearby, but he could not think where they were.

Chapter 13: Castalia

It had taken them almost twelve days to reach the outskirts of Castalia. The ride should have taken them no more than seven, but the travelling had been slow. Alaric wasn't sure, but he thought Ra'naroz was deliberately riding slowly. It was in fact not the case. It was the stallion that could not keep up the pace. The Dark Knight would have been happy to ride the horse into the ground, but he did not think Alaric would be too happy if he did. He could have easily stolen another horse at one of the farms they had past once they had left the forest. He could not understand the filthy creatures' fondness for such animals. Give him a horsling and he could ride all day and all night. That was a beast that was worthy to carry one of the Chosen across the Seven Kingdoms.

They had found water on the first day, but that didn't really help much as the pouches were almost full. It was a good opportunity to water the horses, but that was about it. The small stream led towards Castalia, but only for a few leagues before it ended in a small lake. The hope that had filled Alaric quickly disappeared. He had thought his luck had changed, but it still seemed to be running in the same direction.

Although the trees gave them protection it also slowed the journey. They could not travel along the road in case someone was looking for them. Once they were out of the trees they were able to move more freely, but they were still out in the open. The hills gave them some protection, but it also made it easier for those above to see them. Alaric always felt as though there were a pair of eyes watching them as they rode.

The rolling grasslands also made it difficult for Alaric to catch food. The only animals, besides those of the farmers, were rabbits. They were harder to catch as they were well used to farmers trying to kill them. On one occasion Alaric had to sneak onto a farm and steal a sheep. He could not waste any more time searching for food. He felt bad he could not explain the situation to the farmer, but he was sure he would understand. Their mission was there to save everyone and it was one way that the farmer could contribute.

Alaric breathed a sigh of relief when they crested a hill just after noon and saw the massive city/kingdom of Castalia. He was in awe at the sight below him. He had heard of the magnificence of Castalia, but he still could not believe what he was seeing. The books had given it no justice at all. He took a moment to breathe in his surrounding. It also gave him a chance work out his next move. He knew he needed to gain entrance into the Grand Cathedral to see the High Chancellor, but he could not do that with Ra'naroz in tow. He would need to find somewhere to leave him. He needed to find someone he could trust and that was not going to be easy.

At least he was able to get a good view of the city from where he was. He tried to remember the history he had learnt of Castalia when he was a child.

Castalia stood on the edge of the Great Southern Desert. Originally the city had started from the edge of the desert, but as it grew larger and into a kingdom in its own right it made sense for it to expand.

The kingdom of Castalia was completely surrounded by the kingdom of Remidia. In the early days Castalia was the southernmost city of Remidia. It was founded by a religious zealot looking to bring the church to the south. He was a follower of the God King Topaz and felt that his wisdom needed to be spread to those of lesser minds. Little did he know there was no one for him to preach to, except for the small congregation he had brought with him. The Zealot was not dissuaded and figured if he built a great cathedral then people would come to him. He quickly got his followers working. He was lucky he had competent men who used to be engineers, carpenters and other tradesmen in the king's castle to have around.

The first cathedral took ten years to build. It had been mostly constructed of wood, which was the most readily available resource for building, and some stone which they had brought with them. The Zealot was pleased with what he had built, but did not live long enough to enjoy it. Only three years later he contracted a case of dysentery. The only water supply running to the small religious community was a dirty stream from the north. He was not the only one who had died from the disease.

On his death bed the Zealot spoke to a young man who he had preached to since he was a small boy. The Zealot had liked the boy and had treated him like a son. Since the boy's family had died on the journey south the Zealot had assumed the role of father. He spoke few words, but the ones that had lasted through the ages were pertinent. "Take my dream and make it your own." And that was exactly what the boy did. His name was Castal and there was no guessing who named the city.

With the scare of dysentery running through the congregation it was imperative for Castal to find a new source of water. With everyone paranoid to drink from the stream things did not look good for Castal. Since there was only desert to the south and no sign of water from the north, there was only one choice. Castal had everyone stop what they were doing to dig. Their only chance of survival was to find an underground source of water.

If the Zealot had concentrated more on survival and had not been so concerned with his cathedral then he might have lived a longer life. It only took them three days to find a good water source. Underneath where they had started to build their town was an extensive underground river system. There was more than enough water for what they needed. In fact there was enough water for substantial growth.

With his new found success there was no stopping Castal's enthusiasm. He had plans to make his small village into a great city. The only problem was that they were miles away from anyone. They needed an excuse to bring people to Castalia. It was an idea that Castal would have to come up with on his own. As far as the congregation were concerned they were still there on a religious experience.

It was pure luck that brought the solution to his problem. They had been living quite a mundane life for over a year when a small group of dwarves stumbled upon them. They had lost their way and were grateful to get water and food. Once they had found water they were able to cultivate the land and created a farming community. Even though they were on the edge of the desert the land was quite fertile.

It was around this time that Castal decided he needed a new cathedral. If he was going to make his mark on the world then he would need a new place of magnificence. The dwarves had spoken about the wonders of sandstone. There was nothing like it in the Seven Kingdoms, but they had studied it and rumours said that there had once been a magnificent palace made from it. Castal did not need to hear any more. He waited a day before he suggested a way the dwarves could repay the kindness Castalia had bestowed on them. Of course the dwarves were more than happy to help as they had nowhere else to go.

As if Castal's luck couldn't get any better it did. The dwarves began mining on the edge of the desert. After a few days they had found no sandstone, but had uncovered the mouth of a cave that had been buried under the sand many centuries before. Before they ventured into the cave they thought they should report to Castal. His initial report was to move on and continue to search for his sandstone. Once he had his cathedral built then he would worry about what was in the cave.

It did not take long for the dwarves to find the mineral deposit they were looking for. About half a mile into the desert from the cave they found what they were looking for. Since the dwarves were being fed and looked after they didn't mind working for Castal. They had gone unrewarded for searching for treasure for so long they were happy to have a purpose again. They could even stomach the sermons that came from Castal at dusk. If they wanted to they were allowed to keep working, which was a fair trade off. Although they did not openly worship Horinga, the God of Dwarves, they did so in private.

One night, not long after the sandstone cathedral had been built Castal woke in a cold sweat. He had a feeling something was calling out to him, as if on the edge of reality. Once he had woken he lit a torch and walked out into the night. The town was deathly silent. There was no sound and no wind to carry it on. He walked between the shanty houses seeing if anyone was in trouble. Before he knew what had happened he found himself in the mouth of the cave. He could not remember walking so far, but he knew he had to enter. The answers he was looking for were inside the cave.

He took one step into the cave and slipped on something slimy. He slid down along hard rock further into the darkness. The torch fell from his hand, but landed nearby, still lit. He shook his head and picked up the torch. He had no idea how far he had fallen or what he had slipped on. When he looked around he could see something glistening in the torch light. This new conundrum caught his full attention.

At first he thought he was still dazed from the fall, but as his eyes refocused he realised it was not the case. There was something in the rock walls that was sparkling. He didn't know what it was, but he knew it was of some importance. As he looked closer he thought it was just a simple clear rock and he turned to walk away. As he did he had a bad feeling that he was missing something very important. Castal was sure that Topaz himself was leading him and he would not be appeased until he found what it was. Taking another look at the stones in the wall he still could not see their importance. Sure, they looked pretty in the torch light, but they could not have any significant value. He turned to leave again and again he had a feeling he was missing something.

In the end Castal knew he was not going to get any peace until he took one of the stones back with him. If nothing else it would make a nice paper weight. He might even be able to convince one of his parishioners it was worth something

Removing one of the stones proved harder than he had originally thought. At first he thought they would come away easily, but once he tried he knew it would not be the case. It seemed as though the stones were fused to the rock wall. The only way he would be able to remove them was with the aid of the dwarven mining tools. He figured if they were all asleep they wouldn't mind if he borrowed a small pickaxe. When it was said and done he was doing the work of Topaz and no one could deny him that.

When he returned with the appropriate tool he started chipping away at the rock around the clear stone. It was nearly dawn when he finally wrested the stone from its resting place. As soon as he started he couldn't think of anything else. The stone was larger than he had imagined. It was about the size of a baby's fist. He tossed it gently in his left hand as he thought. He was sure there was a way he could trick someone into thinking it was valuable. There was something about the stone that mystified his mind and started to cloud his judgement.

Castal sat in the original cathedral and stared at the rock. At first he thought that it was worthless, but the longer he stared at it the more he thought it might be worth something. The more he held the stone the more he convinced himself it was valuable. His next problem was to find out what it was without everyone knowing where he found it. It was not that anyone would have rushed into the cave without his permission, but he was starting to become paranoid. His plans were starting to come to fruition and that worried him. He didn't know who he could trust.

Eventually curiosity got the better of him. He decided the person he could trust the most was the leader of the dwarves named Denoch. He did not know why, but he felt as if he had an affinity with the dwarf. In the end his decision was right. Denoch took one look at the stone and instantly knew what it was.

"Where did you find that?" he asked in astonishment.

Castal did not want to reveal that information straight away. He wanted to know what he had and by Denoch's reaction he knew he had something important.

"What is it? I have never seen anything like it before," he asked casually.

"It's a diamond!" Denoch didn't notice Castal shunning the question.

Castal looked at the stone in Denoch's hand with confusion. He had seen diamonds before, but they were always small cut jewels in rings or crowns of high nobles and royals. He was sure that Denoch must be mistaken. There was no way that rough stone in his hand could be a diamond.

"Surely it is something else. This could not possibly be a diamond." Castal didn't want to doubt the leader of the dwarves, but he could not believe what he had been told. "I have seen diamonds before. They are small beautiful stones, not rough and large like this one.

"There can be no doubt that this is a diamond, although I must admit that I have never seen one this large before. I can only imagine how much it is worth," Denoch explained.

They were the words that Castal wanted to hear. A broad smile crossed his face, but was soon followed by another confused look. He still could not work out why the diamond in Denoch's hand was so rough. He had never seen a diamond look in such bad condition.

"Why is this one so rough?" he asked.

Denoch had to laugh. It was obvious Castal knew nothing about gem stones. Castal didn't see the funny side, but he waited quietly for his answer.

"All gem stones look this rough when they are mined. It is a great skill to cut and polish them. The end result takes many hours of painstaking craftsmanship. That is why a cut diamond is so much more valuable than a rough diamond." Castal's face dropped slightly when he heard the news. "Don't get me wrong. This stone could keep you and yours very well off for the rest of your life."

The news brought the smile back to his face. Now he had to work out how he was going to get the stones cut. If there was money to be made then he wanted it. He was sure that Topaz had meant for him to find the stones. It was all part of his master plan.

His next problem was securing the cave. At it stood anyone could wander into the cave and find his diamonds. He needed to take Denoch into his confidence. He knew that dwarves were infatuated with gems.

"The cave that you unveiled the first day you were mining is filled with diamonds," he spoke quietly, not that there was anyone within earshot.

Denoch burst out laughing. Castal could not understand the dwarf's mirth. He did not think it was funny at all. Again he waited for Denoch to speak.

"There could not possibly be a cave full of diamonds. Diamonds are the rarest gem in the world. In my many years of mining I have never seen more than two in any one mine." Castal could already see the gold piling up. "I don't mean to laugh at you my friend, but I believe that you must have been hallucinating."

"I will take you to see, but I must warn you not to tell anyone. This will be our little secret and I will cut you in for a quarter of the profits." Castal seemed to think it was a good deal. As much as he didn't want to give away his prize he knew he needed an ally. He needed help and Denoch seemed trustworthy.

"Okay," Denoch chuckled as he spoke. "If there is a cave of diamonds I will help you." He still did not believe it was true.

"We shall wait till nightfall. We don't want anyone else to know what we are doing," Castal said, still paranoid.

"Very well." Denoch stood and shook Castal's hand before leaving. He was still chuckling on his way out.

Castal spent the rest of the day watching the mouth of the cave. He could not sleep even if he wanted to. When anyone asked what he was doing he simply said he was pondering the majesty of Topaz. Nobody questioned his reasoning. In truth he was making sure that Denoch did not try and sneak into the cave.

Once everyone had gone to bed Denoch and Castal snuck into the cave. Castal made sure they kept the torches unlit until they entered. He did not want to risk anyone seeing the lights and coming to investigate. Until he had the diamonds secured he did not want to risk anyone stealing them.

Denoch stared in awe as they reached the first diamond filled cavern. He could not believe what he was looking at. There were more diamonds than he thought existed in the world. When he came back to his senses he saw there were three tunnels leading off from the cavern. He could not dare to dream what wonders led down them.

"So do we have a deal?" Castal asked.

"I will do whatever you want." The thought of stealing from Castal didn't even cross his mind. Even a quarter share in the mine would give him enough wealth to last a hundred lifetimes.

"The first thing we need to do is find someone to cut the diamond," Castal explained.

"I know someone in Zenza City who can cut diamonds. I think it would be good to keep this out of the capital cities. A diamond this size will bound to get people talking," Denoch explained.

It did not take Castal long to come up with the solution. "Take the diamond to Zenza City. Once the stone has been cut then kill the jeweller. There will be no one to start any rumours. I am sure no one will question the smaller ones."

Denoch could not believe what he was hearing. Castal was a man of the church, but he had to admit it was a good idea. The sight of the diamonds was starting to have the same effect on him. If people knew about the mine then it would only be a matter of time before they tried to take it away from them.

"Then you will need to hire an army to protect us." Castal had thought about his plan.

Denoch was pleased with what he heard. Castal was a ruthless man and he was glad they were on the same side. He did not think it was worth crossing him. Things would be so much easier if he just played along.

Castal's plan went off without a hitch. No one questioned why Denoch had left, the dwarves continued building the cathedral and the congregation continued their meagre life. Castal was left to plan his next move. The wheels were in motion, but if he was going to survive he needed to stay ahead of the game. There was still much to be done.

It was not long after Denoch had left that Castal became more paranoid. It was not that he believed the dwarf would run away with his diamond, that would not make any sense, but he was afraid that someone would stumble into the cave and discover his secret. The cathedral project was only just off the ground, but there was more important work to be done. He needed a defendable wall built around the cave to stop people getting in. The only thing was that he couldn't tell them why.

He pondered on the idea for over a week. He spent all his time in meditation. Everyone was amazed with his dedication. Little did they know the real reason for his contemplation. In the end he came up with an idea he thought would be plausible. He decided it was not fair that Topaz was the only God King being worshipped. He decided Castalia, although it was still not known by that name, should be a place for all the God Kings to be worshipped.

He was surprised to get such a great response from his parishioners. If the madness of greed had not already started to set in he might have been upset with their willingness to pray to other gods. In his mind nothing else mattered, but the job at hand. He would make himself the richest ruler in the world.

Once everyone was happy with his plan he ordered the dwarves to stop building his cathedral and start building his wall. He made sure it encompassed the cave. Castal claimed the cave was a place of holy recognition and he told his followers that he had seen Topaz himself.

His plan was almost complete. Once the wall was finished then the cathedral would be completed and the other gods would have their respective halls of worship built. None would be as magnificent as the one to Topaz, but that would be expected.

It took many years for the wall to be built. Denoch had returned two years after he left with a small army and bundles of gold. By this stage the madness had taken hold of Castal. He believed himself to be the true prophet of the gods. He had moved away from the worship of Topaz and began preaching the word of all the God Kings. He had started calling himself the High Chancellor of the Gods. Denoch was not happy with this change of events, but he was still happy to go along with the plan.

It took over six years for the dwarves to finish building the wall. By the time it was complete Castal and Denoch had gathered all the people they needed for the next stage of their plan. They had decided there was no point in starting to mine the diamonds until the wall was finished. Their supply of gold was almost at an end and it was time for them to reap the rewards for their patience.

Once they started to mine the diamonds it did not take long for the rumours to spread throughout the other kingdoms. To hide the fact of the cave Denoch and Castal look a number of small diamonds and buried them in the sand where the other dwarves were still mining. It was Denoch's idea and as much as it pained Castal to give away his treasure he had to admit it made sense.

When the diamonds hit the marketplaces of the other kingdoms word spread even faster of the wonders of Castalia. Not only the rumours of wealth, but also the wondrous religious experience one could gain from the city. Rumours of miracles, pure lies made up by Castal and Denoch, also made it out of the city.

In ten years the city became the most populous of the entire world. Castal, who was now completely mad, declared Castalia to be a kingdom in its own right. He did not do this, however, before he had a second wall constructed around the rest of the city. This again pushed back the construction of his great cathedral.

King Brand II of Remidia did not like such a revolution, especially not from his wealthiest city. He had not even begun to collect taxes from Castalia and there was too much gold to be taxed for him to let it go. Unfortunately for King Brand a lot of his army had already been recruited by Castal. It was not only the Remidian soldiers he had recruited, but also those from the other kingdoms. With the added numbers of the residing dwarves the strength of his army added with the strength of the walls made it a futile exercise.

The war lasted for almost five years as King Brand tried to breach the city walls. No matter what he did there was nothing he could do. Once Brand had made his decision to declare war on Castalia, Castal had the dwarves reinforce the walls.

In the end Brand had to concede defeat. There were rumours there was a threat from Hondin Lel and with most of his army in the south his borders were wide open. What forces he had left in Remidel would not be enough to stave off an attack. He had no choice but allow Castalia its sovereignty. Castal sat on top of his unbuilt cathedral and cackled at the sky when the soldiers started to leave.

His victory in battle was due to master planning and foresight on Denoch's behalf. Castal could not see this. He thought it was the will of the gods that he remained in control of Castalia. At this stage it was Denoch who made all the decisions on Castal's behalf. He was doing a great job until Castal found out that Denoch was countermining his orders and creating his own. This did not go down well. Castal thought he was the divine messenger of the God Kings. He did not listen to a word his old friend and advisor told him. He simply ran Denoch through with his sword.

Castal then turned his full attention to the cathedral. It was only a few feet off the ground and he wanted it finished. He had spent too much time worrying about walls and mines that he had forgotten his main purpose in life. He was to build his cathedral in honour of the God Kings. He had completely forgotten that he had begun everything with worshipping just one.

Everyone knew what he had done to Denoch. Unfortunately a good proportion of the city believed that he truly spoke for the gods and they were enough to keep Castal in power and those who supported Denoch in check.

The other places of worship went up around the cathedral as it was being built. Castal didn't want the temples to be anywhere near as magnificent as the one they were building for him. He made them ship in iron from the southern Cloumid Mountain Range to mix with the sandstone. The iron turned the sandstone from a brilliant yellow to a brown-red colour. The temples were still respectful, but not anywhere near as grand.

In the beginning the temples were a place for the miners to stay. Castal would convince the devoted that it was their duty to work in the mines. He would make sure that all their meals were provided for them, but he would not let them leave the 'holy circle' as he called the inner city. In the end they were little better than slaves. He made sure the soldiers posted on the gate were loyal to him and no other. The only way he could do that was to make sure that they were well paid.

Towards the end of his life the religious aspect of the city was almost as profitable as the diamonds. Even in his maddened state he was still able to come up with an idea. He had the miners collapse the mouth of the cave and build a tunnel connecting to the basement of the cathedral. He charged a fee, which he called a donation to the gods, for those who wished to come to worship at the temples. It was not long before small groups made regular pilgrimages. All Castal needed was his cathedral to be finished and his life's work would be complete.

The cathedral was only half finished when Castal finally died. He lived to the age of one hundred and seven, but it was not enough to see his life's work complete. He died with no wife and no children to pass on his legacy. Like the Zealot before him he had grown close to a young boy. As the High Chancellor to the Gods he took the right to adopt the boy as his heir. He changed the boys name to Castal. His parents were more than happy, although they were all starting to see the madness in the Castal's eyes.

It took another two generations before the cathedral was finally finished. Like the three High Chancellors before him the current High

Chancellor had been adopted. None of the other High Chancellor's had taken a wife. The first High Chancellor to sit in the Grand Cathedral was the first to break that cycle. He had fallen in love at young age and married when he took the position.

Many years later the King of Remidia, whose name was lost to the ages, tried to regain Castalia to his kingdom. It was said that the king was slightly crazy and it would make sense. There was no good reason why he needed to attack Castalia. Not only was Castalia well renowned for being a religious kingdom it was also known for having the largest army and the strongest defences.

The battle lasted for almost a year and in the end the Remidian forces were completely annihilated, including the king himself. The fact the king had perished stopped Remidia from being completely destroyed. The Castalial forces could have easily marched into Remidia and taken over the land, but the High Chancellor at the time was a very pious man who took his role as the Gods' representative very seriously. He accepted the new king's apology and understood that the old king was insane.

In respect of the attack the High Chancellor decided it would be wise to build a third wall. The city had outgrown the second one that Castal had built. All the houses in the outer city had been destroyed by the Remidian forces as part of the senseless destruction by the king. Even as the last of the occupants were scrambling through the gates the king ordered the houses to be burned. Those that could not be burnt were destroyed by other means. The king also used the rubble to hurl at the walls, but to no avail.

As with all the other High Chancellors before him he eventually became insane himself. He was remembered throughout history of being the wisest and most merciful High Chancellor. Even in his insane years he still held the respect of the people of Castalia. He was well loved by all.

Over the years as the city expanded so did the outer wall. It was an ongoing project. When the city outgrew the last outer wall they started building a new one. At the same time they started to pull down the middle wall and reused the sandstone bricks. The only wall that remained untouched throughout the years was that around the Holy Circle.

Castalia was the largest single city with the largest army and the best defensive walls. Due to the sensitive nature of what lay hidden underneath the sand it was well justified. Diamonds were not the only resource that made Castalia wealthy. The sand was perfect for making glass. To the south of the Holy Circle great factories pumped out great clouds of smoke into the sky. The heat required to melt sand into glass was more intense than that made from a wood fire. A coal fire was required and luckily they had materials to trade with the dwarves from the north. The King of Remidia was much happier as he could tax the coal as it moved through his kingdom and the glass on the way out of Castalia.

No King of Remidia was happy with the expansion of Castalia. The growth of the city meant the decrease in Remidian land. If any other kingdom tried to expand into Remidia then it would be grounds for war, but that was not the case. They knew there was no point in starting a war with Castalia. No King of Remidia had even broken the outer wall and there was no point in even trying. Risking a war with Castalia, without help from at least one other kingdom, would be suicidal.

Now the city stood between Alaric and his goal. The sight from atop the small hill was awe inspiring and a little intimidating. He took a deep breath before he gently tugged on Adelanta's reins. The stallion slowly started down the hill towards the great city. He could feel his master's angst and trod carefully. He wanted to be aware if there was trouble ahead. Adelanta knew there was something important ahead of them.

Chapter 14: Into Castalia

"I do not think that it would be a good idea for us to ride straight into Castalia like this. I am sure people are going to start talking when they see me bound." Ra'naroz had been pleading his case ever since they started their approach to Castalia.

Alaric had simply chosen to ignore him. He had already thought about the dilemma. The last thing he wanted was to start rumours. He decided the best way to play it was to wrap Ra'naroz in a cloak and pretend that he was deathly ill. It was not uncommon for the ailing and infirmed to come to Castalia for the miracle of healing. Alaric didn't think there would be a problem in getting inside the city, but he didn't want Ra'naroz to know that he had a plan. Whilst he was complaining it kept his mind off other things.

The problem Alaric had was what to do once they were inside the city. He could not leave Ra'naroz by himself and he could not take him with him. He needed to find someone he could trust. He didn't know how it was going to happen, but he had faith. He didn't think the prophecy would lead him astray. All he could do was continue and believe that things would work out for the best.

As they approached a section of the wall that had not been completed, Alaric revealed his plan to Ra'naroz. The Dark Knight had to admit he was impressed with Alaric's guile. It did not make things any easier for his escape, but it would get him a step closer to his goal.

"Halt!" a gruff voice spoke as they approached the border of the city.

The sudden noise made Alaric jump in his saddle. He had not seen anyone around and had not expected the sudden noise. When he turned around he saw a soldier dressed in shining armour. On the breast plate was a large yellow sun. The sun was the crest of the Castalial regular soldiers.

"Where do you think you are going?" the soldier barked.

"My friend is sick. We are going to the Holy Circle to pray for his redemption." Alaric already had his speech prepared.

The guard laughed briefly before he spoke again. "I see this is your first time to Castalia. Where have you come from?"

Alaric was a little reassured by the soldier's mirth, but he was also a little concerned. He did not see what was so humorous. He had to be careful not to fall into a trap. He could see the soldier was setting him up for something and he would have to answer the questions very carefully.

"We are coming from Jarrat." Alaric kept his answer short.

"You are a long way off the road from Jarrat." The soldier sounded suspicious.

"We were attacked by bandits on the way and had to leave the road. They took most of our possessions, but we would not give them our lives," Alaric explained, a touch of fear in his voice to accentuate the point.

The soldier did not look convinced. The two men did not look as though they had been attacked in the past seven days and there was no reason why they should be off the main highway. He had a feeling that something was not as it seemed with the two men before him. He thought about detaining them, but on the other hand he did not get paid enough to worry about such affairs. The soldiers at the eastern gate could deal with them. That's what they got paid to do. He just got paid to make sure no one sneaks through the unfinished wall.

"The eastern gate is not far from here. You will have to enter that way. You need to report what happened with the bandits to the guards. They will see that the men involved will be brought to justice." He didn't want to waste any more time.

"Thank you." Alaric showed deference, he thought it was the best way to appease the soldier.

They moved on once the soldier had given them leave. Alaric was glad to be away from the man. There was something about the soldier that didn't sit right with him, but at least they were heading in the right direction.

To Alaric's surprise there was no queue to get into the city. He thought in troubled times that everyone would be flocking to Castalia to avoid salvation. It was the safest place to be in the Seven Kingdoms, but they were the only ones who were seeking entry. Alaric was not sure if this was a good sign or a bad sign.

"State your names and home town," the lieutenant barked when they reached the gate.

"I am Alaric from Arsiliac in Remidia," Alaric thought there was no point in lying about his own identity. He didn't think anyone in Castalia would recognise his name. "This is my cousin Nevil. He is from Jarrat in Entero. He has taken sick and no one can heal him. We are here to pray at the temple of Topaz." The lie was starting to take shape.

The soldier looked at Alaric and then at his companion. It had been a long time since someone had arrived from the east. He was not sure if he completely trusted their story. Not to mention the fact they had come via the wall and not the highway. Normally if someone came to him with such a story he would simply let them pass, but on that day he was not so sure. He thought it would be cautious of him to question them further. The High Chancellor had been in a strange mood recently and he didn't want to do anything to enrage him.

"That is not the way from Jarrat. You have cut through the countryside. It is not the safest way to travel. Why have you come this way?" he asked slowly, thinking of the question as he spoke.

"We were attacked by bandits on the highway. The only place for us to escape was into the forest. Once we were safe we didn't know how to get back. It was by pure luck that we managed to make it safely here," Alaric sounded almost exhausted as he recalled the events that never happened.

The soldier still wasn't sure if Alaric was telling the truth, although he was a little more convinced. He still couldn't shake the feeling that something was amiss. No one had come through the eastern gate in almost a month. There had to be a reason behind it.

"I would not have thought that bandits would be on the highway anymore. It has been over a month since anyone has come this way."

"I suppose that is why the bandits were so brutal when they attacked us. I was forced to kill two of them before we got away. They took everything we had that was not attached to me and my friend's horse. We were lucky to get away with our lives." Alaric hoped that he would get away with his excuse.

The soldier thought on it for a moment. Something still didn't seem right so he pulled aside his crimson cape to reveal the crest on his breastplate. There was a crescent moon with five small stars to make a full circle. The crest indicated he was part of the High Chancellor's holy guard. Even Alaric knew the holy guard only guarded the Holy Circle. The situation must be dire indeed for one of the holy guard to be posted on an outer gate.

"What is a lieutenant of the holy guard doing on post?" Alaric asked before the soldier had a chance to question him again.

"There are enemies all around us. We can ill afford to be remiss about our defence. With the outer wall incomplete we are at our most vulnerable." That was not to say that they weren't well protected. "Security around the city is as tight as it has ever been."

It did not sound good to Alaric. He needed to get access to the Grand Cathedral. He needed to gain some more information before he entered the city. The guise of Ra'naroz being his sick cousin would work perfectly.

"So how will that affect us getting into the Holy Circle?" he asked, the concern in his voice was genuine.

"That all depends." There was a smile of the lieutenant's face.

"Depends on what?"

"It depends on how fat your gold purse is," he laughed as if it was a wonderful joke.

That was going to be a concern. Although Marina had not taken all the gold coins, she had taken most of them. Alaric had a few coins hidden away and it would be enough to see them out for a week or two, but that was not including brides.

"How much will is cost to get into the Holy Circle?" Alaric asked. He did not want to pause too long or the soldier would realise he did not have much gold.

"Well the normal tax to enter the outer city is two silver marks. The inner city charge is one gold mark and to enter the Holy Circle for salvation is four gold marks. That is the normal charge. In these days I would think you could at least double that," the lieutenant explained.

Alaric had to assume he was speaking Castalial marks. The Castalial coins were the most valuable of all the kingdoms' coins and Alaric had none. Most of the gold and silver he had with him were Enteroite crowns. It took twelve Enteroite crowns to equal one Castalial mark. He did have two or three Remidian marks and a handful of Darshivallian crowns, but not many. He was not sure if he would even have enough gold and silver to get him into the Holy Circle. The copper coins that he had would not be worth anything inside the city walls.

There was nothing he could do. At least he would have to pay the lieutenant four silver marks, the equivalent of one gold half-mark. Alaric pulled out his smaller coin pouch from his pocket. He looked inside until he found six Enteroite gold crowns. He handed them across to the lieutenant. The soldier tossed the coins in his hand. No matter how many times he saw the Enteroite mark he could not believe how small and light they were.

"Very well. You may enter the outer city, but mark these words. Just because I let you through these gates it doesn't mean they will let you in at the next one. Times are tough and security is even tougher as you approach the Holy Circle," the lieutenant warned as he stepped aside and let the two of them enter the city.

The outer city was not as densely populated as Alaric had expected. The outer city contained the farms and farmland that supported the inner city and the Holy Circle. One thing that he did notice was that there were a lot of soldiers moving around. The lieutenant had been right. With all the soldiers it would make it much more difficult to gain entrance. It also increased their chances of getting caught. If the Dark Knight who resided in Castalia found out about Ra'naroz then he would be in great danger. It was then that he realised he didn't know the name of the Dark Knight he was about to face. Once they were away from prying eyes he would question Ra'naroz on his brother's name.

The soldiers didn't seem too worried with the strangers moving throughout the outer city. They were used to people who they did not recognise coming and going. It was their job to make sure no one got out of control. If someone was inside the city walls then they had to assume that they were meant to be there. If someone started trouble then they would be quickly marched out of the city and if they were not so lucky they would be spending at least one night in one of the many prisons.

The gate they needed to enter the inner city was not in a straight line. The first gate was due east where the second gate was north-east. It was a deliberate design to make it harder for invading armies. It increased the amount of time their soldiers needed to cross from one wall to another.

"I think we should stay in the outer city tonight," Ra'naroz spoke after another soldier moved out of hearing distance.

"And why would that be?" Alaric was always suspicious whenever Ra'naroz opened his mouth.

"The day is wearing on. I don't think we are going to achieve anything inside the inner city today. The prices at the inns and taverns will be much more expensive in the inner city than the outer. If nothing else we will be able to save some gold. Then we can make a fresh start in the morning." There was something matter-of-fact in his voice that made Alaric very nervous.

Regardless of what he thought of the Dark Knight he had to admit that his words made sense. Unless he was able to find someone friendly to his cause he would run out of gold very soon. That would be disastrous. If he did not have enough money to find somewhere for them to stay then he had little chance in keeping Ra'naroz prisoner. He needed somewhere out of the way to stash the Dark Knight whilst he tracked down the Topaz stone.

"Very well. I suppose you know somewhere for us to stay?" Alaric deliberately made his voice sound suspicious.

"As a matter of fact I do, but I don't think that you are going to listen to me anyway, so I will just let you decide." His words renewed Alaric's distrust in the Dark Knight. Ra'naroz was saying all the right words to ease Alaric's mind. All he achieved was to make Alaric even more suspicious.

Alaric was tempted to just ask Ra'naroz where they should stay. It would be easier that way, but he would not give the Dark Knight the satisfaction. He was sure he would be able to find them somewhere cheap and comfortable. Preferably he wanted something close to the north-eastern gate.

"Excuse me!" Alaric spoke as they approached a small group of soldiers on horseback.

The soldiers simply ignored him and kept riding. For some reason Alaric took offence to their rudeness. He turned his horse around and called out again. This time he put a more forceful tone in his voice.

"I wouldn't do that," Ra'naroz kept his voice low. He was not sure if Alaric heard him, but he was not going to draw any further attention to himself.

The soldiers kept going for a moment before they stopped. It took them a moment for them to realise what had happened. When they did they turned around and rode back to where Alaric was waiting. Three of the five soldiers had already drawn their swords. They did not look like they were interested in conversation.

"Who are you and what are you doing here?" the lead soldier asked.

Alaric noticed they wore the same crest with the crescent moon and stars. There was a difference though. Their armour was black, not steel grey. Suddenly Alaric wished that he had chosen a different group of soldiers to ask for directions, it would not be good start if he had to disarm five elite soldiers.

"I am sorry, but we have been travelling for a long time and we are just looking for somewhere to stay. My friend is ill and he needs somewhere to rest." Alaric tried to be as submissive as possible.

"That was not the question. Who are you and what are you doing here?"

Alaric was about to give his name, but then thought better of it. For some reason he did not like the five men in front of him. There was something not right about them. He only hoped that the Dark Knight would remain quiet. It would be a perfect opportunity for him to cause some mayhem.

"My name is Dyrk," he used the alias that Tancred and Richmond had given him when he was in Bellarome. "This is my cousin. He is sick and we are hoping for salvation in the Holy Circle," Alaric kept his head down as he spoke. He wished he could look them in the eyes and gauge a response, but he was afraid that they would see through his deference.

The soldier thought for a moment. He didn't worry about conferring with the other four men. He would make the decision on his own. Alaric assumed he was a general or some other high ranking officer. It took all of Alaric's will power to keep his head down.

"I see. Well I suppose I can let you off with a warning this time," there was something in his voice that told Alaric this was not over. "The next time you pass the High Chancellor's elite guard I suggest that you show the proper amount of respect."

"Of course, I am very sorry. I didn't mean to offend you." Alaric saw his opening and didn't want to waste it.

"Hmmm," the first the solider did not sound happy with the apology. "Very well then, move it along and be quick about."

As much as Alaric wanted to know where the nearest inn was he did not want to push his luck. He simply turned Adelanta around and moved in the direction they had been travelling. He was sure he would find someone soon enough to give them directions. He was just grateful they had not ended up in a prison cell.

"I think you were lucky to get out of that one," Ra'naroz commented casually, as if they were friends.

Alaric chose to ignore the comment. He found it easier to ignore the Dark Knight than to indulge in conversation. He didn't think any good could come from conversing with Ra'naroz. The Dark Knight would certainly have more to gain from it than he did.

It did not take them long before they found a small group of farmers on the road. They were leading a small herd of goats towards the city. Alaric rode up beside them and leaned over the side of Adelanta to speak.

"Excuse me, I do not mean to bother you, but can you tell where the closest inn to the north-eastern gate is please?" Alaric thought deference was a better approach from the start this time.

The farmers looked up at him and laughed. Alaric was not quite sure how to take the response, so he remained silent. The farmers did not stop moving their goats. The lack of assistance irritated Alaric even more, but he remained quiet. He kept Adelanta at the same pace as the farmers, which was to say not very fast. Eventually one of them had to speak.

"I don't think that you would want to stay at an inn in the outer city. I doubt they will be up to your standard, my lord," the farmer sneered at Alaric as he spoke.

The comment forced Alaric to have a look at himself. He did not think he looked that influential. He had been on the road for a long time and had not had a chance to change his clothes for a couple of days. It had been almost a week since he was able to bathe.

"Don't worry. There are not too many who travel these days. It's not like you look like you just walked out of a palace, but we can tell those of higher birth," the farmer explained when Alaric looked confused.

The comment almost made Alaric laugh. If only the farmer knew where he had come from and what he had been through to get this far. There was also something disturbing about his words. He could not see why the farmer would think he was noble born. He had spent time in the palaces and castles of the various kingdoms and those who didn't know him too well called him lord, but that was the extent of his nobility.

"I am not a noble," was all Alaric could reply.

The farmers all burst out laughing. Alaric did not think he had said anything funny. He was getting more annoyed by the minute. He tapped the hilt of his sword as he waited for the laughter to die down. Luckily his sword was on the opposite side of his horse to the farmers. The men would not have liked such an action and would have quickly found some guards.

"If you say so. There is a small inn this side of the north-eastern gate. It is called the Last Chance." At the sound of the name the farmers starting laughing again. "But don't forget that I warned you."

When the farmer finished speaking he directed the goats off the road towards a small farm house. Alaric pulled on the reins causing Adelanta to stop as he watched the small group lead their animals. He did not know what to make of their encounter. He had received the information he required, but he still did not feel right. There was something strange about the way the farmers treated him.

"Is there something the matter?" Ra'naroz asked when he noticed Alaric was no longer moving forward.

"Oh, nothing." Alaric was deep in thought and didn't really hear him. He forgot he was ignoring the Dark Knight. "Let's get moving. We want to be well and truly settled before nightfall." He was about to continue talking before he realised who he was speaking to.

Without an explanation for cutting his conversation short Alaric started Adelanta moving towards the wall. Although the farmer had been vague with the location of the Last Chance inn Alaric thought it would be easy enough to find. He soon realised that was not going to be the case. He wished he had asked for better directions, not that he thought they would have given them anyway.

The buildings close to the wall were a lot denser than those in the farming land. Alaric could not believe how quickly the landscape had changed. The rolling farmlands suddenly changed to a bustling town. He could only imagine what it was going to be like on the other side of the wall. The inner city would be much more populated.

"Do you know where this inn is?" Alaric finally asked when they approached the north-eastern gate.

"I am sorry, are you speaking to me?" Ra'naroz had an annoying habit of being sarcastic.

Alaric had to do something about the Dark Knight's attitude. He was getting a little too comfortable with the situation and that could only cause problems. The more Ra'naroz became familiar with Alaric the harder it was going to be for him to make the Dark Knight bend to his will.

"Answer the question or you will taste the back of my hand," Alaric spoke between clenched teeth as the street was becoming crowded and he didn't want anyone else to hear. He also wanted to prove his point.

"I do not know the Last Chance, but if you are looking for my advice I could easily suggest a place to stay." Ra'naroz pushed his luck.

"Then it is a good thing that I do not want your advice. We are staying at the Last Chance."

There were a number of soldiers guarding the north-eastern gate. Alaric thought they would be the best ones to ask for directions. He was about to approach before he remembered the conversation with the Elite guard. He did not want to risk upsetting the gate guards. He was sure someone else would be able to give him directions.

It was harder than he'd thought to get someone's attention from Adelanta's back. The streets were noisy and his voice was not carrying. He did not want to yell, that would draw too much attention to himself. It was the last thing that he wanted to do, especially since they were so close to the gate. He had a bad feeling if he upset the guards then he would not be able to enter the inner city come morning.

It was the first bad feeling he had since entering the new outer city. As soon as they had passed through the first gate into the outer city he could feel the prophecy tugging at him again. The only problem was he could not feel the direction. All he knew was that he had to keep moving towards the Grand Cathedral. Since he did not feel right trying to enter the inner city he was happy that he was doing the right thing. The further they moved away from the gate the better he felt. The fact Ra'naroz was not happy with his plan made him feel he was doing the right thing. He did not trust the Dark Knight and he didn't think he ever would.

Alaric tried to get someone's attention as they rode away from the gate, but no one was taking any notice of him. The crowded streets were noisy, but Alaric did not think that was the reason why no one answered him. All the residents walked with their heads lowered. They all wore dark robes with the hoods over their heads. The weather was not too hot and the sun was behind the clouds. The robes gave them protection from the sun, but were unnecessary at that time of day. At the peak of the day the sun could burn straight through someone's skin.

"I know somewhere we can stay tonight. It is starting to get dark and it will start to get very cold soon," Ra'naroz had a playful tone in his voice.

"I know it will get cold soon. I have been in desert before. I know about the extreme temperature changes." He didn't want to speak with Ra'naroz, but he was so frustrated he couldn't help himself. "I am sure we will find the inn before then."

If there was one thing Alaric knew it was that he could not listen to Ra'naroz. He had to find the Last Chance inn. He was sure he would be able to find someone to help him. There was an easier way to get someone's attention, but he did not want to risk causing a scene. He still had a bad feeling he would upset the guards if tried to be forceful, but time was running out. If he did not find the inn soon he would be forced to accost those still on the streets.

The pull from the prophecy was still as strong as ever, but it was not helping at all. It did not give him an indication of which direction he should be travelling in. Alaric wished if it was going to tell him what to do then it would be more specific. All he knew was that the inn was south of the gate.

Finally, just before the sun was about to set, and they were doing their third lap of the streets, Alaric had had enough. He was not going to find the inn on his own. He had resigned himself to that fact. The people on the street were starting to thin out and it was clear everyone was rushing to get indoors before the sun set. The thick robes would give some protection from the cold, but the thin garments they wore underneath would not be enough. Although the night was not going to get as cold as it had been in the wasteland it would still be very uncomfortable. During certain times of the year it had been known for people to die of exposure being out in the dead of night.

Without caring who he spoke to Alaric jumped down from Adelanta's back and stood in front of the first person he saw walking towards him. The man tried to move out of Alaric's way, but that was not going to deter him. Alaric stepped out to block the man from getting past.

"Excuse me, I need your help," Alaric said as he moved in unison with the man.

"I am sorry, but I don't think I can help you." The man kept his head low.

Alaric thought it was a strange response. Something was not quite right with the situation. For a city which made so much coin from foreigners the people seemed to be very rude. He could not understand it. He needed to find out what the problem was.

"Why will you not speak with me?" Alaric asked, a little more forcefully than he had intended.

"Please let me go," there was fear in the man's voice.

"Tell me where the Last Chance inn is?" Alaric didn't think it was worth pushing him further for answers, but he needed to find the inn.

"It is not far away from here. Follow this street through three crossroads and then turn right. It can be no more than one hundred paces on your left," the man spoke quickly and quietly. He didn't want anyone to know they were speaking. It was something that disturbed Alaric even more.

"Thank you," Alaric thanked the man before stepping out of his way.

The man was quick to move on once his path was free. He looked around nervously to see if anyone was watching him. It was a hard task. Everyone was still wearing their thick robes with the hoods drawn. If someone had seen them talking there was little chance he would know until it was too late.

"Well that worked out well," Ra'naroz spoke when Alaric was back on Adelanta.

Alaric wanted to ignore the comment, but he really wanted to discuss what had happened. He wished that Marina had not left him. It would have been good to speak to her about his dilemma, but Ra'naroz was the only one he had. The Dark Knight was better than nothing, at least he hoped so. Revealing too much could work against him, but he thought that Ra'naroz would have noticed the man's strange behaviour.

"Something very strange is happening. It is as if no one here wants to be seen with us. Do you think that is the case?" he resisted the urge to cringe as he asked for Ra'naroz's opinion.

The Dark Knight thought for a moment. He wanted to make a show of it, but with the hood drawn there was no point. He was surprised by the question and he was not ready to answer it. He knew if he took too long that Alaric would become suspicious. If he was quick enough then he could gain Alaric's confidence and that was the most important thing.

"I do think there is something strange." The more he thought about it the more he thought that his brother, Za'aroz, had something to do with it, but he didn't want Alaric to know that. Until he was able to reason things out for himself he did not want to give Alaric any unnecessary information. "I am sure it is just due to these troubled times. If you have not noticed already there are not many travellers in this part of Castalia. I am sure there is something in that." Without giving too much away Ra'naroz was sure that he had appeased Alaric.

Alaric had to admit that the Dark Knight was making sense. He could not find any deceit in his comment. He shook the feeling off. One thing he could not do was trust Ra'naroz, but he had a nagging feeling that he was being honest with him and he did not like it.

Before he knew it they were at the inn. He had been so engrossed in his dilemma with Ra'naroz that he had not even noticed the intersection they must have turned down. It was lucky that Adelanta knew the way. He continued on his own when he realised that Alaric was lost in thought. He stopped when he recognised the smell of hay from the inn's stables.

"I think we need to be careful in here. If they do not like outsiders then I doubt we will get a warm greeting," Ra'naroz warned.

Ra'naroz was right and Alaric knew it. He had a problem though. How was he going to keep the Dark Knight securely tied whilst he gathered information? He needed to spend time speaking with the occupants of the inn before he entered the inner city. He did not think that leaving Ra'naroz tied in their room was the best of ideas. The only option he had was to untie the Dark Knight and take him with him. That was not an option that he liked, but there was nothing else he could do. He wished he had someone with him he could trust. He could have struck Ra'naroz as he thought about what he had done. If it wasn't for his treachery then Marina would still be with them, although he was not sure if she was the best person to place his trust. In the end he might have done him a big favour. Again he had to wipe that thought from his mind. If he actually started to believe Ra'naroz then he would be in trouble.

There was no time for Alaric to worry about the past. He had to concentrate on the job at hand.

He wished he had brought the prophecy with him. He was sure there would be a passage that would tell him what to do.

"Shall we go in?" Ra'naroz asked when they were still standing out the front. "I think people will become suspicious if they see us loitering out the front."

Again Ra'naroz was right, but that did not make his decision any easier. Alaric wished he had more time, but he didn't. He had to make a rash decision and hope it was the right one. He took a deep breath before he replied.

"Okay, let's go see what this inn has to offer us," Alaric's voice was flat. There could be no doubt he did not like what he was about to do.

Chapter 15: Last Chance

The inn was not at all what Alaric was expecting. He thought since the outer city was mainly farmland the inn would be very rural. It was in fact the opposite. It was an inn he would have expected to find just outside the palace walls of a major city. It was clean and presentable. Alaric was more than happy with its appearance. He thought if the inn looked nice then its patrons would be the same. Unfortunately he was wrong.

The instant that Alaric and Ra'naroz walked into the inn all eyes turned on them. Instantly Alaric felt uncomfortable. He felt as though they were not wanted. He could feel the hate radiating from the patrons eyes and as he looked around the room he could not see a single foreigner.

Although the citizens wore heavy robes during the day their skin was darker than those from other kingdoms. It just proved how much power the sun had so close to the desert. The sight was a little daunting to Alaric. He had seen Castalials before, but never in such large numbers. He wished he had remembered some of the names of the merchants he had dealt with in his previous life. A friendly face would be nice to see.

At first Alaric had planned on asking his questions in the inn's common room, but he quickly changed his mind. He thought it would be pertinent to get a room and stay there. There would be time for him to question the innkeeper in the morning. At least that way it would limit the amount of time Ra'naroz was out in public.

Unlike the rest of the inn the innkeeper was happy to see Alaric and Ra'naroz. With the state of the city there was not a lot of business passing through. Most travellers preferred to stay inside the inner city wall. Business was not good at the Last Chance.

Alaric pressed his luck and arranged for some food to be brought to their room. The innkeeper was more than happy to comply. He understood completely how they felt. The tension was thick in the room and it would not leave until the two visitors had left. The innkeeper was quite happy for them to eat in their rooms. It was better than risking a brawl.

Alaric kept Ra'naroz tied up for the night. The innkeeper had given them a room with two beds. Alaric had thought about ordering a single bedded room and make Ra'naroz sleep on the floor but decided it would be too suspicious. If he was going to keep up the ruse that Ra'naroz was a sick cousin then he had to look after the Dark Knight, but if he did anything to upset him then there would be consequences.

Ra'naroz was surprised to be given a bed to sleep on. Even with the bed in the room he would have expected Alaric to make him sleep on the floor. He knew he was starting to have an effect on Alaric. If he could get the man to trust him then it would be easier to manipulate him. That would be the best way to facilitate his escape.

It was a restless night's sleep for Alaric. Although the innkeeper had been amicable it didn't mean the other patrons felt the same. There was a risk they could be in danger in the middle of the night. Alaric slept lightly and woke when ever he heard something stir outside.

In the end Alaric decided there was no point in trying to sleep. Ever since he had been cut of from the source of magic he had needed more sleep and a lack of it was something that he did not need. He could not risk someone trying to enter the room. An attack would give Ra'naroz a chance to escape, or worse someone might kill him.

Eventually the night passed without incident. Ra'naroz woke as the sun was starting to rise. He had slept throughout the night. Even bound like he was he was happy to be sleeping in a bed. It was a luxury he had grown used to in his time in Jarrat, although the inn's bed was nothing like that of Queen Oriana. He failed notice that Alaric had been awake for most of the night.

Alaric tried to look as fresh as possible. He could not let the Dark Knight know he was tired. He could not show any strain. That would only strengthen the Dark Knight's resolve. That was something that he could ill afford to do. He had a long day in front of him and he could not lose his focus. He needed all the strength he could muster.

"What is the plan for today?" Ra'naroz asked as Alaric changed his clothes.

Alaric had been wearing the same clothes for the last week. Although he would wear his heavy robe once he was on the street he thought it was appropriate to have fresh clothes underneath. He did not want to look and smell like a street urchin. He did not think the guards would let him past the gates if that was the case.

"You will keep quiet why I try and gather information. If you speak out of line then you will suffer the consequences." The comment was overly harsh, but Alaric didn't care. He was not in the mood to deal with Ra'naroz.

Ra'naroz felt like objecting, but he thought better of it. Something had changed overnight and Ra'naroz didn't know what it was. He would have to watch carefully to see what had happened. Until he knew he decided to take Alaric's suggestion and keep his mouth shut.

To the relief of Alaric the common room was empty. He did not think he could handle the hatred he had felt the night before. He was tempted to go back to the room and sleep, but he had a job to do. He needed information from the innkeeper and it seemed to be his best opportunity. He did not think the innkeeper would be so forthright with everyone else in the inn.

"Good morning, Sirs, I hope that everything was too your liking," the innkeeper greeted them.

Alaric wanted nothing more then to tell him about the terrible night he had had, but that would prove nothing. He had to hold back his irritable attitude and act pleasant. It was the only way he was going to achieve his goal.

"It was lovely, thank you. I have not slept so well in a long time," he couldn't help but lie.

"Will you be staying for another night?" the innkeeper was hopeful, but the fact that Alaric held their packs was not a good sign.

"Unfortunately not, my cousin is sick and we need to make our way to the Holy Circle," Alaric explained.

"That is disappointing, but if there is anything I can do for you whilst you are still here all you have to do is ask." The innkeeper was hoping to make some more gold before they left.

"I could use some information." Alaric recognised the look on the innkeepers face. "Will you be able to help us over breakfast?" he was not going to get what he wanted without spending more money. He could simply bribe the innkeeper, but he thought he may as well get something for his gold.

The innkeeper was happy with Alaric's suggestion. There was no one else in the inn and it was best way for him to make some coin. His wife was in the kitchen ready to cook, like she was every morning. It had been over a week since anyone had ordered breakfast. He moved into the kitchen with a renewed spring in his step.

"I think you might have overlooked something," Ra'naroz spoke when they were alone. "It is going to be hard from me to eat with my hands bound."

Ra'naroz was right, but there was no chance of Alaric untying him. Alaric had thought about untying the bonds around the Dark Knight's arms, but decided it would be better to keep him in his robe. If he was trying to claim Ra'naroz was sick then it would make sense and would prove to solve two problems. He knew he would have to untie him eventually, but that was a problem for another time.

He thought for a moment before he replied. "I will tell the innkeeper you are too sick to eat this morning. All you have to do is keep your mouth shut, like I told you to."

As much as Alaric wanted to strike the Dark Knight he also wanted to keep up his pleasant ruse and he kept his hands down.

It did not take long for the innkeeper to return. He brought with him three steaming mugs of tea. It was at that point that Alaric realised he had not given Ra'naroz his medicine. As the thought entered his mind his heart started to race. He did not think it would be long before the power started to return to the Dark Knight.

"I thank you, but my friend cannot drink tea. If I could get a mug of hot water I will be able to give him his medicine?" Alaric sounded apologetic. "Also he is not eating this morning. He is not feeling well at all."

The innkeeper looked disappointed with Alaric's comments. He placed the mugs on the table, but did not leave straight away. It was obvious he wanted to say something, but could not find the words. It took Alaric a moment to realise why he was waiting.

"If you have already started preparing the food then of course I will pay for the inconvenience," Alaric hoped he had guessed right.

The innkeeper looked relieved when Alaric had spoken. "Yes, my lord, I will inform the cook." He thought that cook sounded better than wife. If she had heard his words then he would have received a box around the ears.

Alaric seemed happy with the result, although he had to find a way for Ra'naroz to drink. He thought that it would be too suspicious if the innkeeper saw him feeding the Dark Knight and he still could not untie him. He had to work out a way to get the innkeeper to leave the room. It was the only way he could administer the elixir, but first he needed to gather the information he required.

When the innkeeper returned Alaric poured in the evil herb and mixed it with the hot water. When he was done he placed the mug in front of Ra'naroz, who in turn did nothing. The Dark Knight was unsure what he was supposed to do. All the while the innkeeper watched with anticipation.

"He will need to wait for the water to cool. His stomach is sensitive to the heat," Alaric explained and everyone understood.

It wasn't until the food arrived that Alaric asked his first question. He thought the innkeeper would be more amicable when there food was on the table. With the innkeeper eating with them Alaric hoped he would be distracted enough not to really listen to the questions. He wanted answers that the innkeeper would not be able to recall to others.

"It seems as though we are not welcome here?" He thought that would be the most appropriate way to start.

"Of course you are welcome in my inn. I only wished you could stay longer." It seemed as though the plan had worked well. The innkeeper was not about to answer the real question.

"Thank you, but I mean in Castalia," Alaric replied slowly.

"Now that is a tricky question. In the outer city we do not get direct information from the Grand Cathedral. Most of what we hear are rumours and innuendo." The innkeeper looked around to see if anyone had entered the inn. He continued when he was sure no one was listening. "What I have heard is that the High Chancellor is not himself. For the last month or so he has been making wild new laws. One of them was to ban all foreigners from the Holy Circle. I find it very hard to believe since it is mainly foreigners who enter the Holy Circle." Alaric did not like what he was hearing. It sounded as though his job just got a lot harder. "He has decreed that all foreigners cannot be trusted. Although they are allowed into the inner city that is as far as it goes. There is speculation he is planning on having foreigners banned altogether, but I can't see that happening."

Alaric could feel the hand of the Dark Knight in this. There was something extremely off about the situation. If the High Chancellor was in his right mind then there would be no chance of him making such a law.

"I suppose he is concerned about the happenings in the other kingdoms. We have heard the Evil One has broken out of his prison. His spies are everywhere. If we let even one into the Holy Circle then there is no telling what might happen," there was genuine concern in the innkeeper's voice.

If only the innkeeper knew the truth. The enemy was already inside the walls of the Holy Circle and it seemed as though they were taking control. Alaric wished he could go to a kingdom and not have it under control of a Dark Knight. At least his home kingdom was free. That was something.

"That doesn't sound good," the innkeeper had paused and Alaric felt that he needed to say something. "Is that why your patrons were so hostile towards us last night?"

"Ah, no, not exactly," the innkeeper sound somewhat abashed. "That, I am afraid, is the usual clientele of the Last Chance. Since the travellers have stopped coming here I have had to open my doors to the less savoury characters of the outer city. They do not like outsiders."

"When I was speaking to someone trying to find this inn they were almost afraid to speak with us," Alaric pushed a little further.

"That, I cannot explain. As I said the High Chancellor has made some crazy laws, but there is nothing that should have that effect." Alaric watched the innkeeper closely to see if he was holding anything back. He could not see anything.

"So do you think there is any chance we can get into the Holy Circle?" Alaric asked, changing the subject before the innkeeper had a chance to think.

"It's hard to say. Some rumours say yes and some say no," the innkeeper spoke around a mouthful of food. "I personally believe you will get in, but it might cost you a lot of gold."

That was something, although gold was going to be an issue. Once he was inside the Holy Circle it didn't really matter. Getting into it was only one of a number of trials they faced. The hardest test would be gaining entrance into the Grand Cathedral.

It seemed as though he was not going to gain all the information he required from the innkeeper. He thought the innkeeper would have been of more use. The next question he had should have been an easier one for him to answer.

"Do you know of somewhere we could stay once we get inside the inner city?" It was a tough question to ask an innkeeper who was obviously struggling for work.

"I am afraid I can't help you there. I don't go into the inner city much anymore. You could always come back here." Even as the words came out of his mouth the innkeeper knew what the answer would be.

"Thank you, but I do not think it would be a good idea passing in and out of the gate. I really need to find somewhere closer to the Holy Circle." Alaric did not want to upset the man.

"Of course. Well now that you have finished your breakfast you should be on your way." The innkeeper stood.

"Yes, thank you. I will just wait for the water to cool sufficiently." Alaric looked at the water in an attempt to ignore any more conversation.

The innkeeper cleared the table when it was obvious Alaric did not wish to speak further. He found Alaric's attitude to be strange and he wondered if he had upset him. He wanted to apologise, but he thought that would only upset him more.

Alaric saw the reaction out of the corner of his eye. He felt bad, but he needed the innkeeper to leave the room. He had to force feed the Dark Knight and then be on his way. He could feel the prophecy tugging at him and he had to get moving. He had felt it ever since he sat down for breakfast. The more he tried to ignore it the worse it got. He knew that it was time to go. With any luck the prophecy would lead him in the right direction.

When the innkeeper left the room Alaric did not waste anytime in pouring the foul liquid down the Dark Knight's throat. It came as such a shock that Ra'naroz started to choke. The sound brought the innkeeper from the kitchen.

"Is everything alright?" he asked.

"Yes, my cousin will be alright. He will not die yet, we have come too far." It was easy for Alaric to cover. "Now we must be going."

Suddenly Alaric had a bad feeling. He could feel the blood racing through his head as the prophecy screamed at him. He did not know what it meant, but he knew he was in for trouble. At first he thought it was Ra'naroz, but the Dark Knight remained calmly seated. It was something else and sitting in the inn was not going to bring it a head.

Alaric said a quick goodbye to the innkeeper. The feeling inside him was causing a slight twitch in his left eye. He hoped the innkeeper did not notice it. Although his visit would be memorable, purely because they were his first customers for a long time, he didn't want the innkeeper telling anyone.

It wasn't until they walked out of the inn that Alaric realised what the bad feeling was. He knew instantly he should have left when he felt the prophecy's tug. Now he had a completely new conundrum to deal with.

Outside the inn was what Alaric could only call a lynch mob. As soon as he stepped outside the pull of the prophecy and the bad feeling disappeared. He knew the men knew who he was, even with the hood of his robe pulled close. There was no point in trying to pretend he was anyone else. They made no move towards him, which was a fair indication they wanted to speak before they started any trouble. It was a good sign, if only a thin one. At least he would have a chance to talk his way out. He only wished he had gotten a good night's sleep. He was both physically and mentally tired. Neither were promising for the trials he had before him.

"What can I do to help you?" Alaric asked.

There was laughter from the mob. For some reason they felt that Alaric's words were funny. The lead mobster waited for the laughter to die down before he stepped forward. He was quite prepared for a discussion with Alaric, although it would be a one way conversation.

"You are not welcome in Castalia," the man's voice was hoarse. It was obvious he had been up most of the night drinking.

"Then let us be on our way," Alaric kept his voice calm. He wanted to walk away to accentuate his point, but he did not think that it was a good idea.

"I don't think so. I know you are heading towards the Grand Cathedral. I don't believe the High Chancellor wants to see any foreigners. We are here to see you outside of the outer wall."

"I can't allow you to do that. My cousin is sick and he needs help," Alaric explained, knowing full well that it would not work.

"We shall see about that," the man did not sound sympathetic.

Alaric gripped the hilt of his sword before looking closer at the group. He could see the grooves of swords underneath five of the seven men's robes. He couldn't see signs of a weapon on the other two men, but he knew they were there. He couldn't make out faces from under their robes, but he thought the men were in the inn the previous night. He could feel the hostility radiating from them.

Normally Alaric would have no problems in taking on the seven men in front of him, but in his weakened state he was not so sure. The fatigue from lack of sleep was starting to make him question his own abilities. Either way he had to be careful. Getting killed was not going to solve anything.

Standing out in the street was starting to draw the attention of passer-bys. That was not helping anyone. Although the mob felt as though they were in the right they did not want attention from the guards. It was a contradiction that they didn't see. They believed they were doing the work of the High Chancellor and that was all that mattered.

"Move inside the inn. This is not something we need to do in the street," the man spoke quietly.

Alaric didn't want to move, but he had to agree. He didn't think the guards would take too kindly to him if they were found. Even though they would be the ones being attacked he didn't think the guards would care, they were foreigners after all. Things just got even more difficult for Alaric.

"Okay, let's just relax," Alaric held up his hands as he spoke.

Alaric backed his way to the inn's door. He fumbled with the door knob until he opened it. He did not want to turn his back on the mob. Although he did not believe that they wanted to kill him he was not going to take that risk. He thought that paranoia was better than death.

"Come on, cousin, let's see what these men want." Alaric waited for Ra'naroz to enter the inn before following.

"What is it I can help you with?" there was a promising tone in the innkeepers voice.

It did not take him long to realise why they had returned. It was not going to be a profitable experience. He only hoped they were not going to break his property. He had seen the mob in action earlier in the week and things had gotten out of control. The man, a traveller from Hondin Lel seeking spiritual guidance and did not want to leave. The mob did not take kindly to his failure to comply. After severely beating the man they hung him outside the city walls. The body was left there for two days before the guards finally cut him down. The guards had seen the man kicking and struggling for life, but did nothing to help. They thought it would deter foreigners from starting trouble. With the body being visible for so long the stories would soon be spread throughout the city.

"Now I cannot leave before we enter the Holy Circle," Alaric started to speak when the mob entered the inn.

He was about to continue with his explanation when he was interrupted. The innkeeper was trying to disappear through the kitchen door. He had a bad feeling that things were going to get messy.

"Where do you think you are going?" the man spoke in a commanding voice.

"Ah, nowhere," he said, his voice extremely nervous. "I just thought that you might like something to eat."

"I don't think so. Come over here and take a seat. You can watch what goes on," the man spoke again. "If you are going to house foreigners then you need to see the repercussions."

"You have no idea what you are doing," Alaric continued when the man's attention was returned to him.

"I know exactly what I am doing. The High Chancellor has made an edict and we are following that." The man pulled his hood back so Alaric could see his face.

"This is not what the High Chancellor wants, Japheth. You cannot honestly believe what the gossips are saying. There is no way he would command such a thing," the innkeeper spoke from the safety of the other side of the room.

"This is not any of your concern, Tovah. You do not leave your inn. How would you know what is happening in the city," Japheth barked back.

"Please, do not involve yourself in this matter. I can take care of myself," Alaric warned Tovah to remain quiet.

"And just how do you propose to do that," Japheth signalled to the rest of the mob.

This was the moment they had been waiting for. As one the rest of the mob removed their robes. Four of them wore swords whilst the other three had crude looking clubs. The situation just got better, if only slightly. Alaric didn't think there would too many problems taking out the three men with the clubs. He didn't want to kill anyone, but he didn't think he was going to have a choice. He had seen that crazy look in a man's eyes before and he could see it in all seven. He didn't think he was going to be able to talk them down, but he would have to give it shot.

"Untie me and I can help you defeat these men." Ra'naroz made sure Alaric was the only one who heard.

"Not a chance. At least if things turn bad you will be killed too." Alaric also kept his voice low.

"What was that you said?" Japheth asked, more confused than angry.

Alaric didn't respond. He pretended like the leader of the mob was speaking to someone else. He didn't have an excuse and he couldn't be bothered coming up with one. All his attention had to remain on more important matters. At all costs he wanted to leave without a fight.

"Now, I think things have gone a little too far." Japheth, although he was displeased with Alaric's silence, wanted to move on. "I have given you an opportunity to leave on your own. I see the message I left for you foreigners didn't get through. Maybe I need to leave another one."

Alaric didn't like the sound of Japheth's words. He had an idea what the mob had done and it did not sound pleasant. It seemed as though someone had sent a message to all those who wanted to be like Japheth. The Dark Knight was twisting the mind of the High Chancellor and in turn controlling the men in front of him. Although they were not openly evil, they were supporting the rules of the Evil One. It was a stretch, but it was enough to give Alaric the justification he needed.

"I will give you one last warning." Alaric decided there was no point in trying to talk them down. Aggression was the best chance he had to get the mob to back down, although he was not holding his breath for a victory. "We have to get into the Holy Circle and there is nothing that is going to stop us. Now I don't want to make an example of you, but I will if I have to. I am sure it will be a deterrent to anyone else who wants to follow in your footsteps," Alaric sounded confident.

Japheth was suddenly not so sure of himself. He had not expected such a response. He had thought the man would be grovelling for his life. He had to be very careful if he wanted to stay alive. He still thought he held the upper hand with seven against one strong and one sick man. He had no idea if they would all survive. If someone was going to die he did not want it to be him.

"We are only doing what the High Chancellor has commanded. He is the great prophet of the God Kings. He is the divine communicator." Alaric yawned as Japheth reeled out the names of the High Chancellor. "I do not think you should treat his edict so cavalier. You will burn in the pit of the Evil One if you do not listen to his teachings."

Alaric almost laughed when he heard Japheth's words. The man was starting to babble. He might be a zealot, but Alaric could see he wasn't insane. As he looked at the other six men he was not so sure about them. This made Japheth even more dangerous. Alaric could have understood him blindly following the High Chancellor's words if he was somewhat crazy, but doing so in his state of mind was unforgivable.

"Enough of your zealous propaganda. I do not care to listen to your ramblings," Alaric interrupted Japheth as he was in mid-speech. "It seems to me we are at an impasse. I will not leave and you will not relent."

"Then it seems as though you will hang from the city walls by nightfall," Japheth smiled an evil smile.

Alaric believed there was something more to Japheth than met the eye. Whilst he spouted wild doctrine the other men would follow him blindly, but there was something more in Japheth's eyes than his words suggested. He knew more than his ramblings let on. There was something very dangerous about the man. Alaric was sure he could not leave such an enemy alive.

"Now, I don't know if that is what the High Chancellor had in mind," one of the other mobsters spoke. He had a slur to his voice that made him seem a little slow.

"You don't know what the High Chancellor has said. I have met with him..." Jaspeth trailed off, as if he was divulging too much information for those in the room.

"You have not met with the High Chancellor," Tovah stood as he spoke. "I have known you for a long time, Japheth, and you have never spoken with the High Chancellor. Now I think it is time for you to leave before you make a bigger fool of yourself."

The words cut into Japheth like a knife and he took two commanding steps towards the innkeeper. Alaric was not going to let Tovah get in harm's way, not on his behalf and quickly drew his sword and levelled it at Japheth. Although he was not within striking distance he had made his point. Japheth didn't think that he could make the distance across the room to Tovah without Alaric skewering him. For the moment the innkeeper would have to wait, but soon enough he would feel Japheth's wraith and the point of his sword.

"Very well. I don't think there is anything to discuss," Japheth took a step backwards as he spoke. He wanted to make sure the other men in his lynch mob attacked first.

"No, indeed there is not." Alaric took a more aggressive stance.

He needed to make sure he didn't let anything happen to Ra'naroz or Tovah. He felt some sort of responsibility towards the innkeeper. The man had looked after him when he did not have to. Regardless of Tovah's motives for assisting him he felt like he had to protect him.

"In the name of the High Chancellor, kill this heathen," Japheth motioned for the others to fight.

As Alaric had expected the six men were not skilled in the art of combat. They all came at Alaric at once. Ra'naroz had retreated towards the back of the common room during the discussion. He did not risk leaving the room as it would draw unnecessary attention to himself. It was the perfect opportunity to escape. The only problem he had was the innkeeper. The man was standing next to him blocking his exit. He also didn't think it would be a wise decision to leave especially as he was still bound. The citizens didn't like foreigners at the best of times, but one that had his hands tied would look too suspicious.

Alaric deftly defended the attacks. The six men had no hope of fighting as a unit. Alaric was surprised they had not killed at least one of their own in their attempt to kill him. They waved their swords and clubs wildly in front of themselves in an attempt to look dangerous. There was little chance that Alaric was ever going to get struck. Japheth remained on the opposite side of the inn. He did not want to be in the firing line. He had a very bad feeling it was not going to be as easy to beat the two men as he first thought. If things turned bad then he wanted somewhere to escape to.

At least the High Chancellor would reward him for the news of the strangers. There was something different about them. He had felt it when he first saw them, but had taken no notice. Now, as he watched the fighting, he wished he had brought the information to the High Chancellor first. He had made a mistake by acting independently.

It was not long before Alaric had disarmed one of the fighters. It really wasn't all that difficult. One of the men had lost his grip on his sword, due to his wild swinging of it. Alaric simply tapped the sword out of his hand. When the man realised what had happened he dropped to his knees. He knew there was no chance of recovering and he didn't want to die. One of the other men kicked him out of the way. He thought about taking up his sword again, but he thought better of it. He realised he had no chance of defeating Alaric. He had been given a reprieve and he was not going to waste it.

The other five men kept attacking. There was still a crazed look in their eyes. There was a chance Alaric was going to be able to disarm them all and defeat them without killing them. That would be a better option. Besides Japheth he did not think any of them were evil.

The rest of the battle didn't go to plan. He tried his best not to kill anyone, but that was not as easy as it sounded. The first death wasn't really his fault. He had deflected a weak attack by one of the swordsman and he knocked the sword in the way of a club attack. The sword bounced off the club and slashed the throat of one of the other men. It did not kill him instantly, but the wound was fatal. He dropped to his knees and made a gurgling sound as the blood sprayed from his throat.

The death of their companion made the other mobsters wary. They could see the death that awaited them and they were not quite as passionate with their attacks. They watched Alaric a little closer, not that they knew what they were watching. They had no formal training with their weapons and they were no match for Alaric.

The next victim was just a matter of Alaric's training. He had tried to avoid killing anyone, but that was not to be. He blocked one attack and narrowly missed having his head knocked off with a club. When he recovered he only had a moment to defend against another sword attack. His initial thought was to attack in return. If the man had been more proficient with the sword he might have been able to defend the attack, but he had no idea it was coming. Alaric's blade sunk into his chest. The man dropped to the floor as Alaric pulled the blade out ready for the next one.

The man who had lost his blade had already made his escape leaving three left. Japheth was still standing in the room watching the fight. He wanted to get a good idea of what Alaric was like before he reported back to the High Chancellor. He couldn't help but watch in awe of what was happening in front of him.

Alaric kept fighting with ease as his three attackers struggled to keep up the pace. They all knew they were outmatched. It was only then did they realise their leader was not fighting with them. All at once they dropped their weapons and ran out the door. Alaric had to let himself laugh, even though two men had lost their lives. They looked like young boys running away from an angry parent. He quickly composed himself and looked to where Japheth had been standing. He soon found the man was no longer in the room.

"He left shortly before the other three," Tovah explained when he saw the look on Alaric's face.

"Damn it," he cursed quietly to himself.

"I think with all that has gone on it would be wise of you to stay another night." There were only ulterior motives to his suggestion. He did not honestly believe it would be a good idea for them to stay. He was only thinking of the extra gold.

Alaric waited a moment to catch his breath. Although the battle had not been too stressful on him he was still tired from the ordeal. Sweat poured down his face and he was paler than before. Both Tovah and Ra'naroz thought he was going to collapse, but he remained on his feet. There was nothing Alaric wanted to do more than sit down and rest, but there was no time. He knew once he was seated it would be too great an effort to get up again. He also knew that Tovah was not offering accommodation for their wellbeing. His motivation was purely selfish.

"I thank you for you offer, but we need to keep moving," Alaric thought he should be polite regardless. "There is something not right with Japheth and I need to find him. I have a few questions that need answers."

"I can tell you he has always been a strange character, but he has always been harmless enough. At least he was until the last month or so. It's like someone has climbed inside his brain and stirred everything around," Tovah explained. "He was once one of my closest friends. Now it is like I don't even recognise him. He comes in here spouting crazy words and then announces that it is the High Chancellor's edict. I would have banned him, but as you see he has his own group of followers. At least he is only here once a week. He spends time at the other inns of the outer city. We all put up with him because we fear the consequences. I hope that you can bring him to justice before he hurts anyone else."

"I will do all that I can, but we need to leave now. He already has a head start and he knows the city. I will do whatever I can to bring him to justice." Alaric moved to leave the inn, he could ill-afford to waste any more time.

Tovah went to speak, but Ra'naroz shook his head. He indicated that the conversation was over. He was beginning to get annoyed with the innkeeper's behaviour. It was like he was deliberately wasting time. The Dark Knight wanted to know what was going on. Something had changed in the city and he didn't like not knowing what it was. He could feel the hand of his brother on this one. He knew for certain that Za'aroz was behind it, but he didn't know what he was doing. He was going to have to stay close to Alaric if he was going to find out more. All thoughts of escape would have to go on the back burner until he found out what was happening.

Chapter 16: The Inner City

Alaric was glad to be out of the Last Chance and on Adelanta's back again. He had to help Ra'naroz onto his horse, but with their back story he didn't think anyone would take notice. Nothing had gone right for them since arriving. Somehow the situation had turned from bad to worse. He had to leave two bodies for Tovah to clean up. He had to give the innkeeper some more gold to keep him happy, although he did not really see how it was his fault. The men had accosted him and he had only defended himself.

They had not left the inn for more than five minutes before Ra'naroz started to plead his case. He was not going to be any use in his current condition. If he was going to gather the information that he needed then he would need to be untied. He would need to communicate with people in the city.

"I think it would be a good idea to untie me. If we get into another confrontation then I would be able to help you. You might have been able to handle a group of unskilled men, but a group of trained soldiers will be a completely different story. Things are worse than what we originally thought. You could use my help," Ra'naroz spoke as they rode towards the north-eastern gate.

Alaric knew the Dark Knight was right, but it was not the point and that was disturbing in itself. He had a feeling Ra'naroz wasn't looking to escape, but he still could not take the risk. Two Dark Knight's working together was something that wasn't worth thinking about. He would have to resist the urge to release Ra'naroz. Nothing good could come from it.

He didn't reply. It was not worth opening his mouth and showing the Dark Knight how unsure he was. He was still feeling the stress of the fight and lack of sleep. He was going to need all his senses once they reached the gate. He did not think the guards were going to be too accommodating. He would need to be on his game if he wanted to get into the inner city. Then he would need to find somewhere else to rest and hopefully leave Ra'naroz. It was almost a full blown conclusion that there was a Dark Knight in the Grand Cathedral controlling the High Chancellor. The last thing he could do was to take his prisoner with him. Until he found the Topaz stone he had to be very careful.

"Where do you think you are going?" the guard asked when they arrived at the gate.

Alaric spoke the lies that he had rehearsed so many times. He had told it that often that he was starting to believe it himself. It was easier that way and made his telling more realistic. With what he had already gone through he was not sure if his story was going to work.

"I see." The guard looked at Ra'naroz with some doubt in his eyes. "I am afraid the fee to enter the inner city has doubled. It is now two gold marks to get in." He didn't think they were going to be able to come up with the fee.

Alaric foraged around in his money pouch. He was starting to run out of coins. His stay at the Last Chance had cost him more than he had budgeted. He found his last three Remidian gold marks. That would be enough to see them into the inner city. From there he would need to find another source of income if they were going to survive. At least he had a good feeling they were heading the right direction.

"Now you need to pay for your friend. It is two marks each." The guard smiled as he took Alaric's gold.

Alaric could not believe what he was hearing. The second fee would almost completely wipe him out of coin. It did not sound right to him. It was always one fee for the group. If it was a large group there would be a slightly higher fee, but that was too be expected. Alaric wanted to say something, but he didn't think it would do any good. He just wanted to get past the gate. At best he would risk losing the gold coins he had already given them.

Alaric found the appropriate coins to make up the two gold marks. All that he had left was a Remidian gold half mark and a handful of Darshivallian silver crowns. He hoped that would be enough to secure accommodation for the next few nights. He knew it would not be enough to gain entrance into the Holy Circle, but that was a problem for another day.

"I think they were taking advantage of us," Ra'naroz insisted on speaking no matter what Alaric said.

Again Alaric resisted the urge to comment. Speaking with the Dark Knight would prove nothing. It would have been nice to voice his concerns, but that would only give Ra'naroz an insight to what he was thinking. He did not want to give Ra'naroz any further advantage. It would dampen his spirits and let him remember his place. It would also make Alaric feel better, but it would solve nothing. In the end it gave him more risks than it was worth.

"I know a place we can stay. It is cheap and nice," Ra'naroz suggested as they aimlessly rode the streets.

Alaric looked around in awe at all the buildings. He had been in all, but one of the other capital cities, but Castalia was something different again. He did not believe so many people could fit in such a small space. Although the capital cities of the other kingdoms were impressive they had nothing on Castalia. He didn't know how he was going to find Japheth in such a place. There was little chance without assistance. It was that assistance he was desperate to find, but trusting Ra'naroz was not the way to find it.

Alaric had a feeling he was heading in the right direction. That was somewhat comforting, but not by much. He used the Grand Cathedral as his marker. As long as he was heading towards it he felt as though everything was going to be alright. He felt as though things were finally becoming promising, but again it did nothing to help solve their current dilemma. He desperately needed to find somewhere he could use as a home base. It would be easier for him to get into the Grand Cathedral by himself.

"I know where we can stay. It is a small inn near the wall. It is cheap and it is clean," Ra'naroz spoke again when Alaric made no sign that he knew where he was going.

"That is alright. I will know where to stop when I get there. All you need to worry about is remaining silent and playing your role. Just remember for now you are more valuable to me alive, but that will not always be the case." The threat was underlying in his words, but Ra'naroz knew what they meant.

He wanted to reply, but he thought better of it. There was something wrong with Alaric and he didn't want to provoke a response. He was happy with what he had already achieved. It seemed that Alaric was letting the prophecy lead him around the city. There would be a way he could use it to his advantage, but he was yet to work out how. When he did it would be more than advantageous for him.

Alaric took them up and down many streets and side-streets before he finally stopped outside and old looking building. It was close to the Holy Circle wall and looked as though it was well maintained. On the sign hanging over the front door was a picture of a man on his knees praying. It was the inn of the Penitent Man and the place where Alaric needed to make camp. He could feel the prophecy pulling him inside. It had to be a sign that it was the place he was looking for.

"I don't think that you want to go in there," Ra'naroz warned when Alaric dismounted.

Alaric ignored Ra'naroz's words. If the prophecy wanted him to go inside then that was what he would do. He had no idea where he needed to go, so the prophecy was a good a sign to follow as any. He also knew the prophecy would not stop tugging at him until he reached the location it wanted him to be in. He didn't know if Ra'naroz's warning was a good sign or a bad one.

"This is the inn of the Penitent Man. It is an inn that holds mainly zealots and holy men. At a guess I would say it is full of people like Japheth. It will be dangerous," Ra'naroz warned.

"Then we should be extra careful," was all Alaric said as he handed Adelanta's reins to a stable boy.

It was good advice, but he was not going to give Ra'naroz any credit. With the new information he thought the inn would be the perfect place to locate Japheth. With a little luck the man would already be inside, although Alaric did not think it would be the case. He was almost positive the zealot would be inside the Grand Cathedral getting false information from the Dark Knight. He wished he had taken care of Japheth when he had the chance. He had a bad feeling he would come back to cause him no end of trouble.

No one took any notice of the two when they entered the inn. They still wore their thick robes with the hoods drawn over their faces. It was impossible for the patrons to realise they were foreigners. Alaric thought about leaving his robe on, but it was too hot inside the inn. No one else in the common room wore their robes and it would be too suspicious if his left his own on. Of course he was still using the same excuse for why Ra'naroz still wore his.

Once Alaric had removed his robe there was a hushed silence throughout the room. The innkeeper was quick to move over to where Alaric was standing. He had a concerned expression on his face. Alaric was beginning to wonder why the prophecy wanted him in the Penitent Man. It didn't seem like it was going to be a safe place for him to stay.

"Hello, I am Feivel the owner of the Penitent Man. Can I get you a room?" he spoke quickly and looked around nervously.

"I don't know," Alaric was not sure he was meant to stay at the inn. "I am looking for information."

"I don't think you will find anything here. If you do not want a room then I think that you should be on your way," Feivel sounded somewhat relieved with Alaric's response.

Alaric knew he had to remain in the inn. There was something that he needed and if that meant he had to get a room then so be it.

"How much is a room?" Alaric asked after a moment's thought.

Feivel had already started to move away when Alaric spoke. His shoulders dropped at the sound of the question. He thought he had gotten rid of the strangers. He had heard about the troubles in the outer city. Although there had not been any trouble in the inner city it was only matter of time. The Penitent Man was a holy inn. It was filled with pious men, not troublemakers, but even the holiest of men could get swept away with zealousness.

"One gold mark per night," he said quickly.

The regular price was a half silver per night, but he thought if he bumped up the price that would make them leave. He didn't want them there and he thought overcharging would be the best way to do so.

"Very well, I assume that you offer free meals with that price." Alaric knew what was happening and he would not be completely ripped off. If he let Feivel know how desperate he was then there was no telling how far he would go.

"Oh, no, ah, I mean yes. You do get a free meal with that cost," he didn't want to relent, but he saw the look on Alaric's face. He didn't want to get into a fight with the foreigner.

"Very good then, have your stableboy take our bags to our room and we shall have something to drink," Alaric commanded.

"Of course, what would you and your friend like?" Feivel asked, remembering that he was an innkeeper.

"I shall have an ale and my friend will have some water. He is not feeling the best," Alaric added as an afterthought.

There was one table left free in the common room. Alaric motioned for Ra'naroz to take a seat before he did so himself. He thought about sending the Dark Knight to their room, but he didn't want to risk leaving him alone. There would be too many chances for mischief. It was better if he could keep an eye on him.

"Now what do we do?" Ra'naroz asked. "There is still plenty of daylight left. We can make our way into the Holy Circle."

"I am not going to rush into the Grand Cathedral. It is clear to me there is one of your kind in there, pulling the High Chancellor's strings," Alaric kept his voice low. He figured if he was going to gain information from Ra'naroz then he had to give some.

"Yes, I believe that Za'aroz is now in control of Castalia." Ra'naroz offered the information freely.

If Alaric was surprised at his words he did not show it. He kept a stone cold gaze on the Dark Knight. It was more for the benefit of those around them than Ra'naroz himself. He didn't want them to know the severity of their conversation. He wanted them to ignore him altogether, but that was hoping for a little too much.

"Here are your drinks, my lord." A young lady said. She curtsied and smiled shyly at Alaric after she placed the drinks on the table.

"Thank you." Alaric didn't take much notice.

It wasn't until after she had left the table did he realise what she had done. He found her attitude to be quite strange. Everyone else in the common room acted as though they had contagious diseases, but at least they weren't starting any trouble. That was the last thing that Alaric needed. She was a little more than friendly. Her attitude had Alaric's interest piqued. He wanted to go and find her, but he couldn't leave the Dark Knight by himself.

"Go and find her. I will stay here," Alaric, even though he couldn't see under Ra'naroz's hood, knew that the Dark Knight was smiling.

Alaric didn't like the tone in his voice or what he was insinuating. Sure enough the serving woman was attractive. In another situation Alaric would have been tempted to sweet talk her, but that was not his concern. There was something else about the woman that caught his eye. He didn't know what it was, but she seemed out of place. It was as if the curtsy and the smile were put on for his benefit. She didn't look comfortable at all and that disturbed him.

"I don't think so. I don't think you would be safe if I left you by yourself." It was not that Alaric really cared for his safety, but it seemed like a reasonable response.

He sipped on his ale and watched the kitchen door for the serving woman to return. There were three other serving women, working that day, two were young and one a lot older. He assumed the older one was Feivel's wife. Each time the door opened Alaric hoped it would be the first young woman, but it wasn't. He started tapping his right foot in anticipation. His nerves were getting the better of him as he drained his mug.

Before he knew what had happened the serving woman was back with another ale for him. She placed it on the table and took his old mug away. Alaric watched her leave the table and go back into the kitchen. As she walked away she looked over her shoulder and smiled at him. The situation did not seem right at all. There was something askew, but he could not place what it was.

Again the serving woman did not come out until Alaric's mug was empty. He did not order another one, but she was there all the same. This time he didn't let her leave without speaking to her.

"I am sorry, but do I know you?" he asked as she took his empty mug from the table.

She giggled before she replied. "I don't think so," and then she left again.

Alaric watched her leave again, but she did not look back. Alaric didn't know what to make of her. There was something there. He knew she was important to him, but he did not know why. He only hoped she had the information that he required.

"Are you sure you don't want me to leave you alone," Ra'naroz spoke as if he was Alaric's friend.

The Dark Knight's familiar attitude upset Alaric. He had let Ra'naroz become too comfortable. Even though he was clearly a prisoner his attitude did not reflect that. There was no telling what trouble he was planning. Alaric had to be very careful. The situation was getting out of his control and he did not like it.

"I think that it might be time for you to retire for the evening," Alaric suggested.

As much as Alaric did not want to be left alone in the common room he also did not want Ra'naroz to see what he was doing. There was a risk the other patrons would become aggressive if he was by himself. Unfortunately it was a risk he had to take. He needed to find out more about the serving woman.

"Very well, but at least give me some warning if you are going to bring her back with you." Ra'naroz sniggered underneath his breath.

That was all Alaric could take. He had to refrain from hitting him in the common room, but that would not stop him once they made it to their room. Ra'naroz would learn his place one way or another. Beating the Dark Knight would definitely make Alaric feel a lot better.

"Come on now. I think you are feeling too poorly to eat tonight. You should get some rest," Alaric stood from the table as he spoke.

Alaric let Ra'naroz walk in front on the way back to the room. He wanted to keep a close eye on the Dark Knight. Until he had him secure there was still a chance for him to cause mischief. They were already in a precarious situation and it didn't need to get any worse.

As soon as the door was closed Alaric struck Ra'naroz across the side of his face with his fist. It caught the Dark Knight by surprise and knocked him to his knees. He had thought they had been getting on well together. Never did he think Alaric was taking him to their room to strike him. Even if his arms weren't still bound he would have remained on his knees. Any attempt to stand would bring another blow.

"Why did you do that?" Ra'naroz asked. If he had a free hand he would have rubbed his jaw.

It seemed as though one strike was enough to prove his point and he didn't bother with a response. He wanted to beat Ra'naroz within an inch of his life, but he did not have time for such indulgences. He needed to return to the common room and see what the serving woman had to do with his current dilemma. He didn't want to risk missing her. He quickly tied Ra'naroz to the bedpost. He was about to leave when he thought he better double check the knot. The last thing he wanted to do was have Ra'naroz escape because his mind was preoccupied.

When he was confident Ra'naroz could not escape from the room he left to find his mystery woman. Ever since he saw her he couldn't get her out of his mind. He knew she was the one he was looking for, although he did not know why. She did not look like she would be able to restrain the Dark Knight if that was required so there had to be another reason why he was drawn to her.

When he arrived back at the common room he felt something had changed. At first he did not know what it was, but as he tried to make his way back to the table the other patrons moved to block his path. No one physically challenged him, but it was obvious what they were doing. Alaric could feel the hostility radiating from them. It was the same feeling as the one he felt at the Last Chance. Whatever was happening inside the Grand Cathedral was having an effect on the rest of the city.

The serving woman was nowhere in sight so Alaric stopped his approach to the table. He knew when he was not welcome and he did not want to start another fight. He had already shed too much blood for one day. He turned around to leave the common room and he bumped straight into the serving woman. Luckily for Alaric she was not carrying anything or he would have knocked it out of her hands.

It was like he seeing her for the first time. She wore a simple cream cotton dress under her white serving apron. He long brown hair was tied in a ponytail to avoid any hair getting in her patron's food or drink. Her face was young, but Alaric felt it belied her true age. There was something in her deep blue eyes that made Alaric think she was older than she looked.

"I am sorry," Alaric spoke before he realised it was her. He was going to speak again, but he lost his words.

"That is alright," she giggled again before whispering in his ear. "Meet me outside. It is not safe for you in here." She walked away before he had a chance to respond.

Alaric stood and watched her disappear into the crowd. There was something spellbinding about her. It wasn't until someone bumped into him before he returned to reality. He didn't believe it was an accident, but the man had already moved on. The words the serving woman whispered to him echoed throughout his mind. The sound of her voice was very soothing. He had forgotten the fact that he was deathly tired and in a dangerous position.

There was no chance for him to make his way out of the inn through the front door, at least not without getting into a fight. He would have to find a rear exit. He left the common room the way he had come in and looked for a way out. It took him a little while to find the door he was looking for. It led to a small courtyard at the back of the inn. The walls were over ten feet high and there were no doors to the outside. He thought about trying to climb the walls, but there were no good handholds. Instead he turned around and walked back inside.

"What are you doing?" the woman was waiting for him in the doorway.

"I was looking for a way out," Alaric explained.

There was a noise from somewhere behind her. She looked around nervously before pushing Alaric out of the door and back into the courtyard. Alaric was becoming suspicious. Her behaviour was less than normal. He needed answers.

"Who are you?" he asked before she had a chance to speak.

"My name is Minerva Veneficus," she spoke quietly. "If you haven't guessed it already, you are in great danger." She quickly shut the door behind them.

The name sounded familiar to Alaric, but he could not place where he had heard it. It seemed as though she had the information he needed, but now he had to work out a way of prying it from her. She didn't look too happy.

"I have noticed things are a little off in Castalia," he replied slowly. "What is going on?" He did not want to reveal the fact there was a Dark Knight in control of the city until he knew how much she knew.

"There will be time for answers, but not now. There are people listening everywhere." She looked around the courtyard as if she expected to see someone.

Alaric's shoulders dropped. He thought Minerva was going to help him, but it seemed as though she was just as paranoid. It didn't seem as though he was going to get what he needed.

"We need to get out of here. You have to bring your friend to my house," she explained slowly.

"I don't think so," Alaric replied just as slowly. He didn't want to upset her. He didn't know how she would react. "I think we will stay here. I am sure we will be fine."

A confused expression crossed Minerva's face. She could not work out Alaric's sudden shift. She was offering him help and he was turning it down. She knew he needed assistance and there was no reason why he should not trust her. She knew he would be feeling the pull of the prophecy. She thought about their conversation and suddenly realised what was wrong.

"I thought you of all people would realise that just because you can't see someone doesn't mean they are not there." Her words were doing her no favours.

"I think I should find you a physician," Alaric suggested and moved towards the door.

Minerva simply stepped in his path. She was not going to let him go without an explanation. Alaric didn't want to cause her any harm. It was obviously not her fault that she was mentally unstable. The madness was radiating from the Grand Cathedral and it was affecting people in more ways than one. He felt as though he should get her help.

"I am extremely surprised that Eldred Zauber did not tell you about me." Minerva watched his reaction closely.

It was the first time he had heard Eldred's last name, but that was a side issue. If Minerva knew Eldred then there was more to her than he originally thought. But just because she knew him did not mean she was an ally. His name was widely known on both sides of the war. If she was not an ally then he would be walking into a trap and Ra'naroz would soon be set free. He had promised himself he would see the Dark Knight dead before that happened.

"No, he has never mentioned you. That makes me wonder if you are indeed who you say you are."

"Do you truly believe that?" she asked as she levelled a stare at him.

Alaric had to think. Suddenly he felt like a school boy being scolded by a teacher. He couldn't see the prophecy leading him astray, but he could not rely on that fact alone. There was something about her that was askew, but that was no reason to distrust her. In the end he just had to take in on faith that she was there to help. He only wished he could place where he had heard her name before, but he figured it was still part of his memories that had yet to return. Until he knew exactly who she was he had to be careful.

"Who are you?" he finally asked.

"This is not the place for questions. You and your friend need to meet me at my house," she continued to speak quietly.

That comment didn't sound right to Alaric. If she knew who he was then she should also know that Ra'naroz was not his friend. The doubts crept back into his mind again. His thoughts were clearly written on his face.

"I know who he is, but now is not the time for revelations. You have to trust me. I am here to help you." Minerva had all the answers, even before the question was asked.

"Very well. Tell me where you live and we will meet you there." Alaric resigned himself to fact that he needed her help. If she was not who she claimed to be, not that she had claimed to be anyone, then he would have to be prepared for the worst.

"I am glad you have come around," Minerva smiled. "Now this is how you get to my house."

She explained the location to Alaric. She had to go through the instructions a couple of times before Alaric understood where he had to go. The streets of the inner city were crowded and could be confusing. Luckily for Alaric she did not live far away from the inn. All he had to worry about was leaving. It would look suspicious if they left after just paying too much for their room.

"Don't worry about that. I will have your bags loaded onto your horses. By the time everyone realises you are not coming back there will be nothing they can do about it," Minerva eased his mind again.

"Very well, but be warned Minerva. If you are not who you say you are you will suffer greatly." Alaric felt it was necessary to let her know he did not completely trust her.

Minerva giggled at his words before she opened the door. For a while she had lost the mantle of the inn's serving woman. She slipped back into the role all too easily for Alaric's liking. His interest was piqued. He really wanted to know who she was and what part she would play.

He waited a minute after she had left the courtyard to leave himself. It would get mouths talking if anyone saw them leaving together. Minerva loosened her dress slightly to make it look like a secret tryst. At least if they were going to talk about the meeting then they would be off the track. Alaric was not sure if he liked the rumours it would bring, but he knew that it was better than the alternative. All he had to do was to sneak out of the inn. He was sure it would be easier said than done. The longer he waited to make his move the colder it would become and the greater the risk of them dying of exposure.

Chapter 17: Minerva Veneficus

It was easier exiting the inn than expected. Minerva had started a rumour that the new guests were leaving for the Holy Circle. Despite the hour no one questioned their motives and it did not take long for the rumour to spread throughout the common room. It was still early in the evening and the temperature had not dropped too far. No one believed they would gain entrance into the Holy Circle at such an hour, but no one hindered their exit when they left. Alaric could still feel the hatred as they left and he was grateful to be outside.

Ra'naroz had asked where they were going, but Alaric had refused to answer. Until he knew who Minerva was he was not going to let Ra'naroz know her name or anything else about her. He was sure it would happen once they reached her house, but he would hold any information for as long as he could.

Once they were outside the inn Alaric put on his heavy robe. With the protection of the hood no one would know he was a foreigner. That would make the ride to Minerva's house a lot safer. It seemed as though Japheth's attitude was common throughout the city. They were lucky so far only to come up against the six men from the lynch mob.

The streets had emptied quickly when the sun had set. Those going about their regular business would be home well before nightfall. Those on the streets were either going to a tavern or returning from one. Either way they were quite happy to move out of the way of the two horses. Their journey finished without a hitch.

The first problem arose when they arrived at Minerva's house. She lived in a double storey house that had no stable. There was nowhere for them to leave their horses. Alaric had wished Minerva had mentioned this before they left the inn. They had paid for the night and the horses could have stayed there.

"What are we going to do with the horses?" Alaric asked when Minerva opened the door.

"There is a stable not far from here. Tie the horses to this post. I will take them there a little later," Minerva explained.

"I could have left them at the inn's stable. We have already paid for their services." Alaric sounded annoyed as he tired Adelanta and Ra'naroz's stallion to the post.

"I wouldn't trust leaving them at the Penitent Man. When you didn't return they would have stolen the horses and sold them at the auction yards," Minerva explained as they moved inside her house.

Alaric had to laugh when he heard Minerva's words. Both her and Ra'naroz were confused by his mirth. Neither of them had noticed anything funny in what she had said.

"What's so funny?" Minerva asked when they entered her sitting room.

"I don't think anyone will be stealing Adelanta. He is quite capable of taking care of himself," Alaric explained.

"I see," Minerva thought as she spoke. "I thought he was an elven horse, but I wasn't sure. He is a little grey for a purebred."

Alaric had to laugh again. "We have been on the road for a while and I haven't had a chance to brush him down. I wouldn't mention that when he can hear. He can be quite abrupt when he wants to be."

Minerva also started laughing. It did make sense when she thought about it. It was good to break up the tension with some laughter. They were safe from prying eyes and ears and she hoped Alaric was starting to relax. There was a lot riding on him trusting her. She was sure when she explained who she was he would understand, although she couldn't quite work out why he didn't know. The only problem was that she did not want to reveal her true identity in front of the Dark Knight. She would have to gather more information herself first. As much as she had known Alaric was coming that was all the information she had. Why he was with a Dark Knight was a completely new conundrum.

"And who is your friend?" she asked casually.

Ra'naroz still had his hood over his head, but it wouldn't have mattered if he'd had it off. She was sure his identity would be masked, much the same as hers. That was not the only mystery with the Dark Knight. She could feel no power emanating from him or Alaric. She could not work out how Alaric held him prisoner.

"He is no one to be concerned about." It was a game of cat and mouse between the two. Neither of them wanted to give away any information before they knew more.

"I think it would be good if we could talk in private." She suggested.

It was tempting, but Alaric was not sure he wanted to leave Ra'naroz alone until he knew more about her. She was an enigma. There was something not right with her. On occasion Alaric thought he saw her shimmer. It was only for a moment and only out of the corner of his eye so he could not be completely sure, but he would still keep it in mind. He had no doubt that she could be a very dangerous enemy.

"You can speak freely in front of him," Alaric explained.

Minerva did not like his reply. There was no way she could speak freely in front of a Dark Knight. If he was in fact calling the shots then her life was in great danger. She had been so sure of things when she saw Alaric in the inn, but doubts had crept into her mind. It might have been a better idea speaking with them = there and not in her home.

"Well, okay then. You said you were after information. What is it that you want to know?"

Before Alaric spoke Minerva offered him a seat. There were two large couches in the middle of the room. They were situated around a timber coffee table. There were also a number of chairs and two tables. Alaric brought a chair over for Ra'naroz to sit on. He was not going to share a couch with the Dark Knight. If Ra'naroz thought he was going to relax in comfort he would be sadly mistaken. Alaric then sat on one couch opposite Minerva.

"It seems as though the locals do not like us. There have been a number of rumours, but do you know what is actually happening?" Alaric asked.

Minerva looked at the Dark Knight and then back to Alaric. She did not like the fact that Ra'naroz was still in the room. She was not sure if she could give Alaric the entire story. She could not tell him the truth without actually giving him all the information, but the truth was she did not know what was happening inside the Grand Cathedral.

"The High Chancellor has decreed that foreigners are no longer welcome in the Holy Circle and that has been relayed into the streets that foreigners are not welcome in Castalia. I do not know why he has said such a thing, but I believe it is related to the troubles the other kingdoms have been having." She wanted to make the correlation to the appearances of the Dark Knights, but she thought better of it. If Alaric didn't offer information on his own then she would have to push. She was sure he would be able to read between the lines and understand what she was hinting at.

"I suppose that makes sense," Alaric knew she was keeping information from him, but he needed to know what her agenda was. "I need to get into the Grand Cathedral. Is there anyway I can get in there?"

Minerva thought for a moment. There was a way in, but she did not think the Dark Knight needed to know about it. She had to make a stand, even if it risked her life.

"I am sorry Alaric, but I cannot give you the information with him in the room." She neglected to mention she knew he was a Dark Knight, but she was not yet prepared to show all her cards.

Alaric thought for a moment. She had started something that could not be taken back. He only hoped he could trust her. If not then there would be bloodshed soon enough. Without answering he walked to

Ra'naroz and promptly took the robe from him, revealing that his wrists were tightly bound.

"He is not going to worry anyone." Alaric remained standing in case she decided to attack.

Minerva didn't know what to think. It was a good sign that the Dark Knight was clearly Alaric's prisoner, but it didn't make sense for him to still be standing there. It was as if he was setting her up for a fall. She had gone this far and there was no reason to take a back foot. She only hoped she had read the situation well enough.

"There is information that he doesn't need to hear. If he escapes it will be dangerous information for him to have," Minerva explained.

That was true. Alaric had assumed the Dark Knight would be safe within his custody, but the closer he came to his goal the risk of him escaping grew. Since the cat was out of the bag there was no point in trying to hide it anymore. He just didn't know how far he should go. The prophecy had led him to her, but that was not to say he was meant to trust her. He knew the prophecy was hard to decipher and had a mind of its own.

"Is there somewhere secure we can put him?" he asked.

"Of course. I have a cellar that is completely secure. The only way in or out is via a trapdoor in my kitchen. There is no way he can escape," Minerva smiled as she spoke. There was a hint of the serving woman in her smile, but not much. That persona had almost completely left her.

"Do you have any hot water?" he asked as she stood to lead the way into the kitchen.

"Would you like some tea?" she sounded confused.

"Not exactly. If you could get me a mug of hot water then we can put him to bed." He still didn't want to use the term Dark Knight until he was completely sure of who she was.

She shook her head as she left the room. She did not like not knowing what was happening. She was the one who normally kept secrets from everyone and she was the one who usually held all the cards in a conversation. She did not know what was happening. He was the Chosen One and she had to respect his judgement. She did not know how Eldred was able to put up with him.

She returned shortly after with a steaming mug. She placed it on the table in front of Alaric and then stood back. Alaric took a pouch from his pocket and dropped it onto the table. He had decided whilst she was out that he was happy for her to know what he was doing. She seemed just as concerned to keep the Dark Knight prisoner as he did.

"What is that?" she asked as he placed the herb in the mug.

"It is something that will keep him calm during the night."

Once the herb was sufficiently mixed in with the water he poured the concoction down Ra'naroz's throat. He did not wait for the water to cool down. Ra'naroz's spluttered, but he swallowed the liquid anyway. He knew what would happen if he did not. He was not sure who the woman was and he didn't want her to see Alaric beat him. There was a chance he could use her to his advantage. He knew if he wasn't cut off from the power around him he would have been able to work out exactly who she was and what she part she had to play. Until he was able to flush the evil herb from his system he would just have to accept his lot.

Alaric grabbed Ra'naroz by the scruff of his shirt and dragged him towards the kitchen. Even if Ra'naroz didn't want to show his submissiveness Alaric wanted to show his dominance. He wanted to show Minerva that he was in control. He felt if Minerva saw how he was with Ra'naroz then she would think twice about trying to dominate him. Although he couldn't feel it he sensed there was power in the woman before him. Given a chance he knew she would try and control him and that was something he could not let happen.

There was a small staircase leading down in the cellar. Ra'naroz made his way down without being prompted. Alaric was beginning to get annoyed with the Dark Knight being so accommodating. He wanted to push him down the stairs, but that would prove nothing. He was happy just to lock the trapdoor above his head.

"Now will you tell me what is going on?" Alaric asked when they returned to the sitting room.

Minerva was surprised to hear the words come from Alaric. He was obviously not as easily fooled as she had originally thought. She thought she could have got away with her lack of information, but it was clear she would have to be completely honest. She was much more comfortable since the Dark Knight was safely tucked away in the basement.

"In truth, I don't know. I have a feeling there is a Dark Knight in the Grand Cathedral, but have not been able to gain entrance," she explained. "I know that these new edicts are out of character for the High Chancellor. He would not ban people from coming to Holy Circle. It just doesn't make sense."

"That is what I expected." It was not new information. "The Dark Knight is Za'aroz and he is in the Grand Cathedral."

Minerva was surprised Alaric gave up such information. It was clear he was beginning to trust her. The situation was better than what she had thought. She thought she should reveal her true identity to him, although she was still surprised he had not worked it out for himself.

Once he knew who she was then she was sure he would trust her and that was the most important thing.

"I am Minerva Veneficus. I am one of the seven wizards who sit on the Council of Wizards at Ĉarolija Island." Minerva explained.

Alaric was instantly suspicious. As far as he knew all the other wizards, besides Eldred, were still at their home at the Isle of Wizards. None of his brothers and sisters of wizardry believed in the prophecy. As much as his memory was still sketchy he was sure that was true.

"If you are who you say you are then I would know you would be here," Alaric stared. "You will need to explain yourself if you want me to believe you."

Minerva had not been in Castalia for long and she couldn't really explain why she had left. When Eldred had left no one had believed he was doing the right thing and then one day Minerva knew she had to leave.

She had grown up in Castalia many years ago before she became apprentice to Gwydion, the oldest and most respected of the council. They had travelled the Seven Kingdoms together before Minerva had been raised to a full wizard. It had been a long time since she had returned home, but her house had always been kept for her.

"I have not been here long," Minerva started. "I understand your scepticism. None of us believed Eldred when he left in search of what he called the Chosen One and then one morning I woke up and knew I needed to return home. At first I had no idea what I was doing here, but soon enough I realised that it was you I was going to meet and it would be done so at the Penitent Man." She could see that Alaric was coming around, but he wasn't completely convinced. "If I had been here longer I could have gathered more information, but I didn't know when you would arrive and I needed to assimilate myself in the tavern."

Alaric relaxed a little, but there was still something that was not right. The seven wizards had all lived through the centuries. The woman in front of him only looked to be about twenty years old. There is no way that she could be who she said she was. He suddenly felt very uncomfortable.

"As I said to you before, you of all people should realise that things are not what they seem. This is a façade that I wear. I would not have been given the job if I looked like a five hundred year old wizard," she smiled as she spoke. The question was clearly written on his face and didn't need asking.

"You are five hundred years old?" Alaric asked in surprise.

"I have no idea how old I am. After the first century you tend to lose count." She continued to smile. "I have to admit that I do like this façade. I think that I will keep it for a while."

Alaric had to admit that he liked the façade as well. She was a beautiful young woman. Now that he knew it was a spell Alaric almost thought he could see though it. He knew what the shimmers were he saw earlier. He was happy it wasn't a sign he was going crazy. He thought it was a chance with his lack of sleep. At least he would be able to sleep well under Minerva's roof.

"It is all starting to make sense now," Alaric sounded relieved. "Why didn't you explain yourself earlier?"

"I was not sure if you were a prisoner of the Dark Knight. If that was the case then I would have been putting both our lives in danger. I had to make sure you were safe before I revealed my identity," Minerva explained.

Alaric had to laugh again. They were both playing the same game. At least all their cards were on the table and he no longer had to watch what he said. All the distrust he had felt since they met had washed away. Despite not really being able to know who she was he figured the prophecy would be ringing in his ears if he was making a mistake.

"That is Ra'naroz who is imprisoned here," he went on to explain his background history with the Dark Knight. She listened intently until he finished the story.

"I did not know there was a herb that could block someone's power. That is indeed disturbing." She pondered on the ramifications for a moment. "That is a side issue. At least we know he is not going to get up to any mischief. He can remain here whilst you are in Castalia."

"That is not entirely true," Alaric added. "I have a bad feeling I will need to take him into the Grand Cathedral with me." It was a new revelation that had just come to him.

Minerva did not like what she was hearing. She did not think it was a good idea. If Za'aroz was indeed in the Grand Cathedral then he would surely rescue his brother. It would be disastrous to take Ra'naroz and she could not let him make such a mistake.

"I don't think that is a good idea. To take him inside the Holy Circle can only lead to trouble. He will be safe in my basement whilst we go there," she explained.

"I didn't think that I wanted to take him either, but I guess it is out of my hands. It's something that the prophecy wants me to do. I think it is the reason why I didn't kill him in Jarrat. He still has his part to play, for better or for worse." Alaric continued his train of thought.

Minerva couldn't argue with that fact. Unlike Eldred, who had been a slave to the prophecy for many years, she had only recently felt the pull of it, but it was undeniable. No matter what the other wizards had told her she knew where he destiny lied. She went where the prophecy led her. It had led her to Castalia to meet Alaric. It had already proven itself to be correct. It seemed its next mission for her involved both the Chosen One and a Dark Knight.

"Very well. I will trust your judgement on this one." She resigned herself.

There was still a question that remained unanswered. He needed to know how to get into the Grand Cathedral. He knew that was where he would find the Topaz stone. It was the only place it could be. He was tempted to use the Jade stone, which was in tune with the other six stones, just to confirm his suspicions, but there was no guarantee which one it would point to. There was still too much risk until his abilities and his full memory returned. Until they did he would have to place his trust in those around him. When it was said and done the Dark Knight was the lesser of two evils.

"How do I get into the Grand Cathedral?" he asked again.

"That is not as easy as it once was." She didn't need to say that, but she thought that it would add to the suspense. "The rumours are not wrong. The Holy Circle is shut of to all foreigners. In fact it is shut off to most of the city. The guard is as strict as I have ever seen it."

"That doesn't really answer my question," Alaric pushed when Minerva paused.

The old wizard sighed. She did not know how Eldred could have put up with such an insolent boy. She had to make concessions. He was the Chosen One after all. If one of her students had questioned her in such a manner she would have them punished. She thought about what she could do to Alaric and a smile crossed her face. She was sure if he had not already surpassed her skills that he soon would. It was a sobering thought that someone so young could learn so quickly. If she knew his true state she might not have been so accommodating to his whims.

"There is a mine to the south of the Grand Cathedral. Originally the mouth of the cave was inside the Holy Circle, but many years ago a High Chancellor had the mouth of the cave closed in. He believed there were people stealing his diamonds. That is of course common knowledge and it is thought to be where the story ends. What is not known is that there was a tunnel dug from the basements of the Grand Cathedral that run all the way to the cave. The High Chancellor, as much as he didn't want anyone else to have his diamonds, still wanted the wealth that they brought. Those who mined the diamonds were essentially slaves. They were no longer allowed to leave the basement of the Grand Cathedral."

"This history lesson still doesn't help me get inside the Grand Cathedral," Alaric interrupted. He was tired and the lecture was doing nothing for him.

There was nothing she wanted more than to take the impudent young man across her knee and spank him. It would be a humorous sight in her current form, but it would really prove nothing. She just had to bite her tongue and continue with what she was saying.

"There is another way into the diamond mine. It is known only to a few and it is wrought with danger," she spoke quietly, as if there might be someone listening.

Alaric knew it was not going to be an easy task. Nothing was ever easy, but he did not like the sound of what she was suggesting. In his current state he was not sure if he was up to the challenge. Of course it was not like he had a choice. Alena would die if he didn't recover the Topaz stone. It was the only thought that kept him going. One thing he could not do was show any weakness to Minerva. Although he did not think she would take advantage of him he was unsure what support she would be if she knew the truth.

"I have been through many dangers so far, I am sure that one more is not going to kill me." Alaric instantly wished he had not used those words.

"Well I hope that is the case, but I would not be so cavalier about it. Outside of the walls, in the desert, there is a small mine shaft. It is not so much of a mine shaft as it is collapsed ground. The shaft is about a thirty metre sheer drop. At the bottom there is a maze of tunnels going in all directions. Without warning there are drops of the God Kings only know how far. There is no clear trail towards the diamond mines. It is rumoured there are strange creatures who live in the many caverns, but that could be just superstition," she spoke with an ominous tone in her voice.

"So if it is that dangerous how has anyone lived to tell of its location?" Alaric thought it sounded all too suspicious.

"Well that is also another problem. I know of the hole in the ground, but if it actually reaches the main diamond mine I can not be completely sure. Unless you want to take on half the Castalial army there is no other way in." There was nothing in her words to ease his mind.

"I feel this is not the only good news you have for me." Alaric sighed.

Minerva looked at him. He looked drained. She was not sure if he was ready for everything, but she had already started. There was no point in leaving anything out. She only hoped he would be able to handle it. She just had to work out a way to tell him.

"Would you like something to eat or drink?" Minerva stood as she asked. "I'm going to make myself a cup of tea."

It was nothing more than an excuse to give herself some free time to think, but Alaric didn't notice the ruse. He wasn't hungry, but he thought a cup of tea might be nice. His nerves were on edge and needed something to calm himself.

"Tea would be nice, thank you." Alaric also appreciated the time apart. The conversation was starting to wear on him, but he knew he needed answers before he could rest for the night.

"Once we get into the diamond mines is when it really starts to get difficult." Marina started again when she had served the tea. "The mines are filled with slaves and where you have slaves you have slave masters," Minerva explained further when Alaric interrupted.

"The High Chancellor is supposed to be the supreme holy man. I find it hard to believe he would use slaves in his mines."

"I would be surprised if the High Chancellor knows where his wealth comes from. His has an entire team of administrators to look after that for him. They, unfortunately, are not quite as holy as the High Chancellor. When there is wealth to be had, and extreme wealth like what is generated here, there will always be corruption. Not to mention the fact that the High Chancellors' are prone to madness. I think in the history of Castalia there were only a handful of High Chancellors who didn't go insane in their later years. In fact some went crazy a lot earlier in their lives." Alaric appreciated the history lesson, but Minerva could see she was losing him. "Now for us to move around the mines freely will be next to impossible. We will have to move in stealth and one wrong move will bring down a world of hurt. Once we are in the Grand Cathedral we should be able to move around relatively unhindered. Everyone assumes that if you are in the Grand Cathedral then you are meant to be there."

Alaric did not look happy with what he had heard. There were too many uncertainties for his liking. The fact that she assumed she was going with him was both disturbing and comforting. He had resigned himself to fact that he would need to bring Ra'naroz with him. It would be good to have an extra pair of eyes watching him, but he still didn't like the assumption.

"That sounds easy enough," Alaric thought about telling her about the Topaz stone and decided it would be easier if she knew. "Do you know where the Topaz stone of power is located?"

She looked at him with a questioning expression on her face. It was not a good sign. Before she even opened her mouth he knew what her answer was going to be.

"I don't know what you are talking about," she replied after a short pause.

Since he had started he had to continue. "Ra'naroz told me that the Topaz stone was in the Grand Cathedral. It is the reason why I am in Castalia."

"I have never heard of the Topaz stone being in Castalia," Minerva replied. "I think the Dark Knight might have been lying to you."

Although she had not been in Castalia for long Alaric didn't think it was a good sign. If they had come all the way to Castalia for nothing then Alena would die. If Ra'naroz had lied to him then he would die a slow and painful death. The rage that was building up inside of him outweighed his fatigue. He wanted answers and nothing was going to stop him from getting them. He stood up so quickly that it startled Minerva.

"Where are you going?" as soon as she asked the question she knew the answer.

Alaric didn't bother answering. He could feel the blood pumping through his head as he moved towards the kitchen. He didn't want to speak in case he lost his rage. He needed all of it to keep going. He knew once it left him he would be exhausted. There was no way he could sleep without getting the answers he was after.

Lifting the trapdoor he wasted no time in rushing down the stairs. There was a small lantern hanging from the ceiling offering a small amount of light to the cellar. There was no furniture at all. The Dark Knight was huddled in the far corner. He looked as though he had been trying to sleep. Alaric almost felt sorry for him, almost.

"Where is the Topaz stone?" he asked bluntly.

"What are you talking about?" Ra'naroz sounded groggy, as if he had just been woken.

"You heard me!"

"The stone is in the Grand Cathedral," he replied innocently.

"I have never heard of the stone being there," Minerva spoke from the top of the stairs. "I am sure that I would have."

"Well, Wizard, I guess there are things that you just don't know," there was a smirk on his face as he spoke.

His words took both Alaric and Minerva by surprise. They should have realised he would be able to see through her ruse. It had taken him a while, but even cut off from the power around him he could work it out.

"I don't think this is a good time to be smart. Tell me all that you know about the stone," Alaric moved towards him in a threatening manner, but stopped before he came within striking distance.

"I told you that I will not give away too much information too early. If I did that then my life would be forfeited," the smile left his face as he spoke.

"Well that is the catch, isn't it? If you do not tell me what you know about the location of the stone then I will end your life here and now," there was no bluff in Alaric's threat.

Ra'naroz looked him in the eyes before he replied. All he could see was a steely gaze staring back at him. It was almost as if Alaric was daring him to withhold information. There could be no doubt that Alaric would indeed kill Ra'naroz if he did not reveal the location of the Topaz stone. The Dark Knight still had a trick up his sleeve to keep his head on his shoulders.

"The Topaz stone is in the highest room in the cathedral's spire," he kept his edge as he made the revelation.

"If that is the case then wouldn't Za'aroz already have it in his possession?" Alaric was not going to let him get away with such an answer.

"I wouldn't worry too much about my brother. He is not renowned for being the brightest of us," Ra'naroz smiled. "I doubt he would even think to look for the Topaz stone in the Cathedral. It could be right under his nose and he wouldn't know."

Alaric wasn't sure if Ra'naroz was telling the truth. It sounded like a stretch. If one Dark Knight knew of the stone's location then why wouldn't another? He was sure that Ra'naroz was keeping something from him.

"How is it that you know the location of the Topaz stone and Za'aroz does not?"

"The Topaz stone as been here for well over five hundred years." Ra'naroz resigned himself to fact that he had to explain, although he did have one more ace up his sleeve. "It was discovered in the diamond mine. At first the High Chancellor thought that it was a worthless gem, at least compared to the diamonds. When the stone was brought to him his initial reaction was to throw it away, but just when the miner was taking it away he changed his mind. He could not be parted from the stone. It took hold of him. It consumed him. It took control of the next two High Chancellors as well. They could not control the power that the Topaz stone emitted. The next High Chancellor was wise to the *Stones of Power*. He knew what the Topaz stone had done to his predecessors and he would not have it done to him. The problem he had was that he could not simply throw the stone away. He also could not let anyone else suffer the fate of the previous High Chancellors. He employed the services of half a dozen wizards to cast a spell on the stone to block its power. Now it is trapped in the spire," Ra'naroz explained.

"That is a lie," Minerva spoke louder than she had originally intended. "If there were wizards involved then there would be a record at the academy." She felt like walking across the cellar and slapping him. There was no way there could be wizards involved and her not know about it. Finally the Dark Knight had been caught out.

"That would be true, but five of the six wizards died in creating the spell." the smile remained on his face. They both knew that he was keeping something from them.

"Even so, one wizard would still report back to the academy. If five wizards died creating a spell then it would be well documented," Minerva was starting to lose her temper.

"That is where I come into the story. I just so happened that I was moonlighting at the time as a wizard. I was the sixth wizard who created the spell. I have to admit the spell nearly took my life as well," there was no joke in his voice, although the smile remained on his face. "I also managed to change the spell without the other wizards knowing."

There was clearly more to his story, but Minerva cut in. "What did you do?" there was a certain amount of horror in her voice, although it was a rhetorical question. "The change you made to the spell. Is that what killed the other wizards?"

"It is possible, but I do not think that was the case," he was mater-of-fact with his response. "The spell was supposed to imprison the stone for eternity, but the change makes it possible to get access to it. So if you put it that way then you can thank me for making this all possible."

Although his words made sense there was no way that Alaric was going to thank him. There were too many bad things he had done for one lucky gesture to make up for them. He already knew the answer to his next question, but he had to ask it anyway.

"How do I remove the spell?" he asked.

"You don't. I am the only one who can remove the spell. That is why you have to keep me alive." He was proud of his last comment. "If you kill me then you will never gain access to the Topaz stone and Alena will die."

Alaric was about to speak, but there was no point. He simply turned around and walked out of the cellar. Minerva watched him pass with some confusion. There were still questions that Ra'naroz needed to answer. Minerva had learnt something and it was something she had not expected. She had to find out what it was. There would be time to question the Dark Knight later.

"What is it?" she spoke when they returned to the sitting room. "You left in such an abrupt manner."

Alaric suddenly looked deathly tired. He slumped in the couch where he sat. She wanted to offer him something, but she wanted answers more. She hoped she had made the right decision.

"He set this up from the start," Alaric let his head fall into his hands.

"I don't understand. What has he set up?" Minerva asked.

"He knew if he was captured I would need the Topaz stone to save Alena's life. He is smarter than I gave him credit for. Now things just got even more dangerous," Alaric sounded defeated.

"But there is nothing he can do whilst you keep feeding him that brew."

"That is all well and good, but what happens when we get to the spire. I imagine he has not made it easy for the spell to be broken. We will need to give him his powers back if we want him to break the spell," Alaric's words hit her hard.

There was a long silence as Minerva thought on what he said. It was a revelation she had not been expecting, but for a different reason. She waited as she thought on what to say. It was more the confusion that had her stumped.

"I am sure you would be able to break the spell. At least with my assistance," it was as gently as she could put it.

Alaric had gone so far he didn't think that it was worth keeping anything from her. If he couldn't trust Minerva then there was no point in going any further. He would need her complete assistance if he was going to succeed.

"I can't use magic." he lifted his head to see her reaction. There was a confused expression on her face. It was obvious she needed more information. Alaric continued to explain the entire situation.

"Well that does put a different spin on things," she mused as she pondered what he had told her. "I don't think it would be a good idea to let him off his leash."

"I don't either, but there is no other option, unless you can guarantee you can break the spell?"

"There is a chance I could, but I won't know until we reach the spire."

"And that is where we hit the wall," Alaric didn't sound happy at all. "From what I gather it will take about two days for the herbs to wear off. We can't take a risk that you can't break the spell. We have one chance at this and we can't do anything to jeopardise things."

Minerva would have laughed if it wasn't for the severity of the conversation. "Well I think letting Ra'naroz free would be an even bigger risk. There is no way we can trust him, especially since there is no way for you to control him."

"He doesn't know that and that is the way it will stay. The threat of what I can do to him will keep him in line." Alaric wasn't sure he was doing the right thing, but he didn't want Minerva to know. He could see no other solution.

"Well I guess that is that then."

Minerva had to wonder why she had been drawn back to Castalia by the prophecy. She would much rather be in the academy on Ĉarolija Island. He was not at all what she had expected. At this stage of the journey she thought that he would be a lot more powerful, if what Eldred had told them was true. After meeting Alaric it felt as though she was babysitting a first year novice.

***

Ra'naroz sat in the corner until the trapdoor was shut. He could not wipe the smile from his face no matter how hard he tried. He had successfully turned the situation around. Despite his location he knew he was in control and he liked that. Alaric would have thought he was calling the shots, but that had all changed.

Once he had been left alone he moved as far up the stairs as he could go. He pressed his ear up against the trapdoor. He really wanted to hear what they were saying. It would give him a better indication of where he stood. He wasn't so arrogant that he didn't realise that Alaric was still a dangerous adversary. He had already killed three of his brothers. Even though the balance of power had shifted in his favour things could still turn bad.

To his dismay he could not hear anything. He wished he could tap into the power around him. He would have no problem in hearing their conversation then. As he moved back down the stairway he suddenly realised why he couldn't hear anything. The witch had cast a spell. He would have no chance of gathering any more information. It didn't really matter in the end. They would be discussing how they would have to let him have his powers back. That was something he was looking forward to. The thought of it made him drool. Once he had his powers back then he could really start making plans.

Chapter 18: Recovery

The recovery of the three men took longer than Bern had hoped. His plan to root out the Evil One's agents in Jarrat hinged largely on the recovery of Richmond and Tancred. Hadar was the first one to wake two days after Alaric had left for Castalia. It took him another two days before he was out of bed. He had little memory of what had happened. Bern wasn't sure if this was a good thing or a bad thing. If he had endured what Hadar had gone through he wasn't sure if he would want to remember.

As much as Bern was happy to see Hadar up and about he wasn't the person he wanted. He needed Richmond or Tancred to wake up. They had a better idea of who the traitors were having infiltrated the city and castle before the Alliance had arrived. What information they had would be vital and he could not move forward with his plan without it.

The plan to lock down the city was tedious at best, but it was the only way to make sure none of the agents of evil escaped. It was also putting pressure on the citizens of the city. They had been oppressed for a long time whilst the prince was in control and since they had been freed they were prisoners again. Bern knew he was doing the right thing, but he couldn't help but feel for the citizens of Jarrat.

Captain Tyson had been against the idea from the start and the delay did nothing for his mood. He wanted his people free from their imprisonment. He had been forced to sit back and do nothing whilst they suffered under the yoke of the Dark Knight and just when he thought there was chance for him to do something he was stopped again. In a way it was worse than before. To be able to free his people, but to choose not to was heartbreaking for him. Each day he questioned Bern on the condition of the pair and each day Bern told him to wait one more day.

"This is bordering on ridiculous," Tyson spoke to Bern in the command tent.

It was the first time Bern had left the castle and returned to the command tent since Alaric had left. He knew there would be many questions regarding Alaric's mysterious disappearance, questions he did not want to answer. The truth was that he could not answer. Alaric's destination had to remain secret for as long as possible, at least until he was safely in Castalia.

Not only that, but everyone would want answers on what they were doing. At first the army had been happy for the chance to rest, but with lack of leadership things were starting to get out of control. More and more the soldiers were having to be reprimanded for unbecoming behaviour. Luckily none of the soldiers from the Alliance had tried to gain entrance into the city. There is no telling what would happen if they did.

"Hadar is on his feet again. It cannot be long before Richmond and Tancred regain their consciousness." Bern started.

"I know it is hard for you Tyson, but this is something that we have to do." Jarwe saw the expression on the captain's face and tried to reassure him.

To make matters worse Captain Prewitt had gone missing. As much as he was an inferior soldier he still had followers within the Enteroite army. He knew that Prewitt could be dangerous on the loose, but as much as he did not believe the captain was a traitor he was an opportunist. There was no telling what trouble he would cause, given the chance. Things were not working out how Bern had hoped.

"Is there much point in defeating one tyrant just to replace it with another?" Tyson's comment was out of line, but he didn't care.

"Now you know that is not what we are doing." Sorrell snapped.

"There is more at stake than just Jarrat," Jarwe spoke forcefully.

"That is fine for you to say, general. It is not your home city that is surrounded by soldiers," Tyson returned, raising his voice to make his point.

Bern did not appreciate the conversation, but he did not have the heart to stop it. Both sides needed to vent. Once they had got it all out then he would tell them how it was going to be. He had tried resisting the urge to outrank Tyson, but there was no other way around it. He only hoped that Tyson would understand in time. Bern had been working closely with Duke Xarles in the castle and he knew he had the kingdom's best interest at heart.

"It is not an enemy army that holds your city. The soldiers are in place for the safety of your entire kingdom," Jarwe continued. "Or do you want the enemy roaming freely. I am sure the towns and villages would not put up a great fight against them." Jarwe did not think there was a risk to the rest of Entero, at least not immediately, but he thought it would prove his point.

The argument continued across the table for about half and hour before Bern finally spoke. He did not think it would take so long for everyone to get their opinions across and there was no telling how long it would continue. He thought that they could quite easily spend the rest of the day arguing. On the plus side that would give him another day, but on the down side there was a chance swords would be drawn eventually. The death of Tyson or one of his commanders would prove nothing. In the end he needed Tyson to join his command group. He would be a valuable asset in the upcoming battles.

"There is nothing we can do now. We need to wait until either Richmond or Tancred is awake. They will have information that we need to find the traitors in the city. Until then we will have to keep the soldiers where they are," his voice was firm and everyone listened to what he had to say.

"There is plenty that I can do. I can have the army move out of the city." Tyson did not like what Bern was suggesting. Originally martial law had only been implemented for a short time, but this time it was indefinite.

"Yes, you can move the army," Bern spoked softly. "But then I will move the Alliance into place. I am sure that the citizens of Jarrat would be calmer if your soldiers remained where they were."

"If you move your soldiers into Jarrat then I would have no choice, but to declare war on you." Bern knew the threat was coming, but he didn't know how genuine it was.

"You do not have the authority to declare war," Bern spoke calmly.

That took Tyson by surprise. He knew the queen was still sick, but he had not thought to find out who was in control. Bern had safely kept that a secret. He knew that was all about to change. Somehow he did not think he was going to like the answer.

"Who then has the authority?" he asked slowly, dreading the response.

"Duke Xarles is in command of the city, until the queen is ready to resume her power." Bern knew he had just won the argument. "Xarles has agreed with what we are doing and he has given me control until the threat has passed."

"I do not believe he has given the power of the city to a Remidian." He thought about continuing, but then he stopped and waited for Bern's response.

"He has not given me control of the city, but he does realise that what I do, I do for the good of everyone. If we fail then Jarrat does not stand a chance. Your people will at best be killed and at worst they will be slaves of the Evil One. Is that a fate you want to risk for your people?" That was the jackpot. There was no way Tyson could respond and Bern knew it. He didn't worry about waiting for a response. "Now I will let you know once Tancred or Richmond has woken. In the meantime you need to keep being patient."

It was clear to all it was the end of the discussion. Tyson was not happy, but he could not argue his point anymore. Bern had won and there was nothing he could do about it. The army would remain inside the city until Bern commanded. It would take him a while, but he would realise that Bern was doing the right thing.

"Any word when Alaric will be joining us?" Hulkan asked the question to change the subject and kill the silence.

Bern had hoped he would get away without speaking about Alaric, but there was never any real chance of that. He had decided since he left the castle he was just going to say that Alaric was resting. There was nothing else he could think of. If he mentioned that Alaric had left the castle with Ra'naroz then they would want to know where he had gone. Not only that they would want answers to questions he had no idea about.

"He is resting in the castle. He is still strained from his ordeal with Ra'naroz," Bern lied.

"Is he alright?" Dorn asked, concern in his voice.

"He will be fine. He just needs to rest," Bern didn't sound comfortable.

"What of the Dark Knight?" Hulkan continued to question Bern. "If Alaric is unfit then who is keeping an eye on him?"

"Don't worry about Ra'naroz. He has been taken care of. He won't be causing any trouble anymore." He wished he could have confidence in what he was saying. In truth there was a very good chance the Dark Knight could be causing mischief.

"I would like to see Alaric," Dorn suggested.

"I am sorry, but again no one is to come into the castle. The political state is very unstable. We need to tread carefully to make sure that Xarles remains in control. I believe he is the only one who truly cares about the queen and the kingdom more than his own rise to power." Bern hoped the excuse would still hold.

No one wanted to question him, although the excuse sounded thin. There should be no reason why they could not enter the castle. They all thought they would only strengthen the duke's standing with their presence. They didn't want to mention it and it was clear that Bern was not in the mood for discussion.

"Now I think that I shall return to the castle. There is still much to be done and hopefully Richmond and Tancred have woken." It was the last comment that kept anyone from protesting.

They all wanted the two men to wake. The first reason was to know their friends and companions were alright, but more importantly to have a purpose again. With the battle for Jarrat over and the clean up of the dead bodies done there was very little for them to do. Once the two men were awake they would have a new mission to sink their teeth into.

Bern stood and promptly left the tent. He didn't want to give anyone else a chance to speak. He had done what he had set out to do and that was enough. Now that Tyson knew how things were he would be less inclined to pull the soldiers from in and around the city. The entire exercise would be pointless if they didn't see it through to the end.

"Wait!" a voice called from behind Bern.

He thought about pretending he didn't hear the voice and continue walking, but he found himself curious to see who it was. When he turned around he saw Orric and Kilean walking towards him. They had concerned expressions on their faces. Bern had a feeling he was not going to like what they were going to say.

"Thank you," Orric spoke when they reached Bern. "I thought we might speak with you whilst you return to the castle?"

"Of course," Bern started walking as he replied. The sooner he made it back to the castle the sooner he could finish the conversation.

"I don't think you were telling us the truth about Alaric." Orric got straight to the point.

"Why do you say that?" He kept his voice casual as to avoid suspicion.

Orric looked at Kilean who in turn nodded. "We can feel when Alaric is close. We are connected to him and the prophecy. We know he is no longer in the castle."

Bern suddenly stopped when he heard the words and looked around. They were still walking through the campsite and he did not think it was an appropriate place to have such a conversation. He could see no one, but that was not to say there weren't soldiers inside the tents. When he was confident that no one had heard he moved along quickly.

"We know this is true." Orric continued when Bern did not respond.

"This is not the place for this conversation," Bern kept his voice low and continued to walk quickly.

It wasn't until they were out in the open before Bern slowed his step. Originally he was going to ride back to the castle, but the conversation had piqued his interest. He didn't stop, but he was comfortable to speak about Alaric. He only hoped the elf had not ruined everything. If even one soldier heard what he had said then it would be all over the campsite before nightfall.

"Alaric left four days ago," Bern kept his voice as low as possible, although there was no one within earshot.

"Where has he gone?" it was the first time Kilean had spoken.

"I am not supposed to say. If the enemy finds out what he is doing then he will not be safe," Bern replied.

There was a slight pause as the two elves considered Bern's words. There was no real reason for him to keep the information from the elves and yet there was no real reason why they should know. There was nothing that they could do with the knowledge. At least that's what Bern thought.

"It is important that you tell us," Kilean let Orric speak this time.

"I cannot see how this will help anyone," Bern said.

"Trust me, there is more to this than you know. You need to tell us where Alaric has taken Ra'naroz," Kilean spoke again.

The elf's words sent a shiver down Bern's spine. There was no way he could know that Alaric had taken the Dark Knight with him. He could only imagine the information had somehow been leaked. There were only three people who knew. Eldred had not left Alena's side which only left Xarles. He could not figure out how the information would have left Xarles and reached the two elves.

"Don't worry. No one has spoken about them leaving. Let's just say that Kilean has a strong intuition," Orric explained.

Bern wasn't sure what was happening, but he knew he was losing control of the situation. He did not like what the elves' were saying. For some reason he felt a sudden compulsion to tell them everything he knew. There was a subtle difference to the conversation. The elves were doing something to him. He could feel it. He needed to control himself if he was going to make the right decision. Suddenly he felt faint and his eyes started to flicker.

"I don't think you should be doing that?" Bern's voice had changed.

"What do you mean?" Orric sounded innocent.

"I know the subtle magic of the elves, but that is not the way to get information from a friend," he started lecturing.

"Who are you?" Kilean was the first one realise the change in Bern.

"That is not important," Heryion did not want them to know who he was. He figured if they were strong enough they could figure it out on their own. "Tell me why you need to know where Alaric is going?"

Orric looked at Kilean who again nodded, although this time it was out of resignation. He knew they were not going to get answers until they revealed their own secrets. Alaric was more important than keeping secrets. They needed answers so they had to give answers.

"Kilean can see fragments of the future," Orric started to explain. He was about to continue, but there was a strange look on Bern's face. "What is it?" he asked instead.

"Nothing, I was just thinking to myself." That was a lie. Heryion knew exactly what had caused the expression on his face to change. He had been wondering where Kilean had been. He had not known his name, but he knew of him and what he could do. He had thought since so much time had past that he had been killed. Things were starting to fall into place again. "Please continue what you were saying."

Orric knew there was more behind Bern's eyes than what he was saying, but there were more important matters for him to deal with. They could figure out who was behind the façade later. For the moment they needed answers about Alaric. They needed to know where he had gone.

"We know he has gone somewhere with the Dark Knight Ra'naroz. We also know he is in great danger." Orric revealed information that was already known. "We need to know where he has gone so we can help him."

This was a problem for Heryion, or more so Bern. Alaric had not wanted anyone to know where he was going. If he wanted to make an exception with the elves then he would have said so. The only real question was who was more in tune with the future? Did Alaric have a stronger connection with the prophecy or Kilean? If it was Bern he would have gone with Alaric, but Heryion had a little more information at hand.

"Tell me what you know and I might be able to help you." He had no intention of helping, but he didn't want them to know.

Heryion stopped walking as they neared the gate. There was more to the conversation than the walk between the campsite and the castle allowed. The three of them standing in front of the castle would look suspicious, but Heryion didn't care. He was sure that Bern could talk his way out of any questions.

"We don't know much," Orric was starting to explain, but Kilean cut in.

"I know Alaric is in great danger. It is hard to explain what I see, but I know what I know," Kilean explained nothing.

"Well that doesn't tell me anything. Alaric is already in great danger. Ever since he left Arsiliac he has been in great danger. If I am going to trust you then you need to give me a better reason."

Kilean looked at Bern, as if he was trying to see through the façade. He hoped if he looked hard enough he could figure out who was controlling Bern's body. The one thing he did know was it was an ally. He was comforted by that thought. What was uncomfortable was that he had no idea who it was.

"Anything involved with the Chosen One is sketchy. The future is constantly changing and his more so than any others. I can't see specifics, but I know if we don't get to him in time he will die." Kilean was not too convincing.

"As you said his future is constantly changing. Just because you see danger now doesn't mean that tomorrow you will. You are not convincing me to tell you what his is doing." Heryion was just playing with the elves. He was enjoying his chance to speak.

"Yes it changes, but this is something that has remained constant. There is not much time left," Kilean warned.

"There is no point in keeping this from us. You know we serve the prophecy and we would do nothing to jeopardise the Chosen One's chance for victory. We have as much at stake as everyone else." Orric was starting to become frustrated.

Heryion gave it one more thought. He had previously decided to tell them the truth, but he wanted to be careful. There was much more than his pride at stake. If he misjudged the situation then it would all be over. In the end he agreed with Orric. There was no reason for them to betray the prophecy or Alaric.

"He has gone to Castalia with Ra'naroz and Marina. He is looking for the Topaz stone." He did not think it would be a good idea to tell them about Alena's condition.

"Marina?" Orric looked at Bern and then Kilean.

"She is the daughter of King Unwin," Kilean explained slowly.

Orric still had a confused expression on his face. He knew that Kilean was trying to tell him something, but he could not work out what it was. His fellow elf was going to have to spell it out for him. He was becoming very confused.

"She has power." Kilean continued to give him clues. "She has been travelling with Alaric. They came to us in the south," he looked at both Orric and Bern as he spoke. He wanted to make sure that Bern did not understand what he was talking about.

Heryion almost starting laughing at the intrigue. He knew exactly what Kilean was speaking about and the fact that it was taking Orric so long to realise made things even more comical. He wanted to reveal that he knew what was happening, it would make the conversation go much quicker, but he thought it would be better if he didn't. There would be a better chance of them guessing who he was if he revealed his knowledge. Instead he just listened and waited for the answer to dawn on Orric.

"Oh, I know who she is," Orric stated at long last. It took a moment for his next question to dawn on him. "What about my daughter? She is supposed to be Alaric's companion." Heryion was not sure if there was something underlying in his comment, but if there was he chose to ignore it. At first Orric spoke to Kilean before he turned to Bern. "Where is Alena?"

Heryion had hoped to leave Alena out of the conversation, but it was only a matter of time before Orric asked after her. He was surprised it had taken so long.

"Alena is inside the castle," Heryion spoke slowly.

"Why is she still here? She should be with Alaric, the prophecy demands it," Orric raised his voice at the start and then remembered where he was.

Heryion was not sure how much Orric knew. It was well known to those who followed the prophecy that Alena would be taken prisoner. As far as what happened after that it was a little sketchy. He thought he would skip over the imprisonment part of the story and go straight to her current condition.

"Alena is in a coma. She is the reason why Alaric has gone to Castalia. He needs to recover the Topaz stone to revive her. If he does not succeed then she will die."

"I do not understand. This was not supposed to happen. She was supposed to travel with Alaric once he rescued her from the Dark Knight." Orric looked at Kilean.

Kilean shook his head. He had no idea what was happening. He had not foreseen anything happening to Alena. It was as much as a surprise to him as it was to Orric. That was something that didn't bode well. He had felt his gift slipping away from him in the past year. It was another sign of how bad it had become.

"What happened?" Orric asked when it was clear there would be no answers from Kilean.

"She and Eldred were taken prisoner in Nostalia. They were brought here and tortured in the dungeons. Ra'naroz did something to her. He knew if Alaric came then he could use her illness to keep himself alive. Now Eldred is keeping her alive, but I don't know how long he can keep going. Alaric needs to get back here as soon as possible," Heryion explained.

Orric didn't know what to say. He could not believe that his daughter was on the brink of death. He knew she would be taking risks with her life, but he had never imagined that it would go this far. With the new information he could think of nothing else but to go and see her.

"I have to see her," he spoke after a long silence. "I have to make sure that she is alright."

"That is not possible," Bern said. "Her condition is not well known and it is going to stay that way. As much as I believe we have captured all the followers of the Evil One in the castle there is still a chance that we have missed some. If they know about Alena then there is a chance they will try to take her life as well as Eldred's. For now you have to stay away."

"I have a right to see my daughter," Orric was starting to raise his voice again.

"Calm down Orric," Kilean spoke. "You know this is not the time. There are people looking after her. There is nothing you can do. This is not your battle to fight."

Orric had a wild expression on his face. There was nothing he could do and he knew it. It was the first time he felt completely helpless. Even when the Orglin were laying waste to his home at least he was able to attack. He wanted nothing more than to enter to castle and hold her in his arms, but he knew that would do no good. All he could do was trust the man before him and hope he was doing the right thing. If he knew exactly who or what he was speaking with that would ease his burden.

"We have another job to do," Kilean spoke mysteriously.

Although Heryion didn't know exactly what he meant he had a fair idea. He did not know if it was a good or a bad idea. He had not expected it, but that was not to say it wasn't the right thing to do. If Kilean wasn't able to see the future clearly then there was little chance that he could. There were too many surprises ahead and he didn't like it. He didn't know what the prophecy was doing. It was as if it could not make up its mind.

"So what are you planning on doing?" Heryion asked, as the two argued amongst themselves.

No matter how much Orric wanted to see Alena he knew that Kilean was right. They needed to find Alaric. Not only was it the only way to save her life it was their destiny. He could feel the prophecy tugging at him again. When he arrived at Jarrat the prophecy had given him peace for a short while, but it was time to be on the road again. There was nothing he could do about it.

"We will ride for Castalia," Kilean spoke on Orric's behalf. "We have to help Alaric. We cannot risk his life."

"What about the rest of the elves?" Heryion asked. "They will want to know where you have gone. It could be very disheartening for them."

"They know we go where there prophecy leads us. Lord Pernian will assume control of the elves and then of course he will defer power to you," Orric explained. "This is something that needs to be done."

"Very well. Make sure no one knows where you are going. Even if you don't say you are going after Alaric I am sure that people will work it out when they realise he is gone. I am sure you will be able to sneak out through the forest unseen." It was not a derogatory comment, but it could easily have been taken that way. Luckily both Orric and Kilean were too busy with their own thoughts.

They said a quick goodbye before they all went their separate ways. As soon as Bern started walking into the castle grounds he felt a sudden shift. Heryion's consciousness suddenly went back, deep inside Bern. He almost fell over as his awareness returned. He remembered nothing of the conversation with the elves. He looked over his shoulder and watched them walking away before he disappeared inside the castle walls. Luckily the guards knew who he was and didn't question him. It took him a moment before he realised what had happened. The entity inside him had come out again. Normally he could remember things the entity said, but this time he could remember nothing.

There was still much for him to do. Xarles would need to be updated on what was happening with the Alliance. He would need to check to see how Richmond and Tancred were fairing. As much as he had controlled the situation with Tyson he knew it was not over. If he didn't have an answer for him soon then the situation risked getting out of control.

As he walked through the gates he wished that he knew what he had said to the two elves and what their intentions were. He had a bad feeling he had revealed Alaric's location to them. That was something he did not want to do, but it was too late. The decision had been taken out of his hands and there was nothing he could do about it. He only hoped that the two elves didn't reveal the information to anyone else.

Chapter 19: Richmond Wakes

It was two days later, late in the morning, when Richmond finally woke. Hadar had been watching over him. As much as Hadar wanted to get back to the army he did not want to leave his two comrades in such a state. They had been through a lot together and he could not leave them. It would feel as though he was betraying them.

Bern was in a meeting with Xarles at the time. It had been the first chance he'd had since returning to the castle to see him. He had been avoiding the conversation as much as Xarles had been busy with other affairs. Bern was quite happy to let him get on with it and it was the duke who ended up summoning Bern to his private chambers. He had thought the general would have come on his own, but after two days it was obvious that he wouldn't.

After much convincing from the functionaries around the castle Bern was finally convinced that if he was going to stay in the palace he needed to look the part. His leather riding clothes made him look out of place and on more than one occasion he had been berated for being somewhere he shouldn't.

As much as he didn't have time to spend with the many tailors that were sent to his apartment it didn't give him a reason to procrastinate. Despite everything he still felt very uncomfortable in the finery he had been supplied. He wore a loose fitted, dark blue, silk shirt and despite the quality of the fabric it made his skin itch. Even the fine, black, linen pants didn't feel right. He was never more comfortable than when he was in his thick farming clothes. He couldn't believe anyone could live in such a fashion for all of their lives.

"How did Captain Tyson take the news when you told him?" Xarles asked the first question after the pleasantries had been taken care of.

"He was not happy, but he accepted your ruling. He is headstrong, but he is loyal to the crown. He knows you are a good man and will not lead the kingdom astray," Bern explained.

"That is good to know," Xarles didn't know how to take his last comment.

"Don't get me wrong. If they don't wake soon I am sure he will start having doubts," Bern added

"I doubt that Tyson will go against my command. He is a good soldier and a loyal subject," Xarles rebutted.

"Yes, but don't forget he is loyal to the queen. Just because he accepts your command now doesn't mean he won't change his mind later.

I would hate to see Entero sink into a civil war. I don't think I could handle that happening," Bern explained.

"Be that as it may but I will not let the captain take control of the city. If it comes to the crunch then I don't think I will have a choice," there was something ominous in Xarles' tone.

Bern did not like what he was hearing. He wished that he had not brought up the subject. Xarles had his back up and would be expecting Tyson to do something stupid. If things went bad, Bern would have no one to blame but himself. The last thing he wanted to do was order the Alliance to attack the Enteroite army.

Before Xarles could continue there was a knock on the door and a young serving woman entered. She carried a tray of food and a larger pitcher. Bern looked at her and then Xarles. The duke looked pleased she had arrived. There were two pewter cups on the table in front of them.

She placed the tray and pitcher on the table before leaving. Xarles didn't wait for the serving woman to leave before pouring the dark liquid from the pitcher into the two cups. Bern was surprised to see it was wine. It wasn't even midday and although he was grateful for the food he thought it was too early to drink. It was not the first time Xarles had been drinking early in the day.

"If you had the morning I've had you would understand," Xarles explained when he saw the expression on Bern's face.

Bern let the comment slide. There were more important matters for him to deal with and Xarles potential alcoholism was not one of them. He could certainly empathise with the man. He was in a stressful job and the noble men and women of Jarrat were not making life easy for him. All he could do was make a mental note of it.

Bern took a piece of cheese from the platter, but left the wine alone. He had to admit that the wine was tempting, but there was still so much he had to achieve. The main fear was if he started he wasn't sure he could stop.

There was a knock on the door that broke the uncomfortable silence. Bern was relieved for the sudden distraction as he had still not answered Xarles' comment. Xarles really didn't seem to notice and was more focused on refilling the cup in front of him.

Hadar walked into the room. His skin was still a little pale and there was a small amount of sweat on his forehead. Bern didn't think he should be out of bed. It was clear he was still suffering the effects of the torture. At the time Bern had hoped he'd received the same punishment as the others. After the fact he was glad he hadn't. It would have proven nothing for him to be in the same state as them.

"What it is Duke Hadar?" Xarles asked.

"I thought you might like to know that Richmond has woken."

"Thank you Hadar. I will come and see him once I have finished with Xarles," Bern was grateful for the news.

"You can take your time. He is still groggy. I think it will take some time before he is ready to talk," Hadar explained.

"Thank you. Now it looks as though you could use some rest. Why don't you go and lie down. I will check on Richmond shortly," Bern suggested.

Hadar was happy with that. He was feeling tired and he did need to rest. He also didn't want to be in the room with Xarles. He had struggled to be polite in the first place and Xarles' attitude did nothing to improve his mood. If he remained much longer he didn't think that he would be able to hold his tongue.

"There is not much more we need to discuss," Xarles spoke quickly after Hadar shut the door.

As much as Bern wanted to talk with Xarles it was much more important to speak with Richmond. "I don't think there is much that can't wait. The most important thing is to get the information from Richmond and then hunt down the traitors. That will stop any problems with Tyson." Bern had already started to stand before he finished speaking.

"Okay, you can go, but we need to speak again soon. There are still many troubling issues that we need to fix," Xarles replied as Bern made his way out of the room. It seemed as though Xarles was more concerned with the pitcher of wine anyway. It was a disturbing thought, but one for another time.

Bern thought that Duke Xarles would have been able to run the castle without his help. Despite his penchant for a wine or ale he was still doing a good job. Bern had enough on his mind without having to worry about the running of the kingdom. He was considering going back to the army campsite and staying there. He would if he could, but it was not realistic.

He had to find the traitors in the city. He needed to make sure they were all taken care of before Alaric returned. Once Alaric was back they would need to be ready to march. Until then the army could not leave Jarrat. He knew that to be true.

When he arrived at Lady Amilie's apartment he found the physician leaving the room. With the Dark Knight defeated and Xarles in command the physician was a lot nicer to Bern. He was still arrogant, but he was not as standoffish as he had been. He knew that Bern was close to Duke Xarles and that would make him a dangerous adversary.

"How is he?" Bern asked.

"Lord Richmond is conscious, but that is all that I can say about him. He is not responsive to any of my tests and he is yet to say a word." The physician did not instil any confidence in Bern.

"What about Tancred?" Bern asked, already knowing the answer.

"No change. I still think he doesn't want to recover. His wounds were no greater than the others. There is no other reason why he should not be getting better." The physician had a puzzled expression on his face. "I am doing all that I can for him, but I am at a loss."

"Thank you," was all that Bern could say.

The physician walked away. He was still uncomfortable around Bern, he knew the man could kill him on a whim and that was very disturbing. Even though things had calmed down in the castle he was still unsure of what Bern was capable of. Bern knew the physician felt this way and he played on it. He could have done plenty to ease his mind, but he thought it was better the physician feared him. There was less chance of being betrayed that way.

The room inside the apartment was dark except for one small lantern lit in the corner. Richmond lay on the couch in the sitting room, his head propped up by a number of pillows. He didn't move when Bern entered. It was only after closer inspection that Bern realised he was even breathing. Although his eyes were open there were no reactions from the rest of his body. Bern wondered if he had even recovered at all. There was more to being awake than having your eyes open.

"Richmond!" Bern called out as he stood over him.

As he expected there was no response. He didn't know why Hadar had come to get him. He sat down in a chair opposite Richmond and looked at him There was no significant change and that was what he was looking for. He was not going to gather any more information whilst Richmond was in such a state.

"There is no need to yell," the voice was hoarse, but there was no doubt that it was Richmond.

"It is good to see you." Bern didn't know what else to say.

"It is good to see you too, but can you keep your voice down. I have a killer headache." He held his head as he spoke.

Bern wanted to jump up and down, but he controlled himself. He didn't think the sudden movement would do anything to help. He was just happy Richmond was talking. Although he wasn't sure if he was up for questioning Bern didn't really have time to waste. He hoped Richmond would remember the information he needed.

"I need you to answer some questions for me." Bern watched him closely.

"I will do what I can." Richmond tried to sit up, but that didn't work. For the moment he would have to remain where he was.

"When you came to Jarrat you met with some agents of the Evil One. I need you to tell me who they are." Bern cut straight to the point.

"I'm sorry, but I think you might have me mistaken for someone else. I have not been to Jarrat for at least five years." Richmond tried to sit up again, but couldn't. He was clearly becoming agitated.

Bern had expected him to be somewhat disorientated. He even expected a certain amount of memory loss, but this was more than that. If he did not recall coming to Jarrat then there was a good chance he did not remember Bern. He just wondered how far back his memory went.

"What is the last thing that you remember?" Bern asked slowly.

Richmond looked more closely at Bern. He tried to focus on the man before him, but when he did his head hurt. There was something wrong with the situation. The man in front of him was not right for some reason. He looked for as long as he could before he had to close his eyes.

"Who are you?" he asked finally when he realised what was wrong. "You don't look like a doctor."

Bern didn't know how to respond. He had a bad feeling that Richmond would not remember who he was. He thought about calling for the physician, but decided to see if he could gather some information first. There had to be something he could gauge from the conversation.

"I'm not a physician. I am a friend of yours."

"I don't know you." He tried to focus on Bern, but again his eyes hurt his head. Although he could not focus on the man in front of him he knew he did not know him.

"What is the last thing that you remember?" Bern asked again.

Richmond tried to think, but it was harder than trying to see. His head ached whenever he tried to focus on the past. He couldn't remember why he was in such a state. Normally it would have been from over consumption of wine, but he knew that was not the case. His current condition was something completely different from a hangover. When he tried to focus on a thought scorching pain ripped through his head.

"I don't know," his voice was strained as he spoke. "I can't seem to remember anything."

Things were much worse than what Bern had thought. There was nothing else he could do. He had to call for the physician to return. He tugged on the bed pull and waited for a servant to arrive.

To Bern's surprise it was not a servant, but the physician himself who entered the room. He was glad to see the man, but surprised nevertheless.

"I knew you would be calling at some stage. I told the servants to get me as soon as the bell pull rang," the physician spoke before Bern could ask the question.

"I am glad that you did. He has been awake for about half an hour now. He can't remember anything," Bern explained.

The physician walked to where Richmond was lying. Richmond had his eyes closed and initially the physician thought he was sleeping. When he crouched down beside him Richmond opened his eyes. The physician watched him closely. His eyes only stayed open for a second before he shut them again.

The first test the physician did was to force Richmond's eyelids open and examine his eyes. Richmond didn't like what he was doing, but he did nothing to resist. He knew something was seriously wrong. The man who had been questioning him seemed quite concerned. The fact he was in pain and he could not remember anything made matters worse.

"What do you think?" Bern asked when the physician was finished with his examination.

"There doesn't seem to be any permanent damage. I think he just needs time to recover." he thought for a moment. "I will have someone bring some medicine for him. That should help the healing process."

"What do you mean 'should'?" Bern did not like the sound of that.

"I don't exactly know what is causing the amnesia, so I can't be exactly sure how to fix it. All I can do is try and hope for the best," the physician explained.

Bern still did not like the sound of what the physician said, but he could understand. The Dark Knight had done something. It was more than just a beating that they received in the dungeons. He had been suspicious of it at the time, but now he was sure. He wondered if Eldred was able to help. That would be his next option.

"Thank you for your help. I am sure the medicine will help." Bern ended the conversation.

The physician left happy, but Bern was not so sure on his own feelings towards the man. He knew the physician was doing the best he could, but he could not shake the feeling the results should be different. In the end he was just hoping he was not right about Ra'naroz. If he did something magical then there was a chance they would not recover and he would have to make a very tough decision. That was something he could worry about later. He would gather advice from Eldred before he made any rash decisions.

He moved quickly through the corridors towards the room where Eldred would be watching over Alena. He wanted to make sure no one stopped him for conversation. The nobles, both minor and major, were starting to recognise his face. They also knew that Xarles was staring to defer decisions to him. If they wanted something done they could go behind Xarles' back and try and sweet talk Bern. Bern had tried to explain that they were wasting their time, but they didn't seem to get the message. They were too consumed with their own intrigues. That was even more frustrating.

He found Eldred hunched over Alena's bed. At first he thought the old wizard was asleep, but as he walked into the room he lifted his head. Bern had to take a step back when he saw Eldred's face. He could not ever remember Eldred looking so old. His face was covered with thick wrinkles and his eyes were dark and sunken. Bern almost didn't recognise him.

"How is everything?" Bern thought it was the most appropriate way to greet him.

"It could be a lot worse." There was no strength in Eldred's voice and the humour was lost.

Bern moved closer to have a look at Alena. She looked pale and frail. He could not believe it was her lying in the bed. She had always been so strong when they had travelled together and now she looked as frail as a new born baby. Her chest didn't rise and fall and instantly and Bern thought she had died. Eldred's posture did nothing to refute the point. Bern didn't know what to say.

"What is it that I can do for you?" Eldred finally asked when Bern didn't speak.

"Ah, I came to check to see how Alena was fairing," Bern was almost too afraid to speak the words.

"She is fine. She will remain fine as long as my spell remains up," Eldred explained.

"Are you sure, it doesn't look like she's breathing?" Bern could hardly bring the words out of his mouth.

"She's fine. I have her in a state of stasis. It is the only way to keep her alive," Eldred sounded washed out.

Bern was not sure Eldred should be speaking. He did not sound as though he should even be awake. His voice was strained and he looked as though he should be in bed. He didn't think Eldred was going to be able to help with his problem. He wasn't sure if he should even mention it to him.

"But I do not believe that is the reason you have come here," Eldred puffed as he spoke. "Why don't you tell me why you are really here?"

Even in his weakened state he was still able to comprehend the situation. He could tell there was something else on his mind. He was not really up for questioning, but he would do all he could to help. He knew his mission wasn't the only one pertinent to the survival of the Seven Kingdoms. If Bern needed his help then that's what he would do.

"I don't think it is that important. You look as though you have enough on your plate." Bern didn't want to burden him any further.

"Just spit it out. I don't have time to waste." Eldred snapped.

"Richmond has woken, but he can't remember anything. Tancred is still unconscious and he seems to be getting worse. The physician doesn't know why. I was wondering if you think that Ra'naroz did something to them?" Bern asked.

"I don't think there is much I can do. All my energy is being used keeping Alena in her current state. If you have them brought here then I could have a look." It was all Eldred could do.

Bern thought on it for a moment. The wizard did not look as though he needed any extra stress. He wished he had never mentioned it. He had to think up an excuse not to offend him.

"They will be fine. I don't think either of them are in any condition to be moved. I am sure I am just being paranoid. Hadar is up and about and he is fine." That wasn't exactly true, but he didn't want Eldred to worry.

"Well, you know where I am if you change your mind," Eldred tried to sound jovial, but in his current state it didn't work.

Bern simply walked away. Eldred had let his head drop back into his hands. He didn't think there was any point saying goodbye. He doubted that Eldred would even hear what he said. Things were not looking good for the Alliance. Things had been running smoothly, relatively speaking, until they reached Jarrat. Things weren't getting any better and there was a very good chance he would lose some of his new friends. The physician really had no idea and there was no one else around to help.

As soon as he left the apartment he was met by some minor noble. He recognised the woman, but could not remember her name. She was already speaking to him before he noticed her. He couldn't really hear what she was saying. He was too busy thinking about how he was going to get the information he required.

"So, what do you think?" They were the first words he heard.

"Yes, whatever," He just wanted to get rid of her and those words seemed to do the job. There was no thought to the implications of his words.

He was relieved when she walked away. He did not have the energy to deal with minor nobles. There were more important things for him to do. Once she had left he quickened his pace. If anyone else had the same idea then they would be sadly mistaken. He was not going to indulge anyone else. He needed to get back to Richmond. He was hoping he might be able to jog his memory.

Richmond didn't look happy when Bern entered the apartment. He was sitting up, which was a good sign, but he didn't look well. His skin was pale and he was sweating. Bern wouldn't have been surprised if he had been overdoing things. It was a good sign, nonetheless. He was clearly getting better.

There was a plate of food on the small table in front of the couch where Richmond was seated. It looked as though the food had been moved around, but nothing had been eaten. He would have figured Richmond would be ravenously hungry. He couldn't remember the last time he had eaten.

"You should eat something. It will help you build your strength," Bern spoke like he was speaking with one of his children.

"I am not hungry," Richmond panted as he spoke. "I just want to rest."

Bern knew it was the right thing to do. Richmond looked as though he needed to rest, but Bern could not allow it. He needed to try and gather more information. He had to try and help Richmond regain his memory.

"Do you know who I am?" Bern asked.

"No," was Richmond's response.

"Do you remember anything that happened to you recently?" Bern pushed further, even though it was clear that Richmond did not want to speak.

"No," Richmond spoke between clenched teeth.

Bern was getting nowhere, but he had to keep pressing. He hoped if he kept pushing he would be able to spark something inside Richmond's mind. He didn't think letting him rest was the answer, or at least it would take too long.

"You have to remember something. A lot has happened to you recently," Bern continued.

"What do you want from me?" Richmond raised his voice. When he finished speaking he started coughing.

"I want you to remember. A lot of lives are resting on your memory," Bern pushed harder.

"I can't." Richmond suddenly grabbed his head and cried out in pain.

Bern wasn't sure if he should try and help. He didn't know what he could do, so he remained standing where he was and watched Richmond writhe in pain. After a minute had past he thought about calling for the physician, but as he moved to the bell pull Richmond stopped. He panted for air and there was a slight moan to his breathing. Bern felt sorry for him, but he could not let him rest.

"Do you remember anything?" Bern asked again.

"No, why are you torturing me?" he sounded in pain.

Bern was about to speak again, but he noticed something had changed. It was more than the fact that Richmond was now lying on the couch again. There had been a sudden shift in his demeanour. Bern hoped he had remembered something, but he didn't dare to ask. He just watched and waited for Richmond to respond.

"Torture?" it was a question.

"Yes, you are remembering something?" Bern responded.

"Why?" he cried out. "Why is this happening?" Richmond was obviously in distress.

Bern didn't know what to do. He had not been expecting such a response. Richmond was writhing on the couch as if he was in great pain. Something had gone seriously wrong. All Bern could do was stand and watch. There was nothing that he could do to help.

Richmond cried out in pain for over five minutes before he finally calmed down. When he had finished screaming he curled up in a ball and whimpered. Bern didn't know what was worse. He looked so pitiful. Whatever had caused his anguish had caused him pain. Bern needed to know what had happened, but he was not sure he should push so hard.

"What do you remember?" Bern was almost afraid to ask.

Bern's words made Richmond look up. He looked as though he was surprised to see Bern standing before him. It was like he was coming out of a dream. It was like coming out of a nightmare. He looked relieved when he realised where he was.

"What happened?" the questions kept going around in circles.

"I think you remembered something." Bern was slowly beginning to understand what had happened. It seemed as though he made the realisation before Richmond did.

"That can't be real." Richmond was slowly remembering. "Why would I be in a dungeon? Why would I be getting tortured? It doesn't make any sense."

It was time for Bern to fill in the blanks. He hoped once he started that Richmond would be able to remember the rest. As much as the painful memory had been disturbing it was also a good sign. It meant he was slowly starting to recover.

Richmond listened in awe as Bern explained what he had been doing. Although Bern didn't have all the information since he left Bellarome there had been enough to amaze him. He didn't speak until Bern had finished.

"So I am Lord of Bellarome?" the question sent a shiver down Bern's spine.

He had not figured that Richmond's memory was so far gone. He did not know how long Richmond had been Lord of Bellarome, but he figured it had been for a long time. Just when he thought the situation had become better it suddenly became much worse. There was very little hope he would remember the information that Bern needed. Bern's recital seemed to have had no effect at all.

"I think it is probably time for you to rest." Bern wasn't sure what else he could say.

"I am sorry that I can't help you, but I seem to be missing a great deal of my life." Richmond tried to think. There had to be something from his past that he could remember. Suddenly a name came back to him. "Is Tancred here?"

Bern was about to leave when he asked the question. He had skipped over Tancred's condition deliberately. He didn't think it would do Richmond any good. Since he brought up Tancred's name there was nothing Bern could do. It was another sign his memory was returning and another positive step. He only hoped he would be able to handle the truth.

"Tancred was also in the dungeons with us. He has not yet recovered from his injuries. He is resting in the bedroom," Bern explained, leaving out a few details.

Richmond didn't know how to respond. The memory from the dungeon was still thick in his mind. It was all too real. He could still feel the pain. He could only imagine what Tancred had gone through to still be unconscious. He could tell that Bern was leaving something out. At first he didn't want to know, but the more he thought about it the more he wanted to know what was missing.

"What are you keeping from me?" he asked the question slowly, as if he was still unsure he should ask it.

"It is nothing pertinent to your condition." Bern did not want to reveal the true extent of Tancred's condition. He feared that Richmond would slip into a malaise and that was something he could not afford.

"I need to know." There was something in the back of Richmond's mind that was irritating him.

"The physician does not believe that Tancred's condition is entirely due to the physical stress that he endured. There is a chance that his mental state is causing him to remain unconscious."

Richmond had to take some time to think on the new information. He knew Tancred was close to him, but he could not remember why. He also knew the reason why Tancred would not want to recover, but he could not remember. The more he thought about it the more he had a feeling it was bad. It was frustrating that the information was in his head, but it was too far away for him to reach. Just when he thought he had found it, it disappeared.

"Tell me what happened? The memory is in my mind, but I just can't reach it," Richmond pleaded.

Bern was about to speak, but then he stopped. If the memory was in his head then he would have to find it for himself. He needed to be able to remember and it seemed like the logical progression. If he kept feeding him the answers then he would never have to work them out for himself.

"You need to think harder. All the answers are in there. You just have to find them." Bern stayed firm on his decision.

Richmond started smacking the side of his head. He hoped he would be able to knock the answer out. It was a silly plan. He kept going until his head started to ache, but the answer didn't come to him. There was nothing he could do.

"I think I am going to sleep now." Richmond didn't bother with getting off the couch. He simply stretched out and closed his eyes.

The sudden finality of his decision astounded Bern. He wanted to berate him further, but he stopped just as he opened his mouth. In the end he did not think he was going to get any answers. There was nothing more he could do. He sat and watched Richmond until he was sure he was asleep. He though if he sat and watched long enough then the answers would magically come to him. Bern laughed as he stood. The entire idea was ridiculous.

Chapter 20: Trouble in the Castle

The next day, Bern was woken by a knock on the door. The sudden noise was enough to get his heart racing, he had not been expecting anyone. He walked sleepily to the door. The light of dawn had yet to creep through the window. He rubbed his eyes as he moved.

He was surprised to see a young pageboy standing on the other side. He had not requested someone to wake him up and the boy held nothing in his hands. There would have to be a good reason for him being there. If there wasn't then he would make sure that the boy was punished. Bern had not slept well and he did not appreciate being woken.

What the boy had to say to him both intrigued and angered him. Duke Xarles had summoned him to his personal chambers. It was the first time the duke had ordered his appearance. Previously when someone had come for Bern it had always been in the form of request. He wondered why Xarles would all of a sudden command his presence. There was no point in taking his anger out on the pageboy, but Xarles would definitely hear about it.

Bern stormed through the hallways as he made his way to Xarles' apartments. No one was going to talk to him. One minor noble was about to speak as he went past, but he saw the look on Bern's face and decided against it. It would not take long for the rumours to spread through the castle, but Bern did not care. He was sick of the silly little political games the nobles played. Although they called him general and lord he was not suited for life in court. He was much happier when he was at the end of a plough. That life seemed like a lifetime ago. It was a much simpler time for him.

The door was shut when he reached Xarles' apartment, but that did not stop him. Bern did not give the duke the courtesy of knocking on his door. It would be a sure sign of submission and that was not something he was prepared to do. He pushed the door open and stormed into the room. He was about to start his tirade, but something stopped him. There was an air in the room that did not feel right. It was not what Bern was expecting. He wanted to know what was happening before he spoke.

Xarles sat with his back to Bern. He was staring out the window as if he didn't see him enter. That was even more intriguing. Bern wanted to speak, but he could not bring himself to break the silence.

"At what point did you think that it was a good idea to promise Lady Jocelin the estates of Lord Silvain?" Xarles kept his back to Bern, but his tone set the scene for the conversation.

Bern's curiosity quickly turned to confusion. He had heard the names, but he had no idea who they were. It was like he had walked into a conversation that wasn't meant for him. He thought, with Xarles' back turned to him, that might be the case. When he didn't respond and Xarles turned around the situation became even more surprising.

"I have no idea what you are talking about. It would be nice if you would explain," Bern kept his tone level.

The question should have put Xarles on the back foot, but he did not miss a beat. He had been expecting such a response. Not the exact words, but something close nevertheless.

"I have it on good authority you were speaking with Lady Jocelin yesterday. She has claimed that you have given her the estates of the late Lord Silvain. Now I think that it is in bad taste to leave a grieving window and her two children nowhere to live," there was a certain amount of smugness in his voice.

Bern did not know how to reply. All the anger he had felt about being summoned was now gone. He had to think about what the duke was accusing him of. He had no recollection of speaking with a Lady Jocelin. He didn't even know who Lady Jocelin was... and then it dawned on him.

"There was someone who was talking at me yesterday. I had a lot on my mind and I wasn't really listening to her." Bern had to admit.

"Well there in lies the problem. She asked for you to give her possession of Lord Silvain's estate. He was one of the richest nobles in Entero, until he was killed on the battlefield," Xarles explained.

Bern didn't think that his words sounded correct. "I didn't think that any of the nobles had fought in the battle."

"A few had gotten mixed up in the madness. That is one of the jobs that I have the painful task of sorting out. It seems as though some of the nobles believe they can go behind my back," Xarles did not sound impressed.

Bern was slowly starting to catch up with the conversation. He had never wanted to get involved with the politics. He had never wanted to be in command of the army. There was a lot happening in his life that he didn't want, but that was no excuse.

"I did not agree to anything." Bern hoped that was the right answer.

"Then why would she claim that you did?" Xarles' anger was starting to dissipate, although it was still there.

Bern had to think back, but the answer finally dawned on him. "She was talking incessantly at me and I thought the best way to get rid of her was to agree with what she was saying. I had no idea what she was talking about."

Bern's honesty did nothing to calm Xarles' anger. In fact it made things worse. The duke could not believe what he had heard.

"I can't believe you would do something so carelessly." He chose his words carefully. "You cannot simply pass off the nobles by ignoring them. Now she is spreading the word that she is taking over the estates. The castle is in an uproar." Xarles was trying to vent his rage, but it was not subsiding.

The tirade continued for almost five minutes. Bern simply sat and listened to his words. Until Xarles had finished there was no point in trying to defend himself. He knew the duke would not listen to anything he had to say.

"I am sorry, but I am not to blame." It was a long shot. "I have no power in the castle. Nothing that I say can have any bearing."

"I know that is true and you know that is true, but what the rest of the castle believes is a totally different story. People are starting to believe the rumours they are hearing. Think what will happen when people start moving around today." Xarles was still not happy. "Now I have to put away all the things I had to do today to put this little fire out."

"I wouldn't worry too much about it. All that Jocelin has at the moment is her word that I gave my word. Now I don't know too much about court politics, but I do not believe that is enough for her to take control of Silvain's estate." Bern's words made sense and Xarles knew it.

The duke had not thought completely about the situation before he berated Bern. In the end he was just upset that he had more work to do and he needed someone to vent his anger on. Now he had the embarrassing task of admitting that he was wrong. He should have slept longer on his problem. His head was still reeling from the wine he had drunk the day before. Another drink would ease his pain, but knew that wasn't an option. He had a long day ahead of him and he needed all the wits he had left.

"I am sorry, you are right. This is going to be a long day and I need to reserve my anger for the appropriate people." Xarles dropped his head as he spoke.

"I wouldn't worry too much about it. We all have a lot on our minds. I think you should make it known that I have no power within the castle. That should solve both our problems," Bern explained.

"That will only help in the short term. Whilst the nobles believe you have power they will give you the respect that you need. The trade off is that they will pester you." Xarles was right.

Bern didn't like it as much as Xarles didn't, but there was nothing they could do. Bern needed to be looked upon as a leader within the castle. Even though he would not be able to make any real decisions it was important that everyone thought he could.

"How is the queen?" Bern thought it was a good chance to change the conversation.

Xarles looked suddenly sad and Bern wished he had not asked the question. "There have been no signs of improvement. All she does is sit in her apartment and stare out the window. She will not feed herself, she will not use a toilet. It is like she has just given up the will to live." It was obviously having an effect on him.

"How did things get this bad?"

"It is the affect the Evil One is having on the world. There is only so much that we can do," Xarles responded in kind.

The feeling in the room had turned morose. Neither of them knew what to say. The immensity of their situations was starting to get to them. There didn't seem to be any light at the end of the tunnel. Without information from Richmond there was no way for Bern to move forward. Xarles was trying to keep the castle in order until Oriana was able to recover, but he was drowning in all the paperwork. Everyone wanted to take and no one wanted to help. The vultures were hovering over the carcass of the kingdom.

"I better get going," Bern suddenly suggested. "Hopefully Richmond should be waking. With any luck he will start remembering things."

"Of course, we all have things to do today," Xarles didn't stand whilst Bern left the room. He needed something to eat before he braved the throne room. He rang the bellpull next to his chair as soon as Bern had left.

Bern quickened his step once he was out of Xarles' apartment. The last thing he wanted was to be stopped by another noble. He had already done enough damage and he knew the nobles would be looking for him. They would see him as an easy target.

There was nothing Bern could do to avoid being stopped in the corridor. He tried to ignore the first nobleman as he walked past, but the man kept following him, snapping at his heels. He would not leave until Bern had given him his ear.

"My name is Earl Marlon, I understand that you have granted Lady Jocelin the estates of Lord Silvain?" It was a question that was not a question.

"I do not know where you would have heard such a rumour. I have not granted anyone anything." He slowed his pace, but Bern would not stop.

"That is very interesting news." Earl Marlon thought as his walked. "I do not understand why she would say such a thing. She must know that once we learned the truth she would be run out of the castle."

Bern had not realised a simple dismissal of agreement could cause such a ripple effect. Now he felt bad for Lady Jocelin. Although she was trying to be sneaky and manipulative she did not deserve what she had coming. With those few words she would be ostracized and ridiculed by her fellow nobles. When it was said and done she had no one to blame but herself. Bern wished he could explain what had happened, but that would be detrimental to himself.

"I am sure it was just a misunderstanding. I would not be so quick to plan her demise," Bern spoke carefully.

"Ah, yes, I am sure of that." It was clear Marlon had not listened to a word that he had said. "I thank you for you time, I must be moving on now."

Bern wanted to say more, but he was happy the conversation was over. He understood why Xarles had been so upset with him. He had inadvertently caused an uproar within the castle. Each time he opened his mouth he seemed to make things worse. It would be much easier if he did not say anything at all to the nobles, but that would not solve anything. He just had to make sure he watched what he said.

It did not take long before another noble sidled up to him. Bern didn't want to speak, but he knew he had no choice. He had started something that ignorance was not going to fix. He had to think of a way to find a solution to his problem. It was the only way he could make it up to Xarles.

He spoke to three more nobles before he reached the door to Amilie's apartment. Each time he tried a different tact, but each time the noble left licking their lips. It didn't matter what slant he put on the situation they all saw things to their advantage. He hated to think what would happen to Lady Jocelin. He kept the thought in his mind that she had brought things upon herself. Her greed was her undoing. It wasn't much, but it was enough to make himself feel better.

There was nothing that Bern could do about the situation. As he opened the door he knew he had to concentrate on his own problems. He had to get the information that was locked inside Richmond's mind. That was the only chance to stave off a revolution. He doubted very much that Tancred would recover in time. There was no guarantee he would recover at all.

"Good morning, Bern," Richmond greeted him as he entered the apartment.

It was a promising sign. Richmond was standing, something he had not been able to achieve on his own the day before. There was plenty of colour in his cheeks and he was not sweating. All in all Bern thought he looked much better. A renewed hope filled his chest. He was confident he was going to get the answers he was searching for.

"Good morning Richmond, how are you feeling this morning?" He could hardly bring himself to ask the question.

"I am feeling much better, but I am still not completely better. I can only remain standing for a short period of time," Richmond replied.

"What about Tancred? Has there been any change to his condition?" Bern was avoiding the question he really wanted to ask.

"There has been no change. He is still in a coma and it doesn't look like he is going to return any time soon." It was a good sign that he was remembering his old friend.

"How is your memory?" He held his breath as he waited for the response.

"Some things are coming back to me now. I remember what I am doing in Jarrat and I remember what brought me here," he explained.

It was like Richmond was deliberately being obtuse, but in reality he didn't understand what Bern was insinuating. The conversation was frustratingly slow, but Bern did not have the heart to come straight out and ask the only question he needed the answer to. He could only dance around to the subject for so long before he just came out and asked.

"Do you remember coming to Jarrat?" Bern asked.

"I remember coming here. I have been here many times. The most recent visit is still hazy. I know that we came here on a mission, but I can't remember what it was. I don't know how we ended up in the dungeons, but I can remember the pain. It is the pain that is foremost in my mind," Richmond explained.

The answer deflated Bern's hope. As much as he didn't want to keep pushing there was no other option. He had one more day before he had to report back to the Alliance. Tyson would not be happy if he did not have an answer. In fact no one would be happy if he didn't come back with a solution. The army would be getting restless again. Although it was still suffering from the losses of battle it would not be long before they were ready to march again. Everything was starting to snowball and there was nothing he could do about it.

"You came here to spy for the army. You came here and met with someone from the enemy. I need you to remember the name of that person. Things are rolling out of control and this is the only way to make things better." Bern just came out and said it.

There was a blank look on Richmond's face. That was not a good sign at all. It was clear he had no idea what Bern was talking about. Bern had hoped his words would jog Richmond's memory. It didn't work and now he was running out of ideas. It was getting to the fact that he was going to need to come up with another solution.

"You have to remember something," Bern pleaded when there was no response.

"I am sorry Bern, but my head is still sketchy. I am sure it will come back to me in time. I have already gained so much of my life back since yesterday. I am sure it won't take long for the rest to come back," Richmond explained.

It was after his speech that Richmond suddenly sat down. The movement took Bern by surprise. He stood and watched Richmond waiting for an explanation. Richmond thought it was obvious, but by Bern's reaction it was not.

"I still have dizzy spells. I try and stay upright for as long as I can. That means when I run out of energy I suddenly drop. The physician said it was the best way for me to recover. Once I feel better I will stand up again." Richmond explained.

"So is there anything you remember about your time in Jarrat?" Bern asked. "Even the tiniest of details might be useful."

Richmond tried to think. Again all his thoughts were scattered amongst each other. It was more controlled than the day before, but he still could not summon the memories he required. Again they were on the edge of his mind, but just far enough away that he could not reach them. Suddenly something came back to him. He was not sure if it was going to help, but it was something.

"We stayed at an inn," Richmond suddenly blurted out.

"Excellent, what was the name of the inn?" Bern asked excitedly. Finally they were getting somewhere.

Richmond's face suddenly turned from excited to upset. That was all that had come back to him. As soon as the words left his mouth he realised how stupid the comment was. The memory had come back to him so suddenly that he didn't have a chance to think before he spoke. Now he had something else to occupy his mind. If he could remember the inn then there was no reason why he could not remember its name. He could see the inn in his mind. He could see the innkeeper. He could see everything except for the sign hanging over the door. Whenever he tried to focus on the sign in his memory it disappeared.

"Give me a moment. It is there, I know it is, but I just need a moment," Richmond sounded genuine as he spoke.

Bern sat down as he waited for Richmond to remember. After a minute had passed Bern doubted the memory was going to come back. He wanted to speak, but he couldn't bring himself to break Richmond's concentration. He needed something from him and it seemed as though it was the best chance he had.

"I have it," Richmond cried out after about five minutes. He had racked his brain until the answer finally came to him. "We stayed at an inn called the Royal Watchman." He seemed pleased with himself.

Bern stood from where he was seated. Finally he had remembered something. Bern was excited, but only for a moment. There was nothing he could do with the information by itself. There had to be more inside Richmond's head. With the new memory he hoped there was more to follow.

"Is there anything else? That really doesn't give me much to go on." Bern pushed when there was no further information.

"I am sorry, but that is it," Richmond sounded resigned.

Bern was not happy, but at least he had something to do. He could check out the inn and hope that the innkeeper had some information for him. It was a long shot, but it was better than waiting in the castle. The longer he stayed inside the castle the more trouble he seemed to be causing. He did not like to think what was going to happen after his various conversations with the nobles.

"Okay, I will go to the inn and see what I can find. Are you sure there is not something else you can tell me? Any information would be helpful." Bern thought it was worth a shot.

"No, that is it. There is nothing more for the moment."

He had tried to remember more about his time in Jarrat, but there was nothing. Before, when he remembered something, he knew it was in his mind. The memory was always just out of reach, but now there was nothing for him to grasp at. He would just have to wait for his memory to come back on its own.

"Thank you Richmond." Bern also resigned himself to the fact that was all the information he was going to get for now. "I will let you rest. Hopefully I we get some more answers inside the city."

Bern was not looking forward leaving the room. He was sure there was more than one noble who would be looking for him. The rumours would have spread throughout the castle. All the noblemen and women who had not spoken to him already would want confirmation of what they were hearing. It was going to be a difficult task for him to ignore them all, but it was something he was going to have to do. He would just have to deal with Xarles when he returned from the city.

"Why have you not left?" Richmond asked as Bern stood at the door.

"Things are not quite that easy," Bern replied. "There are a lot of people who want to speak with me and I don't particularly want to speak with them."

Richmond started laughing. "Welcome to the world of politics. If you like this you should try being a noble in Darshival. We take intrigue to an entirely different level. If you were in Bellarome now there would have already been half a dozen attempts on your life. Be thankful that all they want to do to you here is speak with you."

Bern did not really see the funny side to the conversation. He was not noble and he didn't want to be. He took a deep breath. He was going to have to brave the outside. There was nothing he could do to change his situation.

As he expected the corridor was a hive of activity. It was getting close to the midday meal time, which meant there were also a large number of servants about. Bern hoped he would be able to disappear into the crowd, but unfortunately in his new finery that would not be the case. He wished he had dressed in his travelling leathers, but he figured that would be just as conspicuous. It was not long before there was a group of nobles buzzing around him. They were all speaking at once and they all expected their questions to be answered first.

By the time Bern made it to the courtyard of the castle the sun had passed its peak. Some of the incessant nobles dropped off the convoy, but most of them stayed. Bern gave small responses every now and then, just to appease them. He figured it was better than just ignoring them. The problem would not leave if he just brushed it aside. At least when he reached the main gate they would have to leave him alone. None of them were allowed to leave the castle grounds. It was the only chance he would have for solitude and he was looking forward to it.

As Bern expected the small group of nobles tried to pass through the gates with him. The guards all knew who he was and were happy for him to come and go as he pleased. The head guard shot him a questioning look when he saw Bern approach with his entourage. Bern simply shook his head and smiled.

"Okay you lot," the captain boomed. "You know the rules. No one leaves the castle grounds."

At the sound of their captain's voice the other guards moved into place. With the crowd that had gathered he would need the support. The nobles did not look as though they liked being turned away and without the extra man power a riot was more than likely to erupt.

"Thanks," Bern spoke over his shoulder as he walked out through the gate.

The simple word put a smile on the captain's face. At first he had not liked a foreigner making decisions in the castle, but the man was growing on him. He could see strength in Bern that he had not seen in a long time. As long as everyone else was happy with his position the captain of the Guard would do nothing to rock the boat.

Being out of the castle was a relief. It was like a weight had been lifted from his shoulders. He had never been so happy to be out in the open, which was the part of his life as a farmer that he liked the most. As he walked towards the city he thought about returning to the army and not the castle. The thought made him happy for a moment before he realised it was not possible. He had too many responsibilities and returning to the army would only be a quick fix. Soon enough things would become much worse for him.

It was fine leaving the castle, the guards knew who he was. Entering the city was an entirely new issue, one that he didn't see coming. It was not until he reached the north-western gate that he realised how complacent he had become. On one hand he didn't like the fact that everyone knew who he was, but on the other hand it did make things easier for him.

"I am sorry, but no one is allowed in or out of the city," it was a lower level guard who spoke to Bern.

This was a problem he had not foreseen. He stood in front of the guard without knowing what to say. That did nothing to instil confidence in the guard and only proved to make things even harder from him. Silently he cursed himself for not sending word of his arrival to the main gate. On the other hand if the agents of the Evil One knew of his impending arrival then they would go to ground and make his life even harder.

"I think you should get your captain," Bern said after an uncomfortable silence.

"I don't think that will do you any good. The law is strict and no one is permitted to enter or leave the city." The guard did not move.

Bern sighed in frustration. The law was there for no one to leave the city not to prevent people from entering. Someone had obviously taken licence on his instructions. It was a logical choice, but it still did not make him feel any better. Standing out of the front of the city was something he did not have time for. The day was already getting away from him and he wanted to get to the inn.

He looked down at the fine clothes he wore and shook his head. If he was dressed in his armour there would be little doubt of his admittance into the city, but again that would just prove another problem. He didn't think he would be able to gather the information he needed if he was dressed as a soldier. Even dressed as a noble would have its own problems, but he could deal with those when the time came.

"I am General Bern. I am the one who makes the laws. Now I would kindly ask you step aside. I have pressing business in the city," Bern spoke firmly. As much as he didn't want to reveal his true identity he didn't have the time to try and talk his way. His name would carry weight and it would be the quickest way to get what he needed.

His words made the guard take a step backwards. It was clear he was trying to think if he had heard the name. The look on his face showed he did not. Bern knew what his response was going to be.

"I do not recognise that name. You are not from Jarrat and therefore I do not take orders from you." The guard had not deliberately been offensive, but that was the end result.

Bern wanted to teach the guard a lesson, but the rapier he wore on his belt was more for show than anything else. All his training had been with much heavier weapons and they were suited to his build. He didn't think he would last long with a thin rapier against a trained opponent. The best result would be to speak with the captain. He was sure the captain would know his name even if he didn't recognise his face.

"I think it would be a good idea if you got the captain now," Bern spoke between clenched teeth.

The guard was starting to fear for his life. He recognised the look in Bern's eyes. He had seen it in the eyes of his instructors when he was a trainee. The following results were never good. He had a feeling his current situation was going to end in the same manner. In the end he figured the best way to escape punishment was to get the captain.

Without saying a word the guard quickly disappeared. Bern thought about just wandering into the city with the gate suddenly unguarded, but quickly dismissed the idea. The last thing he wanted was guards chasing him through the streets. He was sure he would be able to talk sense to the captain.

"What is the problem here?" the captain asked when he returned with the guard.

The guard remained standing a pace behind the captain. His presence was necessary, but he did not want to take part in the conversation. If he had his way he would be hiding in the guard house whilst the captain took care of matters.

"I am General Bern, I am sure you would have heard of me," even as the words came out of Bern's mouth he hated saying them, but they were necessary. "I need to gain access to the city."

"Yes I have heard of General Bern, but I cannot say for certainty that you are him." The captain was firm, but not condescending. "I don't want to discount your status, but I am sure you can appreciate my situation. Your name is synonymous with the Alliance. Anyone can use the name General Bern to gain entrance to the city. Not only that, but you certainly don't look the part."

Bern had to admit the captain was right on two counts. Anyone could claim they were Bern. He had not thought to bring appropriate documentation to prove who he was. His movement between the castle and the army had made him complacent. Not for a moment did he think he would have trouble entering the city. His dress, although it still played on his mind, had not been a concern. Only full dress uniform would convince the captain of who he was and that would defeat the purpose of entering the city in the first place. All he could do was hope he would be able to talk his way through the situation.

"Of course you are right, but you have to look at it from my perspective. I don't think a soldier from the Alliance would dare to use my name to gain entrance to the city. No one else is allowed to leave the castle and that is clearly where I have come from." Bern thought that he was on the right track.

"Is that true?" he asked the captain.

"Ah... I am not sure." The guard was taken aback by the question.

"What do you mean you are not sure, Private? How long have you been out of training? You have been posted to guard those wishing to gain entrance to the city. That means that you have to take notice of people outside the city as well as those within," with each word the captain raised his voice. Of course the questions were rhetorical.

"I...I...I know sir, but..." The guard did not know what to say.

"Spit your words out boy or you will spend the next week in the stocks." The threat was only half true.

"There hasn't been anyone come to this gate in that last two days. I guess that I just lost concentration." He knew his excuse was only going to get him in more trouble, regardless of the truth.

"That will be all private. You can return to your barracks. You are dismissed. I will deal with you later." The captain was fuming.

"Yes, sir!" The guard saluted quickly before rushing off towards the barracks.

"I am sorry that you had to see that," the captain apologised. "But that doesn't really help us with our little dilemma."

Bern had hoped the captain was going to see his point of view, but that did not seem to be the case. He didn't really know what else he could say. It was a small mercy that at least they were taking their job seriously. That was something he could sleep easy on, but he still needed to gain entrance into the city.

"I don't know what else I can tell you. I am General Bern and I have important business in the city." Bern explained again.

"What is it you need to do in the city," it was obvious the captain wanted to believe Bern, but he needed to be convinced.

Bern had to think for a moment. There was no real secrecy with what he was doing, but he did not want the captain to know. He wanted more answers before he revealed his plan to anyone. If the enemy knew what he was doing then they would go to ground and that would make it even harder for him to find them.

"I am sorry, but I can't tell you." Bern knew that was not going to get him inside the city, but he had to stay firm.

"Hmm…" the captain made a sign of thinking. "I am sorry general, but I don't think I can let you in. I am sure that you understand."

Bern understood, but it did not make things any easier. It had taken a great effort to reach the city and now he was going to be turned away. When it was said and done he had no one to blame but himself. He should not have been so complacent about gaining entrance. He would need to get documentation from Xarles and try again.

As he walked backed towards the city he was still cursing under his breath. He could not believe he could have made such a mistake. He had been hoping that upon returning to the castle he would have an idea of where to start looking for the traitors, but he was in no better position than when he left.

Chapter 21: The Royal Watchman

It had taken Bern longer than he expected to convince Xarles that he was doing the right thing. He had no idea why the duke was so opposed to him going into the city. He did offer an excuse, but Xarles pushed him nonetheless. In the end he begrudgingly wrote out a letter of passage. Once he had the letter in his hands `Bern couldn't wait to get out of the room. He knew it would only be a matter of time before Xarles would bring up his conversations with the nobles. That was a conversation he wanted to ignore for as long as possible and with a little luck they would be long gone before it had to happen.

There was little time left in the day for him to achieve his goal. The sun was half way down from its pinnacle and would almost be set by the time he returned to the city gates. There was nothing he could do. At nightfall the city gates would be shut and not even the queen herself would be allowed entrance. Not long after nightfall a curfew would be put in place and would not be lifted until the gates were opened again for all to move in and out, or at least that's what the citizens had been told. In reality nothing would change until Bern was confident all the traitors had been captured.

In the morning Bern woke before the sun. He wanted to make sure he didn't get held up by the nobles again. Even after his meeting with Xarles it had taken him over an hour to get back to his apartment. No matter what he tried he couldn't get rid of them. He was sure once he was spotted in the corridors he would be harassed again. He had already lost a day and he could ill afford to lose any more time.

His planned worked perfectly. The only people in the corridors, beside himself, were servants and they moved past him as if he was not even there. Of course they made sure not to get in his way. They knew all too well the repercussions of running into a nobleman and again Bern was dressed for the part. If only to himself he had to admit that he was getting used to the fine clothing and the expensive material no longer made him itch. In fact he was starting to understand the comfort such clothing.

The sun was only just starting to rise when he reached the castle gate. He passed through without any problems. He only wished it had been so easy to enter the city. The one plus was that he was making good time. With any luck he could have the answers he was looking for by midday.

When he reached the north-western gate he met a different guard. The man was just as young as the guard from the day before. He had a bad feeling he was going to have the same conversation and he hoped the guard in front of him was more adept than the last.

"I am General Bern. I wish to speak with your captain," Bern spoke with a commanding voice. He hoped he would be able to circumvent any delays.

"Of course, sir, he is expecting you." The guard saluted before rushing off to the guard house.

Bern let out a deep breath and relaxed. He didn't realise until that point he had tensed all his muscles. He could relax now that he was getting somewhere, although that luxury would not last for long. Once he was in the city he would need all his wits about him. He had to keep his appearance in the city a secret. He did not want anyone else to know he was there.

"Good morning general, I hope you have to appropriate documentation." The captain was not being sarcastic. He truly didn't want to disallow entry to Bern again.

Bern pulled the document out of his pocket and handed it to the captain. The captain unfolded it and checked carefully. His face gave no reaction, which did little to settle Bern's nerves. He didn't know what he would do if the captain tried to block his path again. There was no longer time for him to be delayed.

"This all looks in order," the captain sounded relieved. He could tell by Bern's demeanour he would not accept anything else. "Enjoy your stay in the city. Be sure to be out before nightfall. Once the gate is closed it cannot be opened for anyone."

"Thank you, but I will not be staying long. I hope to be out again by midday," Bern replied as he took the right-of-passage papers back.

The captain looked as though he was going to say something, but then thought better of it. Bern wondered what it was, but he did not have time to waste. He would just have to put it out of his mind.

The streets of Jarrat were relatively deserted. Bern had expected to see more people since they weren't allowed out of the city walls. There was no reason why everyone would be staying inside. As soon as that thought came into his mind he realised how wrong he was. The state of martial law was having its affect on the residents. Bern finally understood why Tyson had been so against the idea. The thought steeled his resolve. He needed to find an answer and he needed to find it fast. It was the only way he could release the people of Jarrat from the yoke of the Evil One.

One advantage to not being allowed entrance the previous day was a chance to get directions. Richmond had not been able to remember the location or any real details about the inn. Bern had spoken to a number of servers. Although they didn't know the exact location they gave him a good idea where to find it.

There were a few inns in the commerce district, but it did not take him long to find the Royal Watchman. He found the front door locked, so he moved around the outside of the inn looking in the windows, but he could not see anyone inside. He banged on the door, the walls and the windows, but there was no response. The sudden surge of adrenaline when he found the inn quickly disappeared. Although there seemed to be no one inside Bern was not about to give up.

Taking a run up, Bern put all his weight against the door. He had hoped to open it with his momentum, but instead he bounced off the heavy wooden door and went crashing onto the ground. He looked around, but the street was still empty. He was grateful for small mercies. The pain in his shoulder meant he was not going to attempt breaking down the door again. He had not wanted to break one of the windows, but he didn't see any other choice.

Using the hilt of his sword Bern struck the first window to the left of the door. Once he had cleared away the left over shards of glass he climbed through. He was not prepared for what happened next. It was by pure luck he avoided getting his head cracked open. As he clambered through the window he slipped and stumbled into the room. Once he was inside he was struck across the back of the shoulder, which helped him on his way.

Although the first blow had come as a surprise he was prepared for the second. He rolled out of the way as the large club came crashing down. It thumped onto the floor and Bern scampered out of the way. Before a third attack could come Bern was back on his feet. His shoulders ached, but he was not going to let that hinder him. He quickly drew his sword and prepared for the impending attack. He could only hope that he looked the part and whoever was attacking him would think twice about continuing.

"Get out of my inn," Gage screamed at the top of his voice. He still brandished his heavy wooden club, but he made no move to attack. "I have had enough of being robbed."

Bern relaxed a little when it was clear the innkeeper was not going to attack again. He lowered his blade, but not enough to be taken by surprise. If the innkeeper tried to attack then he would be ready to defend himself.

"I think you have misjudged the situation. I am not here to rob you." Bern was taken aback by the accusation.

Gage wanted to move across the room and bash Bern's head in, but he knew it would not end that way. He had seen enough fights in his time to realise that his opponent was a superior fighter. Even with that in mind he would defend his inn to the death.

"Then get out," Gage was not sure how else to respond.

"I am not here to hurt you. I am here because I need to speak with you," Bern spoke softly. He wanted to calm the situation.

"I have nothing to say to a robber. You can kindly take your questions somewhere else," Gage was not going to drop his guard. He knew it was the best way for him to end up with the sword through his belly.

Bern was not sure how he would be able to settle Gage's mind. He thought his best move was to introduce himself. He doubted the innkeeper would have heard his name, but it was worth a shot.

"I am general Bern of the Alliance army," Bern continued to speak softly. "I am not here to hurt you."

Gage thought for a moment. It was clear he recognised the name. Then the answer dawned on him and it was not the response that Bern was hoping for. He could see Gage's expression change from pensiveness to anger.

"So you are Lord Bern? It is you who has caused this atrocity," Gage hissed his accusation at Bern.

Bern cringed at the mention of his makeshift title. He could never get used to being called 'Lord', 'General' was bad enough. It was not the response he was looking for, but at least the innkeeper knew who he was. He had hoped revealing his name would have made the innkeeper lower his club, but that was not the case. He looked ready to strike at any moment.

"I am sorry, but I don't understand." Bern didn't know how to respond. "Can we lower our weapons and speak civilly."

Bern didn't want to force a confrontation. In the end he thought he would be better off sheathing his rapier and fighting the man single handed. Even with the cudgel he thought he would be able to defeat the innkeeper.

To add to his statement Bern lowered his sword. When Gage made no move to lower his club Bern knew he had to do more. He took a risk and sheathed his sword. If he was going to gain the trust of the innkeeper he needed a show of faith.

Once Bern had sheathed his sword Gage changed his demeanour. Slowly he started to lower his club. He figured in the end the general was bound to overpower him if he wanted to. It seemed as though Bern was not there to attack him.

"Thank you," Bern said when Gage lowered his club, although he kept it in his hand. "Now would you tell me what has been happening?" He thought it was a better question to start with.

"Take a look around," Gage said.

Bern did as he was told. He saw for the first time the reason why he had not been able to break down the door. Beside that fact it was a heavy oak door there were also boards nailed to the inside. He was not entirely sure, but he thought there was dust starting to form on the tables and chairs in the common room. Things were not as they seemed.

"What has happened here?" there was a slight amount of shock in his voice.

"This is the result of not letting anyone leave the city. People were fine with it for the first couple of days, but now things have turned bad. Some of the more unsavoury types in Jarrat have taken to looting and worse to fill their days. The city is falling into chaos. With no travellers my business has gone to ruin. Since everyone knows there are no patrons it makes us the perfect target for theft. We are saving all the food and drink for ourselves. There is no telling when we will be able to replenish our supplies. Now I fear for the safety of my family," there was an edge to Gage's voice. He was trying to stand firm, but there was a great amount of underlying sorrow in his voice.

Bern took a step backwards. He had known things were going to get tough when he made his decision, but he had no idea things would get so bad. He needed to move even quicker to gain the information. If he did not have answers by the end of the day then he would have to release the city.

"I am sorry, but there is a good reason I did what I did," Bern tried to explain.

"And it is daytime now." Gage didn't seem to hear Bern's words. "Night time is even worse. That is when I truly fear for my life."

"This is the reason why I have come here. I need information," Bern explained. "I am doing everything I can to change things."

Gage thought for a moment. It was clear the man in front of him meant no harm. If he was who he said he was then he was to blame for his current predicament, but Gage's anger was starting to dissipate.

"Well, you better come in and have a drink. My name is Gage and this is the Royal Watchman." It was a belated introduction. "I think I still have a good bottle of wine somewhere."

Bern was going to refuse the offer, especially since it was still early in the morning, but Gage had already left. Instead he simply took a seat in the common room, looked around and took in the severity of the situation.

"Here we go." Gage plonked the bottle of wine and two goblets on the table.

He poured the wine and then sat down. Bern took the goblet Gage handed him and paused before he took a mouthful. Even though it was so early the wine still tasted sweet. Bern thought it was strange, but he put it to the back of his mind. He had more important matters to deal with.

"I need to speak to you about two men who came here," Bern suddenly forgot his train of thought. His mouth was suddenly very dry. Without thinking he took another sip of wine. "There is something I need to speak with you about," Bern's head suddenly felt very heavy and his eyelids started to droop.

Gage stood when he saw Bern start to waver. Suddenly a thought came into Bern's mind. He could not believe he had been so stupid. That was the last thought that went through his mind before his head dropped on the table.

***

The dim light in the room burned his eyes when he could finally open them again. His head ached and he was disoriented. The room he was in didn't look familiar, but something else was wrong. He tried to rub his head, but he could not move his arms. It was at that stage that he realised what had happened. The innkeeper had drugged the wine. When he was unconscious Gage had tied him to a chair. He had no idea how long he had been unconscious.

"It is good to see you could join us," Gage sounded pleased with himself.

There was a candle in front of Bern's eyes, which kept the rest of the room dark to him. He could hear more than one person in the room. He had a bad feeling that Richmond had missed some valuable information. If Gage had been their contact then he was in grave danger.

"What do you want with me?" his voice was hoarse.

There was the sound of muffled voices around him. His head was still suffering from the drugs and he couldn't catch the words. He did know they were talking about him. He tried his arms again, but they wouldn't move. He was completely at the mercy of his captors. It was time for the entity to take over, but he knew it didn't work that way. The entity never appeared when he really wanted it.

"We want to know what gives you the right to take control of our city?" It was not Gage's voice. "One dictator is much the same in my book."

"Who are you?" Bern answered.

"You are not in a position to ask questions. Your life depends on how you answer the questions we ask." It was another voice again.

There was very little choice for Bern. If they were indeed agents of the Evil One then he could not tell them his plan. He knew once he did they would kill him anyway. If he kept his mouth shut then he would also be killed, but at least he wouldn't have given away any secrets. When it was said and done he knew what he had to do.

"I will not tell you anything until you tell me why you have imprisoned me?" Bern spoke firmly.

"I am sure the army would pay a handsome reward for him," a fourth voice spoke.

"And how long do you think it would take for the army to march in and take him." Gage was the voice of reason. "We are here for a purpose and that is not for gold."

Bern remained silent. He was trying to figure out what was happening. He was sure that there were only four men in the room. Although he could not see them he could hear very well. Along with the four voices he could only hear four people breathing and moving around. He didn't wonder about his suddenly heightened senses. He was too busy concentrating on what was going on around him.

Suddenly Bern felt something hit him across the back of his head. The blow caused him to see stars. He thought for a moment that he was going to lose consciousness again, but he stayed in the room. The further the conversation continued the more he was sure they were agents of the Evil One.

"What is it that you want with me?" Bern spoke when his senses returned.

"We want you to release the city. We have never been under the rule of a tyrant and we don't plan on starting now. You are killing the city," Gage explained.

"Be quiet Gage. He doesn't need to know anything. All he has to do is answer our questions," the first voice spoke.

"That is enough Henri, we are not kidnappers," Gage spoke firmly, but there was an air of uncertainty in his voice.

"Thank you for revealing my name," Henri barked at Gage. "We could have gotten away without our identities being known."

"I don't see why I should be the only one he knows. We are all in this together," Gage returned.

The argument continued until one of the other men broke it up. Bern was starting to wonder if his first judgment was correct. If they were agents of the Evil One then he thought they would hold more confidence in what they were doing. A slight amount of hope filled Bern and he thought he might just survive the day. If they were not agents of the Evil One then there was a good chance he would indeed.

"Now I think you should answer our question. We do not want to hurt you," the third voice spoke.

"What was the question?" So much had happened that Bern had forgotten what it was.

"What gives you the right to invade our city?" There was a slight change to the question, but the end result was the same.

"The decision was made to protect the citizens of Jarrat. Things are not what they seem." That sounded like the best response without really giving any information away.

"That doesn't tell us anything now, does it?" the third voice spoke again. "I would think very carefully before you speak again. We do not wish to cause you any harm, but if you give us no choice..." It was clearly a threat.

Bern could not reveal any information until he knew they were not agents of the Evil One. He could not tell them his plan if they were. He really couldn't tell them his plan anyway. If the word leaked out before he succeeded then he would have no chance. There was only one thing he could do, but that did nothing to ease his mind.

"That is as much as I can tell you," Bern spoke firmly. "If you do not mean to bring me harm or harm to your fellow Enteroites then you will let me go. I have important work to do and I am already out of time. What you are doing here will only extend the lock down of the city and potentially lead Jarrat into a civil war."

Bern's words gave the four men something to discuss. Things had not gone to plan. They had hoped to already have the information they required from Bern and they would be making plans to rectify the situation. Instead the man in bonds seemed to be controlling the conversation. That was something they would have to rectify.

"What do we do now?" a voice whispered in the corner of the room. Bern could not decipher who had spoken. "This is not going to plan."

"We can't let him go," another voice whispered even softer than the first. "He will bring soldiers in to kill us."

"We can't keep him here. That was never the arrangement." Although Bern could not recognise the voice he knew it was Gage who spoke. "There has to be a way to get some information out of him. What about torture?" He did not sound confident as he suggested it.

"We are not barbarians. I am sure we can convince him to tell us what is happening."

"If neither of you have the stomach for this then I will do what is necessary. I will not let this foreigner tell me what I can and can't do in my own city. If he does not speak then he will feel a pain like nothing he has felt before," Henri spoke loud enough for Bern to clearly hear him.

"I would not be so hasty," Bern spoke confidently as he heard the sound of footsteps coming towards him. He was confident now that he knew they were not agents of the Evil One. If they were then they would have no qualms in torturing him. That still did not mean he could reveal the information they required. "Do not do something here that you can't take back later."

Henri paused for a moment before continuing his approach. To start with he smacked Bern over the back of head. It was not as hard as the last knock he received, but it was designed to let him know they meant business. Bern had hoped his words would have had their effect, but it didn't seem as though they did. He would have to try a different tact.

"Be very careful what you are doing." Bern had managed to loosen the ropes slightly whilst the men were talking. It was not enough to escape, but it was a promising sign. He thought if he had enough time he would be able to free his arms. "You know this is not right. I am the commander of the Alliance and I am not your enemy."

"Of course we know this is not right. We are not animals, but things are tough at the moment. These are tough times and tough times mean tough decisions. We have to do things that we normally would not for the greater good. We have to protect our own," Henri would not be dissuaded.

Bern had to admit his words made sense. "The sooner you let me go the sooner I can release the city." Bern hoped his change of tactic might work.

"Things have gone too far," there was something different in Henri's voice. Bern recognised the fanatical tone. "If we let you go then you will have us killed."

"What are you talking about Henri?" there was shock in Gage's voice. "You said that we were simply going to get answers from him."

"I know what I said, but things have changed now. We have gone too far. We must do away with him," Henri argued.

"But we haven't even gotten any information from him," the third voice spoke.

"I had expected such a response from Orvil, but not from you Vachel," Henri almost spat the words.

There had been a complete change in Henri's disposition and it took the other three men by surprise. It had been Henri's idea from the start. No one had found it strange that he knew Bern would be arriving at Gage's inn. When he explained his plan it had always been in the hypothetical, none of them had actually thought it would come to fruition.

When Bern had arrived at the Royal Watchman they had all thought it was a coincidence. It was beginning to seem there was another force at play.

"This is over Henri," Gage said what the other two were thinking. "I am setting him free."

Bern only heard the sound of one footstep before he heard the sound of a blade being drawn. By the sound it was only a dagger, but that would be enough to do some serious damage. Bern's heart started to race. He needed to escape and he needed to do it in a hurry. If Henri got his way it wouldn't be long before he was dead.

"What are you doing Henri?" Vachel asked in amazement

"I am doing what has to be done. Now get out of my way." There was no doubt in Bern's mind Henri was coming to kill him. He didn't think the other three were going to do anything to stop him. "I don't want to hurt you, but I will if I must. There is more at stake than you know."

There was a lot of shuffling of feet. Bern did not know who was moving where. He took the distraction as another opportunity to undo his binds. As much as he wiggled he could not loosen them enough to escape.

"We cannot let you do this," Gage spoke firmly.

That was the last word spoken. Bern could hear a scuffle starting behind him. He thought it sounded as though they were wrestling for control of the dagger. He hoped that was the case. He didn't think Henri would have much chance against the other three men. With any luck they would set him free. At the very least he would no longer have to fear for his life.

It didn't take long for the fight to finish. It ended with the sound of a body crashing to the ground. Bern hoped it was Henri and not one of the other men. If that wasn't the case then he would surely be dead.

He felt someone grip the back of his chair. His heart started to race again as the fear of death refilled his body. Gage swung the chair around so he was facing the rest of the room. It took a moment for Bern's eyes to adjust to the change in light. When he did he could see three sheepish looking men standing before him. He was surprised that they had not already untied him.

"If we untie you will you promise not to kill us?" it was a long shot, but Gage thought that it was the best approach.

"I think we should just leave him here," Orvil spoke nervously. It was obvious that he had no confidence in his words.

"I promise you that no harm will come to you if you release me," there was nothing else Bern could do to calm their nerves.

The three men looked at each other. Bern watched their exchange nervously. He was confident they would release him, but he did not want to do anything to negate that fact. Until he was released he still had to plan for the worst.

"Well, we can't keep him here forever," Gage spoke finally.

With those words the decision had been made. There was no other option to them. Slowly the realisation that Henri had used them for his own gain was dawning on them. The only chance to reprieve themselves was to let Bern free.

Once Bern had been untied the three men retreated to the back of the room. Bern would have been in his rights to give them all a good beating. He did think about it, but in the end it would prove nothing. He still needed information from the innkeeper and he would be better off keeping them on side.

"I think we can all agree that this didn't happen," Bern thought it was the best way to get what he wanted. "But we do need to have a chat."

"Of course general, whatever you need." Gage was quick to answer. He would do anything he could to remain out of the dungeons.

The innkeeper wanted to suggest moving to a more comfortable setting, but he didn't want to risk offending Bern further. He would wait for the general to suggest a change of location. Gage would be happy if he was able to leave the room alive. Only after Henri had been knocked out and bound did he realise how insane their plan had been. He couldn't believe he had ever listened to Henri's madness.

"A few weeks ago two men came here," Bern decided there was no point in beating around the bush. He could follow up on what had just happened later. "It was Lord Richmond and Tancred." He paused and gave Gage a chance to remember.

At first Gage was taken aback by the question. It was not at all what he had been expecting. As he thought about it the answer dawned on him. When he made the realisation a look of horror appeared on his face. He remembered the words that Tancred had spoken about the Alliance. He did not want to betray the man's trust, but he also wanted to save his own neck.

"Yes I remember. They stayed here for a few nights before they left again." Gage kept his description vague.

Bern knew there was more to the story. The innkeeper was acting very strange. "I think you should tell me what happened."

"He told me the Alliance had attacked Kiarome." Gage continued to tell about Tancred's tale of deceit.

When the story was finished Bern felt like laughing. Gage was shaking with fear. He obviously didn't know that Tancred had been lying. He would have laughed, but that would have been inappropriate. That was not the information he required.

"Did they go anywhere whilst they were here?" he asked without being too obvious.

"They went to the castle, that is all I know." Gage looked as though he could lose consciousness at any moment.

"Are you sure?" Bern was not completely confident that Gage was telling the truth.

"They left to go into the city, but he they didn't tell me where they went. That's the truth."

Bern sat back down in the chair he had previously been bound to. He had hit another dead end. He would have to go to the Alliance and tell them that he had failed. There was no longer time to wait for Tancred's memory to return.

"What's the matter?" Orvil dared to ask.

"They met with an agent of the Evil One when they came to the city. I need to know who it was." Bern felt that there was little point in secrecy. Although he wasn't sure he could trust the three men he thought the threat of the Alliance marching in and taking them away would be enough to keep them from spreading rumours.

The room was shrouded in silence. They all thought on Bern's words. They all wanted to have the answer to the question. They felt it was the least they could do and the best way of escaping with their lives.

"What about Henri?" Vachel was the first one to speak. His voice was a whisper, as if he was afraid to voice his thoughts.

"Be quiet Vachel." Gage was quick to react. He didn't want to give Bern a reason to notice them.

Bern shook his head and laughed. He had been so focused on getting an answer from Gage he didn't realise the answer was tied up in front of him. There could be no doubt that Henri was an agent of the Evil One. Until the man regained consciousness he would try and gather as much information as he could.

"What is your connection with Henri?" Bern asked quietly.

The men were in shock at Bern's reaction. It was the last thing they expected. No one knew what to say. Bern had to do something to calm the three men. He didn't need to have them fearing him anymore. They would tell him what he wanted to know regardless.

"You don't have to worry. The stories that Tancred told you were lies. They were deliberately trying to feed you misinformation. I will not do anything to harm you." Bern tried to ease their tensions.

"Henri is the owner of the Disgruntled Pig in the poor district. He is part of the Innkeepers Guild, but we have only really known him recently," Gage started to explain.

"He came to us and told us you were coming here," Vachel cut in.

"His words made sense at the time, although now they seem so suspicious. If we had known then we would not have gone along with it," Orvil spoke quickly, not wanting to be left out of the conversation.

Bern took the information in, although it only confirmed what he had already thought, he knew what he had to do next. The only question was whether he would allow the three men to witness it. He thought they had no business remaining in the room, but in the end he figured they already knew too much. If he didn't let them see it through until the end then they could only guess and that meant that they would speak about it. The more they discussed the matter the greater the chance of the information being revealed.

"Okay. This is not going to be pretty, so if you wish to leave then do so now, but be warned that you may never speak of this again," Bern warned them.

None of the men moved. Bern didn't think it was because they wanted to stay. It was purely because neither of them wanted to be the first to move. They all wanted to leave, but in the end no one did. Whatever Bern was about to do to their friend, or at least the man they had once considered to be a friend, they would stand witness.

When Bern was happy that they were going to stay he moved to where Henri was bound on the ground. He was still unconscious. Slowly he crouched down besides the man and slapped him across the face. He hoped it would be enough to wake him, but it did not have the desired effect.

"Somebody get a bucket of water," Bern ordered when he stood again.

At first no one moved. Bern, even though he had his back was turned, knew that no one was doing as he commanded. Their fear was starting to annoy him. He needed to get things done and he needed them to do what he asked.

"I don't care who does it, but if you don't move soon I might just change my mind." He didn't need to elaborate any further.

The three men almost fell over each other to rush out of the room. Orvil managed to make it out the door first. The other two men wanted to follow him, but they thought it would be better if they stayed. If they all left then Bern might think they were trying to escape. They couldn't get the thought that they might be prisoners out of their mind.

When Orvil returned Bern wasted no time in throwing the water over Henri's head. It did the trick and Henri woke with a start. He shook his head in surprise. When he realised that his arms were tied behind his back he started to struggle.

"I wouldn't worry about that," Bern spoke. "You aren't going anywhere."

Henri looked up and suddenly realised the severity of his situation. With Bern standing over him he knew he was trapped. He had shown his true colours too early and now he was paying the price. There was little he could do. If he wanted to get out of the situation alive then he would have to tell the truth, although if he did he didn't know how long he would remain that way.

"Now I would advise you to answer honestly as I don't have time to waste," Bern spoke sternly, but had an evil smile on his face.

"I don't know what you are talking about." Henri thought he would test his luck.

That was not a good decision. Bern was true to his word. Without warning Bern struck him across the face with the back of his hand. The blow was enough to topple him over. With his arms bound he could not bring himself back up to the seated position.

"Now I think you should rethink what you are going to tell me." Bern paused for effect. "You are an agent of the Evil One and I need to know who else in the city follows your beliefs."

"I still have no idea what you are talking about," he cringed as he spoke.

Bern wasted no time again. He kicked Henri in the stomach making him cough and splutter. He gasped for breath which was made even harder with his arms tied behind his back. When he finally caught his breath Bern gave him no time to relax. He didn't bother re-asking the question. He simply kicked him again before quickly dragging Henri up onto his feet. He was not allowed to double over, which his body was desperate to do. Just when he thought he was about to die air rushed into his lungs.

"Now I think you might have a fair idea how this is going to play out. You can make life easier for yourself or we can continue to play this game. Either way I will get the information that I want from you." Bern kept smiling, as if he was enjoying himself. On the inside he was desperate for the information he required.

"You can beat me to death, but I can't tell you what I don't know," Henri responded.

It was Henri's standoffish attitude that told Bern he was lying. If the man was innocent then he would be begging for his life. Bern knew it would not always be the case, but there was something about Henri that didn't sit right. He knew Henri was the key to finding the traitors in the city.

If Henri wanted a beating then Bern was happy to help. Bern lent backwards before punching Henri in the face. He continued with a flurry of blows as Henri went crashing to the ground.

"Get my sword," he ordered no one in particular.

"Please, Bern. If he knew anything he would have told you." Gage stepped forward, but stopped before he was within reach. "Please don't spill any blood in my inn."

"It has gone well beyond that now. We will see if he speaks after he loses a finger or two," there was something icy cold in his voice.

His emotionless tone forced Gage to move. It caused Henri to rethink his tactics. The strength of character Henri was showing quickly shrunk away. There was fear in his eyes, but he still remained quiet. Bern had hoped his threat would have worked. He really didn't want to start severing fingers, but it was something he was prepared to do.

"Please rethink this," Gage pleaded as he handed Bern his sword.

Bern wanted to give Henri another chance to speak, but he could not weaken. He had to steel his resolve if he was going to go through with the torture. There was nothing for it. He rolled Henri onto his stomach and put his knee in the small of the man's back. Slowly he picked up the little finger on Henri's left hand. He paused for a moment, giving Henri a chance to confess. When no words came Bern quickly severed the finger and threw it on the ground in front of him. Heri cried out in pain. He had not expected Bern to go through with the threat.

Once the finger was off Bern returned to his feet. He wiped the blood off his blade with the corner of a bed sheet. There was hope that he would not have the cut another finger off. Henri was whimpering on the floor. There was no way he could soothe the pain he was feeling.

"I tell you I know nothing." Tears started to roll down his face.

Bern was not going to waste time re-asking the question. He would simply continue the torture until Henri confessed his crime. It was not something he wanted to do, but it was the first finger that was the hardest.

It took three more fingers before Henri admitted he was a follower of the Evil One.

"Very good, now we can move on," Bern wiped the blood from his sword as he spoke. "I want a list of all the traitors in the city," Bern almost sounded relieved as he spoke.

"I don't know who they are," there was unadulterated fear in his voice.

Bern actually believed him that time. He did not think Henri was going to lie to him again, but he was sure there was some information he could get.

"You better tell me something quickly or I will start working on your right hand." There wasn't the same confidence in his threat as there had been, but Henri didn't notice.

"I can tell you who I report to, that is all I know." Henri leaded, hoping that would stop the torture.

"That would be a good start," Bern knew that would be all the information, but he didn't want Henri to know that.

"There is a man name Coyne. He is a farrier in the commerce district. He gives me little tasks to do. I am not allowed to know anyone else," Henri was weeping as he spoke.

"Very good, now that wasn't so hard was it," Bern had to admit his tactics worked. "I think that you should patch up his hand before he bleeds to death."

"And then what will we do with him?" Orvil asked.

"Keep him tied up here. I will have someone come and get him," Bern explained.

"What are you going to do?" Gage asked as Bern walked towards the door.

"I have some business to take care of." Bern smiled as he walked passed.

Chapter 22: Time for a Plan

Bern walked through the streets with a new spring in his step. He was glad Gage was able to give him directions to the farrier's shop. He had a new lead and things were finally moving in the right direction. Things had worked out surprisingly well despite what he had to do. He pushed the thought of the torture out of his head. He was not proud of what he had done, but he knew that it was necessary. He was not going to let that dampen his high spirits.

The sun had just started its downward trip in the sky. Bern had eaten a small meal at the inn before he left. He thought it was the least the innkeeper could do for him. He paid for the food, however, a he thought that the man had suffered enough.

Even though it was early afternoon the streets of Jarrat were all but empty. Bern was getting a true picture of what he had done to the city. It seemed as though people were afraid to walk the streets. He had only just entered the commerce district when he was stopped by a small gang of men. They didn't look much more than a ragtag bunch of hooligans, but there were enough of them to be dangerous.

"I thought the nobility knew better than to wander the streets of Jarrat," the leader of the gang spoke. "These are our streets now. I think you should empty your gold pouch and I like the look of that sword."

Bern counted twelve men. They all held makeshift weapons ranging from clubs to boards of wood. Bern didn't think they knew much about fighting. They would win their battle by pure weight of numbers. Against regular people that would suffice, but against a trained soldier that was another story. Bern wished he had his axe or at least a broadsword. The thin rapier would be no use to him. His dress belied his true position and he doubted the men would believe he was a general.

"I don't want any trouble. I have business in the commerce district. Once I am finished I will leave again." Bern remained calm, although his hand gripped the hilt of his sword. Even though he wasn't comfortable with the weapon it was better than nothing.

Their leader started laughing and the other men followed suit. By the way the men looked toward their leader Bern thought it might just be a simple case of cutting off the snakes head, although that may also be wishful thinking. The men looked as though they were ready to fight to the death. Bern hoped it would not come to that.

"Well it seems as though trouble has found you. Now if you would empty your pockets then you can be on your way." The man was not going to be dissuaded.

Bern knew that talking was not going to get him anywhere and he took a few steps back so he was closer to the wall. He didn't want any of the men to get around behind him. Whilst they were in front he could keep an eye on them. It also limited the amount of people who could attack him at any one time. When he was happy with his location he drew his sword. Strangely the rapier felt comfortable in his hand. There was nearly no weight to the blade, at least not compared to the weapons he was used to.

"You should walk away now. I do not wish to take any more lives, but I will if I have to," there was no bluff in his voice.

The confidence in Bern was enough to make the men hesitate. They had been pillaging at will since the city was in lockdown. Those who had stood up to them didn't for long and they were used as an example to the others. There were many gangs roaming the streets of Jarrat, but these men were the worst. They had the run of the city. Even the other gangs stayed out of their way.

"I don't think you realise who you are speaking to. We are the law in Jarrat now and what we say goes. Now give us your possessions," the man boomed his command.

Bern simply shook his head. When it was said and done it was his law that had created the gangs, therefore it was his responsibility to fix it. He had no idea what they had done with their lives before the lockdown, but they were now clearly criminals. With that thought in mind Bern justified what he was about to do.

"Looks like we will have to take it from your corpse." The leader said as he indicated to the men to begin their attack.

They tentatively moved towards Bern. They had not fought anyone armed with a sword before and although the man was dressed like a dandy he had the build of a soldier. They had the common sense not to underestimate Bern's ability. Their leader seemed to be the only one who didn't care.

"Move it you dogs. He is only one man," the leader barked.

The insistence of their leader did nothing to urge the men forward. It didn't matter what punishment their leader dished out it would be better than death. There was no point risking their lives for a pouch of gold. The sword would be handy, but still not worth the risk. They all moved a little closer, but remained outside of striking distance.

"I'll give you one more chance to leave or else I will start taking heads," Bern almost had a jovial tone to his voice, as if he was looking forward to the fight.

His nonchalant manner had its desired effect. As one the gang started to retreat, but their leader was not prepared to relinquish what he thought was such a great bounty.

"We are not leaving here without his gold. Now fight!" he boomed at the top of his voice.

The command had the exact opposite effect. In unison the gang dropped their weapons and ran down the street away from Bern leaving the leader standing by himself. The sudden movement of his men left him in shock. He should have run away himself, but he couldn't get his legs moving.

"Well it seems it is just you and I." Bern took a number of steps towards the man, tapping the blade of his sword against the palm of his left hand.

The leader, of the now dispersed gang, started to shake. There was a clear sign of fear across his face. Bern had no doubt that the man would not stay and fight, he just didn't want to get too close Bern really didn't want to have to kill him. The man was a criminal, but it was Bern who had created him.

Bern stopped just when he was just out of reach. The man stood before him, shaking in fear. Bern almost started laughing at the sight. He had been so brave with all his men around him, but now he looked as though he had seen a ghost.

"Boo!" Bern leant forward as he spoke.

The sudden movement and noise urged the man into action. He quickly turned around and ran back the way he had come. By the smell that followed him Bern figured he had left something of himself behind as well. Bern had to laugh as he continued towards the farrier's shop.

It wasn't until a new thought entered his mind did Bern stop laughing. There had been something bugging him the city ever since he arrived. He had been too focused on the job at hand to realise what it was. He noticed that there was no military presence in the city. For a city that was supposed to be under martial law it seemed extremely odd. There was no wonder the city was in chaos. He would have to have a serious word to Tyson when he returned to the campsite.

He did not see another soul on the streets on his walk to the farrier's shop. In a way he was grateful. As much as he wanted to see happy people wandering the streets he knew if he saw anyone they would be out for no good. He was lucky to get away from the last gang without a fight. He was not so sure he would be so lucky a second time. He was not afraid of being attacked. He was afraid of having to kill someone who didn't deserve to die.

Once he arrived at the shop his mind refocused on the job at hand. Coyne was the link he had been looking for, he was sure of that. At the very least Coyne would be able to point him in the right direction. He took a deep breath and prepared himself for the ordeal he would face.

The door swung open when he pushed on it. The lock had already been broken off. He drew his sword without thinking before he entered the shopfront. He could feel something was wrong. He was hit with a gust of stale air and his nose twitched as the rank smell filled his nostrils. He quickly shielded his nose as he continued further into the shop.

It was the room behind the shopfront that Bern found the source of the smell. Lying face down on the bed was a limp body. There were a number of flies buzzing around and it looked as though some had already started to lay eggs. Bern guessed the body had been there for at least five days. Covering his nose he moved in further to investigate the corpse.

Once he had rolled the dead body over he knew it was the farrier, Coyne. The body wore a dirty leather smock, obviously what he had been wearing when he was working. There was no sign of a struggle and there was no blood or any cuts on the body. He also didn't look as though he had been strangled. Bern could only imagine that he had poisoned himself. When that thought came into his mind he spat in disgust on Coyne's lifeless body.

Bern deduced that once the city had been surrounded Coyne had taken his own life. He was too afraid to face up to the consequences of his actions. It also meant that Bern had hit another dead end. He could go back to the Royal Watchman and try and get more information from Henri, but he only thought that would waste his time.

Before he left he thought it would be a good idea to search the house for any clues to the whereabouts of the other traitors. He was hoping that Coyne might have a list. The more he looked though, the more he realised he was not the first person to go through Coyne's possessions. Someone had been there before him. If there had been a list it was sure to be gone. The more he searched the more he began to doubt if Coyne had even taken his own life or whether someone else had done the job for him. If the latter was the case then maybe someone was killing off the traitors. It was a long shot, but there was a chance that someone was doing his job for him. The only problem was that he doubted that Henri would still be alive.

The difference in the air outside the farrier's shop was amazing. Bern took a number of deep breaths. He was glad to be outside again. The stench of death was starting to get to him. With each breath he was able to think more clearly and finally the realisation came to him. If someone was killing the traitors and they had Coyne's list then there was a good chance they would be paying the Royal Watchman a visit. He didn't think the three innkeepers would be a match for a trained killer.

Bern hurried his way through the streets. Again the fact the streets were empty was a great benefit to him. There was no one to slow his progress. His heart was racing as he moved, but it sunk when he reached the inn. The front door of the Royal Watchmen was swinging open. He remembered how hard it had been for him to try and break it down. Whoever had done it was powerful indeed. Bern drew his sword a carefully walked into the inn. For some reason each time he drew the slender rapier it felt more comfortable in his hand.

He had only taken one step into the inn before he knew something was wrong. He moved through the various rooms until he came upon one that wasn't empty. The sight before him made him want to be sick. It was nothing like the passive way he had found Coyne's body. There was blood splattered on the walls and large pools had grown on the floor. The bodies of Gage's wife and children were strewn across the room. Limbs had been hacked from bodies. Bodies were slashed and maimed. Bern could only imagine the pain they had gone through right before they died. He could not stay in the room any longer. He needed to keep going. If the murderer was still in the inn then he would pay for what he had done.

He searched the inn and found Gage and his friends in a similar condition to the woman and children. Bern coughed at the sight, but the contents of his stomach remained inside his body. He moved out of the room and as he did he heard something moving towards the front of the inn. Bern wasted no time leaving the room, but when he arrived at the front door there was no one there. Whoever it had been was gone. Bern looked out into the street, he thought he saw the wisp of a robe around the corner of a building, but he wasn't sure.

There was something in the air, a strange smell. It was not the smell of death or blood, he knew that. It was something else. It was familiar, but not in a comforting way. He wanted to remain until he could figure out what it was, but he knew he didn't have the time. He needed to report the bad news to the Alliance.

As he walked towards the north-western gate he wondered if it was in fact bad news or good news. If someone was killing the traitors he wasn't sure if he needed to say anything at all. He knew it was the wrong thing to do, but it was tempting. A few more days and all the traitors would be dead, all at least, except one. He had a bad feeling that that was the one he needed to find.

The north-western gate was not the closest to the Alliance, but Bern figured it would be quicker if he did not have to explain himself at another gate. The guards knew who he was and would let him through. It would also give him more time to think. He needed to come up with another solution to his problem. He could no longer keep the city prisoner, but he could not let the remaining traitors go free.

The guards didn't stop him when he reached the gate. The captain had given them his description and informed them not to delay him. Bern was grateful for that. He really didn't have the energy to argue with anyone. The day was wearing away. He had already lost so much time.

The campsite was a hive of activity and Bern was glad to see the soldiers were busy. Soldiers with too much time on their hands inevitably got up to mischief. That was the last thing Bern needed.

"So, do I give the order to release the city?" Tyson asked when everyone had arrived.

Bern had made a point of waiting for everyone before getting the meeting started. Tyson had been trying to get information from Bern ever since he returned. He had been one of the first to arrive. Once Tyson had heard Bern was back he came running.

"Things are not as simple as that." Bern had still no answer for his question. "I have been into the city to investigate a lead."

Bern continued to explain what had happened. He left out the details about the innkeeper's family being hacked to pieces. He didn't think it was necessary and he didn't want to relive it. It would skew their opinion on what had to be done and he couldn't risk that.

"So someone is taking care of the traitors for us? That has to be a good thing," Tyson was the first to speak. There was passion in his voice. "He will track them down and take of them."

"That will not solve anything," Orric spoke calmly. "If there is one able to kill them all then he is the one that we need to find. Once all the traitors are dead he will leave."

"Do you know who it is?" Bern asked. He recognised something in the elf's voice.

"I have an idea, but I don't want to say anything until I know for sure."

"Well, that is a side issue anyway. Whilst this is going on I am loathed to open up the city." Tyson was about to interject, but Bern silenced him with a wave of his hand. "But I do not believe we can keep the city surrounded. I need ideas of how we can make this work."

They spent the rest of the afternoon discussing the situation around the group, but nothing ever seemed to make sense. Their ideas were either too harsh or too soft. It wasn't until they were eating their evening meal that Dorn spoke for the first time.

"I have an idea." It was the first real chance for the dwarf to speak. Once he had their attention he continued. "What if we open the gates, but still insist that no one leaves the city." Dorn noticed a lot of confused expressions, but he had only just started. "We will then notify everyone that we know who the traitors are and we will be coming to get them. Now the one who is murdering the traitors will know that Bern must have been there. He will also think that Bern has more information than what he actually does. Then we slowly send soldiers into the city. Those who try to flee will be the traitors," Dorn sounded happy with himself.

Everyone around the table thought on the idea. They had to admit it was the best they had heard all day. At face value it seemed perfect, but they needed to be careful. Whatever they chose to do they had to make sure it was correct.

"How will we know it is only traitors who will flee the city? From what Bern said things are pretty bad inside the city walls." Jarwe didn't sound confident.

"If they are not traitors then they should remain in their homes," Dorn explained.

"That is just as bad as what is happening at the moment, if not worse," Tyson barked.

"I don't think we have a choice," Bern sighed. Things were about to get much worse for the citizens of Jarrat, but there was nothing he could do about it. He knew it was the right move and that gave him no choice. "We can't wait for Richmond to remember. Even if he did remember the name of his contact there is ever the chance he has already been slaughtered. This is the plan that we have to go with."

"What about if they claim they are not traitors?" It was the question Bern was hoping Tyson wouldn't ask.

"We have to assume they will all be traitors. I doubt any of them are going to confess." Bern didn't want to voice the words, but they all knew what he meant.

"You mean torture?" Tyson was not going to let it go.

"These are serious times and we need to do what we can. There are more than civil liberties at stake here. We have to make tough decisions for the greater good." Bern's argument was thin, but it was all he had.

"That is not good enough." Tyson stood and banged his fists on the table. "You do not have the right to torture innocent civilians. I will not allow it."

"Bern is right. If they are innocent then they should obey the laws. We have to weed out all the traitors. Especially the one who is killing the others. It will only be a matter of time before he starts killing innocent people." Sorrell was in defence of the plan. He didn't like it in theory, but knew that it was necessary.

"That is easy for you to say Darshivallian, but these are not your people being tortured," Tyson looked around the room wildly.

"Sit down Tyson," Jarwe boomed from the other end of the table. "This is not about individual kingdoms. This is about the Seven kingdoms in general. If we fail then we all fail."

Tyson knew he was right, but it didn't make things any easier. If he sat down then he would be submitting, but if he remained standing then it would be just as bad. He waited as long as he could before returning to his seat. It would do him no good to get everyone off side, but he could not be seen as a push over. He needed to remain in the command group if he was going to make sure things didn't get out of hand.

"Okay, so how do we do this?" he asked when he had calmed down.

"We need to set up a detention camp. I don't want to take anyone to the dungeons, at least not yet," Bern explained. "Those who do not co-operate will be sent there as a last resort."

"What if they are innocent and simply cannot give us any information?" Tyson was still not convinced.

"This army has some of the best interrogators. We can only put our faith in them and hope they make the right decision," Jarwe spoke.

"I will sit in on the interrogations to make sure that they don't get out of hand," Tyson continued.

"I don't think that is a good idea," Jarwe returned. "Things may need to get, 'out of hand', as you put it."

"I cannot allow that to happen. The people of Jarrat have rights."

"These people gave up their rights when they decided to betray us." Jarwe was arguing just as fervently. "They will get what they deserve."

"What about the innocent people? What have they done to deserve such a punishment?" Tyson retorted

The argument went back and forth for almost half an hour before Bern finally spoke. He thought it was better to let them vent for a while. They were solving nothing, but he thought it was good for the soul. The argument was still in full flight when he finally spoke. The tent suddenly went very quiet.

"None of us are happy with the situation, but we do not have a choice. The innocent will have to suffer so the Seven Kingdoms doesn't fall to the Evil One. If there was another way we would do it, but there is not. The city is falling apart and we have to act now," Bern spoke firmly, but calmly. "I am sorry Tyson, but we will do what we have to do."

"We shall see what the queen has to say about this. I am sure she will not agree," there was an edge to his voice that Bern did not like.

"There is no need to make threats," Bern's voice turned icy cold. "Duke Xarles is still in command whilst the queen is unfit to rule. This is something he will agree with."

Tyson wanted to speak, but the words would not come out of his mouth. There was something about the way Bern had spoken to him that made him silent. He did not know what it was, but he knew he did not like it. He wanted to continue arguing, but he knew it was futile.

"Very well, I think this meeting is over. It is too late in the day to make the decree, but we can get word to the town cryers. In the morning the soldiers will enter the city and start routing out the agents of the Evil One, slowly of course. The Alliance will set up ambushes in the forest. We will catch anyone who tries to leave." Bern summed up the details of the meeting. "In the mean time we will have the remaining soldiers build the detention compound. That should keep them busy for a while."

When Bern had finished the summary the meeting was adjourned. No one felt like staying in the tent and making small talk. Even though they had come to a decision it was not a pleasant one. Even those who supported the idea were not happy. They had just agreed on a plan that would cause a great deal of suffering. That was something that they would have to live with.

The sun had almost completely set as Bern made his way back to the castle. It had been a long day and now that the adrenaline of the meeting had worn off he felt suddenly very tired. The day had not at all turned out the way he had thought. He didn't know if it had been a success or a failure. It was a result and that was all that really mattered. He was able to free the city, even if it was only an illusion.

Bern had one more stop before he could go to bed. In truth he had a lot of stops to make, but there was only one he was going to make. He wanted to see if Richmond could remember anything. If there was some more information then it might help them know who the traitors were and save the innocent citizens a lot of unnecessary pain. There were a few nobles in the corridor when he reached the castle, but he simply ignored them. Even when they tried to block his path he pretended as though they were not there. Some took longer than others, but eventually they realised that they should leave him alone.

Richmond was resting in his room. He looked up when Bern entered. He smiled and although he didn't stand he did sit up. There was a new strength in his eyes that Bern had not seen in a long time. It seemed as though Richmond was finally starting to get better.

"It is good to see you Bern," Richmond greeted him. "I have remembered something that might be helpful to you."

The adrenaline started to pump through Bern's body again and he was suddenly wide awake. There was a chance he could prevent the torture of innocent people. He listened intently, waiting for Richmond to speak.

"I have remembered the name of the person Aimon asked us to meet. His name is Coyne and he is a farrier in the commerce district." Richmond seemed pleased with himself.

Bern was suddenly deflated. The hope that he had felt was suddenly dashed. Coyne was dead and there were no other leads. The new plan would have to go ahead.

"What is it Bern? I thought you would be happy with the news." Richmond still had a smile on his face, but it was starting to diminish.

"Coyne is dead. Someone is in the city killing off the traitors," Bern explained.

"That is a good thing, isn't it?" Richmond didn't see the concern.

"There are also innocent people being killed in the process. Whoever is doing the killing will not let anyone get in his way. He is a dangerous man," Bern explained. He was glad to get his little secret off his chest. Ever since the topic came up he had wanted to tell someone.

"I see your point. Do you have a plan to draw him out?" Richmond asked.

Bern explained what they were planning. If Richmond was recovering then he would be a handy advisor and with what they were doing he needed all the help he could get.

Chapter 23: A Plan in Action

On the first day the plan didn't seem as though it was going to work. Everyone in the city was obeying the standing law that nobody was to leave. It was the first time that Bern was upset with the citizens for obeying him. The bluff would only work for another day at most before the residents knew they did not know who the traitors were. Bern could not believe things could get so bad.

Slowly, but surely, people started to leave the city. The traps were set inside the forest so no one knew what was waiting for them if they tried to escape. Bern was able to relax a little when things started to work. There was still a long road ahead, but at least they did not have to go back to the drawing board. Things were going to get worse before they got better.

It had not taken long for the rumours of the murders to circulate throughout the city. It was those rumours that caused the citizens to flee, not the threat of being caught. The first person to leave thought he was home free when he stepped outside of the city. It wasn't until the highway entered the forest did he realise the mistake he had made. The soldiers quickly closed in around him and there was no chance for escape. Once they had the man in custody the soldiers disappeared back into the forest. It was like they had never been there.

"Please," he begged once he was back in the detention centre. "I have a sick relative out of the city. I was only going to visit him to make sure he was still alive."

The interrogator a tall, wiry man named Danin stood over him, not interested in his excuse. "You are a traitor," his voice was as cold as ice. "Confess your sins and you may live a while longer."

"I don't know what you are talking about. I am loyal to the queen. I have been so all my life." It was the way he pronounced the word queen that was the biggest give away he was lying. It was all the interrogator needed to continue his work.

"We are not here to debate your allegiances. If you were innocent you wouldn't have left the city. It is information that I am after," he continued. "I need to know your connections."

"I have no connections. I don't know what you are talking about." His whimpering became worse. "Please let me go. I have to get out of here."

When the man would not reveal any information, the torture started. The interrogator started off slowly, but the man still cried out. He was not used to pain. It wasn't long before Tyson entered the room.

"Okay, I think this is enough Danin," Tyson did not sound impressed. "I will not stand around why you torture this man."

Bern had warned Danin that Tyson may try to stop the interrogations. He had also instructed him not to listen to the captain. It was imperative that he use his own judgement when deciding if someone was guilty or innocent. He was prepared for the interruption, but he did not think it would come so early. He was glad that it had happened with the first suspected traitor. He could nip it in the bud early and hopefully put an end to it.

"This is not your decision to make Captain Tyson," Danin was firm with his speech. He didn't want to give the captain a chance to get the upper hand. "I am in command of these interrogations. I will decide when things are enough."

The words infuriated Tyson. He outranked Danin in the army and he could not accept such insubordinate behaviour. The worst part was that he knew there was nothing he could do about it, but that thought would not deter him from trying. He could not stand idly by while the Alliance tortured the citizens from Jarrat.

"I am the current commander of the Enteroite army and that means I am your superior officer. You will listen to what I have to say. If I tell you to stop this interrogation then that is what you will do," Tyson spoke at the top of his voice.

The man sitting in the interrogation chair had a glimmer of hope. So far the interrogation had been sedate and he knew it was about to get much worse. If Tyson got his way then he was walking away without any real pain.

"This detention centre is run by the Alliance. It is General Bern who has command here. Only he has the authority to stop this interrogation." Danin didn't care if he offended Tyson. He had to stamp his authority in the best way that he could.

Tyson didn't think he could become any angrier. As the words came out of Danin's mouth he could feel the blood rising in his face. He wanted to grab Danin and throttle him. In the end that would prove nothing. In the end he had no choice, but to leave the interrogation room.

Danin was happy to see the captain leave. He knew he was going to suffer once he was back in the Enteroite army, but that was something he could live with. He had been given a difficult task and he was going to do everything he could to succeed.

"Now it is just you and I. I don't think we are going to have any more distractions," Danin smiled.

The man wanted to speak, but he knew there was a greater punishment waiting for him if he did. He had heard the rumours of the deaths in the city and knew that his name would be on that list. If he spoke then he would wish for death. That had been made quite clear to him when he was serving the Great Lord.

"I have nothing to say to you." The fear had gone from his face, he had nothing but resolve.

The strength did not remain long once Danin brought out an evil looking whip. The long leather strap had a number of nasty looking knots. There were a number of other tools for Danin to use, but he liked to use the whip first. He was able to cause a great deal of pain without leaving any permanent damage. A few scars would be the only lasting mark.

Danin had thought the man, whose name he didn't even ask, would last a lot longer than he did. He was grateful he didn't have the need to use some of his nastier tools. He much preferred to use his wits to gain the information he required. Most of the time he could talk down his prisoners, but he just did not have the time. Bern had told him that he needed to be as quick as possible. He did not like the order, but he had to do as he was told.

"Okay, please stop," the man cried out after only five minutes, although it had been an intense five minutes. "I will tell you everything you want to know."

"What is it you are doing in Jarrat?" It was not a question that Bern had told him to ask, but he wanted to know anyway.

"Nothing, I just worship the Great Lord. We are waiting for his instructions," the man was sobbing as he spoke.

"You have some purpose?" It didn't make sense to Danin.

"Once the Alliance was defeated we were going to be rewarded for our dedication." There was no lie in his voice, but his words did not make sense.

Danin didn't think that was the case. Since he could not detect a lie in his voice he could only surmise the man was a simpleton. If that was the case he was not going to gain any real information from the man. There would have to be a least one person he reported to and possibly others he worshipped with.

"Who else do you know who worships the Evil One?" Danin asked.

"I was supposed to report to a man named Coyne, he is a farrier in the commerce district. He didn't make the meeting so I returned home. That is when I heard about the murders. I didn't want to wait around to see if I was next." He was openly crying, making his speech hard to understand.

"Who else do you know?" Danin already knew that Coyne was a dead end.

"That is it," he sounded somewhat surprised at the question.

"There must be more. Who do you worship with?" Danin kept the questioning as he brandished the whip.

"I worship at home, but myself. We meet every full moon in the forest to make a sacrifice to the Great Lord." Danin did not want to know what they were sacrificing and was grateful when the man didn't divulge the information. "We were all instructed to wear dark robes with the hoods covering our faces. No one was to know the identity of anyone else. I didn't understand at the time, but now I do."

It was time for the interrogation to finish. The man could not give him anymore information. With the traitors being slowly murdered there was no chance of another sacrificial ceremony, even though the next full moon was only a week away. If they were to wait that long the traitors could easily all be dead. He needed someone else to interrogate. There had to be someone with answers.

A steady flow of people left the city over the next two days. No one escaped the soldiers waiting in the forest. Everyone was instantly shipped to the detention camp where Danin would apply his interrogation techniques. The more who came the greater the chance there would be someone who was innocent of the crimes they were being accused of. With each new interrogation the results ended the same. Coyne seemed to be the only contact they had within the network of traitors. Danin was beginning to believe he was being set up, although he could not be completely sure. Once he had finished with each traitor they were returned to the makeshift cells in the detention camp.

After seven days had passed the detention camp was nearly overflowing. The next decision was whether to move the prisoners to the dungeons or set them free. Neither was a popular choice. Bern had promised he would not send them to the dungeons, but he didn't see what other choice he had. He could release those who were innocent, but there was still a chance they were traitors. If word reached the city of what was happening then it would all have been for nothing.

"You have to release some of the prisoners," Tyson continued his argument. "You heard it from Danin yourself. There are men and women who he believes are innocent."

"That still does not change the fact that if we release them then they will return to the city and tell everyone what we are doing. That is something that we cannot risk." Jarwe put the other side forward.

Bern was happy to let the others argue while he thought. Their arguments were all valid, but they did not give a solution. Bern knew it would inevitably fall on his shoulders to come up with a plan. The only idea that came to his mind was to move some of the confirmed traitors to the dungeons, but that came with its own risks.

"We can't move them to the dungeons. People from the city will be able to see them being transported. That will certainly start them asking questions." Orric put across a valid point, one which Bern had already thought of.

"Then we can move them at night time. I am sure no one will see them when it's dark," Sorrell added his point.

The suggestions and arguments went backwards and forwards for most of the morning. They stopped only to eat before they continued their discussions. Bern remained quiet as he half listened and half tried to come up with a remedy. No matter how hard he thought, nothing was coming to him. He couldn't get the already used ideas out of his head. He always came back to the idea of sending the traitors to the dungeon. That was not going to appease anyone.

It was mid-afternoon when Danin came rushing into the tent. He was sweating and puffing, but he looked like he had some important news. Everyone stopped talking when he entered. It took him a moment to catch his breath. No one spoke. They had been talking in circles for so long they needed something else to concentrate on.

"I have finally got somewhere," Danin was still puffing, but he was able to speak clearly.

"Calm down Danin and tell us what happened," Bern spoke for the first time in a long time.

"Everyone has been saying that Coyne is the contact in the city. No matter how hard I torture them," Tyson cringed as he spoke. "They are all either telling the truth or consistent with their lies. Anyway, that is not the point, the point is I have another contact now and by all accounts she is still alive."

"Would you get to the point," Tyson snapped.

"Sorry!" Danin apologised. "I have never heard of her before. Her name is Valerie and she lives in the poor district. From what I understand she is some kind of apothecary, but he was a little vague on her occupation. He was able to give me instructions to her current location. She is hiding out at a vacant shopfront in the commerce district. She shouldn't be too hard to find."

There was silence in the tent as the information sunk in. It was the good news they had been waiting for. If Valerie had a list of all the traitors then they could let the innocent people go free. Danin could not understand why no one was speaking. They had finally got a lead and they were just sitting there.

"I don't think she will be in the city for long. It can only be a matter of time before she makes a break for it," Danin spoke with urgency in his voice.

"We can ill afford to rush into the city. There could well be traitors still there. If they work out what we are doing then they will go to ground. Catching Valerie is our best chance to end this," Bern spoke his mind.

"What are you thinking general?" Jarwe asked.

"I will go into the city with Danin. We will find Valerie and get the information from her," Bern replied.

"Do you think it is wise to go in with only two of you?" It was obvious that Orric did not think it was a good idea. "By the sounds of it she could be more powerful than the followers we have captured. I would not rush in to try and catch her. It may be you who become captured."

Bern had to admit that the old elf made sense. He really had no idea what he was up against. Rushing in to capture Valerie could be fatal. He did not think there was anyone else who could really help. If the woman was too dangerous for himself and Danin then no one else could help.

"That is not exactly true," Orric spoke as if he was reading Bern's mind, which wasn't far from the truth. "I will go with you. I will be able to help you."

"You will also be very conspicuous inside the city. There are no elves in Jarrat and there haven't been for a long time. I don't think that is a good idea." Tyson did not like what he was hearing.

"I think the people of Jarrat have more on their mindsthan the appearance of one elf. The city is in chaos." Jarwe had been trying to tip-toe around the topic. "There are soldiers all over the place. I am sure no one will notice you three.

Tyson had wanted to speak at the reference to the city being in chaos, but he had already been warned not to. If he was to bring his patriotism to the meeting then he would be removed. He was free to have his opinion, but he needed to be more objective. This was one of those topics that would get him in trouble. If he was going to help his kinsmen then he needed to stay involved.

"I think that is all. We need to get moving. There is not much daylight left and I don't want to be running around in the dark," Bern stood as he spoke.

The others around the table thought there was more to discuss, but it was clear Bern wanted to get moving. He did not want to sit around in a committee now that he had a purpose. He knew they would eat up the rest of the day in discussion and in the end nothing would change.

The city was just as Sorrell had suggested, in chaos. Soldiers moved around the streets to make sure that no one got away. Citizens, who had to be out and about, moved around quickly, trying not to get in their way. The three of them were able to move around relatively unnoticed. Bern had changed into his army leathers and felt much more comfortable. The soldiers all knew who they were and let them pass. The citizens kept their heads down. They didn't want to make eye contact with anyone.

The light was starting to dim as they reached the empty shopfront. It was obvious that Orric was starting to become nervous. That in turn made everyone else nervous. There was something about the elf's attitude that worried Bern. He knew there was something he wasn't telling them.

"What should we do?" Danin asked.

They were standing a few shops away from the vacant shopfront. When they had found the shop they didn't want to just go rushing in. For starters there were people still in the street. Three men, albeit one was an elf, breaking into an empty store front would only draw attention. They needed to make their visit to the city unnoticed, at least to the citizens of Jarrat.

"I think we should wait until dark. Then we will be able to enter the shop without suspicion," Bern suggested.

"I think that is an exceedingly dangerous idea," Orric spoke with his usual ominous tone. "We need to get in and out of there before nightfall."

"What is going on?" Bern knew it wasn't the right time to ask the question, but he couldn't wait.

"There is not time, but I promise I will explain to you later," he almost sounded confused. "I am sure there will be a way in through the back. Let's check it out."

There was a large fence at the back of the store. It prevented any of them from being able to see. They needed to help each other to get over it. Although there was no one in the small laneway at the back of the building it was still a tense few minutes. Once they were in the small courtyard at the back of the shop they were able to relax, but only for a moment. Their next challenge was much more nerve-racking.

The door to the back of the store was not locked, which seemed odd. Instantly Bern got a feeling that something was wrong. There was a stale smell in the room. It reminded him of the Royal Watchman after everyone had been murdered. He did not think it was a good sign.

As they moved through the building they heard something move. It was subtle, but it was a good sign that someone was inside. All three men drew their weapons; although Bern still carried the rapier. As much as he wanted to bring along his claymore he agreed that a large broadsword strapped to his back would be too conspicuous.

When they entered the storefront they were met with an ear-piercing scream. The sound was not at all what they were expecting. The room was dark and they could only see a small shape. It looked like a person was huddled in the corner. They could only assume that it was Valerie. It did not look as though she was dangerous. It did nothing to change Orric's demeanour and that kept the other two men on edge.

Danin found a lantern on the front desk and lit it. The shutter was closed and only let out a small sliver of light. Slowly he opened the shutter to let more light into the room. The woman in the corner had her head between her legs and her hands covering her face. She was visibly shaking. Bern had a feeling she thought they were someone else. That was not a pleasant thought at all.

"Please don't kill me. I have only ever served faithfully. This has nothing to do with me," she pleaded, without looking up.

"Are you Valerie?" Orric asked before anyone else had a chance to speak.

She looked up when she heard his voice. It was obvious by the look on her face that she was not expecting to see the them. She looked at each of them in turn. At first there was confusion on her face, but when she realised they were not there to kill her it turned to relief. She quickly jumped to her feet and rushed towards Bern. The movement was so sudden that he was taken by surprise, something he berated himself for later. She wrapped her arms around him and squeezed him tight. Once she had hold of Bern she did not want to let him go. He had to pry her from his body. When he was free he took a couple of steps backwards.

"Are you Valerie?" Bern re-asked the question. He was now not sure she was the woman they were looking for. He levelled the rapier at her to thwart any further attempt to attack him.

"Yes. Please you have to help me," she still sounded scared for her life.

"What are you afraid of?" Bern was not going to make it easy for her.

"He is coming for me. He will be here soon. We have to get out of here. We have to get out of here now."

Bern was not so sure. There could easily be a trap waiting for them on the outside. He looked at Orric for advice. The elf simply nodded his head. Bern could see a similar look of fear in his face. There was something going on that Bern did not understand and he didn't like it. He was loathed to leave the shopfront until he understood, but he knew that would not be the case. He still had an opportunity to gain the upper hand with Valerie.

"Tell me why we should help you. You are a traitor and worse. I have a good mind to leave you here to die." It was complete bluff, but Valerie didn't know that.

"Please I will do anything you want. I will tell you whatever you want to know. I have a lot of information. I could be very helpful to your cause." Her eyes were wide with fear. She kept looking over her shoulder as if there was someone behind her.

"Okay. We will take you with us, but if you do not tell us everything we want to know then we will send you straight back to the city and into the hands of your murderer." There was no lie in the threat. The dungeon would be too good for her.

"Yes, of course, whatever you need. Only we need to leave now." She was inching her way towards the door, but she would not leave without them. "Now, please, can we leave?"

"Let's get moving," Bern made it sound as though it was his decision.

The sun had almost completely set when they left the building. This did nothing to calm the nerves of their prisoner. She constantly looked around as they made their way towards the gate. She kept moving ahead, trying to rush them, but whenever she got too far in front she rushed back to where they were walking. The further the sun dropped the worse she became. She almost got to the point where she was pushing them onwards.

She relaxed slightly when they reached the gate. Waiting for them were four horses. Before they let Valerie mount her horse they bound her arms behind her back. There could be little doubt that she would try and bolt once she was on horseback and out of the city. There was also little doubt the soldiers would catch her and possibly kill her. They would not be truly safe until they were inside the camp.

They were stopped a number of times by soldiers on the way back to the detention camp. In the dark no one knew who they were. They were just four riders out in the night. It wasn't until they were recognised before they were on their way again. They rode straight for the detention camp and the interrogation room. Bern and Orric both decided to sit in on the questioning.

"So tell us who the traitors inside the city are?" Danin asked when she was secured in the interrogation chair.

"I don't know them all by name, but I have a list," she blurted out quickly.

It seemed as though she was going to be truthful. Danin thought that was a promising sign. He had hardened slightly since he had started the interrogations, but he would still be happy for them to end. He had caused a lot of pain and that was something he would have to live with. He knew it was for a good cause, but that only made it slightly easier.

"I think you should tell me the names of those you do remember." Danin didn't want to leave anything to chance. At least he would be able to start getting the names of those who were guilty. It also meant he would be able to double check her honesty against the list.

Slowly Valerie started to list the name of the followers she could remember. The list was longer than Danin had expected. He recognised some of the names on the list with those in the camp. If they indeed were on the list she had then they would end up in the dungeons. Although Tyson did not want that to happen there was no other place for them. They were guilty of treason and that was punishable by death. There was little doubt in his mind that was what the queen would have wanted.

"Who is after you?" Bern asked when she came to the end of the list.

Danin shot him an annoyed look. They had decided that Danin should do all the talking in the interrogation. It would keep everything simple. Bern didn't like waiting while Valerie listed the numerous traitors. It had been annoying him ever since he had found out about the deaths. It seemed as though Orric already knew and that annoyed him even more.

Valerie started trembling as soon as the question was asked. She was clearly not comfortable with what she was asked. Although she did not want lie or withhold information she could not bring herself to mention the murderer's name. It was more that she could not speak the name which she had uttered so many times. Each time she thought she could recall the name it disappeared again.

"Answer me or you will end up back in the city before sunrise," Bern yelled at the top of his voice. He was tired and did not want to be messed around.

"I can't," she whimpered.

"What do you mean you can't? You said that you would answer all our questions." Bern was not going to let her get away with such a response.

"Please, I can't go back to the city. You have no idea what he will do to me if I return." She started crying.

"Relax Bern," Orric spoke before he had a chance to speak again. "I don't think she is doing it deliberately."

"What are you talking about?" Bern moved his rage onto Orric.

"She has a mind block. Whoever is at the top of this tree is powerful indeed," Orric explained.

"Who is it?" Bern had to keep the rage inside. "I know you know something that you are not telling me."

Orric thought for a moment. He was no longer sure of his suspicions. "I originally thought it was another Dark Knight at work, but now I am not so sure. It just doesn't feel right. I need to know what she knows."

"If she has a mind block then there is nothing we can do. Eldred cannot leave Alena." Bern wished he had not spoken.

"What do you mean he cannot leave my daughter?" Orric picked up on the faux pas.

"I will tell you later," Bern hoped that he would be able to complete what they were doing before he revealed Alena's condition to her father. "We need to concentrate on the job at hand."

Orric knew he was right, but that still did not change the fact that something was wrong with his daughter. He had known something strange was happening with Alena, but no one would give him any answers. He had stopped asking the question in hope that some information would slip out. Unfortunately it was not the right time push any further. Orric decided in the end that he had to keep going.

"I can try and remove the block, but it might take a while."

"That's okay, we have time," Bern replied. "We need answers more than we need sleep."

Orric moved a chair over to where Valerie was bound. He placed his hand on her head and closed his eyes. Bern thought he heard a slight crackle in the air, but he could not be sure. He did know, however, that Orric had started whatever it was he was doing.

It took almost two hours before Orric released Valerie's head. They both looked exhausted when he was done. Valerie's dark brown hair was drenched with sweat and stuck to the side of her face. Her eyelids drooped and she looked like she could fall asleep at any moment. Bern and Danin, who had both almost fallen asleep themselves, were suddenly wide awake. They were dying to find out if things had worked.

"Did it work?" Bern finally asked when no one spoke.

"I think so. I'm not exactly sure. There was something different about the spell. There was a subtle difference, but it was definitely there. I am pretty sure I have gotten rid of it, but we can only know when she starts answering our questions," Orric explained.

"I think that might be harder than you think," Danin said. "She has lost consciousness."

Danin tried to wake her, but nothing was working. He shook her violently, but she did not react. There was nothing they could do. He checked her pulse to make sure she was still alive.

"I don't suppose it will matter if we wait until the morning. It is getting late and we could all use some sleep. I don't think she is going anywhere," Orric suggested.

"I will make sure she is secured overnight and there will be guards posted to keep an eye on her," Danin added.

"Well I guess everything is taken care of then." Bern did not sound convinced. He had a bad feeling, but that was not anything new. "We shall reconvene at first light."

Chapter 24: Disaster Strikes

Bern was exhausted when he returned to the castle. All he wanted to do was crawl into bed and fall asleep, but that was not going to happen any time soon. Duke Xarles had ordered that once Bern had returned he was to be sent straight his apartments. He wanted an update on what Bern was doing.

Although Bern could have denied the request he didn't want to put the duke off side. He would just have to forego some of his much needed sleep.

Once he had finished he checked in with Richmond to see if there was any change in Tancred. As he thought there had been none. Bern doubted that Tancred would ever recover. The physician still came and checked on him, but there was little he could do. Richmond was taking his condition harder than his own. Since his memory had started returning he could remember his relationship with his advisor. He also knew the reason why Tancred did not want to wake up. Bern quickly realised Richmond wanted time to himself and he was happy enough to comply.

In the morning Bern was up before the sun. He had not slept well that night. He could not shake the feeling that something bad was either happening or about to happen. He only wished he knew what it was. With each day he was becoming more in tune with the prophecy. He woke feeling just as tired as when he went to bed. The only thing that kept him going was the adrenaline pumping through his body. Valerie would be awake and he would finally be able to get answers.

Bern rode his horse hard towards the detention camp. The sun had started to rise and the other two men would be waiting for him. There was no time to waste. The feeling that something was wrong had increased once he left the castle. He knew it would not go away until he reached the detention centre.

Waiting for him at the entrance to the camp was Danin and Orric. By the looks on their faces he knew something terrible had happened. He could hardly bring himself to ask the question, but he knew that delaying it would not make things better.

"What has happened?" he asked.

"I don't know how to explain it," there was a slight amount of shock in Danin's voice.

"Valerie is dead." Orric had no problems in finding the right words.

"What are you talking about?"

"We have been trying to work out exactly what happened, but no one seems to know anything," Orric continued when Danin didn't speak.

"How could this have happened? Wasn't she under guard all night?"

"That is what we can't work out. The guards have said that no one entered her cell. There were always at least two guards stationed at any one time. We knew that her life was in danger and we wanted to make sure her life was safe." Danin shook his head as he spoke. He still couldn't believe it happened.

"Well that really doesn't make any sense," Bern was slowly coming to terms with the fact that Valerie was dead, although the severity of the situation had not yet sunk in.

"In fact it makes perfect sense." Orric had been thinking on the matter a lot more than the others. "And the answer is more terrifying than you think," his words were ominous. "Someone very powerful made their way into the detention camp and murdered Valerie without anyone seeing him. There are not too many alive today with that much power."

"Does that mean you know who it is?" Bern wasn't as shocked as Orric had anticipated. He had taken the news surprisingly well.

"Just the opposite. Now I have no idea who it is," Orric was still thinking. "If I wasn't mistaken I would say it was the Evil One himself."

Neither men were expecting him to say that nor did they know how to respond. Orric's words echoed around their heads. They could not really comprehend the ramifications if he was correct. There was nothing they could do to defend against such power. There had to be another explanation. Bern would be happy to hear that the guards had gone for a walk or fell asleep at their post. It would be much better than the alternative.

"So what do we do now?" Danin sounded lost.

"I think it should be much easier to work out who the traitors are. All we need to do is leak word of what happened to Valerie around the camp and they will be falling over themselves to seek refuge," Orric suggested.

"I don't think that would be a good idea. The last thing we need is to have the prisoners panicked. There is no telling what would happen," Bern refuted the idea. "We need to go to her house and find the list. That will tell us who the traitors are. Valerie must have had a lot of information for her to be killed in such a manner."

"I doubt there will be anything left of her house. I am sure it would have been destroyed by now." Orric was playing devil's advocate.

"Well there is only one way to find out. I am going into the city. Who is coming with me?" It was really a rhetorical question, but he thought he would give them the courtesy of asking it.

The three men made the sombre ride to the house. Neither of them wanted to think about what had happened, but they could not bring themselves to speak. All they could think about was what had happened to Valerie and who could possibly have done such a thing. There was every chance the mystery man was waiting for them at Valerie's house. Again that was something that wasn't worth thinking about, although it should have been something they were prepared for.

It took a while for Danin to find her house. Valerie had given him directions, but he was finding it hard to concentrate. He couldn't shake the feeling that someone was watching him. It was extremely unnerving. He had known his position would make him a target, but he had no idea how dangerous things were going to get.

The house looked as though it had been untouched. The front door was still securely locked. It was a promising sign they were the first there. If that was the case then there was a chance they would identify the mystery assassin. That idea was in the foremost of Bern's mind. He no longer cared about the minor traitors. They had all been duped, but he doubted they would be much of a problem now. They would have to suffer a little more, but they would soon be able to assimilate themselves back into Jarrat.

They checked all around the outside of the house to make sure they couldn't see anyone inside. They were no longer concerned about being seen breaking in. Things had come to a head and it didn't matter who knew what they were up to. All their energy had to be given to catching the leader, although they were not sure if that was even possible. At least if they were able to identify who it was then Alaric could deal with them when he returned from Castalia.

Once they were sure there was no danger inside the house Bern knocked the door open. He needed two attempts of hitting the door with his shoulder before he was able to splinter it away from its lock. Bern stumbled into the house, but was able to keep from falling over.

The front room did not have the same stale smell that met them at the farrier's shop. It was a very promising sign, although they already knew that no one had been killed there. Bern was not so sure if the staleness had been that of death or from the one who had been doing the killing. Either way that was not the most important matter at hand.

The house looked to be in a reasonable condition. It did not look like it had been ransacked. It was not going to stay that way for long. They would tear the house apart to find the information they needed and they would have to do it quickly. They did not think it would be long before the assassin would realise where Valerie had been living. They had to be out of the house well before that happened. As much as they needed to know who the assassin was they didn't want to meet him. The man was too powerful for the three of them and they knew it.

They had hoped that the list of traitors would be easy to find. If life was fair it would have been sitting on top of her desk in her study, but that was not the case. They looked everywhere, but there was no sign of any information of her dealings with the enemy. They convened in the bedroom when they had finished their search.

"Does anyone get the feeling we have been set up?" Danin asked.

"It is looking that way," Orric had to agree.

"No. That is not what is happening here. If she had set this up then we would already be dead. She told us the truth. The only thing is she didn't tell us the entire truth. It is the location of the list which she kept to herself. Whether by design or accidentally, but it was here somewhere." Bern did not agree with the other two.

"Then where is it?" Danin asked. "We have pulled this place apart. It's not anywhere."

"We are just not thinking right." Bern sat down on the bed and let his head droop. He was just as much to blame as the others, but he knew he could find the solution.

The other two simply looked at him. They had given up. They figured the assassin had beaten them to the list and it was now gone, but they would not leave until Bern was ready. They did not think it would take long for him to see the folly of his suggestion, but they had to leave before the assassin decided to return for something.

Bern closed his eyes as he tried to reason out the riddle before him. He knew the solution was there. He just had to put his mind to the task. They could not leave without the identity of the assassin. If they did then no one was safe. He had already proved how powerful his was. He would be able to kill of the traitors and leave them with no clue of his intentions.

When Bern opened his eyes again he could have kicked himself. The answer had been staring him in the face all along. Underneath the bed there was a large floor rug. The corner of the rug was frayed and slightly upturned. When he saw it he had no doubt there was something underneath.

"Help me move the bed," Bern commanded as he jumped up.

"I have already checked under the bed. There is nothing there," Danin argued, but there was something in the look on Bern's face that made him change his mind.

Once the bed was out of the way Bern pulled at one side of the rug. As he dragged it away a small trapdoor was revealed. That was what Bern had been looking for. He knew there was more to the house than what they had seen. He was sure the answers they were looking for would be in the cellar.

There was a large rusty lock on the trapdoor. Getting inside would not be an easy task and they had not seen any keys when they were upturning the house. Now they could be anywhere. The place was a mess. They had not been too careful with their searching.

"Now what are we going to do?" Danin asked.

Bern was not going to be put off. They had gone too far to be stopped by a mere lock. Since it was rusted there was a good chance he could break it. Without speaking Bern drew his sword, he was grateful he had decided to bring his claymore this time, and brought it down with all his might on the lock. When the sword struck there was a shower of sparks, but when he looked down the lock was still in place. Taking a wider arc Bern brought the sword down again. There was another shower of sparks and this time the lock snapped.

"Now let's see what is in there." Bern had a smile on his face.

Once the trapdoor had been lifted they were hit with a stench that almost made them retch. They all had to cover their noses to proceed down into the basement. There were a number of torches on the wall and Bern lit them. As soon as he did he wished he had stayed in the dark. The cellar had been turned into an evil torture chamber. Even in the profession Danin was in he was shocked with what he saw. There were pools of dried blood on the floor as well as chucks of dried flesh. The walls were also splashed with blood. Bern could only imagine what kind of atrocities were carried out in such a room.

The urge to turn around and leave the cellar was compelling. The only thing that kept them going was the desk on the far side. There was suddenly a gleam of hope in their eyes. Bern knew the list would be in that desk and yet he didn't want to cross the floor to check. None of them had moved since they had lit the torches closest to the staircase.

"What is happening?" Bern asked.

"I believe that there is a spell on this room stopping us from crossing the floor," Orric surmised.

"Then we have come to a dead end." Danin had already given up, although he was excited at the prospect of leaving the cellar.

"Not yet," there was a pensive tone to Bern's voice.

He knew he could break the spell. All he needed to do was concentrate. It would be his will power that would force him to the other side of the cellar. He closed his eyes and concentrated on taking one step forward. Each step would be a challenge and the closer he came the harder the movement would become. Slowly he started to move. With each step there was an uncontrollable urge to turn around and run. A great fear filled his body which threatened to break his spirit. He knew it was only the spell, but that only made it slightly easier.

When he opened his eyes again he was standing in front of the desk. Orric and Danin were still standing on the other side of the room. They could not believe that he had made it, their hearts were filled with horror, it was all they could do to keep from running back into the house. They wanted to see if Bern was able to find anything useful on the other side and that was the only thing keeping them in basement.

The desk, unlike the rest of the cellar, was clear of blood. There were a number of sheets of paper on the top of the desk, but none of them were a list of traitors. Bern pulled open the top drawer. It took a great effort and was the one draw that he had a bad feeling about. He knew it was the right one. If something was telling him to stay away then he should do the exact opposite.

There were two sheets of paper inside the draw. They contained the list of traitors they had been looking for. A sudden compulsion to rip up the paper and throw it away came over him. He knew it was only the spell working its evil. He would not feel right again until he left the cellar. He looked back across the torture chamber. It looked like such a long journey and he couldn't bring himself to take a step forward. His resolve had finally been broken.

"Come on Bern," Danin couldn't believe the words came out of his mouth. "Just take one step at a time."

That was easier said than done, but it was Danin's encouragement that urged Bern forward. Once his legs started moving again it was easier to push on. He knew if he stopped he would not be able to get moving again. He didn't pause when he reached the other two. He just kept moving up the stairs and back into the house. Danin and Orric shot each other a quick look before following Bern up the stairs.

No one could relax until the trapdoor had been shut tight. Bern wished he had not broken the lock. He would like to seal that room from everyone. No one should have to go through what they just experienced. If he had time when things were over he could come back and burn the house to the ground.

"What is written on the list?" Danin asked quickly.

Bern looked down at the two pieces of paper. The list was longer than what he had thought. There were many more names than those that Valerie had confessed to the night before. There were two names towards the top of the list. They were Valeria and Coyne. Above their names there was a large question mark. It was the question mark who was in charge of the traitors.

"It looks like the trail ends with Valerie. There is no mention of the assassin. Not even a clue," Bern sounded morose.

"At least we know who all the traitors are," Orric didn't sound convinced with his own statement.

"We better get moving before the assassin comes to get that list." Danin was clearly nervous.

"If we wait then it would give us a chance to find out who he is," Bern suggested, although he did not know why.

"I don't think that would be a good idea. We are no match for the assassin. All we will end up doing is dying," Orric kept his voice low, as if he spoke too loud then someone else would hear him. "We need to continue with the original plan. That is something we can do."

"Okay. You take the list back to the camp. I will return to the castle and see what Duke Xarles want to do with the traitors. I think it would be best if he makes the decision. If he wants to move them to the dungeon then that is what we will do," Bern added as they left the building.

"And what if he decides to let them all go free?" Orric returned, a lot happier to be out of the house.

"I will do my best to convince him otherwise, but I can't really see that he will want to release them," Bern replied.

"You are putting their lives at risk," Orric continued his thought.

"I think that their lives are forfeited anyway. I am sure they will all be convicted of treason and hung," Danin didn't sound so concerned. "Either way they will be dead before the end of the month."

Bern had to accept the fact that Danin was right. As much as he hoped they could be saved there was no chance. One way or the other their fate had been sealed. It would be more humane if they were hung than what the assassin would do to them. He hoped that Xarles would see it the same way.

Bern left the two to take the list back to the detention camp. Those whose names were not on the list would be set free. That was one bonus to come out of the day. In fact it was better than that, although it did not feel that way. Bern had set out, once he had left the detention camp, to find the name of the assassin. They had come no closer to their goal. He needed to return to the castle and speak with Eldred. He was Bern's last chance. If Eldred didn't know who the assassin was then he was out of ideas.

Once again he had to run the gauntlet when he returned to the castle. The nobles were roaming the corridors and when they saw Bern they rushed in to speak with him. Bern was in no mood. He knew that Xarles had told him to be civil, but with what he had experienced that day he had no time. Some of the nobles took it on face value, but others would not be so easily dissuaded. Bern almost had to be physical to persuade those nobles not to bother him. He was prepared to go so far, but luckily it did not come to that. He didn't want to think of the ramifications for Xarles if he had struck one of the nobleman, no matter how much he had wanted to.

He found Xarles in the throne room. It was almost completely full with nobleman and other officials. It was certainly not the best chance to speak with him. He didn't think it would matter if the duke waited to hear the news. There would be no huge problems with the detention centre now that they had the list. Once the innocent citizens of Jarrat were set free there would be plenty of room for the new occupants.

The real reason he was happy to leave the throne room was that he wanted to speak with Eldred. He could not concentrate on anything else. He needed to know who or what he was up against. He only hoped that Eldred would have the answers to his questions. He needed some good news. He felt like he was getting nowhere and there was only so much time he had left. If he didn't figure things out soon then the situation would turn dire.

Eldred was still keeping his vigil in Alena's room. He looked even worse than the last time Bern had seen him. His skin was pale and wrinkled and his clothes were drenched with sweat. His eyes were open, but there looked as though there was no recognition in them. His breathing was slow and laboured. Bern didn't think he had much life left in him.

"Come in Bern," his voice was hoarse. "I still have life left in me," there was a jovial note to his words that was belied by his tone.

"I am sorry to disturb you Eldred, but things have just become more dangerous." Bern was taken aback by Eldred's speech.

"I know and there is no need to apologise. It is good to be able to speak with someone again," Eldred replied.

Bern wasn't sure if Eldred would be able to continue the conversation. He sounded as though he could lose consciousness at any moment. He had never seen the man so weak, even when he first came out of the dungeons. Bern was concerned for his wellbeing, but he was also concerned for Alena. If Eldred failed then she would die. She still had a part to play in the prophecy, he hated to think what would happen if she died.

"How is Alena?" It was a silly question, but he thought that it was one he should ask.

"She is still alive." There was nothing else he could really say.

"And how are you?"

"Getting worse each day." He was honest in his bluntness. "I don't think I will be able to keep this up for much longer. It seems as though I am not as strong as I thought I was. That said I think that Ra'naroz is craftier than we thought. He has done something to make my power wane," Eldred explained.

"How long do you think you can keep her alive?" Bern did not like what he was hearing.

"I don't really know. A day, maybe two, but I wouldn't think much longer than that," Eldred did not sound happy.

That was not what Bern wanted to hear. He had no idea how far away Alaric was, but he didn't think he would be back in time. It looked as though the enemy was going win and Alena was going to die. That was something that he did not want to think about. If it was true then he would have to let Orric into the city. He did not want to be responsible for not letting him see his daughter one last time.

"I am sure that Alaric will be back in time," Bern tried to sound optimistic.

"Was there something else that you wanted?" Eldred wanted to change to subject.

Bern thought for a moment. He wasn't sure if he wanted to lay such a task on Eldred. The old wizard obviously needed to concentrate on Alena. He did not want to distract him, but he did need to know who he was up against.

"It's not that important." Bern decided against the question.

"It's okay Bern. I can see that you need something. Ask the question and if I can help then I will." Eldred pushed a little harder. He knew there was something on Bern's mind and a little distraction would be good for him.

Bern was grateful for Eldred's assistance. He started by explaining what they had been doing. Eldred listened intently to Bern's tale. When Bern came towards the end of the story he could see concern written on Eldred's face. He knew that when he finished he was not going to like what Eldred said.

"It sounds as though there is another Dark Knight in the city." Eldred was thinking as he spoke. "It just doesn't make any sense."

"What do you mean?" Bern asked.

"I couldn't see one of the Dark Knight's living in squalor in the city whilst Ra'naroz was living in the castle. That said there is a lot that has happened that doesn't make sense to me. I guess that it is possible," Eldred did not sound convinced.

"Orric said that it didn't feel like a Dark Knight," Bern said when Eldred had finished.

"Then that puts a whole new light on matters," Bern could see that Eldred was trying to think hard. "I am sorry. I can't seem to grasp what is rattling around in my head. One thing I can tell you is to be very careful. Whoever it is they are very dangerous," Eldred warned.

There was not much else Bern could do. Eldred looked as though he needed to rest. Bern would have to move on. There was still more for him to do and the day was starting to get away from him. He needed to do something to keep himself busy. If he didn't then he would worry about the assassin and that would get him nowhere.

Chapter 25: Things Get Worse

The meeting with Xarles went as Bern had expected. At first he was relieved when he heard they had found a list of traitors, but that quickly turned to anger over the thought of the innocent citizens being tortured. Bern did his best to appease the duke. The interrogations were necessary, but that didn't make things any easier for him. It took Xarles a while before he calmed down again and was able to get back to the point. He agreed the traitors should be transported to the castle dungeons before they would be tried and hung for treason. He wanted it all done before the queen recovered. He knew she would blame herself and would want to go easy on them. As much as he didn't want to execute so many citizens there was nothing he could do about it. If he didn't seek retribution then he would lose all power within the castle. That was something he could not afford to do.

The sun had set by the time Bern left his meeting with Xarles. He had wanted to return to the detention camp to see what was happening, but he didn't see much point. His lack of sleep was starting to get to him. He didn't think he was going to gain anything by exhausting himself even more and there was nothing that couldn't wait until the morning.

Orric and Danin had taken the list straight back to the detention camp. They did not want to keep the innocent locked up any longer. They would have to make sure they were properly compensated from the royal coffers. They were sure that neither Xarles nor Oriana would deny them. It was the least they could do.

The main problem was what they were going to do with those who were guilty. With the assassin still on the loose they didn't know if they would still be there in the morning. If he could sneak into the compound, kill Valerie and leave again without being seen there was no telling what he was capable of. As much as they were traitors neither of them believed that they deserved that fate.

They posted every available soldier to guard the detention camp. Orric's theory was the more soldiers the stronger the spell had to be to get past. They wanted to do everything they could to keep them alive. There was still a chance they could get valuable information from them.

The city of Jarrat was back in lockdown. In the morning the soldiers would hunt out the remaining traitors on the list. Once they had completed the task the city would return to normal, then they would be finished in Jarrat. After that was done they would need to know where they were going next.

It was another restless night for Bern. His dreams were haunted by the face of the assassin. During the night he tossed and turned and in the morning he woke up feeling just as tired as when he went to sleep. The worst part was the memory the assassin had left him. Whilst he was sleeping he was sure it was the man they were looking for, but when he woke he couldn't quite remember. He had to put the thought out of his mind. Without the entire memory there was no point dwelling on it. He had enough things to worry about.

When he reached the detention camp the final part of their plan was in motion. The soldiers had moved into the city and started removing the last of the traitors. Bern was relieved to find out that no one else had been murdered. There was a slim chance that Valerie had been the last one, but Bern thought there would be more.

"What do we do about this assassin?" Bern asked when he met with Orric and Danin.

"I don't see there is anything we can do. There is nothing to give us any clues to his whereabouts. Unless he strikes again," Orric replied.

"There has to be something we can do." Danin was not happy with the response. "What happens if he gets bored killing off the traitors and starts on regular citizens?"

"What would you have us do? We have no way of finding him and if we did find him we have no way of stopping him." Bern's words were not promising.

"There has to be something we can do. By mere force of numbers we should be able to kill him," Danin suggested.

"Whatever we can do will play out in time. At the moment there is nothing we can do about him. We have to concentrate on the job at hand."

"Bern is right. We have to make sure we round up the rest of the traitors, so they will face the justice of Enteroite law not that of the assassin," Orric agreed.

There was a steady flow of traitors coming from the city from mid-morning until late afternoon and there were still a few names on the list as the sun started to set. The command group convened for a meeting. They had all heard rumours of what was happening.

"So our time here is finally coming to an end," Jarwe commented when Bern finished explaining the situation.

"And the city can finally be set free again?" Tyson sounded suspicious.

"That is all true. Once we have everyone accounted for on that list we will return control of the city. As far as the army leaving Jarrat, well we need to wait for Alaric to return," Bern continued. "We cannot go anywhere until then." It had taken a long time, but he knew that was true.

"It will not be long before the soldiers start getting restless," Sorrell repeated the old problem.

"We can have them stationed around the detention camp. I am sure that Xarles won't mind if we hold onto them for a few more days. That should keep them entertained for a while." Bern suggested.

"Then I guess everything is taken care of," Jarwe sounded somewhat disappointed.

Bern was grateful to be out of the meeting. There was a good chance that things could have gone wrong. He was lucky they had not pushed him for more answers. He still did not know what they were going to do. He had also neglected to mention the assassin. He had just advised the detention camp needed to be strongly guarded. The threat of a riot, even though there was not one, was enough to convince everyone that it was the right decision. In truth the traitors were grateful to be in the protection of detention. They didn't care what fate awaited them once they were inside the castle dungeons as long as the assassin didn't get his hands on them. They all knew someone had been killing the followers of the Evil One inside the city and the rumour had been spread through the detention camp. Bern was grateful the rumour had not reached the command group, but knew it would only be a matter of time. With a little luck Alaric would have returned before it happened.

Bern had only just started to ride back to the castle when he heard someone approach from behind. He slowed down. He had a feeling he knew who it was so he didn't bother looking around.

"We need to talk," he recognised Orric's voice.

"I had a feeling I would be speaking with you tonight."

"I think you should have told them about the assassin," Orric rode up next to Bern.

"There is nothing to tell them. I don't think it would really benefit anyone to tell them that a mysterious assassin is killing off the traitors, oh and he can do it whilst a prisoner is heavily guarded. I don't think that would prove anything, but I don't believe that is the reason why you are here." Bern wanted to change the subject.

"No, you are right. I need to know how Alena is?" his voice was soft, almost as if he was afraid to ask the question.

Bern didn't know what to say. He knew he could not lie, but he also didn't want to tell the truth. He didn't know how Orric would take the news. There was a good chance that Alena would die and he doubted that Alaric would be able to make it back in time, but he did not want Orric to know his concerns.

"She is not doing well," Bern was honest. "Eldred is starting to wane. There is something more to her condition than what he originally thought."

Orric rode in silence as he let the information sink in. There was something in Bern's honesty that disturbed him. He wanted nothing more than to see his daughter. He didn't think it would be an issue him entering the castle anymore.

"I would like to see her. If there is a chance I could help her to get better I have to do it." Orric was almost pleading.

Bern was a little taken aback by his attitude. He did not ever think he would see Orric being subservient. He had already decided it would be alright for Orric to enter the castle. If Alena was going to die then her father should be at her side. If anyone within the castle had anything to say about it then they would have Bern to answer to.

"I think it would be a good idea for you to accompany me to the castle. I am sure that Eldred would be happy for assistance," Bern answered.

They continued on to the castle in silence. Neither of them wanted to speak. It was an uncomfortable silence, but they were both happy not to say anything. There would be enough time for talking once they were inside.

The sun had well and truly set by the time they reached the castle. There was a chance that the corridors would be empty, but Bern did not think he would be so lucky. Most of the noble men and women should be in the dining hall or eating in their own apartments, but he knew there would be some scouting the corridors. They knew that he came and went as he pleased and some would be looking for an opportunity to catch him unawares. With Orric by his side he thought that might dissuade them from approaching him.

As Bern had expected there were a number of noblemen in the corridors. When they saw Bern their eyes lit up, but then that all changed when they saw the elf walking next to him. The seriousness on both their faces deterred the nobles from approaching. Bern was grateful for small mercies. He didn't want to have to turn the nobles away in front of Orric. He was just happy they left them in peace.

Eldred didn't bother looking up when they entered the room. It was not that he knew who they were, although he could have guessed, it was that he did not have the energy. He didn't think it really mattered. Whoever it was would identify themselves soon enough.

"Orric is here," Bern spoke when it was clear that Eldred would not.

Again Eldred didn't bother looking up. "I thought it was only a matter of time. How are you my old friend?"

"That is neither here nor there. It is how you are that matters?" Orric replied.

"Getting old, Orric, getting old. I am not as young as I used to be and it seems as though I am aging quicker and quicker with each passing day." Bern was not quite sure what he meant, but Orric did.

"Is there anything I can do to help?" Orric cut straight to the point.

"Unless you have studied to be a wizard all your life I don't think so." It was an attempt at humour, but he failed miserably.

Orric moved closer into the room so he could see Alena. He could not believe that the elf lying in on the bed was his daughter. There was very little resemblance. For a moment he hoped they had been mistaken with her identity, but when he thought about it he knew it was not the case. He wanted to rush to her side, but he refrained. He needed more information on her condition.

"What is wrong with her?" he asked.

"If only we knew. Ra'naroz has done something to her, but I cannot work out what it is. All I can do is keep her alive," there was no emotion in his voice.

"You have to have some idea." Orric did not believe Eldred's excuse.

"As you know I am not renowned for my skill with the medicinal side of magic. That is Althea's specialty," Eldred sounded deflated as he spoke.

"Do you know where she is?" Orric asked with a sudden passion.

"At a guess I would say she is on Ĉarolija Island with the other wizards. If there was time I would have sent for her in the first place."

"Of course, I didn't mean to suggest anything." Orric felt bad for accusing Eldred. "I just wish that there was something I could do."

"All we can do know is pray for Alaric to return." Eldred sounded very weak all of a sudden.

"I think we should leave now," Bern suggested.

"I would like to sit with my daughter for a while. My presence may help her stay alive. I will not disturb Eldred," Orric faced Bern as he spoke.

"Ha," the sound did not sound right coming from Eldred. "I still have some life left in me yet. It will be good to have some company for a while," Eldred almost sounded jovial for a moment.

"Okay then. I suppose you are both old enough to make your own decisions." The words sounded strange coming from Bern, considering he was over a hundred years younger that the two. "I think I will retire for the evening, as I am no longer required."

Bern was glad to be on his own again. His first job was to have some food delivered to his apartment. He was starting to get hungry and he wanted to eat before he slept. The two thoughts were fighting for control of his body, but it would be the hunger that won.

When he reached his apartment it was strangely dark. Normally one of the castle's servants had lit a least one lantern for him. That was not the only strange thing. He thought he caught a stale scent in the air. It was not as strong, but very similar to what he had smelt in the Royal Watchman. He was not able to put the two together straight away. It wasn't until he felt another presence in the room did he realise what it was.

"I was wondering if we were ever to meet," Bern kept his voice calm, although his heart was racing.

"I wouldn't worry about doing that?" The voice hissed at Bern as he reached for a lantern. "The light will not touch the room until I leave."

That was frustrating for Bern. In the dark of the room he was not able to see who it was before him. The figure wore a robe with the hood drawn. There was something familiar about the voice. Again he wished the entity would take over his body. He was sure it would be better suited to handle the situation.

"What is it that you want," Bern stepped away from the table and placed his hand on the hilt of his rapier. He didn't know if it would do any good, but he wanted to be prepared. He wanted his claymore, but he had left it at the campsite. The large sword strapped to his back would be too conspicuous in the castle.

"You can relax. I am not here to kill you. If I wanted to do that then you would already be dead," the voice hissed again.

It was frustrating that his opponent could see his movements in the dark. Then Bern recognised the voice. It was not the same as he remembered, but he was sure he knew who it was. He just needed to work out how he could use it to his advantage.

"I did not think that I would see you again, Viper," Bern almost spat the words.

There was a moment of silence as the words crossed the room. Bern thought they would have their affect, but without a response he was not sure. He thought he heard the sound of laughter. He did not even know if a serpentant was capable of laughing.

"I am not Viper," he spat as he spoke. "I would not associate with that traitor."

Bern thought it was an interesting choice of words. He had to admit he did not know much about serpentants. The memories of the entity were mixed with his own making him remember things he had never actually experienced.

"Then who are you?" Bern thought he would keep the line of questioning going.

"I am Adder, a much superior creation," there was a certain amount of pride in his voice.

"I find it interesting that you call Viper a traitor and yet you are the one doing the work of the Evil One. I would have thought you would be the one who was the traitor," Bern continued.

"I do the work of the Goddess and no one else. Remember that, it might just save your life," Bern did not know how to take Adder's words.

"Well then. I assume you didn't come here to discuss the comings and goings of your life. I hope you have some useful information for me," Bern suddenly changed the topic.

"Well that is very interesting. But I am not here to help you," Adder continued to hiss as he spoke.

"Then what is it you have come here to do?" Bern was starting to become annoyed.

"I have a message for you to pass on," Adder said, but didn't elaborate.

"Are you going to make me guess or are you going to tell me?" Bern tried to sound as casual as possible. Even though he was starting to relax his heart was still racing.

"Tell your Chosen One to meet me at the top of Mount Scorpio. I have an important message for him," Adder spoke softer, as if he didn't want anyone else to hear.

"Why would I want to do that?" Bern replied and then instantly wished he hadn't. If he had just agreed then the serpentant would have left.

"You have already seen what I am capable of. If he does not meet me there I will lay waste to his home town of Arsiliac." His words changed Bern's feeling from fear to anger.

"What makes you think he will give in to a threat like that?" Bern's hand gripped the hilt of his sword. He wanted nothing more than to draw it and run it through Adder's chest.

"I have important information for him. He would be wise to listen to my threat. He has until the waning of the next full moon to meet me on the summit. If he does not then all of his family and friends will suffer," Adder concluded.

Bern knew that Alaric had no ties left in Arsiliac. Bern's family were the only ones who liked Alaric and who he liked in return. He was not sure if that was enough to make him keep his appointment. On the other hand Bern still had a lot of ties to Arsiliac. He could not imagine what he would do if the serpentant made his family suffer. Again the urge to attack Adder rose up inside of him, but he knew it would be a fruitless effort. Unless the entity came to help him he had no chance against the creature.

Suddenly Bern looked up when he heard a knock on the door. The room was lit, although he did not recall lighting any of the lanterns. He had been lost in thought and had no idea what the time was. Something important had happened, he knew that. He looked around the room for an answer when the knock came again.

As much as he didn't want to see who was on the other side it would be rude of him not to answer. Waiting for him was a servant with a plate of hot food. He did not recall requesting any food to be sent to him, but he was grateful. He could also not explain how hungry he was.

When he returned to where he was sitting he suddenly remembered what he had been doing. Adder had given him a message to pass on to Alaric, but he could not remember the serpentant leaving his apartment. At first he thought it was strange, but then he remembered the attack on the detention camp. He had certainly underestimated Adder's power. That was something he should not do again, although he really didn't know how he could stop it. His next problem was what he was going to do when Alaric returned. He did not know if it was the right idea to give Alaric the message or not. There was a struggle inside him. There were good points for both sides.

As he ate his meal he wished that Alaric would appear. There was nothing he could do until his friend returned to Jarrat. Not only that there were many lives depending on his safe return. It was a sobering thought that everything was now out of his hands.

Chapter 26: Problems with the Law

Minerva and Alaric spent the next day planning how they were going to get into the cathedral. It was not going to be an easy task, especially since they had to keep a close watch on Ra'naroz. The Dark Knight was going to be the weak link in the chain. It would not be long before the evil herb would wear off and he would have his powers again. The only saving grace was that Ra'naroz did not know that Alaric could not draw in the energy around him. Minerva would be a capable adversary, but Alaric did not think she would be able to defeat the Dark Knight.

They had kept Ra'naroz in the basement. They did not want to risk him escaping before he helped them retrieve the Topaz stone. They didn't think he would, but they did not want to take the risk. They needed the Dark Knight more than they were willing to admit. If he escaped before they reached the cathedral then it would all be for nothing. One thing Alaric was not going to let happen was to let Alena die. The prophecy had said she would be there at the final battle with him, but the prophecy was ever changing and he knew he could not take what he read as fact.

The following day, as the sun rose, they left the house. Ra'naroz's powers were starting to come back, but it would still take a while for him to reach full strength. They thought it was better that way. There was less chance he would risk escaping until his powers had completely returned. It was a fine line they were walking, but there was no other option.

They all set out dressed in the dark robes. Although Minerva was known to the guards she felt as though it would be safer to be kept hidden. It would look less suspicious if they were all covered and the last thing they wanted to do was draw attention to themselves. It would not be long until the thick robes would be a requirement to stop their skin from burning. Minerva could cast a spell that would prevent the sun from burning her, but she needed to save her energy.

Without the horses it would take them a lot longer to reach the outer city, but they could not take the horses with them. The animals would not be able to survive outside of the city. Even with the intelligence of Adelanta, Alaric was loathed to leave him behind, but there was nothing he could do. He was sure that Adelanta would be able to handle himself if someone tried to steal him.

Even in the early morning the temperature in the city was rising. Minerva explained it was not always so hot in Castalia. During the cooler months the temperature was quite pleasant. It never got very cold during the day, but it did become a lot nicer. The desert, however, always remained uncomfortably hot. It would get a lot hotter once they left the city.

They passed through the north-eastern gate without being stopped. It was not the closest gate to the desert, but they didn't want to make things too obvious. Three people walking straight out into the desert would look too suspicious. If anyone realised what they were doing then it would all be for nothing. Stealth was the only way they would succeed.

Once they were in the outer city they slowly started to make their way west. Again they did not want to head due west. It would again be too suspicious. Minerva led the way through the streets. They had kept Ra'naroz bound, but once they reached the entrance to the mine they would have to untie him, but they would not do so a moment earlier. It looked a little suspicious, but they were willing to take that risk.

"Halt," a commanding voice called out behind them when they were no more than one hundred paces from the desert.

Alaric's heart sank. He recognised the gruff voice and he knew it was not going to be good. As he turned around he saw the black armour with the crescent moon and stars emblazoned on the breast plate. Alaric kept his head lowered so the soldier could not see his face.

"Take your hoods off," the soldier barked.

It was the last thing Alaric's wanted to do, but there was no way he could get around it. If he declined then the soldiers would forcibly remove them. Slowly Alaric pulled back his hood before motioning for the others to do the same. With his hood back he looked the soldier in the eyes. That was his first mistake.

"So it is you again. It doesn't look as though your manners have improved at all," the soldier had an evil smile on his face as he spoke.

Alaric knew he was thinking something that was not good. He couldn't imagine what the soldier was planning, but he knew it would not be pleasant. He had no time to be held up. He could feel Alena slipping away from him. The feeling had started the previous night and was getting much stronger. He did not know what he would do if the soldier wanted to detain them. It was something he could not allow to happen.

"Captain Cassius, I might have expected it to be you," Minerva spoke before things could get out of hand. She could feel the intensity of the situation and thought it best to act early.

The captain shifted his gaze to the other two. At first he looked at Ra'naroz. There was something off about that man, but he couldn't put his finger on it. He didn't want to waste his time on him. He wanted to see the woman who not only knew his name, but also spoke to him in such a common manner. It did nothing to calm his demeanour.

"Lady Minerva." He sounded surprised as he spoke her name. "I haven't seen you in, what, about two years?"

"When I returned to the city I thought it was made clear that I was not to be waylaid." Minerva spoke as if she was scolding a child.

"I am sure that you made the command, but that doesn't make it law. You still speak to me as if I was a child. It is time that you learnt you are not the master of this city." Alaric did not like the tone in the captain's voice. "I think that a night or two in the cells would do you some good."

"You would not dare." Minerva could not believe what she was hearing. "You know the consequences if you do such a thing."

"Lieutenant Marcellus," the captain boomed.

"Yes sir!" the young Lieutenant stood to attention.

"Would you be so kind as to tell these strangers what we do with insubordinate civilians?" Cassius did not bother look at Marcellus.

"We string them up, Sir and teach them some manners," the response was very clinical.

"I think you could use some manners Minerva and I am sure your two friends could use some as well." Cassius watched the three carefully. Normally when he made such a threat there was fear written on his opponents faces, but there was no emotion at all on any of the three.

"Your threats are not going to make us cringe. We do not have time to deal with your idleness. I am sure you could find someone else to pester." Minerva was not going to back down.

Suddenly the sound of armour clanking came from behind them. Alaric spun around quickly to see another dozen soldiers marching towards them. His hand moved instinctively to the hilt of his sword, but he did not draw it. He didn't want to do anything that would start a fight. The advantage had shifted towards the guards.

"As you can see I have the manpower." Cassius was still annoyed there was no fear on their faces. Although their expressions had changed it was clear they were just trying to sum up the situation. "I think you should come with us now."

"This is not something you want to do," Alaric warned Cassius as he let his attention shift back to the captain. "We are on our way out of the city. We don't want any trouble."

Cassius did not like the way things were going. Alaric had been very subservient the first time they had met. Now there was something different about him. There was a confidence that made the captain wary. The numbers were sixteen to three, but that did not seem to deter their confidence. He felt as though his advantage was starting to slip. He could not let them go now. If he did then he would lose the respect of his officers. He didn't think he had any other option.

"Tell me why I should let you go?" Cassius asked. He needed to find a way to let them go and not lose face. If he was to attack and lose that would be even worse.

The question took Alaric by surprise. He had not expected such a diplomatic question. He had not really thought any further on why they should be let go as he did not think that he would have a chance to explain further. All of a sudden he had to think on his feet.

"We have done nothing wrong. We simply wish to leave the city." It was a weak explanation, but it was also somewhat true.

Cassius had felt there was something wrong with the situation as soon as Alaric had started talking. At first he could not place what it was, but the further the conversation went the closer the realisation came until he finally understood.

"I thought you were trying to gain entrance into the Holy Circle. There is no way you would have gained entrance so quickly. Not to mention that your friend's recovery seems to be rather quick," there was an accusatory tone to his voice.

"That is simple to answer. My friend simply got better. We did not need to go into the Holy Circle. Someone might say it was a miracle. I don't know about that myself, but I do know that he will now survive and that is all that I care about," Alaric explained calmly.

"I don't believe you. No one comes here on the off chance that their friend is deathly ill. You are up to something and I am going to get to the bottom of this." Cassius had found the solution to his problem. "Now are you going to come along quietly or are you going to make trouble?"

That was the question Alaric had been asking himself. There was something that was telling him not to fight. He did not think the soldiers would be able to beat the three of them, but there was something else. Ra'naroz would become suspicious if he didn't use magic and that was something he could not risk. He now needed an excuse to succumb to the elite guards.

"What do you think Minerva?" Alaric pushed the question to the wizard.

"I think that Cassius is a fool," she sneered at the captain. "But I don't think it is worth making trouble in the street. It will prove nothing if we defeat the elite guard here. I am sure it will bring down the morale of the outer city and that is not something that I want." Minerva was being as offensive as she could.

"Then give up your weapons and come with us," Cassius concluded.

"We will not give up our weapons. We will come with you, but not as your prisoners." Alaric was happy that Minerva spoke. He was not prepared to give up his sword and more so the Jade dagger which was strapped to his belt.

"I don't think this is going to work," Cassius was not sure where things went wrong. The situation was slowly starting to slip through his fingers.

"It is either that or you suffer a defeat in the streets in front of everyone," Minerva warned.

A crowd had started to gather around them. That was not good for either side. Alaric had hoped they would have been able to sneak out into the desert unnoticed. It quickly seemed as though that was not going to happen. The elite guard did not need to be seen taking a hit. They needed to move things along. At least if they were going to be undermined it was better that it didn't happen in public. Cassius was going to have to accept the fact they would remain armed.

"Let's get moving." Cassius indicated to the other soldiers that they should keep a safe distance.

Things would be better once they reached the outer city command post. There would be more soldiers and no chance for them to disobey him then. He will have their hides if they didn't answer his questions.

Alaric knew it wasn't the greatest of ideas, but at least it got them out of the streets. They would be even more outnumbered once they reached the command post, but he was hoping he would be able to talk his way out of the impending fight. It seemed as though Minerva knew the captain and that was a promising sign, although their relationship didn't seem too good.

"How well do you know the captain?" Alaric asked as they walked.

"No talking," the captain barked back, although he didn't hear what Alaric had said.

Alaric didn't let Cassius have the last word. He did not consider himself to be a prisoner. If that was the case then they were free to talk. He would keep up that pretence right until they reached the command post. Once they were there he would need to change his tact, but until then he would not back down.

"Not well at all. As you already know it has been a long time since I have been home, but the city remembers who I am. When I arrived I made it known to the Elite Guard I was back. Captain Cassius didn't sound overly pleased, but he was shut down by his commanding officer. I guess Cassius took it to heart. I don't think he will do us any favours," Minerva explained. "From what I could gather he is a fairly inept soldier. He only rose to rank of captain because his parents were well known. It is rumoured they pulled strings to make sure of his position before they died suddenly," she raised her voice so Cassius could hear her.

"I don't think I like what you are insinuating, Witch." Cassius was not going to let her get away with her scathing comment.

His words brought a smile to her face. She had infuriated Cassius and that would put him off guard for what was to come. It was more to the point that his soldiers had also heard her jibe.

They continued in silence until they reached one of the many outposts used by the Elite Guard. Like most of the outer city the outpost had only recently been constructed. The large stone building had been designed not only to house soldiers, but prisoners as well.

The three were lead straight to a large cell where they were locked inside. Alaric paced around while the other two found somewhere to sit. It was certainly not the place Alaric wanted to be. He had thought they would have been able to speak to someone with greater authority than Cassius and then they would then be on their way.

"What are we going to do now?" Ra'naroz asked.

"We wait," Alaric replied. "We do not want to create a scene. That is not the best way to remain anonymous."

"That is fine, but now we are imprisoned." Alaric was about to speak, but Ra'naroz continued. "Whether you want to believe it or not we are now their prisoners! Look around you, this is a prison cell if only a holding one. Even though we still have our weapons we are still their prisoners," Ra'naroz sounded frustrated. "I don't have my powers back yet so I can't help you, but I am sure between the two of you there should not be a problem."

"We are not here to hurt anyone," Alaric spoke quickly. "We will get out of here without having to fight."

The door opened when Alaric stopped talking and Cassius walked into the cell. Alaric thought he would have brought more soldiers with him. It wasn't a good sign that he didn't bring his commanding officer. Cassius brought a chair with him so he could sit during his interrogation. The others would either have to stand or sit on the cold, stone floor.

"Before you get any ideas there are over a hundred highly trained soldiers in and around this post, so I wouldn't advise you try to escape," Cassius explained.

"I didn't think we were prisoners," Minerva didn't sound impressed.

"That is not a matter of perception. You are our prisoners whether you would like to believe it or not," Cassius almost snarled the words at Minerva.

"What are we being charged with?" Alaric quickly asked the question.

"I don't have to charge you with anything. You are here because of your suspicious behaviour. These are troubling times and we need to be extra careful of who we let wander around the city," Cassius sounded pleaded with himself.

"I have told you. We have finished with the city and we are on our way back to Jarrat," Alaric tried his best to sound frustrated.

Cassius thought for a moment. There was another piece to the puzzle that he was missing. He had thought that Dyrk's friend's health was the only abnormality, but the more he thought about it the more he knew there was something else. Then it suddenly dawned on him.

"If you are leaving the city then where are your horses?" Cassius smiled. He had caught them out in their lies.

"We had to sell them. The rates in Castalia are through the roof. We needed coin to buy food and shelter. I wish we still had them. It is going to be a long trip back to Jarrat." Alaric was ready for the question. He was surprised it took so long to come.

"That is very convenient. Where is all the gold you received from selling your horses?" Cassius wasn't about to give up on his line of questioning.

"We have already spent it, I already said that." Alaric didn't miss a beat.

"I see." Cassius had hoped he would have caught them out, but Dyrk was a more accomplished opponent than he first thought. "It seems as though there is more to you than I originally thought."

"Will you just let us go?" Alaric thought it was worth trying. "We have done nothing wrong and we mean you no harm."

"That is a matter for debate. You have yet to convince me you are not up to no good," Cassius stood as he spoke. "Consorting with the likes of her has done nothing to help your credibility."

"You know you can't keep us here," Minerva also stood as she spoke. "I still have standing within the Grand Cathedral."

"That might have been true at one time, but I do not think that is the case anymore. You and your kind have been out of favour in the Grand Cathedral for a long time. If you had been here you might have realised that instead of hiding on your island. I do not think that you will be getting any help," Cassius scoffed as he spoke.

If only the captain knew the truth. It was ever since the Dark Knight had taken residence had she lost her favour. If only she had returned earlier she might have been able to prevent such a disaster from happening. She had been too caught up in her own life and the missives she had received told her nothing of the state of the city. Za'aroz had been able to take control of the High Chancellor. There was no telling what changes he had implemented.

"Be that as it may I am sure that Augustus will be displeased to hear you have detained me." Minerva deliberately used the High Chancellor's chosen name. "I don't need to say that if you detain me much longer he will be very upset."

Cassius was taken aback by her words. There was something in the way she spoke that warned him to be careful. He had heard rumours of the mysterious wizard. As much as she hadn't lived in Castalia for a long time the stories were still fresh. They were folklore amongst the city. He knew that he could not take anything she said on face value.

"If you are indeed on a mission for the High Chancellor then I am sure you have the appropriate paperwork?" Cassius was confident he was able to read between the lines and knew exactly what she was hinting at.

"You know very well if I was on a mission for the High Chancellor there would be nothing tying me to him. I am not on a mission for the High Chancellor, but what I am doing is very important. It is important to all those in Castalia." That was the truth.

"You have to let us go," Alaric spoke before Cassius had a chance to process what Minerva had said. "There is a great deal depending on what we have to do."

Cassius did not like what he was hearing. The situation was getting out of his control. To make matters worse his prisoners were still armed. That was something he did not like, it gave them a certain amount of power. He was sure he would have already gained the truth if they were not. He needed to give himself time to think.

"I will give you some time to think about your answers. The next time I return I want the truth. If you continue to lie then things are going to get a lot worse for you," Cassius warned before he left the cell.

They waited until Cassius left before they spoke again. They were not sure if they were winning or losing the battle. It didn't seem to matter what they told the captain he was not going to believe them. Alaric doubted if the truth would appease him either. There had to be another way to convince the man to let them free.

"Well this is working out great," Ra'naroz made the snide remark. "If you had just killed them we would already be in the mines by now."

Alaric chose to ignore the Dark Knight. He really wanted to strike him, but that would be a little hard to explain if he was caught. Ignoring him was the only option. They had to come up with a viable solution.

"Is there any way we are going to convince him to let us go?" Alaric asked, keeping his voice low in case someone was listening on the other side of the door.

"He is a stubborn man. He has a tendency towards cruelty. I think that is why he was promoted through the ranks so quickly. In his mind he thinks we are guilty of some terrible crime. Our one advantage is that he is not completely sure. There is doubt in his mind. If we give him any indication that we are lying then he will try and keep us here forever." Minerva's description was very in-depth considering how little she actually knew of the man.

"Well that isn't going to happen. We need to escape without hurting anyone, but if that's not possible then we shall do what we have to. We cannot waste too much more time here. We need to get into the Grand Cathedral." Alaric was as much speaking with himself as he was the others.

"I will try and reason with Cassius as soon as he returns. Besides that I don't know what else I can do," Minerva already sounded defeated.

It was another hour before Cassius returned. Alaric had started pacing around the interrogation room. He hoped to already be on his way to the mines. He knew the captain was deliberately making them wait. It was a ploy to make them confess. Cassius knew they were in a hurry to get somewhere, whereas he had nothing but time. He was making it his mission to make sure they had no other option but to tell them what he wanted to know. The captain was unintentionally playing right into Ra'naroz's hands. If he regained his powers before they reached the mines then it would give him the perfect opportunity to escape. Ideally Alaric didn't want Ra'naroz regaining his power until the very last minute, but on the other hand he would be able to unleash the Dark Knight. The blood would effectively not be on his hands.

"Now, are you ready to tell me the truth?" Cassius spoke when he returned.

Alaric wanted nothing more then to draw his sword and wipe the arrogant smile off the captain's face. There was a chance if he killed captain then one of them would die and he needed both of his companions alive. He resisted the temptation and returned to back of the cell. He wanted to remain as far away from the captain as he could. The urges would be easier to control if he was out of arm's reach.

"All you need to know is that we mean you no harm." Alaric was the first to speak. "You must let us leave."

"I *must* do nothing," he raised his voice as he spoke. "You must do what I tell you to do. That is the only way you are going to leave this prison cell. If you don't then your next move may just be to the hangman's gibbet. I wouldn't advise that," there was an evil tone to his voice. It was as if he was enjoying himself.

"That is enough, Captain Cassius," Minerva almost spat when she said his name. "You have proven your point. Now it is time to let us go. I might be out of favour with the High Chancellor, but I still have friends in the city. Despite my absence I always have agents to do my bidding and to keep me informed with what is happening."

"Why should I do that?" He did not like the way she was speaking to him.

"Because you know it is the right thing to do. Something has changed in you. From the stories I have heard about you this is not something you would do. You were tough, but fair. This is completely out of character," Minerva kept her voice level.

"Things have changed. I am a Captain of the Elite Guard. The enemy is all around us. They were simpler times those years ago. Now we have to be cautious. Any stranger should be considered a spy for the enemy until they prove themselves to be otherwise. Especially strangers who are acting, well, as strange as these two," Cassius explained.

"We are not enemy spies." Alaric wanted to explain the truth, but with Za'aroz inside the Grand Cathedral he couldn't risk the information getting back to him. "In fact we are just the opposite."

"What do you mean by that?" Cassius didn't sound convinced.

"They are gathering information for the Alliance," Minerva cut in before Alaric had a chance to speak. "There have been rumours that there is a Dark Knight in the Grand Cathedral."

"That is ridiculous," Cassius interrupted. "There is not a Dark Knight in the Grand Cathedral. I have never heard anything more preposterous in my life. I should have you all whipped for saying such a thing."

Alaric almost laughed at the captain's ignorance, but that would not be appropriate. He thought he knew where Minerva was going with her conversation and he didn't want to do anything to ruin it. There was nothing to be gained by revealing what was really happening to Cassius. He would not believe it anyway.

"I know," Minerva spoke again when Cassius had finished his rant. "If you would let me finish, I will explain." Minerva paused. When Cassius didn't speak she continued. "As I told you before, these two came here to investigate the claims that there was a Dark Knight in the Grand Cathedral. They did not find any evidence to support those claims. When they came up with nothing they came to me. I told them the same thing. There never has and never will be a Dark Knight in the Grand Cathedral," It was Ra'naroz's turn to repress his laughter. He knew for a fact the statement was false. Again he needed to feign compliance if he was going gain Alaric's trust. "I am purely travelling with them as evidence when they return to the Alliance. They felt it would be more believable coming from me."

Cassius had not been expecting such a comment. It had completely taken him by surprise. If he had been prepared he might have been able to see the inconsistencies in the tale. It explained a lot, but it did not explain everything. The captain had to think. There was now a plausible reason to let them go, although that was not something that he wanted to do.

"You have given me something to think about, I will give you that much." It was obvious he was desperately thinking as he spoke. "I think I should ponder on this information."

No light from outside was allowed into the room, but it had to be getting close to midday. They needed to be on their way very soon. He remembered the afternoon sun in the Southern Wasteland and he did not want to be out in such extreme temperatures. They had to leave now.

"That is not good enough," Alaric barked. There was something about his voice that made everyone in the room stop and listen. "I am afraid I have been polite enough." Minerva did not like what she was hearing, but Ra'naroz started to lick his lips in anticipation. "You know we are not a threat to your city. There is no reason to keep us here. If you do not let us go then there will be trouble." He didn't want to make the threat, but it seemed appropriate. He had a burning urge to draw in the energy surrounding him. The only thing that was stopping him was knowing how he would feel if he did.

"Do you think that making threats will make me release you?" Cassius was trying to regain control of the conversation, which had seemingly slipped away from him.

"I don't really care what you think. We are leaving and there is nothing you can do about." Alaric continued his line of threats.

This was not something that Cassius had thought would happen. He couldn't let them go, but he was not so sure he was doing the right thing. There was something about the way Alaric was threatening that made him stop and think. There had to be another way out where he kept his strength.

"You have taken things too far." Minerva could see what he was thinking. "You have no way out of this with your pride in tact."

"And what exactly are you going to do?" Cassius stood back with his arms crossed across his chest.

Minerva looked towards Alaric. She was sure they were on the same track, but she wanted to make sure. Alaric simply nodded his head. It seemed as though there were no other options left. He wished he had been able to talk his way out of the outpost, but that dream had well and truly gone. It was their last chance to escape without serious fighting.

Slowly Minerva started drawing in the power around her. She had waited in case there had been another solution. It was obvious that Cassius didn't know what was coming. He simply remained where he was and waited for Minerva's response. Little did he know that the response was coming in the form of a spell. Alaric hoped she went easy on the captain. As much as he wanted to teach Cassius a lesson he did not want to punish him too much.

Once she had released the spell there was a slight crackle in the air. That was the only warning Cassius had that he was about to be attacked. He heard the crackle, but he didn't realise until it was too late. The spell lifted him to the tips of his toes and pushed back across the room until he was pressed against the wall. It was clear he was trying to move his arms and legs, but there was nothing he could do. The spell had him completely trapped.

"This is what I am going to do and I will keep doing it until we are out of the outpost."

"Guards!" Cassius called out.

Two soldiers instantly burst into the room at the sounds of his command. They drew their swords, but made no further move into the cell after they took stock of the situation. They had expected the prisoners to be attacking the captain, but that didn't seem to be the case. Alaric opened his robe and put his hand on the hilt of his sword, but made no move to draw it. Only death would be the result if he did.

"Let me go," his mouth was the only part of his body that could move. "I demand that you let me go." As much as he wanted to call his soldiers to attack he also didn't want to risk any deaths. He had hoped their arrival would have perturbed Marina, but that had not been the case.

"You are not in any place to make commands. If you don't want me to parade you in front of your commander you will listen to what I have to say," Minerva had an evil smile on her face.

"What is it that you want?" it was clear he had resigned.

"I want you to let us go," she started.

"Fine, you can go," Cassius was quick to respond.

"That is not all. I want you to write a letter-of-passage for us. No one is going to hinder our travel anymore." at first she would have been happy at being set free, but she knew that wouldn't last long.

"What makes you think that I would do such a thing?"

"Because you have little choice, that is why.   If you want me to parade you around for all your troops to see I am more than willing. I am sure they will have a great amount of respect for you after that." Again Alaric had to restrain himself from laughing.

The soldiers looked at each other with confused expressions of their faces. They didn't know what they should do. Until Cassius gave them another command they would just watch and wait.

"Fine!" he cried out. "Just let me down!"

Minerva let him down slowly, but she kept him wrapped in the spell. She wanted to make sure if he tried to double cross them she was ready. If he did then he would definitely suffer for his betrayal. She was finished with playing nice.

Once he was free to move he ordered one of the soldiers to get him some ink and some paper. He wanted nothing more than to be rid of the trio. The longer they stayed at the outpost the worse it would look for him. The sooner they left the sooner he could forget it ever happened. He should have known better than to try and muscle Minerva.

"This just proves my point," Cassius spoke as he scrawled out the letter-of-passage. He had never been too good with writing. It was another part of his studies that he had neglected. Normally he would have one of his subordinates do it for him. "I don't understand why you would need a letter-of-passage if you are leaving the city. This just proves that you are up to no good."

"No, we need the letter-of-passage to make sure that you don't try to double cross us. As soon as you set us free you would have your soldiers come after us. Once you sign this letter there is nothing you can do. If you went back on your word then you would lose your command. I don't think you are that stupid." Minerva justified her position.

Cassius grumbled under his breath as he finished writing the letter-of-passage. He had to admit they had him. He knew they were traitors, but there was no way to prove it. If they were then he would have charged his soldiers to restrain them. All he could do is hand Minerva the paperwork and plan for the future. If it was the last thing he did he was not going to let her get away with this.

Chapter 27: Into the Desert

They were all relieved to be away from the outpost. Alaric was worried things were going to get further out of control. He was glad that Minerva was able to find a solution that kept the need for bloodshed. At least they would be able to travel unhindered, although Alaric was sure that Cassius would be planning his revenge. That was something he would have to wait for. As Minerva had said he could not go against the right-of-passage he had signed for them. Even being under duress was not an excuse. He would be risking his career if he went after them and that was something he had worked too hard to achieve to throw away.

As Alaric had surmised it was past midday when they finally left the command post. They had hoped to be inside the mines by midday, but they would be lucky to make by mid-afternoon. There was nothing they could do to make the journey quicker. If they moved quickly through the streets then they would draw too much attention to themselves. If they moved quickly through the desert they would risk dehydration and exhaustion. They would have to be even more careful in the heat of the afternoon sun. The risk of serious heat related injuries were great. Without a pack animal there was only a limited amount of food and water they could take.

Even though they had free passage they still did not want anyone to know where they were going. There was no doubt Cassius would order them to be followed. If he knew they were headed into the desert then he would petition the High Chancellor to revoke their right-of-passage. It wouldn't stop what they were doing, but it would alert Za'aroz to their presence. If he could figure out what they were doing then he could prepare for them. It was something they did not need, at least not until Alaric was able to recover the Topaz stone. Once that was done he was hoping he would be able to use magic again. He would need that if he was going to defeat two Dark Knights.

Once they were out of the command post they found the most crowded street. Becoming lost in the crowd was the easiest way for them to lose any tails. Even losing line of sight for a moment was enough to lose them. With everyone wearing the same dark, heavy robes it was impossible to tell one person from the next.

Once they were in the crowded streets they managed to push their way through. When the opportunity arose they ducked into a side street before disappearing into another street.

It took them another hour before they reached the edge of the desert. Alaric had already started sweating underneath his robe. When he took his first step onto the sand he felt the temperature rise. He didn't know if it was just in his head, but either way it was more uncomfortable.

Minerva and Ra'naroz were not suffering the temperature as much as him. One of the first spells a wizard learnt was to regulate their body temperature. The spell was so subtle that they were able to keep it up without using any energy. Ra'naroz's ability to use magic was slowly starting to return and it was the first spell he created. Alaric saw a small smile on his face.

There was nothing Alaric could do and he had to hide the fact from Ra'naroz. If he showed any stress from the temperature then the Dark Knight would know that something was wrong. He was already starting to gain an advantage and Alaric couldn't give him anything else.

"How long do you think it will take us to find the mine shaft?" Alaric asked as they started into the desert.

"Hopefully it shouldn't take more than two hours, but that all depends on whether I can find it straight away for not." It looked as though Minerva was trying to concentrate on the surroundings.

Alaric had no idea how she was going to find the entrance. There didn't seem to be anything to take reference from. There were a number of dunes, a few rocky outcrops and a number of cacti. There was nothing that looked out of the ordinary. He hoped she knew what she was doing. Her words did nothing to instil any confidence in him. If she was wrong then they were certain to die. He didn't like putting that much faith in someone he had just met, but there was seemingly no other option.

Once they had crossed over into the desert Alaric realised they were not the only ones travelling. At first he could not understand why anyone would be out in such conditions, but then he saw that they all looked similar. Besides the fact they were all dressed in the same heavy robes, they were all short in stature. It didn't take Alaric long to realise who they were.

"I thought the mining was all done through the mines under the city?" Alaric asked, although he kept his voice low. He knew that sound travelled further than expected in the desert.

"That is only for the diamonds. These dwarves are mining for sand. You would be surprised at how valuable sand is," Minerva explained.

Although they were the only ones of regular height no one seemed to take any notice of them. The dwarves all kept their heads low. It was too hot to care what anyone else was doing. They trudged along on their way out to the sand mines. They knew that men in the desert were never a good sign. It was generally someone from the Inner Circle coming to check what was happening in the mines. To gain their attention would result in having to speak to them. If they did not work they did not get paid and it was too hot for nothing.

Alaric was happy with the situation. He was quite happy at being ignored. It was not often he could avoid attention and more often than not it was a hindrance. The last thing he wanted to do was spend any more time in the heat than he had to. He could not wait to be in the coolness of the mines.

"Are you sure that you know where you are going?" Ra'naroz asked when they had been wandering, apparently aimlessly, for an hour.

Minerva chose to ignore the Dark Knight. She was concentrating on her surroundings, not that there was much for her to focus on. Alaric still had no idea how she knew where she was going. He wanted to know the answer to the question as well, but he did not want to side with Ra'naroz. He could only hope that Minerva was heading in the right direction.

"You don't have to answer me, but I might be able to help." Ra'naroz was not going to let it go. "It is not going to do any of us any good if we die of heat stroke." Even with the spells protecting them there was still a chance the heat could kill them. The spell only masked the symptoms. It did not remove them altogether.

"I think you should keep your ideas to yourself," Minerva stopped and snapped at him. "I know how much you like to cause trouble. Don't for a second think I don't know what is at risk. I don't need you bantering in my ear."

Ra'naroz couldn't help himself but laugh. This did nothing to calm Minerva's attitude, but it was Alaric who did something about it. He moved to where Ra'naroz was standing and struck him with the back of his hand. The unexpected blow caught him by surprise. It was enough to knock him back a couple of steps.

In the meantime Minerva had stormed off to stop herself from doing the same thing. She did not want to let the Dark Knight get the better of her so, she walked to the top of a nearby dune. She took a moment to calm herself before she looked at the land before her. She let out a cry of excitement before she managed to compose herself. Alaric was not sure if it was a good sign or a bad sign, but he was not going to wait around to find out. He quickly made his way up the dune.

It did not take him long to realise what had caused Minerva to cry out. In the sandy valley below there was a massive quarry where the dwarves were mining the sand. The operation was larger than expected. It was one of many quarries around the desert, but it was the one Minerva had been looking for.

"What is it?" Alaric asked.

"This is the marker I was looking for. Now it should not take me too long to find the entrance to the mine," Minerva explained.

"I think we should keep moving," Ra'naroz spoke. "We are starting to draw unnecessary attention."

The Dark Knight was right. Some of the dwarves had noticed them. The longer they stood there the more dwarves looked up. Alaric suddenly felt very subconscious. He had a bad feeling that Ra'naroz was right. They needed to move out of sight.

"Why are they all looking at us?" Alaric asked.

"Let's keep moving," Ra'naroz suggested. "We can talk as we walk."

Alaric had to agree, but Minerva did not move. He wanted to grab her by the arm and drag her away, but there was something about her demeanour that made him stop. Although he could not see her face he knew she was thinking. He did not like the way the dwarves were milling around, there was a certain purpose to their movement that had Alaric concerned.

"I really think we should get out of sight," there was a certain amount of nervousness to Ra'naroz's voice.

"I just need a minute," Minerva spoke, her voice distant.

Alaric was torn between the two. Ra'naroz had already started to walk down the other side of the sand dune. Minerva was still standing on the top. He could see the dwarves were becoming agitated with their presence, although he could not work out why.

"Move, now," Ra'naroz's voice was soft, but urgent.

"I have it," Marina sounded relieved.

When she finished speaking she quickly moved down the other side of the dune to where Ra'naroz was waiting. Alaric didn't waste a moment and followed closely behind. He hoped with their presence gone the dwarves would return to their business. He also really wanted to know what was happening.

"Would someone kindly explain to me what just happened up there?" Alaric asked. It was a very dangerous position for him to be in, especially in his current state.

"That sandstone mine is the first marker I was looking for. Now I know where we are going," Minerva explained. "The shaft into the mine is not too far from here."

"First marker? How many markers are there?" Alaric was not completely happy with her answer.

"There are five," she explained as she continued away from the quarry. "Now if you don't mind I am trying to concentrate."

"If you tell us what the next maker is then we can help you find it." Alaric wasn't going to let it go.

Minerva looked at Ra'naroz before she looked at Alaric again. Before she spoke he knew what she was going to say, but he let her speak anyway.

"I do not want him to know what the markers are. This mine is the only way to sneak into the Grand Cathedral. In the wrong hands it could be a very dangerous piece of information."

"I wouldn't worry about him. I doubt he will be living long enough to tell anyone," there was something evil about Alaric's tone. "Things will move along quicker if we all know what we are looking for. I don't want to be out in this heat any longer than I have to."

Minerva thought for a moment as she walked. No matter which way she looked at it she had to admit Alaric was right. The day was getting unbearably hot, even for one who was used to the heat of Castalia. The sooner they were in the mine the better it would be for all of them. She stopped when she decided to tell Alaric what the next marker was.

"Okay. We are looking for a cactus or more so a pair of them." Minerva paused for the information to sink in.

Alaric looked around. He had not seen a single cactus for over an hour, not that he had really been looking for one. There was nothing for as far as the eye could see. He was sure that Minerva must be mistaken, or maybe she was trying to put Ra'naroz off the scent. Either way he did not like what he was hearing.

"These two cacti are very special. They are joined together at their top and they make the shape of a heart. The heart-shaped cacti are the next marker we are searching for."

She was still not sure if she was doing the right thing, revealing the information to a Dark Knight, but as Alaric said there was a good chance Ra'naroz would be dead soon. When it was said and done it was not the first time Ra'naroz had been inside the Grand Cathedral and she was sure he could do it again if he really wanted to. The problem was that he could sneak an army through the mine, and that was what she was trying to avoid.

Once she had explained what they were looking for they started off again. Alaric had to assume she was leading them in the right direction and he did not need to know which way they were travelling. He returned his attention to the dwarves back at the mine. It was clear that Minerva was concentrating on what she was doing. It would be pointless and unconstructive to disturb her. As much as he did not like it, he would have to ask Ra'naroz if he wanted answers.

"Why were the dwarves becoming so agitated?" he put the question out there, so he was not asking Ra'naroz directly.

When it was clear that Minerva was not going to respond Ra'naroz decided to speak. It took him a moment, but he quickly realised the question was for him. That was a good sign that Alaric was starting to trust him. Things were moving along a lot better than he had expected. He could feel his powers starting to return. He wanted nothing more that to draw in the energy around him, but he knew than would only bring him pain. It was almost worth the retribution.

"Things are surprisingly competitive in the desert. There are only half a dozen sandstone quarries. Each quarry is run by a different group of dwarves. Should one of the quarries run out of sandstone then it would make sense for that group to try and take over another mine. They are all run by the Eastern Dwarven Guild, but they are more of a regulatory body than anything else," Ra'naroz explained.

"I would have thought with this much desert it would make sense just to find another source of sandstone."

"That is true, but you have to remember there is only so far you can haul stone through this heat," Alaric had to admit that Ra'naroz made sense. He did not know how the dwarves were able to work in such conditions. "It will not be long before war will break out. That is why the dwarves were looking at us so nervously. They thought we were spying on their operation. If we stayed around too much longer I am sure that they would have come and had words with us." Alaric knew it was a euphemism. If they had stayed on top of the sand dune then the dwarves would have come to deal with them. There was little doubt in Alaric's mind it would have led to some to fighting. "Personally I think it is a good way to do business, but that's just me." Ra'naroz didn't want to push his luck, but he couldn't resist the comment.

Alaric thought on the information. There was a lot about the Seven Kingdoms he didn't know. He could not imagine why he would be the saviour. He didn't know enough to take on the role and yet that was the hand he was dealt. He had to remember he was taking advice from a Dark Knight. That in itself was a dangerous move, but he had to admit it did make sense.

"What does the High Chancellor think of all of this?" Alaric felt like he should try and gather more information. It might be pertinent to what he was trying to achieve and that would be invaluable.

"I would assume not very much." Ra'naroz shrugged his shoulders. "Why would he care what the labourers are doing?"

"It is his responsibility to make sure his citizens are safe. I would imagine he would want to look after them, especially since they make him so much gold."

"He doesn't care what his citizens do. He lives the life of luxury in the Grand Cathedral. I would be surprised if he even knew where the sandstone comes from. No, he will not be doing anything to stop the situation. Things will sort themselves out, one way or another," Ra'naroz sounded pleased with what he was saying.

There was something disturbing in the Dark Knight's words. He had to admit that he did not know much about Castalia, but it seemed as though the High Chancellor should take more interest in what was happening around him. That was a side issue, but he was sure it would be pertinent in the future. There were more important things that he had to concentrate on. He had a feeling that if they did not find the mine shaft soon that at least one of them would die of heat exhaustion.

"There it is," Minerva spoke as Alaric came out of his reverie. She was pointing to the distance in front of them.

Alaric looked to where she was pointing. He could just make out a break in the sand in the distance. He could not work out what it was, but he assumed it was the heart-shaped cacti. They were one step closer to their destination.

"What is the next marker?" Alaric asked when they arrived at the heart-shape cacti.

On closer inspection Alaric could see that the two cactuses were in fact not joined. There was a slight amount of space between the two, but that was not really the point. He quickly returned his attention to Minerva.

"To the west of here there is a small rocky outcrop. That is the next marker," she explained as she looked into the distance.

"Is there anything specific about this outcrop?" Alaric asked as they started west.

"Not really. You will see when you get there," there was something mysterious about the way she spoke.

Alaric wondered at the next marker. He didn't know if Minerva was deliberately being obtuse because she was the one who found the cacti or just to keep them guessing. Either way Alaric did not like it. He was wandering through the desert with no idea where he was going. His life was completely in her hands. As much as he trusted her, he didn't know if he trusted her that much.

Although the sun was on its downward path its intensity had not wavered. Alaric's body was completely drenched in sweat. He wished that he could do something about the heat, but it was too much of a risk.

Although the spell was only small he did not want to risk drawing in the energy around him. Instead he would have to sweat it out. He had already drained one of his water pouches and had started on his second. If Ra'naroz had been paying attention he would have realised something wasn't right.

It did not take long before Alaric realised what Minerva was talking about. There was a small rocky outcrop at the base of a small dune. From above they could see the rocks were positioned in a way that looked like an arrow. The arrow pointed to the south-west. There was no doubt it was the way they had to go.

"Is this natural?" Alaric asked in amazement as they took a short rest amongst the small shade the rocks provided.

"There are many things that are strange in this world," Minerva explained. "But I don't think this is a great mystery. The outcrop is natural. Whether it was just dumb luck, which I doubt, or whether the position of the shaft was made deliberately using the sign post as a marker when it was built will never be known. No one knows the origin of the shaft, but I could hazard a guess." She let the thought trail away.

As much as Alaric wanted to know the answer he did not want to push. It was clear she did not want to reveal her suspicions. It was too hot to waste his energy on such a matter. There were more important things for them to discuss. Alaric wanted to know what the next marker was.

"What are we looking for now?" Alaric asked when they rose to get moving again.

"The next one is going to be the hardest to find. Now that was have our setting we need to make sure we hold it." It was clear her concentration was elsewhere. Her voice was very distant. "We are looking for the twin dunes," she continued when she was happy they were travelling in the right direction.

"Well that shouldn't be too hard to find." Although Alaric did not know exactly what they were looking for, but it didn't sound too difficult. "I am sure we will be able to see two sand dunes."

"The twin dunes are in the valley of another set of dunes," Minerva didn't sound as though she really wanted to be speaking. "The twin dunes are small. They are shadowed by the dunes around them. If we don't climb the right sand dune then we will walk right past them. This is why we need to concentrate on where we are going." Her last comment was directly related to Alaric's questioning.

Alaric was happy enough with what he had heard. He had something to focus on, although he was not so happy with what they were trying to do. It would be too easy for them to walk straight past the next marker. If they did then there was no chance for them to find it. They would have to start again. Whoever had made the mine shaft had definitely made it hard to find. He wondered at the reason behind that.

The three remained silent as they made their way through the desert. Alaric was still the only one who was suffering from the heat. He wished there was something he could do about it, but that would risk Ra'naroz knowing of his weakness. That was something he could not risk. The Dark Knight would not let him live long if he knew the truth.

It was harder than expected to keep a true heading as they trekked through the desert. The sun was the only true way to tell which direction they were travelling, but as it came lower in the sky it was nearly impossible to remember. Alaric could only hope Minerva knew where she was going. He could not see anything out of the ordinary that she could be using for help.

They had been walking for over an hour when Alaric finally had to stop. He rested on his haunches and puffed for breath. He wondered if he had any water left in his body. He had been constantly sweating since he entered the desert. He didn't know if he was going to be able to travel much further. Minerva and Ra'naroz didn't notice straight away. They continued in the direction they had been travelling.

Once Alaric was alone a strange feeling came over him. It took him a moment before he realised what it was. He felt a tug to the north. The further the others walked away the stronger the sensation became. When they stopped walking he thought he could point to the exact spot he was being drawn to, but that sensation only lasted a moment. When the two made their way back to Alaric the feeling widened before disappearing altogether.

"What are you doing?" Minerva asked when she reached him.

Alaric was standing upright again. The feeling of direction had given him a new purpose. The feeling of utter exhaustion, although it had not gone, was at the back of his mind. He knew he had to go north.

"We need to go north," Alaric blurted.

"I don't think so," Minerva did not sound happy. "I am sure the twin dunes are just ahead. We just need to keep going."

"No," Alaric kept his voice strong. "We need to go north." Each word was a struggle. He had a renewed energy, but his mouth was bone dry. He still had one water pouch left, but he didn't want to use until it was absolutely necessary.

"What are you talking about Alaric? We don't have time to be going off on wild goose chases," Minerva sounded annoyed. "If we move off the path there is no way for us to find it again. We will have to go back to the city and we don't have time for that."

"Then you should listen to what I have to say. The twin dunes are to the north. If we continue on our current direction we will be walking for the rest of the day," Alaric kept his voice level.

"What makes you think it is towards the north?" she asked.

Alaric didn't answer. He thought Minerva would come across the answer on her own and he didn't want to waste his words. Begrudgingly he took out his water pouch and took a small draught. Even after taking a mouthful of water his mouth was still dry.

"Very well, but if you are wrong then we are all dead." It was a little extreme, but she had to make her point.

Alaric led the way. Even though he could no longer feel the tug of the prophecy he thought he had a good enough idea of where he had to go. He knew he could make the others wait, but he did not see the point in it. Nothing was going to stop him from reaching his destination. He had renewed energy and he was going to use it.

As Alaric had said it was not long before they crested a large sand dune. When they looked down the other side they could see two small lumps in the valley below. Alaric understood what Minerva had said. If they had not climbed the dune they were on, or one of the surrounding dunes, they would have no idea that the smaller dunes were there.

"Now what do we do?" Alaric asked, a little excited.

"Now we head due east," Minerva explained.

Before they set off again Alaric wanted to know what the final marker was.

"What are we looking for now?" he asked as Minerva was about to leave.

"The next marker is the shaft itself," there was something cheeky in her tone. "From here it is relatively easy. All we have to do is head directly for the spire of the Grand Cathedral."

As Alaric turned around he realised he could see the spire on the horizon. He did not know how long it had been there, but he was grateful to see it. They were finally getting somewhere. He guessed there was only an hour or two before dusk and he wanted to be underground before the sun set.

There was a new spring to Alaric's step as he walked back down the large sand dune. When they reached bottom, the spire was out of sight. With the disappearance of the spire so did the spring in Alaric's step. Although the spire soon returned his spring did not. The day's exhaustion was starting to get to him again. He didn't know if being underground was going to help at all, but he thought it would be better than being under the sweltering sun.

Although they were walking in the direction of the mine shaft it still didn't make it any easier to find. If it wasn't for Ra'naroz nearly falling into it they would have walked straight past. If it wasn't for his cursing the other two would not have even noticed.

"That is it," Minerva sounded excited when she saw the hole in the ground.

The mine shaft was little more than that, a hole in the ground. Alaric doubted it was man made. Its edges were jagged and it looked awfully small. At first glance he did not think that he would even fit. On closer inspection he realised it was larger than he first thought, but not by much. A larger man would not have a chance to enter the shaft.

"It doesn't look like much," Ra'naroz scoffed. "Are you sure that this is the way into the mines?"

"Positive," there was something in her tone that concerned Alaric. It was almost as if she was salivating.

"Then how are we going to get down," Alaric dropped a small rock he had found nearby into the shaft. It took ten seconds before he heard a faint clink in the distance.

"Leave that to me," again there was something mischievous in her voice.

Chapter 28: Into the Depths

There was a moment of silence before Minerva continued to speak. She was waiting for someone to ask the question, but neither of them were going to. Ra'naroz would not indulge her and Alaric did not have the energy to play games. He was already exhausted and the challenge had only just begun.

"Very well then," Minerva revealed a long length of rope she had secreted in her robe.

"That is all well and good," Alaric was the first to speak. "But what are you going to anchor the rope with? It's not like there are any good boulders around." Alaric looked around, but nothing was suitable. "And I don't think that rope is going to be long enough."

Minerva had to laugh. Alaric sounded so concerned she could hardly bring herself to explain things to him, she appreciated the fact that time was wasting away. They had to move and they had to move quickly. She wished there was more time to play with him. She thought he could certainly be brought down a peg or too. He was very arrogant for someone so young.

"I have learnt a trick or two over the years. You should know that just because things don't look like you expect them to doesn't mean they can't change." Although Minerva's hood covered her face Alaric knew that she was smiling.

Alaric put his lack of understanding down to heat exhaustion. As soon as Minerva spoke he knew how stupid his comment had been. He only hoped it didn't give the Dark Knight any ideas. He knew that Ra'naroz's power would be starting to return. If he felt that Alaric was weakening then there was a chance he would try to attack. Alaric needed to be very careful. The more time that passed the more dangerous his situation would become.

Minerva dropped one end of the rope into the mine shaft before slowly feeding the rest in. If Alaric didn't understand her explanation before he definitely did now. She kept feeding the rope into the shaft even though she should have been at the end. When she was confident the rope was far enough in she simply dropped the other end onto the ground. Alaric's initial thought was to grab the rope before it disappeared into the hole, but he stopped himself before he moved. The end of the rope remained in the sand where Minerva had dropped it.

"Well, who wants the honours?" Minerva sounded jovial, although it was a rhetorical question. "Okay. I will go first."

Without warning Minerva grabbed the rope and dropped into the mine shaft. Alaric thought the next thing he would hear was her screams as she dropped to her death, but there was nothing but silence. He really needed to have more faith if he was going to survive. He was still clearly not thinking straight.

"After you." Ra'naroz offered when he was sure that Minerva would be at the bottom.

"I don't think so." Alaric might have been suffering from exhaustion, but he was not stupid. "You will be going in first."

Ra'naroz laughed before responding. "I really wish you would learn to trust me."

He did not wait for Alaric to reply. He knew what the response would be and he really didn't feel like having an argument. As Minerva had done before him Ra'naroz grabbed the rope and simply dropped into the hole. There was obviously something that Alaric was missing. He wasn't sure if he would have the confidence to follow suit.

There was no time for him to think about what he was going to do. Even though the sun was nearly ready to set it still beat down on him. When he was sure Ra'naroz had reached the bottom, although he did not know how he knew, Alaric took the plunge. Once he had picked up the rope he felt a sudden urge to drop into the hole. The feeling was overwhelming and there was nothing he could do to resist. Without thinking he jumped.

What happened next was not at all what he was expecting. He felt a sudden rush around him. He could not explain how he felt, but it was not unpleasant. Before he knew what had happened his feet touched solid earth again. When he regained his senses, it seemed like a dream. There was something very disturbing about that thought.

It was a lot cooler underneath the earth than it was outside. Even so Alaric was still quick to take off the heavy robe. There was a slight cool breeze, although Alaric couldn't think for the life of him where it would be coming from. Nevertheless it felt refreshing against his skin.

Once Minerva had landed in the mine she had created a small light ball. The light from the hole above was not enough to light the cave. She had removed her hood, but had kept her robe on. Ra'naroz had done the same.

"Sorry about that," Minerva said when Alaric arrived. "The rope was completely unnecessary, but I thought it would give you more confidence."

"What are you talking about?" Alaric could feel he was being manipulated and he didn't like it.

"I placed a spell on the mine shaft many years ago when I realised what it was and where it led. Only when I am around will anyone be allowed to pass through," she explained.

Suddenly Alaric understood the situation, but it didn't make a great deal of sense. Slowly a rage was building inside of him, but he thought he better give her the benefit of the doubt, at least until he knew the truth.

"So all the markers, you made them?" Alaric kept his voice level.

"Well, yes and no. The rocky outcrop is actually natural. I made the rest around that," she sounded rather pleased with herself.

"What is the point? If no one can enter the shaft wouldn't it be better to make easier directions?" Alaric did not sound impressed.

"Definitely not," Minerva didn't really understand Alaric's line of questioning. "It is a simple spell. It will protect against those who can not use magic, but even a simple magician would be able to break it. This way it gives a certain amount of protection against everyone."

"Did you make the shaft?" Alaric was still not satisfied.

"No. As I told you it is a mystery to me on who made the shaft. It is possible that it is just a natural crack in the earth." Minerva became defensive.

"This is a nice little history lesson, but it is not getting us any closer to the cathedral." Ra'naroz explained.

"You should put your robe back on Alaric," Minerva spoke before they continued. "It can get very cold in the mines. As you can imagine the sun does not reach down here."

As much as Alaric wanted to leave the robe on the ground he could appreciate what Minerva was saying. They had only been in the mines for a few minutes and he was already starting to feel cold. He knew it would not be too long before it became uncomfortable. The extreme temperature shifts were starting to get to him.

"How do we know which way to go?" it was a silly question, but Alaric asked it anyway.

He looked around and could see no discerning features. He didn't even know which way he was facing. He knew the downward trip had turned him around, but he didn't know which way he landed. He assumed that was part of the spell, although he could not work out why. The only thing that came to mind was the fact that Ra'naroz and himself were now completely at her mercy. He did not know what significance that had, but he was going to keep it in the back of his mind.

"We go that way." Minerva pointed in the direction of the little floating ball of light.

Alaric had no idea how she could decipher which way to go, but that was not the point. She sounded confident and that was enough to convince him. It was not like he had any other choice. He would not have a clue which way to go without her. In his current predicament he had no other option. She had not given him any real reason not to trust her but it was becoming much harder.

They had landed in a small cavern. The walls were just outside the range of the light orb. Not being able to see them made Alaric a little uncomfortable. He felt as though he could feel the walls closing in around him. The thought was disturbing and Alaric tried to put it out of his mind. He was a lot happier when Minerva led them into a small tunnel. The walls were much closer, but Alaric didn't care. At least he was able to reach out and touch them. That was a comforting thought.

The further they travelled the closer the walls and ceiling became. It was not long before Alaric had to duck his head to stop it from scraping across the rocks. After that they all had to walk sideways to fit thought the tunnel. Alaric thought it would not be long before they could no longer continue. Eventually they would have to drop to their stomaches and crawl.

"Do we have to go much further?" Alaric called out from behind Minerva and Ra'naroz.

As much as he didn't think Ra'naroz would escape whilst they were in the mines he also didn't trust him to be at the back. There was too much mischief he could cause if he was left alone behind the two of them. As much as he was pleading his fealty there was nothing in his actions to make Alaric believe him. He knew there was an ulterior motive for his actions, he just couldn't work out what it was and he was not going to give him the chance.

"Not much, but I would advise you to keep your voice low." Alaric knew she was using magic to make her voice carry. "We are getting close to where the miners are. If they hear us then we will be in trouble."

Alaric wished he'd remained quiet. The claustrophobia was starting to get him. He did not like being in such a confined space, especially since he didn't know when or if it was going to end. Minerva was confident that she was leading them in the right direction, but Alaric was not so sure. There was a very good chance she had become disorientated and was leading them to their death. That thought that was thick in Alaric's mind.

As Minerva had explained it did not take long before they came out of the tunnel. There was a small drop on the other side a fact Minerva conveniently didn't mention to Ra'naroz. The Dark Knight did not fall for the trap, even though it was a foolish prank. There was enough light from the orb for him to realise that he was not coming out onto flat ground. When it was Alaric's turn Minerva came to his aid. As much as he could have managed on his own he was grateful for the help.

They did not continue as Alaric had expected. They both waited for Minerva to speak. They were both as keen as each other to keep moving and Alaric could feel that he was getting closer to his goal. The memory of Alena was still in his mind. He needed to get the Topaz stone back to her. He knew she could not have long left. Ra'naroz had his own reasons that would remain secret until he was ready to reveal them.

"This will be the last chance we have to rest. Once we are out of this cavern we enter the mines. I think that we should eat something." Minerva found a stray rock to sit on.

It was clear the matter was not up for discussion. Alaric was not hungry, but he knew it would not be long before he was. He was running on adrenaline and once that wore off he knew he was going to be hungry. As much as he wanted to keep going he was glad that Minerva had suggested they stop.

With the thought of Alena in his mind he did not want to sit around for too long. Once he had eaten he was back on his feet. Ra'naroz didn't waste any time following suit. It was actually Minerva who kept them from moving. If it wasn't for the fact that she was the only one who knew where they were going Alaric would have been tempted to leave her behind. There was absolutely no logic in that thought.

"Now we need to be careful. There are many guards watching over the slaves. They will not take too kindly to us wandering through the mines. We need to avoid being seen at all cost," Minerva kept her voice low, but it did not hide the severity in her tone.

"What will they do if they catch us?" Her reasoning was fairly self-explanatory and he wanted to get moving, but the question came out nevertheless.

"At best they will assume we are slaves trying to escape. They will flog us and then chain us to the other slaves. Then we have a life of mining ahead of us." She watched their reaction before she continued. "Worst case scenario they think that we are trying to poach the diamonds and have us killed."

"I don't think that is exactly true," Ra'naroz surprised them all by speaking. "With our abilities I am sure we can take care of a few guards," he did nothing to keep his voice low.

"That is the catch. Once we reach the diamonds mines our powers will no longer work," Minerva explained.

"That is impossible. I would have heard about it if that was true," Ra'naroz scoffed.

"It is true. I don't know exactly what the reason is, but I think the diamonds have something to do with it."

"I have been around diamonds before and I have not lost my powers." Ra'naroz could not believe what he was hearing.

"That is true, but I think in their raw form and in such quantities they have a completely different effect. Do you really think the Council of Wizards would allow such a place to exist if there was anything we could do about it?" Minerva raised her voice slightly as she tried to make the Dark Knight understand the dangers before them. "If we get caught there is nothing we can do to escape. Otherwise I would not be concerned."

It was her last statement that made the Dark Knight take note. As much as he was still dubious he was not going to question her further. It was something he was not looking forward to. He was only just starting to get his powers back and now they were going to be taken away from him again. On the other hand it would give him an excellent opportunity to escape. He had to keep the foremost in his mind.

"Okay, let's get moving," Alaric spoke when it was clear that the conversation had finished.

As much as it was going to put their lives in danger Alaric was glad they could not use their powers. It might give Ra'naroz the chance to escape, but Alaric thought he would be able to handle the Dark Knight. With everyone on an even playing field Alaric finally felt like he had the advantage. He only hoped that they would be able to sneak past the guards. He was in no state to be fighting anyone unnecessarily. Ideally he would like to rest, but avoiding anything too strenuous would have to be the next best thing.

There was no argument to Alaric's comment. Ra'naroz was surprisingly submissive. When he heard he could no longer use his powers he suddenly became very nervous. Alaric thought it was a strange turn of events. Throughout his captivity with Alaric he didn't look as concerned. That held firm in his mind. He was sure there was something the Dark Knight knew that he didn't. That was not a pleasant thought.

They did not travel far before Minerva's floating light suddenly blinked out. Alaric wished she had warned them before she had done so. With the sudden blackness he did not see Ra'naroz stop and walked straight into him. A cold shiver ran down his spine as he touched the Dark Knight. He was quick to recoil, but the memory remained. He felt sick in the stomach and wanted to double over. It was the same feeling he felt when he tried to touch the energy flowing around him. He took a number of steps backwards and nearly tripped over a stray rock.

Alaric heard the two in front of him slowly starting to creep forward through the tunnel. He hoped it would not be long before there was light again. In the darkness he could feel the walls closing in on him and he could not regain his bearings. Slowly he moved along the tunnel keeping his hand on the wall to keep his balance. The only way he knew where Ra'naroz was, was by the sound of his breathing. He thought it would be the perfect opportunity to run his blade through Ra'naroz's heart. The thought of the feeling he felt when he touched the Dark Knight was still thick in his mind. He wanted nothing more than to end his life, but in doing so he would also end Alena's. It was a frustrating dilemma.

It was not long before they came out into light again. They stopped on a small platform overlooking the main diamond mine. The light came from thousands of torches. Alaric was both amazed and shocked at the sight below him. The torch light sparkled off the wall. At first Alaric thought they were all diamonds, but when he looked at the wall behind him he saw a number of other minor gemstones.

The main mine worked on a number of different levels. There were also tunnels that led off to smaller mines. Not all of those mines held diamonds. Some of them were just test mines. The sight was quite amazing.

What shocked Alaric were the many slaves he could see. Even from the distance he could see there were children working. He could not believe such a place existed. Even more surprising was that it was in Castalia. The High Chancellor was the supreme religious figure in the Seven Kingdoms. He was supposed to be caring and compassionate, but what Alaric was seeing showed neither of those traits. He could not believe the High Chancellor would be aware of such a practice.

"Believe me when I say he does." Minerva knew what Alaric was thinking as if she was reading her mind. "The High Chancellor knows exactly what goes on here and he chooses to ignore it."

Alaric didn't know what to say. He could not refute her words, but he did not want to believe it was true. It was quite discerning, but there was really no other answer. A rage started to burn inside Alaric. But he had to contain himself, it was not the time or place.

"How do we get down?" Alaric looked around and could not see anyway down from the ledge.

"That is another trick," Minerva winked at Alaric. "Just follow me."

She walked to the edge of the ledge against the wall. Instead of stopping she just kept on walking. Alaric watched in horror, but she did not drop to her death. There was magic at work again, but that didn't make any sense. Minerva had told them they could not use magic around the diamonds.

"Just follow me and you will be safe," Minerva turned around and spoke to the pair when she realised they were not following her.

"I don't understand," Alaric was not about to let it go. "You said that we will not be able to use magic?"

Minerva clearly did not want to answer the question. "Let's just say that it took a great effort. Now if you have finished asking silly questions we need to keep moving."

It did not escape Alaric that Minerva had not given an answer. He wanted to ask it again, but Minerva had already started down the other side. Alaric only hoped he had not said the wrong thing. There was something in her tone that worried him.

Once Ra'naroz had started down the invisible path Alaric followed. He was not going to let them get too far ahead. His distrust in Minerva had only increased with her dodging his question. He knew he should trust her, but he could not change the way he felt. As he walked downward he couldn't help but wonder if it was a trick of the Dark Knight. His powers were returning and he could not be trusted. Alaric wouldn't be surprised if he was altering his perception. The spell would have to be subtle or else Alaric would have noticed, or at least that's what Ra'naroz would have thought. Alaric knew he had to be careful.

It was strange walking down the invisible path. Alaric had to keep his eyes up. When he looked down he felt as though he was going to trip over. When he looked up he was able to judge the distance between the ground and his feet, but when he looked down he was not able to judge his step. It was a very discerning walk. He was constantly looking towards the mine to see if anyone had noticed them. It seemed as though they were too busy concentrating on their own lives to worry about anything else. All the slaves worked with their heads down whilst the slave masters kept a close watch. With a little luck Alaric thought that they would make it past unnoticed.

Once they were on the same level as the miners Alaric realised there was more room to hide. From the ledge it looked as though the mine was completely open, but from the lower level he could see there were many corridors and tunnel branching off all over the place. They were in an area that had been completely mined out of diamonds.

"We have to keep moving," Minerva kept her voice low when Alaric reached the bottom. "These tunnels are still in use. Keep your hoods on and your heads down. We need the slave masters to think that we are miners."

The way Minerva was speaking there was no way to avoid the guards. That was not in the original plan. Alaric knew there would be risks, but it seemed as though Minerva was changing the rules and each time she did so things became a lot worse. She had already started to move when she had finished speaking. It was obvious she did not want to answer any questions. It also irritated Alaric. He had a bad feeling he was about to walk straight into an ambush.

On the other hand there was no way he wanted to remain in the middle of a tunnel by himself. That would surely get him into trouble. There was nothing else he could do. He reluctantly lowered his head and followed them. As he started walking he suddenly felt very self-conscious. He looked behind nervously, but there was no one there. The tunnel behind him was dark. It was possible there was someone there, but he could not see them. He put it down to paranoia.

Minerva kept a slow pace. If they moved quickly then the slave masters would know they were not slaves. Alaric was frustrated with the slow pace, but he knew she was doing the right thing. It would not be long before they came out into the main mine. Then it would be imperative that they fit in. Even the slightest abnormality would alert the slave masters to their appearance.

Once they were out in the mine Alaric's heart started to race. If he felt self-conscious before, now he thought he was going to jump out of his skin. They started to pass other slaves who were also trudging through the mines. As much as Alaric wanted to raise his head and look around he knew that was not a smart idea. He could not see any slave masters, but he knew they would be around.

After they were trudging along for about half an hour Alaric started to relax. They all kept their heads down, but that was not enough to avoid attention.

"Where do you think you are going?" a voice barked from in front of them.

Alaric lifted his head slightly, but not enough to gain the slave master's attention. He could see Minerva simply raise her arm and point in the direction they were walking. He hoped that would be enough to get them past, but he doubted it.

"No one is authorised to come this way." It was those words that sent a shiver down Alaric's spine.

"I am sorry, Sir, but we were told to come this way," Minerva made her voice as gruff as possible.

"Who told you to come here?" he did not sound convinced.

"The Master, Sir."

"Hmm…" Although Alaric could not see the man he guessed by the deepness of his voice that he was strong. "I am sure he would have spoken to me if he was sending me some slaves. I think we should go and speak with him." The man took a step before he stopped.

Ra'naroz and Alaric lifted their heads. Neither of them could contain their curiosity. They figured it couldn't cause any more problems.

If they went to see the Master-of-the-Slaves then their identities would be revealed anyway.

"How dare you lift your head to me," the slaver master sounded bemused.

The slave master looked around, but there was no one else to back him up. Already he did not like the situation before him. Never before had a slave stood up to him. Any disobedience was beaten out of the pitiful creatures before they were given to him. He wasn't completely sure of what he should do. He was armed with a club and a whip, but he had yet to draw either.

The slave master's words caused Minerva to turn around. Her shoulder's dropped when she saw Ra'naroz and Alaric standing up straight. The only saving grace was the fact they kept their hoods drawn. There were not many options available to them now. She wished they had just kept their heads down and let her sort it out. There was a good chance they had just made things much worse, but there was nothing else she could do.

"We need to continue." Minerva motioned for Alaric to draw his sword as she spoke. "Would you kindly step out of the way?"

"What are you talking about? I will have your hide for such insolence." He had still not drawn either of his weapons. He was more perplexed than anything. Normally he would simply whip someone who was out of line, but there was something different about the three in front of him.

Alaric drew his sword and stepped forward. It was time for him to take control. The slave master looked at the sword in horror. He had never seen a slave with such a weapon. In fact he had never seen one of his fellow slave masters with such a sword. He knew that he had to be very careful if he was going survive.

"What is this all about? Where did you get that sword?" he asked in astonishment.

"That is none of your concern," there was strength in Alaric's voice. The slave master did not like what he was hearing. "What is your concern is how you are going stay alive. We need to reach the Grand Cathedral. You are going to make sure we reach it safely," there was no doubt in Alaric's voice.

"That is not something that I can do." The slave master was not sure of himself. He knew that he should not allow them in the Grand Cathedral, but most importantly he wanted to remain alive. In the end he would do whatever he had to do.

"I don't think you understand what I am saying to you." Alaric was expecting such a response. "This is not up for debate. Either you help us or you die."

The slave master had never been accosted by a slave before. He didn't know how to react, although he was starting to believe they were not slaves. If that was the case then he needed to figure out where they had come from. Then a thought dawned on him. They must have been sent from the Grand Cathedral. It was a test by the High Chancellor. He had heard stories of such happenings. He was not going to fail. He had heard that those who did ended working side-by-side with the slaves.

"I think you should return to the mines. There are a number of my fellow masters right behind me. They will be here in any moment. If you are still here when they arrive I would say that you will not live to see your evening meal," the slave masters voice was shaky.

Alaric knew he was lying. The slave master looked around nervously. There was no one coming. He could not understand why he did not surrender. He could try and attack with his club and whip, but he would be dead before he made his first strike. He was in an impossible position and yet it did not look like he was going to back down.

"Then I guess this is where you take your last breath." Alaric had no time to waste. He took a step closer to the slave master as he spoke.

Something was not right. The slave master did not know what was happening. He couldn't back down, but it did seem as though the man in front of him was going to kill him. It had to be part of the ruse, but it was getting a little too serious for his liking. He wondered to himself if it would be so bad if just let himself be taken prisoner. Surely it would be alright.

"I think things are getting out of control. Lower your weapon and surrender." He was not yet ready to give up.

Alaric didn't respond. He looked at Minerva who in turn shrugged her shoulders. Alaric returned his attention to the slave master. The man thought he had called Alaric's bluff and a broad smile appeared on his face. He could not have been further from the truth. The reason why Alaric didn't respond was due to the fact that he had enough. The look of pure horror on the slave master's face showed he had no idea what was coming next. Alaric moved forward and plunged his sword into the slave master's stomach. He twisted the blade once before pulling it out again.

The surprise was so great that the slave master didn't even cry out in pain. He simply dropped to his knees with the same surprised expression on his face. Alaric ran his blade across the man's throat to finish him off. There was no need for him to suffer any longer, even though Alaric was completely disgusted with his profession. It was the High Chancellor who he was really upset with.

"Let's keep moving," Minerva suggested. "It will only be a matter of time before someone comes across this body."

No one doubted her words. They moved on at the same slow pace. Alaric thought that it was a moot point, but Minerva wanted to keep up their pretences. He thought it would be better to move along as quickly as possible, but he did not want to argue with Minerva. He was happy to keep to her rules, at least for the moment.

They continued for about an hour before they reached a tunnel that started to slope upwards. Minerva stopped at the bottom. Alaric wanted to keep moving, but it was obvious something was on her mind. He looked around nervously. He thought they could at least move into the privacy of the tunnel. Although there was no one around he did not think it would stay that way for long.

"At the top of this tunnel is the Grand Cathedral. The door leading in is heavily guarded. It is time for a little trickery, but these robes will give us away. It is time to shed them. Let me do the talking, but if anyone asks you any questions just play along," she explained.

"What are we playing?" Alaric thought it would be best to know beforehand, although it didn't seem like Minerva wanted to explain.

"I will explain on the way." And with that she started up the tunnel.

Chapter 29: The Grand Cathedral

They were met at the top of the tunnel by a group of eight armed guards. They looked as though they were well trained. Alaric wasn't sure he would be able to deal with all eight of them. On the way up he realised he was the only who was armed. He knew the Dark Knight was unarmed, but he figured that Minerva would have a weapon. He thought it was especially odd since she knew that she could not use magic.

"Well I think everything is in order," Minerva spoke casually to Alaric when they reached the top.

"Yes, I believe you are right," Alaric agreed.

They pretended like they didn't see the guards. They only stopped when four of them blocked their path. Minerva put on her best annoyed look when she was stopped.

"What do you think you are doing?" she asked with a distained look.

"Who are you and what are you doing here?" the guard spoke with a gruff voice, although it was obvious he was confused at their appearance.

"We were sent by the High Chancellor to check on the condition of the mines."

"I know nothing about this," the captain-of-the-guard looked at his subordinates. They all shook their heads. "And no one else looks like they know anything about it."

"Well it's not my fault you are all group of idiots. How else would we get down here if we were not who we say we are? Think about it for a moment. Do we look like we are miners?" She crossed her arms across her chest and tapped her left foot.

The captain had to think. He had no idea what they were doing, but he had to admit the woman made sense. They did not look like miners trying to escape. The problem he had was there was no notice of their inspection. He knew it was possible the High Chancellor could pull a surprise inspection, but he was sure that someone would have told him. He thought if he heard their names that it would jog his memory.

"What are your names?" he asked

"My name is Minerva." She knew he would recognise her name, but not realise to what extent.

"What about these two?" he asked, as he tried to recall her.

"They are my guard and their names are not important. Do you think I would come to such a place without protection?" She started to feign annoyance. "Now I think you should step out of the way and let us into the Grand Cathedral."

The captain had to think. The situation just didn't feel right to him, but he couldn't come up with a decent reason to stop them. He had to think quickly. He knew he had heard the name Minerva before, but he could not remember where. In the end he had to let them pass. He knew if she was telling the truth then his life would no longer be worth living. If he was wrong then he was sure that he could make up an excuse.

"Very well," the captain stepped aside. "But be sure that if you are not who you say you are you will be back to see me soon." The threat had no substance.

Two guards unlocked the large double doors and pushed them open. Alaric could not believe the ruse had worked. He was sure he was going to have to fight. He wished everything could be so easy.

They moved past like they were on a mission. Minerva kept her head in a haughty manner. She had to keep up the pretence, at least until they were out of sight. It was not hard for her do. She was used to the finer things in life.

They entered the Grand Cathedral's cellars. The first thing Alaric noticed was the absence of prison cells. The second thing he noticed was the rows and rows of wine. He could not believe that such a collection existed. The more he learnt about the Grand Chancellor the more he was starting to dislike the man.

"How are we going to get to the spire?" Alaric asked as they walked through the cellar.

"That is going to be tricky." Minerva stopped and looked around to make sure there was no one within earshot. "We have to go through the main foyer."

"Surely it can't be that hard. We got past the guards easily enough. There has to be thousands of people in the Grand Cathedral. There is no way we will look out of place."

"Although it has been a long time since I have been here I am sure there will be people who will recognise me."

Alaric didn't think that sounded right, but there was something in her tone that made him pause. He wanted to push her further, but it was Ra'naroz who spoke first.

"Why don't you just change your appearance?" He said. Since they had left the mines he could feel his power return and he was not so timid.

"Because if Za'aroz feels it then things will be just as dangerous," Minerva spoke as if she was addressing a child.

Ra'naroz had to admit he had forgotten about Za'aroz. As the herb's affects were starting to wear off Ra'naroz found himself losing perspective. He hoped it was not going to be long term. He needed all his wits if he was going to escape. That was still his main goal.

"Then we shall just have to be careful," Alaric chose to speak before anyone else could. "Standing around down here is not going to get us any closer to our goal. Hopefully most people will have retired for the night."

Alaric's words made sense. Although no one really knew what the current time was they knew that it must be getting late. He could see that Minerva's attitude had increased and in turn it gave Alaric more confidence. There was a chance things were going to work out. It was the first time Alaric had felt that way since they had left the city.

When no one else spoke Minerva started them on their way again. There were many staircases leading up from the cellar, but Minerva ignored them all. It wasn't until they reached the end of cellar did she choose a set of stairs. Alaric noticed it was a lot shorter than the others.

The door at the top of the stairs gave them entrance to the kitchen's meat pantry. There were cured carcasses hanging from hooks on the wall. The room itself was a lot cooler than the cellar. The temperature helped keep the meat from going off. Something about the room made Alaric feel uncomfortable. It was as if there was something evil about it.

"We are going to come out in one of the kitchens. Hopefully all the cooks will have left. At worst there should be only a few scullery maids. They will neither recognise me nor have the strength of character to question me," she sounded happy with herself.

Minerva waited for Alaric to open the door. If they were going to keep up the pretence then Alaric would have to remain as the security guard. He was the only one who was armed even if he didn't totally look the part. Ra'naroz, being unarmed, would have to play the part of a visiting noble. It was not something that he was happy about, but it was better than her original idea that he would be her personal servant.

As Minerva had expected the kitchen was empty besides a number of scullery maids cleaning the last of the pots and pans. They would then have a short break before the crockery, cutlery and glasses were returned by those who had eaten. At first they didn't notice the newcomers. Alaric thought they might have been able leave unnoticed, but that was not the case.

"And you can see it comes out through the kitchen," Minerva spoke as if she had been in the middle of a conversation.

None of the scullery maids were prepared to speak when they saw the intruders. They knew better than to question someone of higher birth, and there could be no doubt they looked the part. Minerva also knew this would be the case, but that was not the reason for their ruse.

Once they were gone the maids would be certain to talk amongst themselves and that was the way rumours would start. If the rumours said there was a group of three sneaking through the kitchens then that would put the real guards on alert. The rumour of a number of nobles roaming the kitchen would not set off any alarm bells.

"I see, that's amazing." Ra'naroz played along.

They walked through the kitchen without looking at the maids. Alaric wanted to see the expressions on their faces, but he could not look. If he did then there was a chance he would give away their ruse. That was something he didn't want to do. In the end all he could do was hope they believed what they were supposed to.

Even though it was not a difficult act Alaric was still on edge. He didn't realise how tense he was until they exited the kitchen. Once they were on the other side of the door he was able to relax. It felt good, if only for a moment. It would not be long before he would have to put his guard up again. He had to take advantage of such moments when they came around. They were always few and far between.

Minerva led them down a maze of corridors until they finally reached the main foyer. They had passed a few servants and a young priest, but no one of any to great importance. Minerva did her best to keep her head high, but also keep it out of view as best she could. It was an art form that Alaric thought was quite handy. If ever he had the opportunity he would have to get Minerva to teach him.

The main foyer was as grand an entrance as Alaric had seen. The floors were made from pure marble, something that Alaric had not been expecting. He thought, like the outside of the Grand Cathedral, the inside would be made from sandstone. He could not imagine how long it would have taken to have all the marble shipped in. To add to the floor there were two rows of columns leading from the main doors to a large staircase. Everything was grandiose. Alaric was getting a better perspective of the original High Chancellor. None of the stories he had heard or the histories he had read could prepare him for the sight in front of him.

"There is no time for sight seeing," Minerva called back to Alaric.

Alaric had not noticed he had dropped behind the other two. He was busy staring at the wonder around him, but Minerva was right, he was not there on a social visit. He was there to do what needed to be done. He wished he was there under different circumstances to enjoy it. He had to lower his head and catch up to the other two. If anyone had noticed his actions they would have realised he was not who he was pretending to be.

Although there were not a lot of people in the foyer it would only take one to catch them out. As Alaric had expected it was mostly priests and other religious figures walking around. Some of them had books or parchment in their hands, but they all kept their heads down. The only people who had their heads up, besides the three of them, were the small amount of nobles. They moved around with more purpose than the priests. They also looked as though they were too busy to worry about the three of them.

Minerva led them up the main staircase. Like in the kitchen she kept up the pretence that she was showing Ra'naroz around the Grand Cathedral. No one seemed to take any notice of them and again that was the point. It seemed the more they spoke the more they blended in. If they had remained silent then they would have been more conspicuous. Alaric was quite happy to play the part of the guard. It meant he could remain silent and be prepared for danger. It was the perfect way for him to hide his tension, or at least justify it.

Once they had left the main foyer the easy part of the journey was over. The higher they climbed in the Grand Cathedral the more conspicuous they would become. The first two levels would be fine, they were accessible to everyone, but the levels above were only for certain religious figures. When Minerva had been living in the Grand Cathedral she had been allowed on all but the top three floors. They were reserved for the High Chancellor and the High Chancellor alone. The only advantage they had was the fact the further up they went the less soldiers and guards they would encounter.

When they reached the second level Minerva quickly pulled them into an open doorway. Once she had shut the door she was relieved to see that no one else was in the room. They had ended up in a small prayer room. An altar was set up on the far side of the room. It was obvious that someone had just finished praying. A number of candles by the side of the altar had almost completely burnt out. Alaric tried to see who the altar was for, but from the other side of the room he could not work it out. There were more important things for his attention so he let it go.

"What are we doing here?" Ra'naroz was growing in confidence. It was not that long ago he would have been too apprehensive to speak.

"There was someone at the other end of the corridor who knows who I am. They did not see us, so I thought it would be better for us to hide in here until they pass by," Minerva explained.

Although Minerva had not been in Castalia long since her return she had spent some time in the Grand Cathedral. The chances of meeting someone who knew her was low, but that was just how the prophecy worked.

"What if they come in here?" Alaric asked as he listened at the door.

"No one will enter a prayer room with the door shut," Minerva explained. "We are safe as long as we are in this room."

Again Alaric took the chance to relax, although he knew it would not last for long. Once they were sure the man had past then they would be back out in corridors again. Alaric was not sure how long he could keep going. The stress was starting to get to him. He needed rest like he had never needed rest before in his life.

"Okay," Minerva spoke after a couple of minutes. "He should be gone by now."

There was no time to check if the coast was clear. Once the door was open they would have to leave. It would be too suspicious if they didn't. Once the door was open then prayer time was over and the room had to be vacated. All they could do was hope the corridor was empty, or at least no one who would recognise Minerva was there.

Luckily the corridor was completely empty when they left the prayer room and Minerva did not waste any time taking advantage of the freedom. She hurried along the corridor until she heard a door open from somewhere behind them. When she heard the sound she slowed to a regular pace. She could not risk doing anything that would draw attention.

The first two levels in the Grand Cathedral were made up of prayer rooms. Alaric was glad there was something he had been expecting. His entire experience of Castalia had been a total let down up until that point. The next three levels were apartments for those who lived inside the Grand Cathedral. The next level was the High Chancellor's personal chapel, followed by his personal offices and then his personal chambers. The top levels were mostly unknown. Only the High Chancellor himself was allowed above his own chambers. Ra'naroz might be the only one alive who had been above, besides the High Chancellor himself.

They made it through the next level of prayer rooms and the first level of apartments unseen. They were half way through the next level when a voice called out from behind. As one the three of them stopped. Alaric's heart started to race even faster.

"Minerva? What are you doing here?" the voice sounded as though it came from an elderly man.

They all turned around together. Walking towards them was a man dressed in a white robe. His hair was pure white and his face was wrinkled. He had a smile on his face, which was not what Alaric had been expecting. He thought their identities had been uncovered and instantly his hand went to the hilt of his sword.

"Linus?" Minerva could not hide her surprise. "Thank the gods it's you."

A look of confusion crossed the old man's face as he moved closer to them. He waited until he was standing in front of them before he spoke again.

"I thought you had been banished from the Inner Circle?" there was a note of surprise in his voice. "I did not know it had been lifted."

Alaric was surprised at his words. She had not mentioned she had been banned from the Grand Cathedral. It was an important piece of information and something she should have shared before they had left the city.

"It hasn't," Minerva looked around nervously as she spoke. "Although that mandate was made many years ago I believe it is still being enforced."

"I think that it would be a good idea for us to get out of sight." Linus was quick to catch onto the situation. "If I can still recognise you after all this time then I'm sure others will."

The old priest led them to his apartment. It comprised of one room, very plain and very simple. It was exactly what Alaric thought it should be. There was a bed on one side and a small round table with four chairs on the other. The only other thing in the room was a small wardrobe. Alaric could only assume that there was a communal bathroom somewhere on the level.

"Now I think you should tell me what is going on," Linus spoke after he closed the door.

Minerva had hoped the question would not come, but she knew it would. Linus was a priest for the God King Jade and an old friend. He was one of the last friends Minerva had in the Grand Cathedral. He had lived there for most of his life and he knew the day to day workings better than most. Although Minerva had only known him when he was young, on a short visit, she had liked the man and he had warmed to her. She almost couldn't believe how old he looked. She was banned from the Grand Cathedral then, but that had never stopped her before.

"Well this is definitely an interesting turn of events," Linus spoke when Minerva had finished speaking.

"I hate to break up this reunion, but we really need to be on our way," Ra'naroz sounded nervous, as if he knew something the others did not.

"I would not be so hasty. Things have changed in the Grand Cathedral since you were last here," the priest's knowing tone surprised Alaric. "Have a seat and I will explain a few truths to you."

There was something comforting in his voice that made Alaric relax. He knew he was being paranoid, but he couldn't shake the feeling it was a spell. That thought made him suddenly uncomfortable. He would remain paranoid until he had his powers back.

"What is it?" Minerva asked when he didn't continue.

"The High Chancellor is a lot more paranoid than he usually is." It seemed like the best way to start. "About a year ago something changed in him, as you well know Minerva. It was about the time he got himself a new advisor." They all knew it was Za'aroz. "More recently though he has changed again. He now has guards posted on all the entrances to his private rooms. This happened about the time his new advisor mysteriously disappeared."

Alaric's ears pricked up. "Where did he go?" there was a little too much excitement in his voice. If the Dark Knight had left the Grand Cathedral then things would become a great deal easier, but he thought that was too good to be true.

"No one knows and the High Chancellor refuses to discuss it. If it were possible I believe the High Chancellor, his supreme holiness, is acting even stranger. I fear there is no chance for you to reach the top room." The news was not good.

"If Za'aroz has left then it should not be a problem sneaking past the guards," Alaric spoke plainly.

"I would not underestimate my brother. I am sure he is here somewhere. He would not have just left the High Chancellor to his own devices. Not if he was in charge. No, I think there is something else happening here." Ra'naroz surmised.

Alaric had to admit that Ra'naroz was right. There was no reason why Za'aroz would leave the Grand Cathedral. By what Linus had told them he still had a hand in things. Just when Alaric thought they were having some luck it had quickly changed. Things just became worse. A hidden danger was much more perilous than an open one.

"So how are we going to get to the top?" Alaric asked

"Do you have any ideas?" Minerva asked the priest.

"I might have been a little overzealous when I said you have no chance to reach the top," there was something evil in the way he spoke. "When the High Chancellor goes to sleep all the guards are shifted to the lower levels. Everyone else is cleared out, which means there is no reason to secure every level."

Alaric liked what he was hearing. He was yet to find out how many guards would be posted, but he was confident he could take them on. There was too much at stake for him to fail. They couldn't use magic or they would alert Za'aroz to their location, which just made things more difficult. It was not going to be easy, but Alaric could finally see the light at the end of the tunnel.

"At any one time there could be up to a dozen soldiers guarding the door to the High Chancellor's chapel," Linus continued.

"What are the least amount of soldiers ever guarding it?" Alaric asked. He needed information if he was going to formulate a plan.

"From what I have heard at certain times there can be as little as two," Linus answered.

That was what Alaric wanted to hear. Two soldiers were much better than twelve. Things just got even better, but they still had to come up with a plan. Fatigue was starting to play its role. Alaric was not thinking straight. He needed to rest, but there was no time.

"Is there any specific time when the numbers are less?" Alaric seemed to be the only one asking questions. Both Minerva and Ra'naroz were happy to listen.

"Not really," Linus replied. "Although I do have an idea," there was something mysterious in his voice. "The soldiers do have a tendency to leave their post to eat. If we have a midnight snack prepared for them then it should be a lot easier for us."

All of a sudden the priest had included himself in their mission. Although Alaric liked the sound of his plan he was not sure he wanted the old man tagging along. He did not think it was appropriate for a priest to be taking part in such a ruse

"I don't think you should come along with us," Minerva also picked up on Linus' words. "This is going to be dangerous."

"Now Minerva, I am not in my grave just yet. You forget that I spent my youth in the army and I spent time in the High Chancellor's guard before I became a priest. I think that you are going to need me if this is going to work," Linus explained.

For the first time Alaric saw Linus. His face was worn with years of experience. There was strength in his eyes. The white robe hung loosely over his body, but Alaric assumed there were muscles underneath. He should not have underestimated the man without knowing him better. He was still unsure if he should come any further than the chapel as things were going to get even more dangerous. He wasn't sure if the priest was up to the challenge.

"This sounds like we have a plan. How long is it until midnight?" Alaric returned to the conversation.

"I still don't think that this is a good idea. It has been a long time since you were a soldier Linus. You are a priest now and should not get mixed up in such things." Minerva was still not convinced.

"I still keep up my training in my spare time. Don't you worry about me, I will be able to hold my own," Linus continued.

"You are a priest now, not a soldier," Alaric wished that Minerva would just let it go. They had more important matters to discuss.

"I think you will just have to trust me. This plan won't work unless I am involved." Finally they were getting somewhere.

"I thought priests were supposed to be gentle creatures," Alaric could have hit Ra'naroz when he spoke. "Isn't it against your faith to be violent," he sneered.

"You should not speak about things that you do not understand." Linus could tell there was something off about Ra'naroz, but he did not know the true extent. "We have pledged to do whatever it takes to protect our beliefs. If that means going into battle then that is exactly what I will do," he spoke with a passion that uplifted Alaric.

"This is all very interesting, but we don't have time. Let's get this plan formulated and maybe get a little rest," Alaric interrupted before Ra'naroz had another chance to speak.

"We've got about two hours before midnight. We are going to need every minute if we are going to get this right," Linus just ruined Alaric's plan for rest.

Chapter 30: Top Floor

None of the guards thought it was odd when Linus came to them to explain that a midnight meal had been prepared for them. There was no reason why the guard should doubt him. There had been no high alert. As far as they were concerned it was business as usual and that meant it was time to eat. If there was a specially prepared meal for them then all the better. It was about time someone showed their appreciation.

That was the easy part of the plan. Linus always had complete confidence it was going to work. The next part was a little harder, but he still had faith. Before they had left to see the guards they had to sneak into the guardhouse and steal two uniforms. They would have to convince the soldiers that Ra'naroz and Alaric were guards and would look after the door whilst they all ate.

Alaric had to admit he was happy to change clothes. The clothes he had been wearing had been drenched in sweat. He felt a lot more comfortable in the garb of the Grand Cathedral Guard. At first he had thought the idea was silly, but since they did not have a better plan he didn't say anything. Once he saw himself and Ra'naroz dressed as guards he quickly changed his mind. He actually thought that Linus' plan might work.

The first problem was that Ra'naroz was now armed. That was something that Alaric wanted to avoid. He told Linus, without revealing who he was, but that just confused him. No one would believe that Ra'naroz was a guard if he did not have a weapon. There was nothing Alaric could do about it. If the plan was going to work then Ra'naroz had to look the part.

Minerva was the next problem. If the guards recognised her then they would know that she shouldn't have been there. Even if they didn't know who she was they would figure that she did not belong. Either way she was going to have to remain hidden until the guards had all left. The only way to do that was to time things to perfection. If she arrived too soon then the guards would still be in place and they would be caught. If she was too late then the same would happen. Linus was confident they would have a long enough window to make it work.

"I do not think we should leave our post," said one of the two soldiers still stationed at the door. They were not so quick to rush off as the others. "I do not know who these soldiers are."

"It's no problem. You should not let the others have all the food." Linus couldn't try too hard or they would be caught out.

Alaric was trying his best not to look nervous. They had already been waiting too long. Minerva was going to be arriving shortly, depending on how accurate she could count time. There was a good margin for error and Alaric knew they were running short.

"We have already eaten." Alaric tried his best to put on a Castalial accent. It was not the best, but the soldier did not notice.

"What is this all about?" the soldier was still suspicious. "I am sure someone would have informed us if there was going to be a special meal tonight."

Linus continued his line of speech. He could not let the soldier get the better of him. It took longer than Linus had hoped, but in the end he was able to convince the two soldiers to leave their post and not a moment too soon. As soon as they disappeared Minerva arrived.

"This is where we part ways my old friend," Minerva spoke to Linus.

"I don't think so. I have come this far. I am going to see this through to the end," Linus retorted.

"Things are more dangerous than you think." Minerva tried to dissuade him. "You should return to your cloister. You will be safe there."

"Something is wrong here in the Grand Cathedral. I have noticed it for a long time and done nothing. Now it is time that I do something about it. I am stronger than you think and not quite as ignorant as you believe."

"We don't have time for this." Alaric was looking around nervously. "If you are coming, then let's go."

That was the end of the conversation. Linus opened one of the doors into the chapel. Minerva was not happy, but there was nothing she could do about it. Alaric was right. If they remained where they were, the guards would return and it would all be for nothing. They needed to keep moving. When the soldiers returned they would wonder why no one was guarding the door. They had to be well and truly gone by the time that happened.

The chapel was not at all what Alaric was expecting. It was still lit by candles in a number of chandeliers hanging from the ceiling. They were nearly burnt out and only had an hour of light left. He thought it would have been a large grand room, but instead it was small and homely. Wooden pews lined the way to a small stage where there was a lectern and a modest throne-like chair. It looked out of place within the Grand Cathedral.

"What will the soldiers do when they find no one is guarding the chapel?" Minerva asked as they made their way to the staircase at the back.

"Hopefully they will moan and complain and then go back to their job. By the time they report what happened we will be long gone," Linus explained.

"What if they don't just moan and complain?" Alaric did not like what he was hearing.

"Then we better move fast," there was no humour in his voice.

As much as his words spurred them on they did not quicken their steps. Linus had surmised there would be no soldiers past the door, but he was not completely sure. There was still a chance that they could run into more guards. They needed to be careful if they did not want to be on the wrong end of a sword.

The stairs at the back of the chapel led to the High Chancellor's private offices. Even though they were sure the High Chancellor had gone to bed there was still a chance he was still awake. If he was awake then he would be in his offices. The last thing they needed was to run in him.

When they reached the top of the stairs the High Chancellor's offices were dark, except for a small amount of light that came in through the windows. It was obvious the High Chancellor was not working, but that was not something they were going to leave to assumption. Regardless of their need for speed the limited light made them walk slowly. The last thing they wanted to do trip over something and make a racket.

Once they were successfully through the offices they had to make their way through his private apartments. That was not going to be as easy as it sounded. Linus stopped them before they started.

"I think we are pretty safe from the soldiers now," Linus whispered.

"Then we should keep moving." Alaric couldn't understand why they had stopped. He was getting so close to his goal.

"I have never been this high before, but from what I have heard there is a staircase as the back of the High Chancellor's bedroom."

"Then we shall have to be extremely careful," Minerva sounded irritated. She was still not happy that Linus had come with them, although she had to admit his advice was invaluable.

The High Chancellor's apartments were split into a number of different rooms. They were separated by a short corridor, but no doors. If the High Chancellor was in any of the rooms and not asleep then he would see them walking past. Linus led the way. Each time he came to an entrance he would peer around the corner before they continued. The going was slow, but it was necessary. Alaric had to contain his nerves.

The apartment was even darker than the offices. Heavy drapes covered the windows, obscuring all but a little light. Alaric wished that

Minerva could create her little ball of light, but he knew that wouldn't work. He was actually glad Linus was with them. Although he had not spent much time in the High Chancellor's private apartment, he had an idea of where they had to go. The bedroom was the last room at the end of corridor.

They moved at a slow and annoying pace. Alaric's eyes slowly adjusted to the light. He knew if he had his powers he would be able to see better, but that was not an option. He had grown so accustomed to his new powers that he hardly believed he had lived without them. Now that he was so close to getting them back he could hardly contain himself.

As they feared they found the High Chancellor sleeping in his bedroom. They could not see him so much but they could hear his breathing. At least it sounded as though he was sleeping. Alaric would have loved to be able to check to make sure, but the risk of waking him was too great. There was nothing they could do except hope he didn't stir.

In the dark it was almost impossible to see inside the bedroom. Alaric could see the outline of furniture around the room, but he couldn't pinpoint anything specific. Linus didn't know the location of anything in the room. He had never been allowed so far into the apartment. It had only been rumours that told him there was a staircase at the end of the room.

Again Linus led the way. They all crouched down, although Alaric could not see the point. Linus had started the trend and all the others had followed suit. Alaric could feel the blood pumping through his head. The adrenaline was also starting to pump through his body. Once they were out of the bedroom they would be able to move freely again. That was what he wanted.

Their movement through the bedroom was painfully slow. Linus had to make sure that he did not trip over anything. If the High Chancellor woke then it would all be over. It would only be a matter of time before the apartment was filled with soldiers. Alaric thought it might be easier just to take him prisoner. If he was under their control he could not call for help. It was a good idea, but there was something telling him that it was not the way to go.

Linus suddenly stopped as the High Chancellor took a deep breath. For a moment they all thought he had woken. Not only that but Minerva nearly bumped into Linus, Ra'naroz nearly bumped into Minerva and Alaric nearly bumped into Ra'naroz. There was no doubt that a chain reaction would have woken the High Chancellor. When Linus realised he had not woken him he continued on towards the back of the room.

The stairs leading out of the bedroom were narrow. They were made out of timber and had not been maintained in a long time. Linus took a tentative step onto the bottom step and heard the timbers squeak under his weight. Once his foot was down he waited to hear if the High Chancellor had woken. When he was sure he hadn't Linus continued. Each step brought a new sound and with each sound there was a chance they were going to be caught.

Alaric was wondering how far away dawn was. It felt like they had been moving for hours. He would not be surprised if he saw the light from the sun creep through a window.

They all relaxed once they reached the top of the stairs. There was a small trapdoor at the top that lead to the next room in the spire. Linus could hardly contain his excitement. To his knowledge no one, except for a High Chancellor and Ra'naroz if he could be trusted, had been above the bedroom in the spire. It was not the reason why he had come with them, but it was an added bonus. He only wished he could see.

As if Minerva was reading his mind she created the same small orb of light she had created in the mines. At first everyone had to shield their eyes until they became accustomed to it. Minerva's sight returned almost instantaneously followed shortly by Ra'naroz. It took Alaric longer than it should for his eyes to adjust to the light and finally Linus' old eyes were the last.

Linus' reaction to what was around him was clear to everyone in the room. At first there was a look of surprise, not that he really knew what he was expecting. It quickly changed to a look of glee. They were in the High Chancellor's personal library. One of the Linus' greatest joys was curling up in bed with a good book. He could only imagine what wonders the shelves held. He took a step towards the nearest bookshelf, but stopped before he moved any closer. He suddenly felt the eyes of the others on him.

"We have to keep moving," Minerva almost sounded sad as she spoke. She too would like to spend time in the library, but that was not what had moved her. "You have come too far to stop now," she felt for the old priest.

"Of course. It is just a shame to see so many books go to waste," there was a touch of longing in Linus' voice.

Alaric could understand how he felt, but that was no excuse for slowing them down. There was still the risk that Za'aroz was still in the vicinity. If that was the case then their lives were at a greater risk than Linus would know. There was no point in explaining things to him, but they had to keep moving. Alaric could almost sense the stone above him and that kept him going.

They walked through the rows of books looking for the next set of stairs leading them forever upwards. Their initial reaction was to walk to the opposite end of the room. When they did all they found was another row of books. They walked back the way they had come, checking between the aisles as they went. As they thought there was nothing they had missed on the way, which gave them an entirely new dilemma. They stopped in the middle of the library to speak.

"Where do we go now?" Alaric asked.

"I don't know. No one except for the High Chancellor has ever been this high." Linus thought Alaric had been speaking to him, when in fact he was speaking to Ra'naroz.

"That is not entirely true," Minerva spoke before Ra'naroz could.

"What are you talking about?" Linus spoke again before Ra'naroz had a chance.

"That is a story for another time," Alaric quickly put an end to the conversation before Minerva had a chance to speak. "You have been here before Ra'naroz. How did you get past this room?"

Again Ra'naroz didn't have a chance to answer. It took Linus a moment, but he quickly recognised where he had heard that name before. There could be no doubt; it was such a unique name. No one in their right mind would name their son after a Dark Knight. He wasted no time in drawing his sword, which he had successfully concealed under his robe. When he was armed he took a number of steps backwards until he was sure that no one could get the jump on him.

"What is going on here Minerva?" he raised his voice louder than he had planned, but that was the least of his concerns.

"Calm down Linus. I can explain everything," Minerva kept her voice low. "Put your sword down. This is not the place for such discussions."

"Be that as it may we are not going to any further until you explain to me why you are travelling with a Dark Knight?" Linus moved his sword nervously, so it took turns pointing at each of them. "Is he calling the shots? Has he taken control, Minerva?"

"We don't have time for this," Ra'naroz took matters into his own hands.

The Dark Knight waved his right hand when he spoke. As he did the sword was knocked out of Linus' hand. The old priest rubbed his wrist as if he had been struck. Alaric could not believe what he had seen. They had all agreed it was too dangerous to use such magic. Minerva's spell had been too small to be really noticed, but he was sure that Ra'naroz's was not.

"What are you doing?" Alaric drew his own sword and moved in front of Ra'naroz.

"We don't have time for this nonsense," Ra'naroz explained. "I am sure my brother would not have felt that. It was really a weak spell."

Alaric didn't know what to think. The Dark Knight was becoming too arrogant. He was still their prisoner, but he was not acting so. There could be no doubt he was getting his full strength back. He was more dangerous than ever. Even so Alaric could not show any sign of weakness. If he did then there was no telling what the Dark Knight would do.

"There is a trapdoor somewhere in the ceiling. It has been a long time since I have been here, so I don't know exactly where it is." Ra'naroz looked up.

Alaric wished he had said something at the start, but he was too excited to worry about it. He had to find the trapdoor and come one step closer to his goal. The problem was that the small orb of light did not light a great deal of space. They all had to follow the orbs path, instead of searching in different directions.

The search was painfully slow. Alaric had to wonder if Ra'naroz had been telling the truth. There was something very suspicious about his behaviour. Then he had to remember that Ra'naroz was a Dark Knight and not an ally. There was always a good reason for him to be deceptive.

Eventually they found the trapdoor above a bookshelf. The dust on the floor showed it had been a long time since it had been moved. Whoever had been there last wanted to make sure that no one else was able to find the trapdoor. There was a good chance the current High Chancellor didn't even know about it. That thought made Alaric feel a little better. There would be little chance of them getting caught.

"I think this is where we part ways," Minerva said to Linus again once they had moved the bookcase.

"What are you talking about?" he sounded confused.

"We are going to need someone to move the bookcase back into place after we leave," she replied as Alaric made his way up.

"That is all well and good, but how are you going to get out?" Linus was not yet defeated.

Minerva had to admit the priest was right. When the bookcase was in place there was no way to open it again. Without that excuse there was no good reason for him to be left behind. She wished he would return to his apartment, but she knew there was nothing she could do.

"Very well. Come along now." Minerva resigned herself to the fact.

To Linus' chagrin Minerva helped him up through the hole in the ceiling. He could have gotten up by himself, but he had to admit the extra help was handy. He wished she had at least asked before helping him instead of assuming he needed assistance. In return he reached down and helped Minerva up. She took his hand gratefully. She didn't think for a moment that he was doing it out of spite.

The next room was even dustier than the one before. Again they were all surprised with what they saw. The room was full of ancient artefacts. Minerva was in awe. She went from one piece to another. As she went the orb followed her. There was no chance of Alaric doing a separate search. He knew the stone was close and he did not have time to waste, but Minerva did not seem to notice. She was too concerned with what was before her.

There were trinkets from all around the Seven Kingdoms. At first she picked up a shield with a strange symbol on the front. There was a circle with eight lines dissecting it into perfect eighths. Above there circle there was a small green dragon and underneath there were three flames, as if there was a fire heating the circle.

"I never thought that I would see anything like this," Minerva's voice was full of awe.

"It's a shield, what's so good about that?" Alaric sounded annoyed. Although he had asked the question he really did not want to know the answer. He just wanted to find the next way up.

"This is an ancient Avlyset shield," she explained. "Avlyset used to be the land which is now mostly made up of Remidia. The land we are on used to be part of Avlyset. All Avlysetian artefacts are very rare and almost impossible to find." She carefully placed the shield back on the table and kept looking through the other items.

Alaric had to admit to himself he was excited to see what else she was going to find, but not enough to distract him from the job at hand. He moved along behind Minerva, looking for a way to get higher up into the spire. If she did not return her mind to the job at hand soon he would have to take command.

She went from table to table, looking in amazement at all the rare artefacts. There were things that she thought that she would never get to see. All she could think about was how she could get the items out of the Grand Cathedral. There were years of study all around her. There was nothing she could do whilst it was in its current location.

Almost half an hour had passed before Alaric had finally had enough. He had seen a small staircase towards the back of the room as they moved around. He had not said anything at the time as he had hoped Minerva would have come to the conclusion on her own. When she did not he knew that he was going to have to say something.

"There will be plenty of time for this later. Right now we have to get moving. I have a bad feeling we have already taken too long," Alaric kept his voice even, although he was becoming agitated.

"Of course," Minerva took one last look at the bounty around her before returning her attention to Alaric. "Have you seen any way up?"

Alaric explained to her about the stairs and they were soon on their way to the top room of the Grand Cathedral. He insisted that he lead the way. He wanted to be the first into the room, but he paused when he reached the door at the top of the stairs. He remembered what Ra'naroz had told them and wondered if there was a spell on the entrance. He did not want to rush in only to find it was a trap.

"Are there any spells on this door?" he spoke to Ra'naroz who was standing between Linus and Minerva on the stairs.

"Not that I have put there," there was something in his voice that made Alaric want to strike him.

He wanted to ask the question again, but the risk of Ra'naroz realising his situation was too great. Instead he would have to take a chance. If there was a spell on the door then his journey would suddenly be cut short. It was the better of two evils. He held his breath as he touched the door handle. Suddenly a shiver passed through his body, but it was not what he was expecting. There was an edge of exhilaration.

When he opened the door the feeling only increased. There was something very homely about the room as he stepped into it. The orb still remained with Minerva and Alaric could not see what was ahead of him. He did not need to be able to see to know that the Topaz stone was somewhere in front of him. He could feel it. He thought he could hear it calling to him. It was a muffled voice, but he was sure that it was there.

When Minerva entered the room a sudden burst of light followed her. The orb was able to light the entire room, although Alaric thought it had increased in intensity. The thought quickly left him as he saw the glass case in the centre of the room. Inside was a small sceptre with a yellow stone at the top. There could be no doubt that it was the Topaz stone.

Chapter 31: More Than One Deception

Alaric stood two paces away from the Topaz stone. He wanted nothing more than to reach out and take it, but that would certainly cause his death. No one else wanted to speak. They were all waiting to see what Alaric was going to do. They were also spellbound by the sight in front of them.

Ra'naroz was the first to recover his senses. The memory of the last time he was in the room came flooding back to him. There was something about the Topaz stone that made him very uncomfortable. He had never liked being in its presence. The first time around it had been a fortuitous experience. Now it was something completely different. He wanted to leave his spell in intact and run. He looked around nervously, as if he had spoken his thoughts out loud, but no one seemed to be taking any notice of him.

It was up to Alaric to make the first move. They were all waiting to see what his reaction would be. Slowly he took a step forward. Minerva thought he was going to reach out and touch the glass. She wanted to stop him, but she could not move. She was mesmerised by the sight of the Topaz stone.

"Remove the spell," he didn't take his eyes from the stone as he spoke, but there could be no doubt who he was speaking to.

"You better move back," Ra'naroz warned as he moved forward. He needed to be within touching distance of the stone for his spell to be removed. "I don't really know what will happen when I stop the spell. It was not designed to be removed."

That comment seemed odd to Alaric. He could not work out why Ra'naroz would create a protective spell on the Topaz stone that couldn't be removed. There was more to the situation than the Dark Knight was letting on. That was something that Alaric did not like at all. He thought about stopping Ra'naroz, but he desperately wanted the Topaz stone. It was the only way to save not only Alena, but himself as well.

"I think you should extinguish your light." Alaric thought he could hear a muffled moan come from the orb, but he shook it off. "The residual magic could cause havoc."

Alaric did not know if he liked the idea of letting Ra'naroz work in the dark. There was no way to make sure he wasn't up to mischief. Minerva thought the same thing, but she also had to agree with Ra'naroz. She was not sure exactly what he was doing, but there was a good chance the orb would cause problems. Minerva muttered under her breath and the light blinked out of existence. It was only at that point that Alaric realised the sun had started to rise. A sliver of light crept in through the window.

"Let's do this." The sudden realisation of time urged him to react. "The sun is rising and we are out of time." He didn't know if that was true, but it seemed appropriate.

"Well step back and let me get to work," there was no confidence in Ra'naroz's voice.

Alaric realised he was the only one who was standing out from the wall. Slowly he moved back until he was standing next to Minerva. It was all in the hands of the Dark Knight. Alaric made himself a silent promise that he would never put himself in such a position again.

Ra'naroz dropped to his knees. He moved so suddenly they were not sure if it was part of his spell.

No one moved. No one would move until the spell was complete. It was half in anticipation and half in fear of what could happen if the spell went wrong. It was just a matter of waiting for the result.

Suddenly Alaric felt a tug. It was so strong that he almost fell forward. He could only imagine the amount of energy the Dark Knight was drawing in to create such a force. If he was thinking straight he would realise that Za'aroz would also feel what his brother was doing. If he was still in the Grand Cathedral then it would not be long before he was knocking on the door.

The spell was more complex than Alaric could imagine. After a minute had passed a subtle glow appeared around both Ra'naroz and the glass case. It was a good indication that the spell was working, at least that was the thought going through Alaric's mind. It would not be long before he had the Topaz stone in his possession. Then he would be able to heal himself and those who were sick in Jarrat. He had not been sure if he was going to survive, but suddenly his mission was all but complete.

As the spell continued Alaric could see the space between Ra'naroz and the stone start to waver. The spell was starting to have its affect. A droplet of sweat appeared on the Dark Knight's face. It was the first time Alaric had seen Ra'naroz start to show any strain. Even when they were battling in the dungeons of Jarrat Alaric did not notice any perspiration on the Dark Knight's body. If he was going to kill Ra'naroz it would be the perfect time, although it would put the Topaz stone completely out of his reach. He could only hope that the end justified the means.

In total the spell lasted for almost ten minutes. When he was finished Ra'naroz dropped to the floor. He looked as though he was completely exhausted. Alaric almost felt sorry for the Dark Knight, but he knew the evil creature's past. He could never feel any remorse for such a vile being. He quickly put the thought out of his mind and returned his attention to the Topaz stone. The glass casing had completely disappeared leaving the sceptre out in the open.

"I think it is down now," Minerva spoke when Alaric had not moved. "It should be safe for you to take the sceptre."

He did not like Minerva's tone. There was no confidence in her words. She did not want to take responsibility if she was wrong. Alaric had hoped for something more, but that was all he was going to get. The sole responsibility fell on his shoulders. As much as he wanted to reach out and take the stone he still did not move.

"The spell has been removed," Ra'naroz puffed as he spoke. It was obvious to all that he was struggling. "You are safe to take the stone. Take it soon because it will not be long before my brother is here."

The warning forced Alaric into action. He took a tentative step forward before he stopped again. Something was amiss. As soon as that thought came into his mind a peace suddenly came over him and he quickly brushed the feeling aside. As he moved closer he felt better than he had in a long time. The closer he came the more the Topaz stone started to glow.

"Take me and strike them down," a voice yelled in his head when he was within touching distance of the sceptre.

Alaric reached out, but stopped when he heard the voice. There was something aggressive in it and it made him pause, but only for a second. He needed the stone and this was the only way he was going to get it. Slowly he gripped the sceptre and pulled it from its resting place. The effects were instantaneous.

The light from the Topaz stone intensified to the point where it filled the room. Not only that, but the bright yellow light shot out of the windows. Anyone who was looking at the great spire would see it. There could be no doubt that something was happening.

Alaric dropped to his knees as a feeling of pure contentment filled his body. The poison that had affected him since the dungeon was completely gone. All the aches and pains of the day disappeared. It was like he was a new man. The feeling was pure ecstasy and he hoped he could hold onto it forever.

It took a lot more effort to return his normal senses than Alaric had anticipated. He tried to dull the effort of the Topaz stone, but nothing happened. The feeling of pure joy was hard to control. He had hoped it would be easy, but that was not the case. As with dealing with all the *Stones of Power* it would take a much stronger effort to take control of the Topaz stone. He needed more willpower because he really didn't want the feeling to end.

Through a great effort Alaric was able to suppress the joy the Topaz stone had created. At first the feeling was slow to dissipate, but the worse he felt the easier it was. When it had completely gone Alaric felt depressed. His first thought was to reach out to the stone for help, but it was Minerva's words that stopped him.

"You have to be strong Alaric. The stone will try and take control of you." They were words he had heard before and they still made sense.

He looked back down at the small pedestal the sceptre had been seated on. He saw there was a small velvet hood that would completely cover the Topaz stone. He knew that was the only way he could dampen the stone's control. As he picked up the small hood the voice returned to his mind.

"Don't do it. I have been silent for so long. I can help you. You need me to help you. You have a long way to go and you will need my help. Don't put me in the dark," the voice was pleading inside his head.

Alaric did not want to reply. He knew as soon as he spoke he would be admitting there was more the stone could do for him. He knew he needed the stone's assistance in healing Alena, but he had to be able to overpower it. The Topaz stone was trying to gain control of Alaric. That was something he could not allow.

"You will do what I say," Alaric gritted his teeth as he spoke with his mind.

There was no answer. Alaric had already placed the hood over the stone and tied it tight. He suddenly felt very tired. The strain of fighting with the stone, had overtaken the strain of the day. He still felt a lot better than he had before he touched the sceptre. His job was complete. Now he was free to return to Jarrat and save Alena's life.

"Are you alright?" Minerva asked.

It was only at then that Alaric realised Minerva and Linus were standing directly behind him. He had neither heard them move nor knew how long it had taken them to get there. When Alaric had not moved for over ten minutes they had started to become concerned.

"Yes, thank you. I think it is time for us to get moving," Alaric turned around and looked to see what Ra'naroz was doing.

To his horror he could not see the Dark Knight in the room. Although the sun had not completely risen there was enough light for them to see clearly. Alaric suddenly felt very stupid. He quickly realised Ra'naroz's ruse. He had truly believed that unravelling his spell had taken all his energy. Now he realised that was not the case. He had his suspicions as whether the drop of sweat had been real, either way he had been duped and he did not like it.

"Where did Ra'naroz go?" Linus was the first one to speak.

"What do you mean?" Minerva was the last one to realise the Dark Knight had gone.

"I think this was his plan all along," Alaric explained. "He has gone."

"Why would he have waited for you to get the stone? I would have thought he would have left a long time ago. Surely he has had opportunities." Linus was trying to work things out.

"I don't know. I thought I was being careful. I don't think I gave him an opportunity to escape." He tried to think back, but his mind was hazy. "I am sure he had his reasons and that makes me very nervous. We need to be very careful now."

It was at the point they all realised there was someone else in the room with them. At first, in the dim light, they thought it was Ra'naroz, but they were soon able to realise their mistake. Minerva and Linus knew who it was, but Alaric had no idea. He wanted to draw his sword, but something told him not to.

"What do you think you are doing here?" the voice sounded less than impressed.

"I am sorry, High Chancellor," Linus prostrated himself as he spoke.

"I am sure you are priest, but that doesn't answer my question," his tone was filled with contempt. "These are my private rooms. No one is allowed up here. Explain yourselves now or I will have you arrested."

Something wasn't right, or at least that's what Alaric thought. He could not work out why the High Chancellor was there. Not only that, but it didn't make sense that he was alone. He knew that something was very wrong, but he could not fathom why. It was right on the tip of his mind. Ever since he had touched the sceptre his mind had gone fuzzy. He could not grasp the simplest of ideas.

No one knew how to answer the question that was asked of them. Linus wanted to speak the truth, but it was not his place. Neither Minerva nor Alaric knew what to say. They could not tell him the real reason why they were there. The High Chancellor would certainly want the Topaz sceptre for himself if he knew of its existence. On the other hand there was no lie that could explain their reason for being there either.

"We just wanted to see how far we could get without being caught," Minerva's excuse was weak.

It was as if the High Chancellor had only just seen the other two for the first time. When his eyes met Alaric's there was a sudden change to his demeanour. At first there was a look of shock on his face, which quickly turned to disgust. He quickly returned his attention to Minerva before he gave too much away.

"I thought you were banned from the Grand Cathedral?" He knew full well that she was banned. "There can be no excuse for your presence."

His last statement was true. There was no excuse for them to be there at all. The High Chancellor's reaction to Alaric was disturbing. Alaric was the only one who noticed as the other two were desperately thinking up excuses.

Alaric was still trying to work out why the High Chancellor should be there. He could understand if there was a group of soldiers behind them, but that was not the case. There was something seriously wrong with the situation.

"How did you know we were up here?" Alaric asked the question before anyone had the chance to speak.

"How dare you ask me such a question?" the High Chancellor sound flabbergasted, but again there was something not quite right with his reaction. "I am High Chancellor Augustus dux Spiritus, you do not question me." He was clearly struggling for words.

"It is a simple question." Alaric was not going to let it go.

"I think you have said enough," there was deep concern in Linus' voice. "We should get out of here."

"I think you are right priest. This is a discussion best kept to my chapel." The High Chancellor was grateful for the distraction.

Alaric was still not happy, but he was willing to accept the change of venue. He was starting to become very uncomfortable in his current surroundings. The room suddenly felt like it was closing in on him. It was like he needed to get further away from the High Chancellor. That thought also disturbed him.

Although they all agreed to leave the room no one moved. They were waiting for the High Chancellor to move first who, in turn, was waiting for the others to lead. He did not want to have the intruders out of sight. It was clear that nothing was going to happen until he spoke.

"I will follow you three down. I will not risk my life to such intruders." His words made sense, although Alaric was still not satisfied.

Minerva took the instruction and made her way down the stairs, followed shortly by Alaric and Linus. Alaric almost had to push his way past the old priest. He did not want the High Chancellor directly behind him, at least not until he knew what was bothering him. He wanted to keep as much distance from the High Chancellor as possible.

The journey to the chapel was done in silence. Alaric still could not shake the feeling that had plagued him since the High Chancellor had arrived. He knew the answer was in his head, but his mind was still clouded. He knew it was the effect of the Topaz stone. It was very tempting for him to take the hood off the top of the sceptre. His fingers toyed with the strings, but he knew it was a bad idea. Once his reliance on the stone began it would be nearly impossible to stop. He knew he would get the answer eventually. All he had to do was stay aware and wait.

The chapel was already starting to fill. Priests were coming in for their morning prayers. They looked up in anticipation when the High Chancellor walked in. To say they were surprised to see the small group would be an understatement. No one was allowed past the chapel and the room was soon abuzz with speculation. It took the High Chancellor a moment to quieten the room. He was less than impressed.

"I know you must all be wondering what is happening," his voice carried throughout the chapel. At first Alaric thought it was the acoustics of the room, but then he realised it was something else. "I have caught these three in my private chamber trying to steal my private possessions." He made a point to reiterate the word private.

As he spoke a number of soldiers entered the room. One nosey priest was quick to send for the guards. Rumours had already started circulating about what had happened during the night, but no one believed that a priest would try and enter the High Chancellor's private chambers. When the guards were advised of the situation they were quick to react. Those who had been on the night shift had already finished, but what had happened would reflect on all the guards. Those who were working had to move quickly if they were going to regain their honour.

The High Chancellor's words brought uproar in the chapel. The priests hollered for blood, although none of them moved any closer. The soldiers also kept their distance. They would not move until they were instructed. Rushing in could get them in just as much trouble as their counterparts.

"No one in my reign has ever been so bold as to try such a stunt." There was still something in his voice that Alaric thought was off. "So I have a problem of not knowing what the appropriate punishment for such an act is."

"Lock them up!"

"Execute them!"

"Send them to the mines!"

"Hang them from the spire!"

"Make an example out of them!"

"No one will do this again!"

Alaric was shocked and amazed at the voices calling out from the priests. He had always believed that religious figures should be passive and forgiving people. For the first time he was seeing a completely different side to them. There was not a friendly word from the crowd. There was nothing but retribution.

"Is this right?" he kept his voice low so only Minerva and Linus could here them.

There was no answer. They knew all too well not speak whilst in the presence of the High Chancellor. If he wanted to know their opinion he would ask. Alaric did not appreciate being ignored, but the High Chancellor had started to speak again.

"We teach compassion and forgiveness," the High Chancellor had suddenly changed his tone. There was something very different about his words. Alaric wished he could figure out what was happening. "Is this not something that we should practice?"

His words brought the crowd to silence. No one knew what to say. They had been so keen for retribution that they had not even thought about their own doctrine. The priests all kept their eyes down, embarrassed at their eagerness for vengeance. The soldiers kept their heads up, but they did not want to say a word.

"I will tell you. Those who try and steal from me are no better than the rats that live in our sewers. They are not men, they are animals. We should treat them like they were animals," the High Chancellor's voice changed again.

When the High Chancellor paused there was still silence from the crowd. No one knew what to think. He was bouncing from one stance to another. After a few seconds had past the crowd erupted again. They didn't really understand what was happening either, but the blood lust was back. The soldiers started to make their way closer to the dais. The High Chancellor raised his hands which stopped both the soldiers' advance and the crowds' cheering.

"Quiet, all of you!" Minerva's voice carried to everyone's ears, even amongst the din. "This is not the behaviour of priests. You are a rabble." Minerva spoke as if she was berating a class of apprentices.

She had stepped forward so she was standing next to the High Chancellor. This was something no one had done before. The entire chapel was shocked by her boldness. Even if anyone wanted to talk they wouldn't know what to say.

"I admit we should not have been in the High Chancellors private rooms, but I can assure you that it was for a good reason," Minerva continued to speak with strength in her voice.

"And pray tell what that excuse might be?" The High Chancellor had not been taken aback by her attitude. "I would really love to hear your excuse," he boomed before she had a chance to speak. "Be careful what you say here," he kept his voice low so only those on the dais could here.

Minerva was taken aback by his words. There was something knowing in his voice, but she couldn't work out what it was. Something wasn't right, but Minerva pushed the feeling aside and continued the conversation

"Our reasons are our own and are not to be discussed in public. If you would give us a moment I am sure you will understand." Minerva still had faith that the High Chancellor would do the right thing. She knew he had changed, but she could not believe that all reason had left him.

"Ha, ha, ha…" he started laughing. "You don't honestly believe that I would trust you alone in my chambers. I am sure you would try and kill me the first chance that you got." his words brought an uproar from the crowd. The High Chancellor was only increasing their bloodlust. "It looks like your time is short," again his voice only reached the other three. There was mocking in his tone. "I will own whatever it is that you stole from the Grand Cathedral."

Suddenly Alaric realised what he had been struggling to see. When the thought reached his mind he instantly drew his sword. It was a knee-jerk reaction that he wished he had not done. His action caused the soldiers to move closer to the dais. They only stopped when the High Chancellor raised his hand. He was not ready for them to attack, especially since things were just starting to get exciting. Alaric made no move to attack, but he also made no move to retreat.

"I see that you are not as dumb as I first thought." The High Chancellor had a smile on his face.

"What are you doing Alaric?" Minerva sounded shocked. "I know the situation is bad, but you can not threaten the High Chancellor."

Alaric kept his stare on the High Chancellor's face. Now that he knew his secret he could not divert his attention.

"Alaric!" Minerva urged.

"He is not the High Chancellor," Alaric's voice was cold. "He is something much worse."

Chapter 32: Za'aroz

"What are you talking about Alaric?" Linus sounded confused. "I must be seeing things, because this looks like the High Chancellor to me."

"Appearances are not what they seem. Ask Minerva. She will tell you how easy it is to create a façade." Alaric kept his stare fixed on the High Chancellor.

Suddenly it dawned on Minerva. She quickly stepped back when she realised who it was. As she moved she also pulled Linus back a step.

"That is the Dark Knight Za'aroz," Alaric kept his voice low even though he knew the Dark Knight had created a spell to stop anyone else in the chapel from hearing them.

"How can that be possible?" Linus was not sure what he was hearing.

"It's simple," Za'aroz spoke for the first time since the revelation. "I was instructed to keep the High Chancellor alive and just advise him on what we wanted him to do. That was working out fine when I first arrived here." Alaric was amazed at how forthcoming Za'aroz was being. He wondered if Minerva had a hand in it, but he doubted she could manipulate a Dark Knight.

The crowd shuffled forward slightly, trying to hear what was being said. There seemed to be something important being discussed, but they were not able to hear it. It was frustrating, but they would just have to wait. They were sure they would get their vengeance.

"It seemed that the willpower of the High Chancellor was greater than I expected," Za'aroz continued. "I tried to control him, but his consciousness kept returning at the most inappropriate moments. He was becoming too much of a liability," Za'aroz explained.

"So you killed the High Chancellor?" Linus asked in astonishment.

"That would have been my preference, but when the Great Lord commands something of you then that is what you must do. He instructed me not to kill the High Chancellor and that is exactly what I did." Za'aroz sounded happy with himself.

"Then what have you done with him?" Linus did not realise the danger of speaking with the Dark Knight. He really had no way to defend himself.

"He is safely tucked away in the mines, working hard like he has made so many others before him. I think it will do him some good to do some honest work." Za'aroz was having no problem giving away all of his secrets.

"That doesn't make any sense. Surely he would have revealed himself to the guards by now," Linus continued.

"Well, I have cast a spell on him that takes away his intelligence. Now as I said he has his moments of lucidity. The guards just think that he is insane and send him back to work. It did not take long for him to lose all clear resemblance to his identity and the guards wouldn't know the difference. All they know is that I am in the Grand Cathedral and some crazy man is in the mines," Za'aroz almost laughed when he finished speaking.

That was all Alaric needed to know. Whether it was Minerva playing with his mind or Za'aroz showing off the conversation had come to an end. There was no further information that Alaric needed. He did not have time to waste. He needed to kill the Dark Knight and be on his way back to Jarrat.

"It is time for you to die now," Alaric took one step forward, but then stopped. There was a look in the Dark Knight's eyes that didn't make sense. "What are you smiling at?"

"Do you honestly think that you can kill me?" There was something unusual in the question. "Look around you, Alaric. These people are not here to help you."

Alaric looked out into the chapel. He had to admit the Dark Knight was right. There were a lot of angry faces, but they were not directed at Za'aroz. Alaric knew there was no chance to defeat the Dark Knight. He would need all his energy to kill Za'aroz and he could not stop a room full of angry men at the same time. It was only then did he realise how perilous the situation really was.

"It's good to see that you finally understand the situation." That was why the smile had never left Za'aroz face. "Now I think it would be a good idea for you to surrender your weapons and the stones."

Alaric looked around for a means to escape. He knew it would not be possible to escape by normal means. A number of guards had moved between the dais and the entrance to the High Chancellor's private chambers. He reached for the energy around him that he would need to create the spell to escape. It was only then that he realised he could not feel anything.

"You are slow, but at least you get there in the end," Za'aroz scoffed.

Alaric looked at Minerva who, in turn, shook her head. The Dark Knight had also blocked her powers. On the plus side it would be taking a lot of his strength for Za'aroz to contain both of them at the same time. Alaric doubted he would be able to cast anymore spells. This was his opportunity to attack. With a little luck he could kill Za'aroz and they would be on their way to Jarrat within a few minutes.

"What is it that you want from me?" Alaric tried his best to keep some strength in his voice.

"It would give me great pleasure to end your life, but it seems as though the Great Lord has different plans for you. He wants me to keep you alive until he gets here. I suppose he just wants to kill you himself. Now that you are trapped there is no chance for you to escape. You will wait out your time in my dungeons," Za'aroz started to laugh.

"And what about us?" Minerva sounded worried.

"You? I don't think that I need to keep you alive. I will have you executed immediately," Za'aroz continued to laugh.

"Alaric, you have to do something," Minerva pleaded.

He knew she was right, but what could he do? Without the ability to draw in energy he could do nothing to defeat Za'aroz. All he could do was hope he was able to gain a chance to escape before Nyrra arrived. As far as Minerva and Linus were concerned their fates had already been sealed.

"That's right there is nothing that you can do." The Dark Knight was loving the fact that he had an opportunity to gloat, that was his downfall.

Suddenly an idea crept into Alaric's head. His mind was still hazy from the after effects of the Topaz stone, but once the thought was there it was not going to leave. He had to use one of the stones to break the hold Za'aroz had over him. The only problem was that he was not sure which stone he should use, or even if one would be enough.

"What are you doing?" the Dark Knight did not sound as sure of himself as he had been.

There was no more time for Alaric to decide. Whilst he had been thinking his right hand had started to play with the drawstrings on the Topaz stone's velvet hood. It seemed as though the choice had been made for him. Now he just had to hope his plan worked. Without a second thought he pulled the hood free and grasped the sceptre in his right hand. The Topaz stone shone brightly and filled the room with an intense yellow light. It was so bright it made those closest to the dais shy away.

"There is nothing you can do with that." The Dark Knight was trying to convince himself more than anyone else. "Put it away!"

Alaric was not going to be dissuaded. As soon as he revealed the Topaz stone a feeling of contentment filled his body. His health was suddenly renewed. He was confident he had the power to defeat the Dark Knight. With the stone much stronger that the spell in place there was nothing Za'aroz could do to prevent him from using the power around him.

"Kill them all. Kill them before they kill you," the voice urged in his head. Alaric ignored the implication and assumed he was just speaking about the Dark Knight.

"You cannot kill the High Chancellor," to Alaric's surprise it was Minerva who spoke. "Not in front of everyone here." Although she wanted nothing more than for Alaric to strike down the Dark Knight she knew that her words were correct.

"You can kill them. You must kill them," the voice increased its urgency.

It took a moment, but soon enough Alaric could feel the energy around him again, but he drew on the power of the stone. Once he had his fill he simply broke the spell the Dark Knight had cast. It was the last thing the Dark Knight was expecting as he dropped to his knees and cried out in pain. If he had been prepared then the result would have been much less painful.

The rage Alaric had been feeling for Za'aroz had now reached its peak. He could feel the blood pumping through his head. It made a rushing sound that blocked out all other noises, except for the voice inside his head.

"That's right. Use the power I offer. Destroy them all. It is your destiny," the voice was very excited as it was coming closer to its goal.

"Alaric!" Minerva cried out, but there was no response.

The crowd of priests and soldiers could now hear everything that was happening on the stage, although they did not fully understand. No one made a move to advance. The addition of the Topaz stone made everyone nervous, although again they did not know exactly what it was. All they knew was that the man before them was dangerous. Minerva's panicked voice only increased their concerns.

Alaric continued to draw in energy from the stone. Za'aroz had not been able to recover from the last blow and was still on his knees. There was nothing he could do to defend against the impending attack.

"Alaric!" Minerva continued to try and gain his attention, although she was loathed to touch him. In his current state she knew that her life was also at risk.

"Alaric!" Linus also called out.

The priest didn't realise the state that Alaric was in. He grabbed Alaric by the shoulders and shook him once. He wanted to shake him more, but Alaric did not give him the chance. He struck the priest in the stomach with his left hand. The movement was so quick that Linus did not have a chance to defend himself. Linus' desperation was enough to bring Alaric back to reality. He looked at Linus and then Za'aroz and then at the rest of the chapel. As much as he wanted to destroy the Dark Knight he knew that Minerva was right. He could not kill the High Chancellor in front of so many people.

Alaric let his shoulders slump. There was only one thing he could do. He tried to push the voice out of his head. Whilst it was screaming at him he could not create the spell he needed. The voice was not happy, but Alaric was determined. He could not completely silence it, but he was able to muffle it enough so he could concentrate.

The next thing they knew they were standing in a quiet kitchen. There was sweat on Alaric's brow, and he looked as if he had just woken. There was no sign he had just gone through a great ordeal. The other two were not taking the situation as well as him.

"What happened? Where are we?" there was a large amount of panic in Linus' voice. He moved around in an erratic manner, trying desperately to work out what had happened.

"How did you do that?" there was surprise in Minerva's voice. She knew what had happened, although she was not sure how.

Alaric did not hear the questions. His body was full of adrenaline. The Topaz stone made him feel so good that he could not believe that his body could feel such a way. There was no time to stop and they needed to be on the move again. Alena's life was relying on him to return. With the Topaz stone in his possession there was nothing he couldn't do. He turned around and for the first time realised there were two other people in the room. Instantly he thought he was in trouble again, but then he realised who they were.

"I think you should cover the Topaz stone again," Minerva sounded concerned.

"I don't think so," there was something different in Alaric's voice.

Not only had his voice changed, but there was something different in his eyes. There was a tinge of yellow circling his irises. Minerva didn't like what she was seeing. She knew the effects a *Stone of Power* could have on someone. It was clear the Topaz stone was starting to take control of Alaric.

"You have to overpower the stone," Minerva continued.

"I am in control," Alaric replied, although she did not know who was really speaking. "I don't need your help. I have to go and save Alena."

Alaric was about to blink out of the room, but there was something that stopped him. A voice in the back of his mind was telling him to remain where he was. The urge to leave was compelling, but he could not bring himself to.

"What is it?" he finally asked. "What is it you want?"

"I want you to think about what you are doing. I know that you want to save Alena, but there is more here at stake," Minerva spoke softly, hoping he would hear her.

"Would someone please tell me what is happening and where are we?" Linus did not like being ignored.

"We are back at my house," Minerva explained. "Somehow Alaric has worked out how to teleport, for lack of a better word," Minerva sounded annoyed at having to explain what she thought was the obvious.

Linus opened his mouth to speak, but nothing came out. He could not believe what he was hearing, but the surroundings spoke for themselves. He looked around the kitchen and spotted a stool behind the island table. He needed to sit down before he fell down. The experience of leaping through the fabric of reality was too much for him.

"What is it that you want?" Alaric snapped at the delay. "I have to get moving. Alena's life depends on it."

"Yes, but there is more to life than just Alena," Minerva did not sound comfortable. "We have to get Za'aroz out of the Grand Cathedral. At the moment he controls that strongest army in the Seven Kingdoms. If the Evil One wants the army to move then it will move. We need to work out a plan."

"That's not right. We have to get going." The voice returned to forefront of his mind. "Alena will die if we don't move now!"

Alaric tried to push the voice to the back of his mind. They both made good arguments, but with the voice in the front of his mind it was impossible to think. He had to push the urges down. He knew Minerva made sense, but there was still no answer to what he should do.

"What do you have in mind?" Alaric finally managed to ask the question.

"Do not do this. They are setting a trap for you," the voice screamed inside his head. "You must destroy them."

"QUIET!" Alaric called out the top of his voice.

His sudden outburst brought silence both inside and outside of his mind. He was glad to finally get some silence. Finally he had a chance to think, or at least try and think. His mind was also still swimming with the glorious sensation of wellbeing. He knew Minerva had come up with a valid point, but he could not work out what it was. He just hoped the voice would remain silent.

"What is it that you were saying?" Alaric asked softly.

"Za'aroz now controls the Castalial army. This is something that we cannot allow. You need to do something to stop him," Minerva re-explained.

"I see, that is a very valid point," the voice was mumbling in the background of his mind as he spoke. "What do you have in mind?"

"I don't know. I know that I have to go and meet with my fellow wizards. They will know what to do," Minerva did not sound confident.

Alaric did not want to think about it. His head was not working as it should, but there did not seem to be any other option. He knew that Minerva was right and that there was something he had to do before he left Castalia. All he had to do was remember what it was.

"What am I going to do?" They had almost forgotten that Linus was still there. "I can't go back to the Grand Cathedral and I don't think I would last too long in the inner city. I am sure that the High Chancellor will have my picture out to all the guards. Can I go to the Island of Wizards with you Minerva?" there was little hope in his voice.

"You know you cannot," Minerva replied.

"Kill him. That is the best thing for him," the voice was whispering inside his mind.

Alaric was about to say something, but then stopped. He could not continually speak aloud to the voice in his head. He did not want the others to know it was there. At least the first time they thought he was speaking to them. It was Linus who had given him the idea.

"You will come with me," Alaric looked at Linus as he spoke.

"No, that is a bad idea. You must kill him," the voice was starting to get louder.

"What do you mean? Where are we going?" Linus sounded confused. It was clearly not the response he was looking for.

"We are going to Jarrat. If we are going to be able to remove Za'aroz from the position of High Chancellor then we are going to have to find the real one. You will have to help us with that," Alaric explained as best he could. His mind was starting to become foggy again and his thoughts were all jumbled.

"I guess that is a plan then," Minerva sounded happier with his decision.

"That won't be so easy. We still need to get out of the city. I am sure if we move quick enough we will be able to escape, but it won't be long before the High Chancellor gets word out." Linus could not bring himself to admit that the High Chancellor was Za'aroz.

"That will not be a problem. We will not be travelling the conventional way." Alaric did not elaborate any further, but Linus did not like the sound of what he had said.

"That's good. I will be able to make my own way out of the city. I think it would be a good idea if you could meet me at Ĉarolija Island. I am sure the other wizards would love to meet you," there was something cynical in Minerva's voice.

"I need to get Adelanta before we go," Alaric's voice was starting to become shaky.

"Of course. I will get him for you and then we all must be on our way. I think in the meantime you should cover the Topaz stone," Minerva sounded concerned.

"You can't do that. You need me," the voice was back screaming in his mind.

"I don't think that would be a good idea, but thank you for your concern," Alaric struggled to respond.

Minerva was not happy, but she also knew there was no time for an argument. It would not take Za'aroz long to realise they were at her house. The sooner they were gone from Castalia the safer they would be. She needed to speak with her fellow wizards. The recent events did not play out like she was expecting and that was worrying.

Linus was not happy at being left alone with Alaric. He was not sure what was happening, but he was not getting a good feeling. There was something different about him. He had only known Alaric for a short period of time, but he could definitely see the change. He was hoping it was the fact that he had not slept during the night, but he doubted that was the case.

Alaric could feel the hold the Topaz stone was having over his body, but he also knew how it felt to cover the stone. It was neither the time nor the place for him to do that. He could not hide the stone away until he had healed Alena. Once he did that then he would be able to crash and crash he would. All he had to do was stay in control until then.

"Are you alright?" Linus had planned to remain silent, but the words just came out of his mouth.

Alaric didn't answer. He didn't hear the words. All he could hear was the voice inside his head. It was trying to take control, he knew that. It was trying to overpower him. That was something he could not allow. If he let the voice take over then he knew there was no chance for him to recover.

"You need my help. This is the least you could do," the voice hissed in his head.

"No!" Alaric spoke with his mind. "You will do what I say."

When he finished speaking he felt a pain in his stomach. He knew the Topaz stone was making him suffer. He wanted to double over, but there were two reasons why he shouldn't. The main reason was that he didn't want the stone to know he was in pain and the second was that he didn't want Linus to know what was happening. He succeeded with the second, but not he first.

"I know you can feel that," the voice started laughing. "I will make it worse."

Alaric had to concentrate, although his mind was still hazy. He could not let the Topaz stone overpower him. He started breathing deeply to try and muster the strength that he needed. The voice screamed inside his mind, even when it was not saying anything. The stone did not want to give Alaric a chance to gather his thoughts. It knew it was starting to gain control and the last thing it wanted was to relinquish that advantage.

"You have to let go. Your mind is tired and needs rest. Once you have recovered I will give you back control," the voice was now sickly sweet.

It was a tempting offer. Alaric had to admit his head was feeling heavy. He had not slept in over a day and he could not remember when he had slept well. It would be the perfect opportunity to rest. The only thing that stopped him was a warning he felt in his heart. He knew that something was not right. He could not trust the Topaz stone. If he relinquished his spirit then there was little chance he would get it back.

"You will not take control of me!" Alaric held his breath and strained to regain the advantage. His face started to go red and a vein started showed on his forehead.

"Are you alright Alaric?" Linus was starting to become concerned.

"Yes, thank you, there is nothing for you to worry about." Alaric was not sure if the words that came out of his mouth were in fact his.

"That is right. There is nothing he can do to help you. I am the only one who can help you." The voice was trying to coax him. "You need rest."

Alaric's eyelids started to close as he took another deep breath. They had become suddenly very heavy. He wanted nothing more than to let them shut and fall asleep. His mind craved sleep, although his body was still rippling with energy. It would be easy to let his mind slip off to sleep, but that would not solve anything.

"I will not let you take control." Alaric clenched his teeth as he spoke with his mind.

"It is alright Alaric. This is the best thing for you. I will look after you." The voice continued to try and coax him. "Just let yourself go."

Alaric fought to keep his eyes opens. They flickered once and then shut completely. Linus watched from the other side of the kitchen, not sure exactly what to think. Alaric had said he didn't need assistance, but that did not sound right. There was something wrong with him.

At that moment Minerva returned. She pushed the door opened and made it slam against the side of the wall. The sudden noise made Alaric's eyelids jolt open. Linus jumped a little when he saw them. The yellow tinge had increased and almost completely covered the irises. It was Minerva who regained his attention before he had a chance to say anything.

"I have the horses. We can get going now." She didn't seem to notice the change in Alaric nor the tension in the room.

"Of course," Alaric's voice was suddenly very cold.

Minerva turned and left the room without really listening to what he had to say. She had a lot on her mind. It would be no easy ride for her to the Isle of Wizards. She would have to ride through Remidia and that was no longer a safe journey.

"I still have to pack, so you will forgive me if I don't see you out." She had moved to her bedroom and was starting to stuff clothes into her travelling pack.

Alaric was more than happy to comply. Now that everything had been sorted he wanted nothing more than to return to Jarrat. He had the strength inside to do the job and it would take a lot to make the leap from Castalia to Jarrat. He had never tried to travel so far in one go, but he was confident he was strong enough.

"Are you coming?" his voice was still cold as he spoke to Linus.

The priest was no longer sure it was the right thing to do. He was sure something had changed in Alaric. He wasn't sure if he trusted him anymore. He was thinking it might be better for him to try his luck on his own.

"We have to get going." He spoke again when Linus didn't move.

Alaric waited at the door. His stare was as icy as his voice, which did nothing for Linus' confidence. There was something very disturbing about Alaric's new demeanour. It could not be the fact that he was lacking sleep.

"Come on Linus. We have no time to waste." Alaric's voice didn't change, although he was clearly urging Linus to move. "Move!" The word sent a chill down the priest's spine. It came out of Alaric's mouth as a growl.

It was enough to get Linus out of his seat. He did not know why, but he was compelled to follow. Alaric's last comment made Linus want to run, but he could not do anything except follow. He knew it was not a good idea, but again there was nothing he could do about it.

They found the two horses waiting out the front. Adelanta looked pleased to see Alaric. That did not last long. Once Alaric touched the mane of the white stallion he shied away. He looked at Alaric with confusion on his face.

"Let's get moving. You might want to keep you eyes closed." Alaric ignored his horse's reaction.

There was no time to Linus to object. Once he finished speaking they blinked out of existence.

Epilogue: Deaths and other Tragic Events

Ra'naroz was happy to be away from Castalia. He couldn't believe how easy it was in the end to escape from Alaric. The Chosen One, as he was known to his enemies, was not as formidable an opponent as he could have been. The Dark Knight neglected to remember the times that Alaric held him prisoner or the time he beat him in the dungeons of Jarrat. All he could think about was how he had managed to out smart Alaric in Castalia.

Now he was walking through a forest in Remidia. He was glad to be away. He had never liked the desert city. There was something about it that never sat right with him. He always liked the comfort of trees and that was something Castalia had very few of. That's why he had enjoyed running the show in Jarrat. He had been completely surrounded by forest. He knew that wasn't the right way for a Dark Knight to feel, but he couldn't help himself. The Great Lord loved desolation and all his brothers were supposed to feel the same.

It was like there had been a weight lifted from his shoulders when he left the city. Now he was not sure what he should do. He could not return to Jarrat, that door had been shut. He thought about heading to Remidel, but he was sure his brother Dargoz would have already set up camp. He had always gotten on well with Dargoz, but that didn't mean he would receive a warm welcome. He was not going to be second to anyone. He would need to find a way to get back in the game, but for the moment it seemed as though he would be left up to his own devices and that meant getting into some trouble.

As he walked through the forest he saw a sight that made his eyes bulge. There was a wooden shack tucked behind a small cluster of trees. Smoke was pouring from the chimney and there was light coming from the window. Although it was the middle of the day the dense canopy made the forest dark. Just the way Ra'naroz liked it. There was a much greater opportunity for murder. With any luck there would be an entire family inside. It had been too long since he had killed someone. Sure he caused many deaths in Jarrat, but their lives had not been taken by his own hand. A slight amount of drool appeared in the corner of his mouth. He quickly sucked it back in before it dripped down the side of his chin.

He approached the small shack with caution. He did not want to scare away the people inside. He was happy he had not given up his disguise when he left Castalia, if he had then the inhabitants would certainly run when they saw him. He was sure they would not be used to visitors calling. Not this deep in the forest. He was a little surprised at the shack's existence. If he had thought further on it he might not have been surprised when he entered.

Ra'naroz knocked on the door when he reached the shack. He thought it was the best way to play things. He liked to toy with people before he killed them. It was always more fun that way. Sure he could kill them quickly, but where was the sport in that?

There was no answer to his knock so Ra'naroz pushed the door open and walked inside. What he found was not at all what he had been expecting. The outside of the shack was made of timber, but the inside was pure stone. There was no fireplace to cause the smoke he had seen from the outside and no windows on the inside. The light came from a single lantern hanging from the ceiling. It was as if he had stepped through a portal to another place altogether. The truth was that was exactly what had happened.

It wasn't until he reached that conclusion did he realise he had walked straight into a trap. The only question was who it was who had set it? That thought in itself was disturbing. He had no idea who would be powerful enough to create such a spell. Not to mention the fact no one should know that he was passing through the forest. It could have been a trap for someone else, but he did not believe that for a second. All the thoughts raced through his mind and none of them reassured him.

Each time a thought ran through his mind it still came back to the same answer. There was only one person who would create such a place for him. But why? He could not work out why he would be summoned by the Great Lord. As he turned around he saw the face of the one he did not wish to see. He instantly dropped to his knees and prostrated in front of Nyrra. There was a mixture of fear and exhilaration coursing through his body.

"What do you have to say for yourself?" the voice was harsh and rasping.

Ra'naroz wanted to grasp at his ears to stop the noise. It was the most beautiful and the most painful voice at the same time. No matter how great the urge his hands remained on the floor in front of him. He wanted to look up, but he knew better than that. He would not rise unless the Great Lord demanded it of him.

"I am here to serve you and only you," Ra'naroz grovelled at Nyrra's feet.

"Stand up, you snivelling worm." Nyrra thought about spitting on the pitiful creature, but he restrained.

"Yes, my lord. I live to serve." Ra'naroz quickly came to his feet.

"Well, that is interesting for you to say," the voice changed to a more wishy-washy tone. "That is not what I am hearing. I told you to trap the Cursed One in Jarrat and then wait for me. I do not believe that you have done this?"

"No, my lord. I tried, but he was too strong for me." That was no excuse, but he could not think of anything else to say. He wished he had time to come up with better answers. "I did all that I could."

"I don't think that is the case. If you did all that you could then you would either have the Cursed One or you would be dead," there was something evil in his tone and yet it was playful at the same time.

There was a pause for Ra'naroz to respond, but he did not know what to say. He could not work out what the Great Lord was insinuating, but he did not like it.

"Well I guess there is no excuse for your failure," Nyrra continued when there was no answer.

"That is not true." Ra'naroz chanced his luck and looked up. He quickly lowered it again when he realised the Great Lord was not looking at him. "When I failed in my task I brought him to Za'aroz. I made it so he could capture the Cursed One." Even Ra'naroz did not believe in his own lie.

Nyrra radiated pure evil at the best of times but since Ra'naroz had lied that evil intensified. Even the Dark Knight, who normally bathed in such evil, had to shy away. He knew it was not a good sign. He was going to suffer a great punishment, but that was nothing new. It had been a long time since he had been punished by the Great Lord, but he would soon be on his way.

"Do you think you can lie to me?" Nyrra's voice echoed through Ra'naroz's head.

"No, Great Lord, I would never lie to you." His arrogance was going to be his downfall.

Nyrra paced around the room, forcing Ra'naroz into the middle. The Dark Knight looked around nervously. There was something different about the situation from the other times the Great Lord had punished him. It was that thought that created fear in his heart. It was the first time in a long time, possibly even ever, that he had felt fear. Even when he was the Cursed One's prisoner he did not feel fear. No matter what he did he always had a plan to get out of trouble, but he was not sure what he could do. Finally he threw himself back on his knees.

"Now you see the truth. Now you know what must happen," there was a mocking tone in Nyrra's voice.

"I only ever served you. What I did I did for you," Ra'naroz's voice was filled with fear.

"Then tell me why you let the Cursed One gain the Topaz stone. I was pleased when you placed the spell on the stone." Ra'naroz did not know how the Great Lord could have known that. When he created the spell the Great Lord was trapped in the North. "You not only led him to the stone, but you removed the spell allowing him to capture it. Now I would love for you to tell me the reason why you let him do such a thing?"

Ra'naroz did not know how to reply. There was no point in lying anymore. That would only get him into even more trouble. The only reason why he had led Alaric to Castalia was so he could escape. He figured once he was gone he would be someone else's problem. He quickly realised the error of his ways. He could not admit the truth, so he just remained silent.

"Now he is on his way to save her. That is not what I wanted," Nyrra's voice hissed again. "She was not supposed to survive. You were meant to see to that. Now you have failed me again."

"But you told me to keep her alive. You said that it was imperative that I kept her alive." He made the mistake of looking up as he spoke. He quickly lowered his head when he saw the fire in the Great Lord's eyes. "I did what you commanded. She is still alive only because it was your desire."

"You are a fool, Ra'naroz. I don't why I ever elevated you to the rank of Dark Knight. You would have been much better off to die like the rest of your pitiful race." Ra'naroz shied away from his comment. The Dark Knights never liked to be reminded of their origins. At one time they were human, just like those they now hated so much. "The only reason why I wanted you to keep her alive was so the Cursed One would come to you. When he was there you should have killed her."

That thought had never come into his mind. If the Great Lord had said to keep her alive then that is what he would do. He knew that something very bad was going to happen to him. He was not so confident that he was going to be alright.

"Yes, that is right. You have failed me for the last time," there was something in his voice that didn't sound right. It was almost like there was laughter in the background.

Ra'naroz stood up quickly to protest, but no words came out of his mouth. His eyes were wide open in fear as he realised he couldn't move. His arms were pinned to his side and his body was stiff. In an instant Ra'naroz was engulfed in flames. A great pain ripped through his body. He wanted to cry out, but no sound came. It was at that point he realised the horror of what was happening to him. The Great Lord had turned his back on the Dark Knight, before vanishing altogether.

Ra'naroz had been tortured by the Great Lord before. He had been surrounded by fire before, but this was different. When the Great

Lord tortured someone he wanted to hear their screams. He would also stay to watch and enjoy his handy work. Once the Great Lord had left the room Ra'naroz suddenly got his movement back. The first thing he did was let out a blood-curdling scream. After that he tried to pat out the flames, but he knew it was a pointless exercise. The flames would only extinguish when the Great Lord wanted them to. He could only hope the Great Lord did indeed plan for them to.

The flames licked at his skin for over fifteen minutes. The pain was excruciating. Although the flames caused great pain they did not break Ra'naroz's skin. It was a promising sign that the Great Lord did not want him dead, which had become more and more apparent as the events unfolded.

When the flames finally died down all that was left in the room was a small pile of ash.

***

Bern tapped on the door before pushing it open. The situation inside had not changed. Alena still remained unconscious and Eldred was only just alive. The old wizard did not look up when he entered the room. Bern was not even sure if he realised he was even there. He had hoped that Alaric would have returned already, but that was not the case. Eldred could not have much energy left.

"How are you Eldred?" Bern asked.

"There is not much left." Bern was not really sure what Eldred was speaking about. "Has Alaric returned?" his voice was dry and cracked.

Bern was not sure what he could say. He wanted to say that Alaric had returned with the Topaz stone, but that was not the case. He didn't think that Eldred would be able to handle the news. He suddenly wished he had not entered the room. He knew there would be no change.

"He has not," was all Bern could say.

"Then I fear that we are out of time," Eldred did not sound well.

"I am sure he will be here soon. All we have to do..." Bern did not get to finish his thought.

Eldred had collapsed on the floor. He had finally run out of energy. Bern knew that it meant the spell he was using to keep Alena alive was finished. She would not have more than a day left. He doubted she would live beyond nightfall if Alaric didn't return soon.

She looked even worse than before. Her skin was completely white and covered in a thin layer of sweat. The only sign that she was alive was the occasional rise and fall of her chest. It was a lot slower and more laboured than it should have been. Bern did not like what he saw, but he now had another problem on his hands. Eldred had completely lost consciousness. If he wasn't careful then he could have two dead bodies on his hands.

Bern quickly put that thought out of his head. He could not let Eldred lose his life. They had come too far. He was not going to let anyone lose their life. He did his best to pick Eldred up and place him on the bed next to Alena. It seemed the best place for him, at least until he could call for the physician.

It took longer than he would have liked for the physician to arrive. When he did the physician did not like what he saw before him. He knew the situation in the room and that there was nothing he could do about it. That was why he didn't rush to the room. When he saw Eldred lying on the bed next to Alena he wished he had moved quicker.

"What happened here?" he asked, knowing full well what had happened.

"Eldred just collapsed. I think the strain just got to him." That was the only explanation he could come up with.

The physician had a quick look over Eldred. There was no response to any of his tests. A concerned expression crossed his face, which did not instil any confidence in Bern. Things had just been going from bad to worse. On the plus side they were well on their way to removing all traitors from the city, but that was a small mercy.

"There doesn't seem to be anything wrong with him," the physician scratched his head as he spoke. "Besides the obvious, that is. He has no energy left in his body, but from what I can tell he will make a full recovery once he has had time to rest."

Bern did not know if that was a good sign or a bad sign. The physician said he was going to make a full recovery, but then again he didn't really know what was wrong with him. At least it was something. Since there was nothing he could do about it he would have to put his mind to something else.

"Is there anything we should do?" he asked as an afterthought.

"Just make sure he is comfortable. Are you sure he should be lying next to Alena?" there was something in the physician's voice that made him think it was not the right idea.

"No. I think we should have another bed brought in. I have to keep on the move. Would you have a nurse come in to look after him?" his mind was wandering as he spoke.

"Of course," the physician was a lot more helpful than when they first met. He knew Bern was in favour with the duke and that was all he cared about.

"Thank you." Bern remained seated when the physician left.

The last thing he wanted to do was leave the room. He knew that Duke Xarles would be looking for him. He didn't have the energy to deal with politics. He had hoped Alaric would have returned by now. The army was getting ready to be on the move again and he had nowhere to move them. He knew he would not know which direction they were heading until Alaric arrived.

It was still Alena's health that was foremost in his mind. He sat and watched her slow breathing. He knew each breath could be her last. As much as he told the physician he had to leave, he did not think he could. He would have to remain and hope that she had the strength to survive.

***

Marina had ridden hard since she had left Alaric. She rested only when her horse was tired or when she needed to sleep. If it wasn't for her horse she would have kept riding through the night. She cursed the mare every time she had to stop. There was nothing else she wanted more than to regain the Sapphire stone. Since it had been stolen by Argoz she could no longer hear its beautiful voice. That was the most painful part. She could not think of another time in her life that she had suffered so much.

When she left Alaric and the Dark Knight Ra'naroz she knew her life would become dangerous. Not so much on the journey, but once she reached Lel Dinion. She had been to city once before when she was a child. Her father had taken her on a royal visit, but that was not the danger. The danger was involved in recovering the stone from Argoz. He would not simply hand it over, but she was prepared to do whatever it took.

Something had changed within her when he took the stone. It was like a piece of herself was missing. There was something building inside her, but she did not know what it was. She knew she could no longer trust Alaric. She could not believe she had thought she loved the man. He had chosen the elf over her and that was unforgivable. He knew how much the Sapphire stone meant to her. She could not believe he had just let the Dark Knight take it and then get away.

It had been a long time since she had felt such a rage. In fact she was not sure if she had ever felt that way. She did not know what she was going to do when she caught the Dark Knight, but he would not live to tell the story, that much she knew.

The mare was on its last legs as she walked it through the city gate. She had been stopped by the guards, but they were not going to let her through until she announced that she was Princess Marina. She had hoped to keep her name out of common knowledge, but that was clearly not going to be the case. She could ill-afford to get caught waiting at the main gate. She showed her royal signet ring and started to cause a fuss. At first they could not believe it was her. She looked a mess from the long ride and she had no entourage, but they were able to recognise the tone in her voice. If she was not of royal birth she was close enough to it. They would not risk their jobs by detaining her any further. They could always deny letting her through the gates. There was more than one into the city.

Marina had no doubt the Dark Knight would be heading straight for the palace. There would be no other place for such a creature. Even if he was not there it would be the best place for her to start. King Lisle would treat her with the respect she deserved. It was a respect that Alaric had never given her. She almost spat when she thought about the man. He had treated her with nothing, but contempt. She was glad she was away from him.

She moved through the city as if no one was there. In fact the city streets were strangely vacant. It was something she didn't notice, if she had she might have been more cautious when she entered the palace. All she had was one thing on her mind and that was regaining the Sapphire stone.

She was stopped at the palace gates when she approached, but as soon as she mentioned who she was she allowed entrance. It was as if the guards were expecting her. They did not question her appearance or lack of forward notice. It was another fact that should have warned her that something was not right in the palace.

A magnificent room had been prepared for her, all a little too quickly. She was able to bathe and fresh clothes had been brought to suit her royal standing. It had been too long since she had been properly pampered. She was beginning to remember what it was like to be a princess and heir to the throne of Darshival. It was a manner she was accustomed to and she needed to be properly attired for her meeting with the king. She had not expected to be entertained by the king, but her own self-importance blinded her to the potential danger.

Once she had bathed, changed clothes and prettied her naturally beautiful features, she made her way to the main banquet hall. The king was having a magnificent feast planned for her arrival. She breezed through the corridors, her ball gown swishing around her. She wore a royal blue dress, cut tightly around her chest and waist. The king had also provided her with a diamond cut necklace and similarly designed tiara. She finally felt like a princess again. She kept her head high and completely ignored the servants scurrying about her.

The banquet hall was all but empty when she entered. There were two men at the main table. Both were eating and talking quietly amongst themselves. It wasn't until that point did she realise how much danger she was in. She reached for her sword, which she had carried with her ever since she had left her home, but it was no longer there. She could not wear a sword with a ball gown. She was completely unarmed. The sound of the doors locking behind her was the last sign that she was trapped.

"Come in, come in," a familiar voice called from the table. "We have been waiting for you."

Marina stayed where she was. She did not want to move any closer. Suddenly her left foot raised and she took a step forward. She tried to stop it but there was nothing she could do. Slowly her body was making its own way to the table. Her head started to become clouded the closer she came.

"I think it would be the right thing to do to curtsey in front of the king," Argoz had an evil grin on his face.

King Lisle did not look up as Marina approached. He continued to eat his meal as the Dark Knight spoke. Marina did as she was told and quickly curtsied. It was an involuntary action, much the same as her walking. There was nothing she could do to stop herself. She knew the Dark Knight was controlling her body. If she had the Sapphire stone she could stop him, but until then there was nothing she could do.

"There is a plate of food for you. I am sure you are hungry," Argoz offered.

Marina sat down next to King Lisle and started eating. She couldn't taste the food as it went into her mouth. She had no idea what she was eating, but she could not stop. The more she ate the more she forgot what she was doing. She knew she had come to Lel Dinion for a reason, but she could no longer remember what it was.

"You have come on a diplomatic mission for your father." The voice jogged a memory in her mind, but it quickly disappeared.

She could not remember why her father had sent her to Lel Dinion, but he must have had his reasons. The memory would return to her eventually and the king didn't seem too worried. His advisor was doing all the talking anyway. She would wait until he questioned her.

"Do you not remember why you have come here?" as he spoke Argoz produced a small velvet pouch from his pocket and placed it on the table in front of him.

Marina thought that the velvet pouch looked familiar. She thought it might be pertinent to her being in Lel Dinion, but she could not work out why. All she knew was that she couldn't take her eyes from it. She wished that he would take it off the table.

"I must be mistaken," he mused as he returned the pouch to his pocket.

All he wanted to do was see if she remembered the Sapphire stone. It seemed as though that thought was completely gone from her mind. She was completely in his thrall and that was what he wanted. He had no further need for the ruse. It was late in the day and he wanted to retire. He also wanted to test another theory.

"I think it is time for us to retire," there was a friendly tone in Argoz's voice.

King Lisle simply stood and left the room. At first Marina thought it was odd, but that thought also soon left her mind. She was struggling to hang onto anything that came into her mind. It was like there was a great roar in her head that stopped her hearing her inner voice. She hated it, but again the thought did not remain for long and once it was gone it was forgotten.

"I will leave too," the words came out, but she was not sure where they came from.

Without waiting for a response Marina rose from the table and moved towards the door she had entered from. She took no more than a dozen steps when she stopped. For some reason she thought that something was not right.

"Where do you think you are going?" Argoz remained seated as he spoke.

"I am going back..." she stopped when she could no longer remember where she was going.

"You are staying with me now," there was something evil in his voice.

"Of course," she turned to walk out of the door at the back of the room. The door led to the king's private apartment.

As she walked towards the back of the room there was something calling out deep inside of her. She knew something was wrong, but she did not know what it was. It was a terrible feeling. The feeling of pure dread increased the closer she came to the door until it suddenly disappeared. Once it was gone it was not even a memory. She only felt content as the king's new advisor got out of his seat and escorted her out of the banquet hall.

***

Richmond sat by his friend and advisor's bed. There was still no change to his condition. The physician said the same things as he had before. There was nothing physically wrong with him. His coma was purely in his mind. That was something Richmond could not bring himself to accept. There had to be something the physician was missing. Tancred had been tortured in the dungeons like the other two. Both Richmond and Hadar had taken different times to recover. He was sure that Tancred would come around.

His best chance to recover would be when Alaric returned with the Topaz stone. Tancred's life depended on Alaric's return as much as Alena's did. As much as Richmond hoped he would recover on his own he knew that would not be the case. All he could hope for was that he was able to hold on. At least nothing was changing. That was enough to give Richmond hope.

Without warning Tancred sat bold upright in his bed, his eyes wide open. Richmond almost fell off his chair with surprise. Once he realised what was happening his called out his friend's name. At first there was no response, but after a few seconds had passed he looked over at the voice. There was no recognition on his face. His eyes were still wide open, but that was the only expression.

After few more seconds Tancred sucked in a lungful of air. It was as if he was a newborn taking his first breaths. Richmond thought it was a good sign that he was recovering until his eyelids closed, his body went suddenly limp and he collapsed back onto the bed.

Richmond was in shock. He didn't know what to think. It took him a moment to realise there was no movement in Tancred's body. His chest was no longing rising and falling. He quickly checked a pulse and found nothing. In a panic he tugged urgently on the bellpull. He did not stop until the physician arrived.

The physician rushed into the room. When he saw Richmond standing over Tancred's limp body he quickly moved into action, but it did not take him long to realise what was wrong.

"I am sorry," the physician took a step back from the body of Tancred. "There is nothing I can do. He is dead!"